ABIDING LOVE

BANISHED SAGA, BOOK EIGHT

RAMONA FLIGHTNER

Beverly,
The Saga continues!
hope you enjoy!
love
Ramona

GRIZZLY DAMSEL PUBLISHING

Cover design by Jennifer Quinlan.

❀ Created with Vellum

CAST OF CHARACTERS

BOSTON:

Richard McLeod- brother to Gabriel, married to Florence, black-smith, father to five boys

Florence Butler – married to Richard, used to teach with Clarissa, mother to five boys

Sophronia Chickering- suffragist, mentor to the McLeod women

Aidan McLeod-uncle to the McLeod boys, married to Delia, father to Zylphia, excellent businessman.

Delia McLeod- married to Aidan, mother to Zylphia, still aids the orphanage

Owen Hubbard: successful Boston businessman, interested in Zylphia

Theodore Goff- married to Zylphia, excellent businessman

Zylphia McLeod Goff—married to Teddy, daughter to Delia and Aidan, suffragist and painter

Rowena Clement- Zylphia's friend, suffragist activist

Morgan Wheeler-Parthena's husband, successful Boston businessman.

Parthena Wheeler- married to Morgan, sister to Genevieve Russell, Zylphia's friend; excellent pianist

Perry Hawke—singer and friend to Lucas Russell

Martin Russell- owns *Russells*- a fine linen shop in Boston; father to Savannah and Lucas

MONTANA:
   Missoula:
   Gabriel McLeod- cabinetmaker, married to Clarissa

Clarissa Sullivan McLeod- married to Gabriel, used to work as a teacher, now works as a librarian; a suffragist

Jeremy McLeod- cabinetmaker, works with his brother Gabriel at his shop, married to Savannah

Savannah Russell McLeod- married to Jeremy, suffragist

Melinda Sullivan McLeod- Savannah and Jeremy's adopted daughter, Colin/ Clarissa/ Patrick's much younger sister; mother is Mrs. Smythe

Colin Sullivan-Clarissa and Patrick's brother, blacksmith

Ronan O'Bara- a McLeod friend, a cobbler, injured in mine in Butte, uses wheelchair

Araminta- friend to the McLeods, helps care for their children and clean their homes

Hester Loken- librarian in town, friend to the McLeods

Bartholomew Bouchard- banker, interested in Araminta

Mrs. Bouchard- sister to Mrs. Vaughan, busybody in Missoula

Mrs. Vaughan- sister to Mrs. Bouchard, busybody in Missoula, blames Clarissa for her family's misfortunes

Butte:
   Lucas Russell- Savannah's brother, a famous pianist, travels the world performing.

Genevieve Russell- married to Lucas, Parthena's sister

Patrick Sullivan- Clarissa and Colin's brother, accountant, married to Fiona

Fiona Sullivan- married to Patrick, has one daughter, Rose

Samuel Sanders – Gabriel's cousin (was Henry Masterson in Boston), nemesis to all McLeods

Mrs. Smythe: collaborates with Samuel Sanders, stepmother to Clarissa/ Colin/ Patrick; mother to Melinda
   Darby:

Sebastian Carling- runs the sawmill in Darby, married to Amelia, great friend to the McLeod's

Amelia Egan Carling- close friend to the McLeod's – lives in Darby

PROLOGUE

The haunting voice echoed over the small group gathered around the gaping hole in the ground. All wore black, and all bowed their heads deferentially as the singer sang *"Ave Maria."* Women swiped at their cheeks while another whispered, "She was too young to die."

The McLeod brothers stood in front of the grave, waiting for the song to end and for the priest to begin his incantations. As they had since the night of their parents' deaths many years before, they formed a wall of solidarity. Now, just as then, they had been powerless to prevent the loss of one they most loved.

As the last syllable of the song was carried away on the soft wind, the priest began to speak. The Latin prayers brought little relief to the overwhelming grief they felt. The self-doubt grew as they wondered what more could have been done to prevent such an untimely death.

And they fought the worst fear of all: was more death inevitable?

CHAPTER 1

"*I*'m surprised to find you in town, Rowena," Sophronia Chickering said as she sat in a comfortable chair at the reception held in Mrs. Beaumont's ballroom after Perry Hawke's performance at the Opera House. The area in the center of the room was crowded with other patrons of the fine arts, while chairs were scattered along the room's edges for those who preferred to sit. Three large chandeliers gleamed, enhancing the glow of the women's jewelry and satin dresses. No one danced as Mrs. Beaumont had not hired an orchestra and did not believe such frivolity acceptable when the country was at war.

Perry Hawke's performance had been highly touted because he sang a wide variety of patriotic songs interspersed with his usual operatic masterpieces. Sophronia, an elderly woman accepted in society due to her marriage and force of personality, had hoped not to live through another war. Up to now, her political focus had been on obtaining universal suffrage for women. She set aside her cane and accepted a glass of champagne while motioning with a tilt of her head for the young woman to sit beside her.

Although nearly eighty, Sophie had a close relationship with many of the young suffragists from Boston and considered them a part of her family. She had mentored them for years, starting with Clarissa Sullivan McLeod in 1900, and they had formed strong bonds. Now, with the suffrage movement demanding their youthful presence in Washington, DC, Sophie had to rely on their letters and infrequent visits to Boston to maintain that bond. She smiled as the young woman sat beside her.

"I will return to Washington soon. Others are as capable of reporting the goings-on as I am," Rowena Clement said. Her auburn hair was pulled back in a stylish but plain knot, and her dress was a pale beige color. She had become closer to Sophronia during the past few years, having first met her in 1914 during a visit to Newport, RI. At the time, no one had realized Rowena's ability as a writer and reporter. However, those abilities had been well utilized in the past year by Alice Paul and the National Woman's Party in their weekly publication, *The Suffragist*.

Sophie frowned at Rowena's plain outfit and unremarkable makeup. "You aren't wallpaper," Sophie muttered. "You must stop trying to blend into your surroundings."

Rowena smiled, her brandy-colored eyes sparkling with mischief at the older woman's disgruntlement. "It's the best way for a reporter to overhear what others would rather have remain unheard." Her smile deepened at Sophie's cackle of amusement. "Besides, I have no desire to be noticed."

"The War will end, Rowena, and soon there will be no need to feel any shame," Sophie said in a low voice. They shared a knowing look about Rowena's desire to hide the fact that her mother had been a well-born German. Since the start of the war, Rowena had acted as though she had not had a mother. Sophie bit back what else she might have said at Rowena's shake of her head. "As for your reporting, I was on the edge of my seat, reading your account of the House vote last week."

"I would think the president's declaration to Congress would have given you more of a shock," Rowena said with a smile. "I never thought the man would be in favor of the vote."

Sophie *harrumph*ed. "I never dared hope he'd see it 'as an act of right and justice to the women of the country and the world.'" She raised a brow as she stared at Rowena. "I was glad to read that Miss Rankin was in charge of the House proceedings for the Anthony Amendment vote. Seems fitting a woman would be the acting floor leader for such a momentous occasion." Sophie set her glass of champagne on a side table and *thunk*ed her cane for emphasis.

"The passage in the House is momentous, Sophie. However, the real struggle has always been garnering the majority needed in the Senate. According to Alice, we are eleven votes short, probably more if the senators change their minds as readily as they change their pantaloons." Rowena sat with her back straight as she watched other concertgoers mingle and attempt to fawn over the aloof and famous Perry Hawke. "I fear it will be a long-drawn-out battle to have Congress approve the amendment."

"Not too long, Rowena. I refuse to be like Susan, dead these many years and denied her right to vote. We must get the Susan B. Anthony Amendment passed in Congress. I want to vote!" Sophie said. She pasted on a smile as Perry Hawke approached them on Zylphia's arm.

Zylphia McLeod Goff was another young suffragist who had worked in Washington with Rowena the past year. Zylphia stood several inches shorter than Perry, with her raven hair contrasting his blond hair. Her blue eyes sparkled with mischief as she acted as his guide.

Sophie glanced around the room, spotting Zylphia's husband, Theodore—called Teddy—a short distance away, watching his wife intently. Sophie focused again on the famous singer who had performed for them that evening. "Hello, young man. You sing quite well."

Perry bit back a chuckle and nodded his thanks. "It was my pleasure to perform for you." His smile impersonal, he turned as though to move on to other patrons of the arts in the room.

Zylphia tugged on his arm, preventing him from moving away.

"No, Mr. Hawke. This is Mrs. Sophronia Chickering and Miss Rowena Clement. Good friends of mine, suffragists, and also friends of Lucas and Genevieve's." Zylphia smiled as Perry relaxed at Lucas's name. Lucas Russell was a famous pianist and cousin of sorts to Zylphia. He now lived in Butte, Montana, with his wife, Genevieve.

"You know Mr. Russell?" Perry asked.

Sophie *tsked*. "I knew him when he hid from his parents, eager to play the piano but just as intent on concealing his talent. Nearly wasted it all to sell linens!" She smiled as her gaze became distant with her memories. "We spent lovely evenings in my sitting room as he tried out new compositions." She focused and speared Perry with an intent gaze. "You could do with a more talented accompanist."

Perry chuckled. "My regular was taken … ill. I should like to hire your Mrs. Wheeler, but I fear her husband would not like the nomadic life."

"You met Parthena?" Rowena asked, her eyes alit with joy. Parthena Wheeler was a good friend to Rowena and Zylphia, forming their own tight little group years ago. Parthena had traveled to Montana to be with her younger sister, Genevieve, who was about to have her first child.

"Yes, a few days ago in Minneapolis. They were stranded there due to a train delay, and I had the opportunity to perform for them and to practice with Mrs. Wheeler." He flushed. "My usual accompanist was not pleased with my praise of a woman and has decided to take his talents elsewhere."

"Fool," Sophie said with at *thunk* of her cane. She eyed Perry with a cagey expression. "Leave it to a man to be jealous of a woman's talents."

Perry laughed. "Artists are inherently jealous and insecure, Mrs. Chickering." They shared a smile. "I fear my accompanist was not used to a woman with superior talent." Perry shook his head. "It was a wonder to sing with her. Her ability to anticipate and to adjust the tone of the piano's notes to match the mood of the piece was remarkable." He shook his head again and sighed with delight. "Her talent nearly equals Lucas's." He looked at the three friends. "Am I foolish to associate with such radical women?"

Zylphia laughed. "Oh, assuredly. But then we know you like radical women." She flushed as Sophie laughed, and Rowena ducked her head in embarrassment.

Perry chuckled. "I admit that Miss Woodward had a fiery temperament and was as committed to suffrage as you are. However, that association is long over." He failed to mask the bitterness in his gaze at his breakup from the famous opera singer a few years ago. It had been the talk of the gossip papers for months as Miss Woodward had leaked salacious details about their relationship to the press. "I can assure you not everything you read was true."

"As a reporter, I already knew that," Rowena said. She flushed as his light brown eyes focused on her for the first time.

"I hope you are generous in your estimation of my talents, miss," he murmured.

Sophie waved away his comment. "She reports important news, Mr. Hawke. She's a suffragist reporter." She saw him half smile in a self-deprecating way at her rebuke. "Now, as you are accustomed to such radical women, I presume you would have no compunction in holding a small soiree as a form of fund-raising for our cause?" Sophie asked. "I know many would delight in hearing you sing again."

Perry's gaze darted from one woman to the next, each one more amused than the last at him having backed himself into a corner. "I would be delighted. However, I fear my schedule is quite fixed at the moment."

Sophie again waved her hand in dismissal of his concerns. "I've spoken with your manager. He is astute but not enough for someone of your stature." She pinned Perry with a severe stare. "You are free two nights from now." She glared him to silence as he attempted to make a feeble complaint about his need for free time.

"My father has a large ballroom, Sophie," Zylphia said as she battled a grin at Perry's discomfiture for being outmaneuvered. "It would be the perfect location, and you know how generous he is in opening his home." She shared an innocent smile with Perry. "He's always in favor of all I do and is eager to support my causes."

"Perfect. Then it is settled. I would hope in the ensuing days you would seek out a new pianist?" Sophie said with the rise of one eyebrow. She nodded as Perry walked away with Zylphia, holding back her chuckle until he was out of earshot.

"That was well done," Rowena said. "Alice will be pleased."

"I want you there, Rowena," Sophie said. "I think a piece in the paper about our efforts could help others see that the struggle continues and that the need for fund-raising is ongoing. Too many will see the president's actions as a sign that we have attained our goal. If we do not continue to bring attention to suffrage, we will never achieve it."

"I will attend, but then I must return to Washington," Rowena said, her gaze tracking Perry's movement through the well-dressed crowd. "I wouldn't mind hearing him sing again." She ignored Sophie's mocking gaze as Rowena watched the mingling guests.

Two evenings later Perry Hawke wandered the glass-enclosed sitting room at the back of Aidan McLeod's mansion. He fingered a palm frond and hummed keys before singing a scale. His voice caught on one of the higher notes, and he cleared his throat before starting the scale over again. After a few more scales he took a deep breath and sang a few notes at full volume.

His mind wandered to the numerous cities he had visited. The concerts he had given. The mind-numbing after-parties where he had been forced to smile at the hostess's inanities when all he desired was quiet. He sighed. Before his accompanist had quit in a fit of rage at being upstaged by Parthena Wheeler, Perry had had a friend and ally in the room. Now he was alone. "Don't think about her," he whispered to himself, banishing thoughts of the woman he had loved and thought he would marry.

He let out a deep breath, forcing his shoulders back and rolling them to relax. He then hunched forward and back, in an attempt to relax the muscles further. He ignored the opening door, accustomed to fans attempting to sneak in to see him. "Please, leave me alone."

"I never thought doing calisthenics was part of preparation for a singer," Aidan teased as he poked his head into the back room. "May I come in for a moment?"

"Mr. McLeod," Perry said with a deferential nod to this evening's host. His alert gaze raked over the man who was almost seventy but appeared a decade younger. His hair was nearly all silver, with a few specks of black in it, and he had wrinkles at his eyes and mouth. Perry wondered if they were from frowning or smiling. Aidan's blue eyes were friendly but astute as he met Perry's assessing gaze. "Thank you for allowing me to perform in your beautiful home."

Aidan chuckled. "From what I heard from Teddy, my daughter Zylphia's husband, you weren't given much choice in the matter." He smiled as Perry shook his head. "I have found that it is often better to allow the women in my life to believe they have outmaneuvered me. It brings me peace."

Perry laughed. "In this instance, I was backed into a corner. It's been a long time since that's happened."

"It will do you no harm to have another successful concert here in Boston," Aidan said. "Although you must know that some of your fans will be disgruntled when they realize the proceeds will go toward aiding the suffragists."

Perry half smiled as he took a sip of water. "Even those against suffrage will have to come to understand that their views go against the tide of public sentiment." He shrugged. "New York ratified their referendum in November. It's only a matter of time until the majority of the states agree. And I'd hate to be the politician to face the new electorate's wrath when they have the opportunity to vote."

"You're a pragmatist," Aidan said.

"Show me an artist who isn't." He paused and then took a deep breath. "Your renown as a financial genius is famous, even among those of us in the artist world. Might I meet with you to discuss my portfolio?" He flushed as Aidan's gaze became penetrating as it

9

studied him. "I beg your pardon. I'm certain you focus your talents on those with more assets."

"Nonsense," Aidan said. "You were gracious enough to agree to this concert for my daughter and her friends. I would be honored to look over your portfolio. If you don't mind, I would like to work with my son-in-law, Teddy. He has an even greater mind for business than I do, and we began working together a few years ago. Might you be able to come by his office tomorrow?" Aidan rattled off an address and a time.

Perry smiled. "Yes, I could. Thank you." He shrugged his shoulders again and then moved to a chair to pull on his jacket. He smoothed down the lapel and then the sleeves and donned an impersonal smile. He stood a few inches shorter than Aidan at six feet tall, and his blond hair was styled with a light coating of pomade. Mild interest shone from his brown eyes. "That Chickering woman seems to like to meddle."

Aidan laughed and slapped Perry on his shoulder. "That is the perfect word for her. What did she do to annoy you?"

Perry raised a brow and looked around the back room. "Besides arrange this evening, she had the gall to proclaim that my accompanist was lacking in sufficient talent."

Aidan grinned. "Sophie's never been known to mince words. And she is rarely wrong." He motioned for Perry to follow him as they approached the door to the sitting room. "I cannot be saddened that she caused this evening to occur as I am always thankful to have my home filled with friends. After the concert, I look forward to introducing you to my wife, Delia." He smiled with wicked humor. "And I'll let you know if your pianist tonight is any better than the previous one at the Opera House." He led the way from the room to introduce Perry to the waiting crowd in his ballroom.

Perry took a deep breath in the hallway, listening to Aidan's concise, yet equally effusive praise of his accomplishments. At the generous applause, he strode into the room and smiled at the crowd seated in front of him. He noted house staff lingering in the opposite doorway, and they appeared to have been invited to listen to him too.

He took a deep breath of rose-scented air, seeing that the roses were all yellow, with purple ribbons around the large vases. He closed his eyes a moment to focus on what he would sing, rather than any distraction from the room. After a moment he nodded to his pianist and lost himself to his music.

~

R owena stood to the side of the ballroom as she watched the immaculately dressed crowd extol Perry Hawke and his talent. She frowned when she saw him speaking with Owen Hubbard, and her frown intensified to a glower to see Parthena's sister, Eudora Tyler, at Owen's side. "What can she be thinking?" Rowena muttered to herself.

She took a sip of punch, sighing with pleasure that it was not overly sweet, and continued to watch the occupants of the room. Her pale blue dress nearly matched the new wallpaper, and she smiled with satisfaction that she blended in. Mrs. Bolinger glared at a vase of yellow flowers and narrowly missed knocking one to the ground by her husband grasping her arm. Mr. Theubes snuck a bloom from another vase and clipped it to place in the buttonhole of his jacket. "I wonder if he realizes what that signifies?" she murmured to herself again. Wearing a yellow rose was often construed as support for the suffrage movement. She shrugged, thankful that one of the leaders in men's fashion had taken such an action and made a note to remark on it in her forthcoming column.

"Some would think you are snooping," Theodore Goff murmured as he stood next to her. He smiled as she rolled her eyes. Teddy was a tall, lanky man who wore his sable hair longer than was stylish in an attempt to conceal scars above his right eyebrow and behind his left ear from wounds suffered while fighting in the Great War for the British Expeditionary Force. His right hand held a tumbler of whiskey, the tips of his three middle fingers missing from injuries sustained in the War.

"Then they would be more astute than I generally give them credit for," Rowena said with a half smile. "I thought you'd be with Zee."

"She's in her element, speaking with another painter about light and texture. I decided to leave her to it." He saw Rowena's gaze following Perry Hawke. "Why don't you speak with him?"

"Oh, I have no need. He's done what he can for the suffrage movement," Rowena said. "No reason to bother him further."

Teddy nodded and took a sip of the amber liquid in his glass. "I suspect he'd rather be bothered by you than by the likes of Mrs. Bolinger. She seems particularly irate that the proceeds are going to the NWP." Most Americans perceived the National Woman's Party, headed by Alice Paul, as a more radical branch of the suffrage movement. Many who supported suffrage preferred NAWSA, the National American Woman Suffrage Association, headed by Carrie Catt.

Rowena rolled her eyes. "Mrs. Bolinger detests either group but just hates Alice more than Carrie. If we donated to NAWSA, she'd spew the same amount of vitriol."

Teddy chuckled. "I know Zee took enormous delight in decorating the room today. She and Delia relished the challenge of finding such a number of yellow roses in January." His gaze found his wife in a corner, waving her arms about as she expounded on some topic.

"I hope the distance between you is not as great as it appears," Rowena said. She felt Teddy stiffen beside her, and she flushed. "I beg your pardon. I have no right to say such things."

"On the contrary, you have every right. I'm not used to others seeing through the carefully constructed facade." His gaze was filled with longing as he looked at his wife. "We still have quite a bit to overcome after the events of last fall." His face clouded as he considered his wife's jail time after protesting in front of the White House.

Rowena knew the loss of their unborn child would forever haunt both Zylphia and Teddy.

"Much was lost that we are still trying to regain."

"You will, Teddy," Rowena said. "Have faith." She smiled at him as he nodded before moving away from her to join a business partner who had called for his attention.

She remained to the side of the room, frowning as she no longer saw Mr. Hawke among the small groups who were mingling. She jolted as a soft, deep voice spoke in her ear.

"Looking for me?"

She turned to meet the challenging, inquisitive gaze of Perry Hawke, his light brown eyes dancing from a joke only he understood. "Yes." When he appeared surprised at her forthrightness, she smiled.

"I escaped the clutches of Mrs. Bolinger and thought I'd attempt to fade into the wallpaper as you do. Do you have a dress to match each ballroom or sitting room you frequent?" He chuckled and took a sip of his drink as she glared at him.

"It is a valuable ability for a reporter," she snapped. "Besides, I can't hope to compete with the women in the room."

He frowned and then looked at the women in the crowd bedecked in jewelry and fine gowns. "I fail to see what you mean. They need baubles to brighten their appearance, whereas your intelligence and curiosity make you shine." His frown deepened as her vivacity faded. "I meant no offense."

"I know what I am, Mr. Hawke," she muttered.

"I don't believe you do. I think you believe what others have told you—repeatedly. I think it would be fascinating if you finally learned who you truly were." He smiled as she flushed and then followed her gaze where she watched Teddy and Zylphia, who were speaking with Zylphia's parents. "An old flame?"

She glared at him. "No, she's one of my best friends. And he's her husband."

Perry was quiet for a few moments and then sighed as he stood tall. "Believe it or not, Miss Clement, I understand yearning for what I can never have." His gaze met hers and was filled with the memory of loss. "I should not take up any more of your valuable time. I hope you enjoy your evening." He nodded to her and moved away.

Rowena watched him join another cluster of partygoers, an impersonal smile and expression on his face as he moved from group to group. After a few minutes Rowena joined Zylphia. "How are you?" she asked her friend.

"Fine," Zylphia said. "It's time I am back in society, and I am thankful I could do something for the movement that did not cause me to return to Washington."

Rowena frowned. "When do you think you will return? I will miss you there, and I know Alice will be anxious for your organizational talents." Rowena absently noted Teddy stiffening at her question.

Zylphia shook her head. "I don't know. I'm still not ready. At least a month, Ro."

"You know, by then, we'll have moved our headquarters out of Cameron House?" She met Zylphia's shocked look. "The house is being sold. There's talk we'll move to a bigger building near Lafayette Square."

Zylphia smiled. "We wouldn't have to march anywhere to protest. We could protest right in Lafayette Square with the White House nearby." She sobered. "Although I will miss Cameron House."

"I won't," Teddy murmured. He shared a long look with Zylphia as though remembering the days after she was released from imprisonment and how he had been separated from her. "I will like knowing you aren't going back to that place."

Rowena flushed with annoyance. "The work is the same, Teddy, no matter the building."

Zylphia nodded. "I imagine, if the persuasion tactics with the Senate do not go well, that there will be more protests. Alice has shown that they are effective."

"Excuse me," Teddy said as he left to approach Perry speaking with Aidan.

Rowena watched Zylphia's gaze track her husband's movement. "He doesn't want you to return to Washington." She took a sip of punch and met Zylphia's tormented gaze.

"He hasn't said that in so many words. Not lately. But I hate how he tenses up every time *Washington* and *Alice* are mentioned. I think he wishes I would remain here." Zylphia fingered her punch glass and feigned gaiety at Sophie's penetrating gaze from across the room.

"You know I want you to return. I hate being in Washington without you, and the work always seems more manageable when you are there." She paused at the torment in her friend's eyes. "But you need to do what is right for you, Zee. For you and Teddy."

Zylphia blinked to clear the sudden apparition of tears. "I know. I just don't know what that is."

Rowena gripped her arm. "You only reconciled with Teddy a few weeks ago. You're barely recovered from what happened in November. Take the time you need, Zee." She looked around in triumph at the room filled with those who had donated generously to the cause. "You've succeeded in helping Alice from here."

Zylphia nodded and then forced a smile as a fan of her art approached. Rowena backed away to retake her position as a wallflower.

~

That evening Zylphia lay on her side of the bed she shared with Teddy. She listened as he moved around the room, and she heard the sound of linen rustling and clothes being set aside, the *clink*ing of cuff links as he placed them on a dish on his bureau. She took a deep breath and relaxed as the mattress next to her dipped when he climbed into bed.

"Night, Zee," he whispered, kissing her shoulder. She felt him turn to his other side, his back to her side.

"Did you enjoy the evening, Teddy?" A long sigh escaped as he turned onto his back. She imagined him staring at the ceiling.

"He sang well, and your father's friends didn't seem upset at parting with their hard-earned money to support Alice and the NWP." Another sigh came. "I'll spend more time with him tomorrow as I have to look over his financials with Aidan."

"They're your friends too." She bit her lip to prevent a tear from slipping out.

"They tolerate me, Zee. That's all they've ever done." He huffed out a laugh. "You should rest, Zee."

"I'm not going back with Rowena," she whispered. Her hand roved in the space between them until it clasped his. "I'm staying here for a while longer." She held her breath until he clasped her fingers and gave them a squeeze.

"How much longer?" His voice emerged thickened, as though by a deep emotion.

"I don't know." She paused as he failed to respond. "Do you mind?"

"Stay, Zee. Stay with me." He rolled to his side and tugged her so that her back was to his front, wrapping his arm around her middle and squeezing her. "I never want you to leave."

"Teddy," she murmured as she rolled over to face him. She traced his cheek, frowning at the deep furrows there and on his forehead. "Even if I were in Washington, I'm always with you." She leaned forward and kissed him softly. "I'll always love you."

"I find that harder to believe when you are away. When you are seduced by your cause." His eyes shone with torment as he admitted his feelings. "I can't make you stay. I won't make you stay." He let out a deep breath. "But I would ask that you tell me first what you plan. I would hate to hear of your decision from a friend or an acquaintance."

"Oh, Teddy," she whispered as a tear tracked down one of her cheeks. "I'll always tell you first. And I've only ever been completely seduced by you. Not by my art. Not by my belief in suffragism. Only you." She smiled as he cupped her cheek and kissed her.

"Come, my love. Rest with me," he murmured, tugging her into his arms.

Zylphia relaxed into his embrace, her momentary joy overshadowed as she realized he had not avowed his love for her. She slipped into a restless sleep, dreaming of a time when she and Teddy were fully reconciled.

Perry Hawke followed the butler into the large office off the main hallway of the mansion in the Back Bay. He held a slim folder in his hands and stood with immaculate posture in his afternoon suit of navy blue with a crisp white shirt. "Thank you for agreeing to see me, Mr. Goff," he said as he sat.

Teddy nodded and leaned back in his chair. The wall space over his chair was blank, but it bore a slight shadow, as though a painting had once hung there. The bow-fronted windows to Teddy's right let in bright sunshine on the late January afternoon, glistening off the pile of snow outside the window. A small fireplace behind Perry and beside the door helped heat the room. Teddy nodded to Aidan who emerged from the area near the fireplace. "Aidan was insistent we meet with you."

Perry rose, shaking Aidan's hand, before he sat again with Aidan now beside him. "I feel foolish, having two of the great financial minds of our time looking over my meager savings. However, if you wouldn't mind?" He handed over the folder, and Teddy clasped it.

Perry fought the urge to fidget as Teddy frowned and then shook his head. After a few moments Teddy passed the folder to Aidan and waited for his father-in-law to peruse the precisely detailed notes.

"Who is handling your money now?" Teddy asked with a tap of an injured finger on his desk.

"A company out of New York but with offices in Chicago and Boston. I was to meet with one of their representatives tomorrow, but I would prefer your counsel." Perry noted how Teddy's eyes seemed to darken to a stormy gray.

"Who were you to meet?" Teddy asked in a clipped tone.

"A Mr. Owen Hubbard." Perry looked from Aidan to Teddy and back again as they both let out hisses and shook their heads. "Should I be concerned?"

"For some reason, you had the instinct to meet with us. Explain why." Teddy leaned forward, his entire focus on Perry.

"I have money saved, but it doesn't seem to earn the rate of return that my friends discuss, even though some of my investments seem risky. And I worry that the management fees are too high." When Teddy raised a brow at that remark, Perry said, "I was advised that it was normal for them to extract a portion of the profits earned as part of their fee."

"Vultures," Aidan said, returning the folder to Teddy. "I'd withdraw my money from their accounts today, if possible. Teddy and I would be pleased to help you invest in more sensible ventures, with equal, if not greater, yields. Hopefully it will be a greater yield, but we cannot promise you anything." Aidan sighed. He pointed at the papers now in front of Teddy. "What you have listed there are all of your investments?"

"I own two houses and some land. The rest is there."

Aidan pulled out a card. "I would recommend you speak with your bank and inform them that you have new financial advisers and to deny anyone else access to your accounts from now on. I know you have little reason to put your faith in us over a large group from New York City, but I fear your carefully saved money could be at risk."

Perry sat in a daze at Aidan's words.

"If I may, Mr. Hawke?" Teddy began. "You excel at singing. I would bet your fortune"—he tapped the pages of Perry's portfolio—"that you have relied on your instinct to survive and then to excel. Trust your instinct that caused you to doubt Mr. Hubbard's group."

Perry frowned. "What would you recommend I do?"

Teddy took a deep breath and shrugged. "My opinion isn't a popular one, but I believe the War will end in one to two years, hopefully sooner. When it does, the economy may do well for a short time, but then it will decline. Although you may lose some money because you weren't aggressive now, you won't lose it all when the economy falters."

Perry rubbed at his chin and saw Aidan nod his agreement. "So you advise caution and risk reduction now, even though there is money to be made?"

Aidan chuckled. "Someone will always tell you there is money to be made as they take it from you. If you want to know, we are following the same advice we are giving you now."

"What in my portfolio do you not like?"

Teddy pointed to three items. "At a quick glance, these. They all depend on defense contracts. What happens when there is no war?"

Perry nodded. "I see." He let out a deep breath. "Will I be seen as against the war effort because I'm not buying this stock? I depend on society's goodwill to sell my music and to sell out my performances."

Aidan's eyes flashed, and he shrugged. "There is that possibility if those without scruples leak your stock purchases. However, what you buy should remain confidential. If there ever is any concern about your patriotism, you should speak of the number of concerts you do to boost morale and about the amount of War Bonds you've bought, and few will focus on your stock portfolio."

Perry sighed and then nodded. "I will speak with my bank and have them telegram you when I have changed financial advisors. I know of you from your reputations as honest and hardworking men, and Lucas recommended you to me." He held out his hand and then paused. "What is your commission?"

"For you, a flat fee of $20 a year," Aidan said with a smile. "Neither of us need the money, and we'll enjoy the challenge of straightening out your finances."

Teddy cleared his throat and looked uncomfortable a moment. "I feel I should inform you that Mr. Hubbard will accuse me of stealing you as a client because I do not like him."

"Is he lying?" Perry asked.

"No, I detest him. He treated my wife, Zylphia, abominably before we wed, and I will never forgive him that transgression. Besides, he's dismal with anything financial. He'll beggar you as he beggared his father."

"Didn't he just purchase a mansion?" Perry asked in confusion.

"War brings profit, Mr. Hawke. Especially to those without scruples. It's doubtful such profits will last." Teddy rose and shook Perry's hand. "Please visit us again when you are next in Boston."

Perry shook both men's hands and then departed. On the front step of Teddy's house, he took a deep breath and gave silent thanks for Lucas's recommendation and for following his own instincts.

Three days later Zylphia joined Sophronia for tea. Zylphia fought a smile as a maid led her into Sophie's back sitting room. "Hello, Sophie," she said.

"No need to be amused," Sophie said. "I happen to enjoy this room." She glared at Zylphia when her younger friend burst out giggling. "I'm having the front parlor redecorated, starting next week."

"Oh, I hope you are not taking your daughter's advice again," Zylphia said as she swallowed the last of her laughter.

Sophronia gave Zylphia a withering stare. "I am using my own decorator this time. I hate to admit that it will be more like it previously was before my daughter's designer destroyed my relaxing room with the horrid shades of blue more befitting a funeral parlor than the calm refuge of my sitting room."

Zylphia looked around the small rear sitting room with a settee, a lit fireplace, a desk by the window and Sophie's chair between the desk and the fireplace across from the settee. "I hope we'll still meet here. This is a comfortable room, and I find I prefer it to the larger more formal front sitting room." Her gaze turned critical as she stared at her painting of the cliffs near a house Sophie had rented five years ago in Newport, RI, where she had first met her husband, Theodore Goff.

Sophie shrugged. "If I weren't expected to host more events, I wouldn't bother with the front room. But, as it is, I don't care to have anyone in that room. Thus, I must redecorate." She waved her hand as though she were tired of discussing her refurbishment plans. "Now, how are things between you and Teddy? There were moments a few nights ago when I thought you were no longer reconciled." Her aquamarine eyes shone with concern.

Zylphia let out a huff of air and shook her head. "I don't know what to do, Sophie. Whenever Washington is mentioned or Alice or the cause, he buttons up. He can't abide the thought of me returning to Washington."

"What do *you* want to do?" Sophie asked. She motioned for the maid who entered the room to set down the tea tray and to leave. When the door closed, Sophie frowned. "I know Alice wants you back in Washington soon, but Alice has a singular focus on the goal of universal enfranchisement. While I can admire her determination, I can also despair her inability to deem anything else of equal importance in her life."

Zylphia shook her head. "I don't know what I want. I feel like I am finally emerging from a fog." She looked into the flames, her gaze distant and mournful. "He won't touch me. Not truly."

Sophie sighed. "Do you want him to?" At Zylphia's nod, Sophie leaned forward and tapped her friend on her knee. "Then you must show him that you do."

"I don't know if I'm that brave, Sophie," Zylphia whispered. "It took almost everything I had to return to our home for New Year's." She swiped at a cheek. "I don't understand how he can forgive me when I still can't forgive myself."

Sophronia nodded. "That is the true problem, Zee. Not that you're afraid of his rejection. But that you don't believe yourself worthy of forgiveness." She waited until Zylphia gave a subtle nod. Sophie sighed and sat back in her chair, deep in thought. "There is no easy answer. You must take time. Try to paint. Find your way again."

Sophie watched as Zylphia battled tears. "I imagine you must be terribly disconcerted as you have always known your path and which way you were charging forward. Now you must be patient with yourself as you learn what you desire while you heal."

Zylphia nodded and then sniffled. "Thank you, Sophie. I have this fear of letting everyone down." She jumped as Sophie grabbed her hand and squeezed it, blanching at the fire in Sophie's eyes.

"The only person you should worry about is yourself. And Teddy. If you never went back to Washington, if you never did one more thing for the cause, I could not esteem you any higher than I already do, Zee." Her eyes glowed with her impassioned truth. "You've sacrificed more than I could ever dream of. Do not feel that you must do anything more. Do what you know to be right. For you and for Teddy."

Zylphia nodded again and then tried for a smile filled with bravado. "Did you give Parthena the same advice before she decided to travel to Montana?"

Sophronia *harrumph*ed, then chuckled. "That girl has always been headstrong. She was intent on traveling there and had booked tickets before ever informing me." She shared a long look with Zylphia. "I'm only thankful her husband showed enough sense to travel with her this time."

"What I wouldn't give to witness that reunion," Zylphia murmured, a smile hovering on her lips as she and Sophie shared a conspiratorial look.

"Oh, yes. That would be something to see."

CHAPTER 2

Butte, Montana, January 1918

Genevieve Russell sat at the desk in her small parlor, absently rubbing a hand over her belly. She shared a large home in Uptown Butte with her husband, the famous pianist, Lucas Russell. A little over two years ago he had helped her escape her father's plan to marry her to an aged lecher, and they had settled in the thriving, tumultuous mining town set in Montana's mountains.

Genevieve stared out the window but glared at the brick wall of her neighbor's house. She closed her eyes, envisioning a large green yard with a rose trellis. She smiled at the unlikelihood of roses blooming in Butte, due to the pollution and elevation, and then smiled further when she heard her husband's chuckle.

"What has my beautiful wife smiling?" Lucas asked. He entered her room and bent to kiss her nape. "Might I hope it had to do with me?"

"No," she said on a breathy exhale as he kissed around to the front of her neck. She tilted her head to allow him easier access. "I was thinking about roses." She opened her eyes as she saw him still. "Not because you haven't bought me any. I was imagining a scene outside my window that is other than a brick wall."

Lucas chuckled again and moved to a nearby chair. He motioned to the pile of correspondence on her desk. "What is the news?"

Genevieve took a deep breath. "Savannah writes that she plans to be here by mid-January. She doesn't want us to be alone as the baby comes."

Lucas frowned. "Why should that worry you?"

Genevieve motioned to the large number of letters on her desk. "Do any of them consider that I might like time alone with my husband and child after our baby arrives?" She flushed as Lucas watched her with gentle rapprochement.

"I'll write Sav and let her know that she should wait for an invitation," Lucas said. When that failed to lift his wife's mood, his frown turned into a near glower. "Vivie? What aren't you telling me?"

"Parthena's coming," she said in a rush. "By the time I received her letter, they'd already bought their tickets."

Lucas nodded. "I'm glad you'll have your sister with you for support. For too long you've had to depend on my family." He shook his head in confusion and tapped his fingers on his thigh. "I don't understand why that would worry you."

Genevieve flushed and looked away. She sat in dejected silence, her hands gripped together on her lap. She shook her head as though unable to speak.

Lucas rose and knelt in front of her. "Speak to me, Vivie. Share your fears with me. For whatever bothers you, bothers me."

"I'm being foolish," she burst out. "It's just that …" She raised a shaky hand, pointing to her body, her curves enhanced from the pregnancy weight, her large belly and swollen ankles. "Look at me. Why would you want me when Parthena's coming?" She kept her head bowed.

He growled in anger and gripped her chin more harshly than he meant to. "Dammit, Vivie. This is why we've never returned to Boston. Have you shared that with your sister?" His hurt expression flit over her vulnerable one. "I love *you*. My wife. My Vivie. Not her. Never anyone else since we wed."

"How can you?" she cried out. "Look at me!" she wailed. When he chuckled, she hit him on his shoulder.

"I am, and I find you gorgeous," he whispered, leaning forward to kiss her on each cheek. "You will never see you as I see you. Lush and beautiful with your pregnancy weight. Precious as you carry our child. Fragile as you tire more easily and your balance becomes more precarious." He traced a finger over her hands before raising one to kiss it. "You are mine to love and protect, as I am yours."

"Oh, Lucas," Genevieve murmured, leaning forward. "I'm terrified of what will happen when you see Parthena again."

Lucas rose, easing his wife to a nearby settee. He sat, enfolding his wife in his arms, his fingers plucking out pins from her chignon. "Nothing will take away that fear until you see us together. Until you realize she's nothing more than a memory for me. And my sister-in-law."

Genevieve shuddered in his arms. "Forgive me. I know you love me. I'm feeling vulnerable."

He smiled as he held her. "I know, and I hope you will always share how you feel with me. I want to share everything with you, Vivie. The good and the bad." He ran a hand over her belly, his breath catching as he felt a kick. "I don't know as you'll ever understand the extent of my joy, knowing that we are to be parents." He continued to run soothing hands over her belly, and she relaxed into him.

"Please invite Savannah. I'd enjoy having her here too." She turned so he could kiss her neck.

"She loves you like a sister," Lucas murmured. "But I don't know how healthy it is for her to be here at a birth. She's never fully recovered from the fact she can't have children."

"Do what you deem right," Genevieve murmured. "I trust you."

Lucas played a soothing lullaby on the piano while Genevieve attempted to find a comfortable position as she listened. He'd tinkered with the piece for weeks and considered it nearly perfect as their baby was due any day. "That's lovely, Lucas," she murmured. "I think the repetition of the melody would calm any colicky baby."

He winked at her over his shoulder as he continued to play. "And hopefully an uncomfortable wife."

She laughed at his comment. Then, at the knock on the front door, she straightened as much as she could. Lucas approached her and gave her a hand to help her rise. He kissed her on the mouth, nodding to her as he met her worried gaze, waiting for her instinctive panic to ease. He smiled before linking their fingers together to make their slow progression to the front door.

When he flung it open, he smiled. "Hello! Welcome to our home." He shook Morgan's hand and nodded to Parthena. He watched out of the corner of his eye as Parthena pushed past Morgan and threw herself into her sister's arms. Lucas shut the front door behind them and hung their coats on the coat rack before motioning Morgan into the main living area.

Morgan seemed to catalogue the details of their rather simple but comfortable home.

Parthena stood about a half-foot shorter than Lucas and her husband, Morgan Wheeler. Her straw-blond hair was held back in an intricate chignon, while her hazel eyes shone with apparent delight at seeing her sister again after over two years. Morgan, only slightly taller than Lucas, had an eagle-eyed focus on his wife and stood with stiff formality in the face of Lucas's exuberant welcome.

"I trust you had an uneventful journey," Lucas said as he stood next to Morgan near the piano and watched as the sisters prattled, hugged and cried.

"We did. Parthena was most displeased at the delay in Minneapolis, but I am delighted to see we arrived in time." Morgan tilted his head toward Genevieve in her pregnant state.

Lucas nodded. "Yes, travel in winter can be unpredictable. However, we are very happy with your arrival." He slapped Morgan on the back before approaching his wife. "Vivie, you should sit and get your feet up." He placed a protective hand around her waist and led her to a chair with an ottoman in front of it. "There, my love." He stroked her ankle as he helped her raise her feet and then winked at her before rising to play host.

"Would you like to see your room and freshen up after your journey?" he asked. When they shook their heads, Lucas smiled and waved at them to sit in the comfortable chairs scattered throughout the room. He poured drinks for everyone and then joined the conversation.

"Were you able to use the tickets I wrangled to see my good friend Perry when you were in Minneapolis?" Lucas asked. "He was there again on tour."

Parthena nodded. "We did. Thank you for so generously obtaining them for us."

"We even met him, much to Parthena's delight," Morgan said with a rare smile among company. "He seemed intrigued with Parthena's abilities at the piano."

Lucas laughed. "I imagine he tried to convince you to tour with him." At Parthena's flush and Morgan's glower, Lucas laughed harder. "Since he is unable to coerce me into joining him, he's trying to find someone of equal talent."

"I thank you for the compliment, but I know I am not near your ability," Parthena demurred.

Lucas raised an eyebrow. "*Yet*, Mrs. Wheeler. Not yet. But you will someday, if you continue to practice." He smiled at Morgan in a friendly, unchallenging manner. "Your wife could be one of the most sought-after pianists in the country."

Parthena shared a quick glance with her husband. "That is a goal I no longer cherish." At Lucas's surprised look, she smiled. "I've found I enjoy my life as it is. Performing and living with public scrutiny would be a tiresome burden."

Lucas watched as Morgan relaxed with Parthena's words. Lucas turned the topic away from the piano. "I'm surprised it is taking this long for your trunks to arrive."

Morgan cleared his throat. "We had no desire to be a burden to you as you are to be new parents. We've rented rooms at a nearby hotel."

"Oh, Parthena," Genevieve wailed, flinging her hand out to grasp her husband's hand. "I wanted you here."

"We won't be far away. We're staying at the Thornton Hotel." Parthena attempted a reassuring smile for her sister.

Lucas watched Morgan closely, their gazes locked for a few moments. "I understand. We'll have plenty of time together, and you are welcome here anytime. Hopefully you will dine with us daily."

"Of course," Parthena said, rushing over her words. "I didn't want to intrude in your home after you had the baby. You should have time together, just the two—then the three—of you."

Genevieve shook her head in disappointment. "But Lucas's sister will be here. It's pointless for you to stay away from us." She gazed at Lucas, entreating him to intervene. When he shook his head subtly, she huffed out a moan and collapsed against the back of her seat.

"We'll be here at least two months, Viv. You'll be tired of us by the time we leave," Parthena teased her sister.

Genevieve reached a hand out to her sister. "I'll never want you to go." Both sisters blinked away tears at her avowal.

Morgan sat against a few pillows in the bed he'd share with Parthena in their room in the Thornton Hotel in Butte. He acted as though he were reading, but his gaze rose to the closed bathroom door every few moments. When she finally emerged, he set aside the book to study his wife. "How are you, Hennie?"

She slipped out of her emerald-green silk robe and climbed under the covers. She lay on her side, and he scooted down so they were at eye level. After a short pause, she met her husband's gaze and spoke. "I think he truly loves my sister."

Morgan frowned at her incredulous tone. "Why should that surprise you? Your sister has been writing of his devotion since nearly the time of their elopement."

Parthena shook her head, her gaze distant.

"Did you believe he wouldn't recover from loving you?"

28

Parthena's startled gaze met his. She flushed and nodded. "Yes, I'm embarrassed to admit, I did. I love Viv, but I always knew I was ..." She broke off before shrugging. "Smarter, prettier, more sought after."

"In my eyes you are, Parthena. However, you must realize how conceited you sound. Your sister has many wonderful attributes, and she and Lucas seem perfectly matched." He leaned forward and kissed her nose. "Even if I do say so myself, as I conceived of the match."

Parthena met his teasing, yet worried gaze. "Why did you agree to come here with me? It can't have been easy with your multitude of businesses, and I know you've never yearned for Lucas's friendship."

Morgan watched her for a few moments. "I knew it would make you happy." He paused. "And I didn't want you to travel alone." He held a finger to her lips before she could sputter a protest. "It's not that I don't trust you. It's more that I'm protective of you." He kissed her softly. "There is little I wouldn't do to see you happy." He caressed her shoulder. "As for my businesses, never fear. I have associates I trust, and I've asked Aidan McLeod and Teddy Goff to keep an eye on things in my absence."

She kissed his fingers as she studied his gaze a moment. "Why else did you come here?"

At her whispered question, he flushed. "I dreaded being separated from you. The last time we were apart, you were incarcerated and treated in ways I can't bear to imagine." His eyes clouded in agony as he beheld her. "I ... I need to be with you."

"Oh, Morgan," she whispered, leaning forward to kiss him. "My ... my desire for us to be together isn't going to fade." She caressed his cheek as she met his tormented gaze. "You have the right to time away from me, darling."

He shook his head. "I've spent enough of my life alone. Now all I want is to be with you."

Parthena curled into his chest and relaxed against him as he tugged her closer, rolling to his back so she could lean against his shoulder. She traced patterns across his chest, rousing shivers from him. "I need to speak with Lucas. One more time," she whispered.

He nodded and kissed her head. "I knew you would." His ease at having her in his arms dissipated, and he tensed. "It's another part of the reason why I wanted to travel with you. I intend to be a constant reminder to you of your recent contentment."

She pushed away from him to look into his eyes. "*Contentment?* Is that what you'd call it?" She frowned to find his eyes guarded as they watched her. Unexpected tears flooded her eyes. "It's so much more than contentment to me, Morgan."

At her whispered admission, he groaned and rolled her so he leaned over her, her face framed by his large hands. "What are you saying, Hennie?" His intense, hopeful gaze seared into hers.

She shook her head. "Make love with me," she pleaded, arching up to kiss him. She kissed away the flash of disappointment in his gaze, dispelling any doubts with her passion.

~

"Why do you have such a large staff working at the house?" Parthena asked her sister. "Even by Boston standards, it's excessive."

Genevieve sat with her feet up and smiled at one of the maids who brought in tea. "There was a horrible miners' strike here last year. When Lucas realized it would last for months and that many of the people of Butte were struggling, he decided that we needed more than an occasional cook or cleaning woman." She waved her hand around. "Now we have two maids, a cook, a butler and a gardener."

"Even though you don't really have a garden," Parthena said with a raised eyebrow. "And Lucas still answers his own door."

"I'm hoping we'll have roses at some point, although I'm uncertain they'll grow in such a harsh climate." Genevieve rubbed at her belly. "I wish we could have done far more for the miners, but Lucas didn't want to anger the rich bosses in town by openly staging a protest."

Parthena curled into her settee and watched her sister with avid curiosity. "What else did he do?"

"He paid the grocer's bills for local families he knew were struggling. He sent money to the churches so they could aid families in need. He held a concert, a rarity for him these days, and helped the miners by giving the proceeds to charity. All anonymously of course." She shrugged. "We have the money, and we couldn't stand watching our neighbors and friends suffer. It wasn't enough of course. Nothing we did could help the thousands of men and their families. But we had to do something."

Parthena snorted. "They chose not to work. And the nation needs copper for the war movement. It does seem rather unpatriotic that they'd choose that moment to stop working."

Genevieve glared at her sister. "Do you have any idea what provoked the strike?" At her sister's blank stare, she said, "Men, brave men—who worked in those mines every day in order to feed their families or who hoped for a better life—went down for their routine shift one night. A horrific fire ensued, and 168 men died. Others were unable to ever work again. And the mining companies didn't care. They don't care about the miners' working conditions. About the suffering of their workers. All they concern themselves with is profit."

Parthena watched her sister with an amused smile. "I thought you'd rid yourself of your radical tendencies when you left university."

Genevieve shook her head with annoyance. "Why should you feel free to march and proclaim all you want about the rights of women and then mock me for my beliefs?" She glared at her sister.

Parthena smiled. "I'm merely thankful that you finally feel free enough, secure enough, to speak your own truths. You were stifled in Boston, Viv."

Genevieve swiped at her eyes as tears leaked out. "I was. Believe it or not, I've never felt more at liberty to speak what I truly believe than since my marriage. Lucas encourages me and delights in my beliefs." She stared at her small wedding band and missed the flash of regret that Parthena quickly concealed. "How are Eudora and Isabel?" Genevieve asked. "I hear so infrequently from our two youngest sisters, and Mother never writes."

Parthena grimaced. "You will never be forgiven for having escaped Father's snare. He still complains of the expense of having chased after you to Minneapolis."

Genevieve shuddered. "Thank God, Lucas and I were already married. Lucas had the foresight to have it all arranged from nearly the moment we arrived in Minneapolis." She focused on her sister. "What aren't you telling me?"

"Eudora is to be married in April to a Boston businessman. He's not as horrible as that old lecher Father wanted to marry us to, but I know him to be a rather nasty person." Parthena shivered. "He's regained his fortune by speculating on the war."

"That's horrible! There shouldn't be profit when men are dying in the trenches."

"A fine sentiment, Viv, but far too many are always willing to profit from another's suffering. And this man is always looking to turn a profit. He's Owen Hubbard. He tried to ally himself to Zylphia, but she threw him over for Mr. Goff."

Genevieve smiled. "I'd think she'd be much better off with her Mr. Goff. He always seemed a rather romantic figure to me."

Parthena snorted. "You would think that. I'm not sure Zee would agree, spending day after day with him. No man is romantic all the time, not when you live with him."

Genevieve shrugged. "Of course I know that. But I'd think she'd be thankful for her lucky escape from a man who only saw a ledger when he looked at her."

Parthena sighed. "Yes, well, this is just the man who Eudora will marry. Unfortunately she thinks herself in love with him and won't be talked out of it, no matter what I say. Mother has had a greater hand in this match than Father, although I know they worked together for it to come to pass."

"Is Father as destitute as when I left a few years ago?" Genevieve rubbed at her belly, grimacing and taking a deep breath before she focused on Parthena again.

Her sister shared a chagrined look with her. "He's one of the vultures profiting off the war." She flushed with embarrassment. "At times I wish I could disavow any connection to our family. And I fear the feeling is mutual, as they are mortified of my involvement with the suffragist movement in Washington."

32

Genevieve looked at her sister and studied her with an intensity that made Parthena squirm. "Are you happy, Parthena?" When her sister remained silent, she asked, "Are you happy with Morgan?"

Parthena's smile was instinctive as she nodded. "I am. After everything that happened in Washington in November, Morgan and I made our peace."

"I'm glad," Genevieve said as she groaned and rubbed her stomach again. "I always thought he'd be a good match for you." She grinned at her sister's astonished expression. "He's strong enough to support your wild ideas and antics, and firm enough to rein you in when necessary."

Parthena blushed. "How well you know me."

"Was Washington awful?"

Parthena nodded as her smile faded and her gaze became introspective. "Yes, at the end. In the beginning it was almost fun. Defying the police and judges, marching out of Cameron House with our banners to protest. The shared camaraderie and sense of purpose was intoxicating in a way."

"And the workhouse?" Genevieve asked after a long quiet moment.

Parthena took a deep breath and closed her eyes. "Was the worst experience of my life. They relished in their mistreatment of us." She shook her head and smiled reassuringly to her sister. "It's not something I ever discuss. That any of us care to discuss."

Genevieve watched her sister with concern. "Perhaps you should. Those kinds of memories can only fester and leave scars. If you speak of what occurred with someone you trust, there's a chance you'll no longer be haunted by them."

"I'll be haunted by my time there forever, Viv. Speaking about it will never change that."

"Was Zylphia equally affected?"

Parthena nodded. "I believe it was worse for her. She nearly lost her marriage over it." She raised luminous eyes to her sister. "Whereas, in a bizarre way, it helped to save mine." She paused as though remembering the days after she was released. "I finally allowed myself to acknowledge what I felt for Morgan and my good fortune in him as my husband."

"He was steadfast in his care of you?" Genevieve smiled with approval.

"Yes, in a way that was wholly unexpected. No one had ever cared for me like that before. Not unless they'd been paid to," Parthena whispered. "Do you remember when I was a little girl and had scarlet fever?"

Genevieve nodded and paled at the memory.

"I was quarantined, and the only people who'd come near me were servants. They'd toss trays at me or clothes and scurry from the room." She closed her eyes as though to erase the memory. "Never was I made to feel important or treasured when I was ill as a child."

"As though our illnesses were a burden, and we needed to over-come them so Father could show off his perfect family to his friends," Genevieve murmured.

"Exactly," Parthena whispered. "Imagine my surprise to find Morgan caring for me personally in Washington. He never left my side." She blinked away tears. "It was the greatest declaration of love anyone could have made to me."

Genevieve clasped her sister's hand and squeezed it. "Oh, Parthena. I'm so glad for you. And you've told him how you feel?"

Parthena shook her head. "Not yet." At her sister's frown of disap-pointment, she slumped her shoulders. "I haven't figured out how to tell him."

Her sister rolled her eyes. "It's not that hard. When you're alone with him, say 'I love you.'"

Parthena glared at her. "You say it's not hard, but it's terrifying to me."

"Is it because you truly mean it this time?" At Parthena's flush, Genevieve smiled. "It's unfair *not* to tell him, but you'll know when it's the right time." She gasped, "Oh!" and rubbed at her belly.

"Are you all right?" Parthena held Genevieve's elbow.

"I just had a very sharp pain. Will you find Lucas for me?" She shared a terrified glance with her sister.

"Sit here and breathe. It will be all right." Parthena rose, moving toward the back of the house as she called out for Lucas.

~

S avannah McLeod emerged from her guest bedroom two days later at Lucas and Genevieve's house and abruptly stopped. As Lucas's only sibling, she wanted to be in Butte to support him and Genevieve at the birth of their child. She lived in Missoula, about one hundred miles away, with her husband, Jeremy, and their daughter, Melinda.

Her eyes narrowed as she beheld Parthena in front of her, a basket of laundry held at her hip. Although Savannah had never met Parthena, Savannah had an instinctual dislike for her as Parthena had broken her brother's heart six months before he had met and wed Genevieve. "I thought they had plenty of maids to do that sort of work."

"I want to help my sister, and she needed more cloths for the baby." She met Savannah's disapproving stare and shrugged.

Savannah moved to block Parthena's passage down the hallway. "Why did you come? There is no reason for you to be here. Lucas and Genevieve have plenty of family here to care for them."

Parthena flushed red and glared at Savannah. "Viv has no one here from her family. She deserves to have someone who isn't biased toward Lucas."

Savannah stared at Parthena. "You don't know us well enough to cast such aspersions on us. However, I can tell you where we are biased. Against you." When Parthena paled, Savannah smiled. "Although in many ways I suspect I should thank you for your fickleness. I've never seen Lucas as happy as he's been since he arrived in Montana two years ago."

Parthena blinked, clamping her jaw shut. "I married to protect my family from financial ruin. As any of your family would have done." She frowned as she stared at Savannah. "Although that's not true, is it? Your family didn't believe you were worth protecting."

35

Savannah gasped and backed up a step. "That's horribly unfair."

"Yes, it is. Just as it is unfair of you to treat me as a pariah simply because I acted to help someone other than myself." She watched as Savannah nodded her understanding. "Don't judge me for what I did, Mrs. McLeod. I'd do it again, if asked, to protect someone I loved." Parthena turned at the sound of her sister calling her name. "If you'd excuse me?" She pushed past a shaken Savannah and moved into her sister's room.

～

Savannah slipped into Genevieve's room later that afternoon to find her *coo*ing to her daughter, Elizabeth. "How are you, Genevieve? Can I bring you anything?" she whispered.

Genevieve looked at her sister-in-law with a radiant smile, her skin glowing and her clean hair pulled back loosely in a braid. "No, we're fine. Please join us."

Savannah sat on a chair near the bed and watched Genevieve with her daughter. "I'm so relieved you are well."

Genevieve groaned. "I'm still quite sore, and the doctors are concerned I have anemia due to the amount of bleeding I suffered, but otherwise I feel fine." She shared a conspiratorial smile with Savannah. "Tomorrow I'm getting out of this bed. I don't care what Lucas says."

"I think he'll fight you. He wants you to recover well first." Savannah's hand reached out as though of its own accord and traced Elizabeth's downy head. "So precious," she whispered.

Genevieve smiled before focusing on the longing in Savannah's gaze. "I'm so sorry. Since the birth, I never stopped to consider how hard this must be on you." She caressed her daughter's feet. "You never had this, did you?"

Savannah raised haunted eyes to meet her sister-in-law's worried, yet curious gaze. "No, I never did. I thought my daughter had died, and I wasn't reunited with her until she was over a year old. I had a few short months with her before … before the typhoid took her." Her tremulous smile did little to hide her grief. "I will always be thankful I held her."

"What did you call her?" Genevieve whispered.

"I named her Adelaide, but her new parents called her Hope," Savannah said around a sniffle. "I think Hope was a fitting name for her."

Genevieve nodded as she bent forward and kissed her daughter's cheek. "I agree. I wanted to name my little one Grace, but Lucas insisted she be named after your charitable aunt Betsy."

Savannah blinked away tears. "You would have loved Aunt Betsy. She died in 1911 after suffering terrible rheumatism." Savannah smiled at Genevieve. "She would have been delighted at Lucas finding such joy with you."

They sat in companionable silence a few moments, the sounds of the house quietly infiltrating their haven. A maid sang in the hallway, while the sound of the piano playing downstairs seeped through the floorboards.

"Parthena's playing," Genevieve murmured. "That doesn't sound like Lucas." She flushed as she met Savannah's gaze. "After living with him for a few years, I've become rather an expert at how he sounds."

Savannah's smile dimmed. "I'm afraid I was rude to your sister earlier. I need to apologize to her."

Genevieve grimaced as she shifted on the bed. She nodded her agreement as Savannah lifted baby Elizabeth and settled her in the bassinette by the bed before focusing on Savannah's comment. "I can't fault you for loyalty, although, from what I heard, Parthena was equally rude."

Savannah nodded. "Yes, although I had provoked her. I hate the thought of anyone hurting Lucas, although I'm delighted he's found joy with you, Genevieve." She shared a chagrined smile with her sister-in-law. "There's no reason for me to attempt to punish your sister for her decision to marry her husband when, due to that, Lucas was fortunate to have met and married you."

Genevieve smiled as she clasped Savannah's hand. "Ironically we have Parthena's husband to thank for that. Morgan arranged for my escape from Boston, with my sister's approval."

Savannah smiled as she squeezed Genevieve's hand before releasing it. "Now, if I could convince Lucas and you to move to Missoula, everything would be perfect."

Genevieve's eyes fluttered as she fought sleep.

Savannah rose. "You should rest while the baby sleeps," she whispered. She eased out of the room, shutting the door quietly behind her.

"Are you happy, Thena?" The whispered voice emerged from the shadows in a rear sitting room where Parthena had gone to think over her interaction with Savannah.

"Lucas," she breathed. She stiffened her shoulders and spine. "What are you doing here?"

He emerged from the shadows, a three-day growth of beard and well-worn clothes highlighting his exhausted state. "I thought to steal away for a few moments as you tended Vivie." He chuckled. "And hide from my sister and your husband."

Parthena smiled. "I wondered why Morgan had time to pore over a report he received from Boston." She traced a hand over the back of a rocking chair. "What is this room?"

Lucas smiled. "This is our private sitting room, although we rarely use it. Gabriel made me that rocking chair, and Jeremy made Vivie hers." He smiled as he looked at them. "We had them in the front room until it became too difficult for Vivie to sit in such a chair."

"She might appreciate it now in her bedroom, to rock the baby to sleep."

Lucas nodded, his gaze roving over the room. "I wonder what we'll have to move so that it will fit in our room," he murmured. "The bassinette takes up more space than I thought it would." He yawned and stretched, his muscles shaking with the movement. "Forgive me. I haven't had much sleep these past few nights."

Parthena watched him as though mesmerized. "But you wouldn't have it any other way."

Lucas tilted his head to the side, contemplating her comment with confusion. "Of course not. My Vivie gave birth to our daughter, Elizabeth. I want to be here and to support her as much as I can. I'm already at a disadvantage as I can do little to nourish her." A wondrous smile bloomed. "But I can soothe her and hold her and let her know how cherished she is."

Parthena bit her lip as she blinked away tears. "You really love her, don't you?"

Lucas nodded, his gaze warm, but with no hint of passion as he beheld the woman he had once loved. "Yes. It didn't take me long to realize what a gift she was. She is." His tender gaze met Parthena's. "Surely you realize that you and I would have driven each other mad within a year. We shared music, but our desire to perform, to excel, would have eroded any regard we had for each other."

She swiped at her cheeks and shook at his words. "I—I must admit I've never thought about it in that way."

"Thena, I won't lie and say that I never loved you. That I was mistaken in my regard for you. I loved you, and Vivie is aware of that. But it's all in the past. Vivie and our daughter are my future." He watched Parthena with a fierce intensity. "I need to ensure you understand that."

She watched him. "I do."

His brows furrowed as he was unable to hide his concern. "I'd wish the same for you."

Parthena attempted a smile, but it was brittle and did little to reassure him. "Morgan and I ... Well, let's say, we've come to an understanding. He's been supportive of me and all I do for quite some time now."

Lucas frowned at the vague description of her relationship with her husband. "I hope it's more than companionship for you, Thena. You deserve more than that." He squeezed her arm. "I must see how Vivie and the baby are." He brushed past her, leaving her alone.

~

Lucas crept into the bedroom where his wife and daughter slumbered. He knew the time soon approached when baby Elizabeth would awaken with a cry, demanding to be fed and changed, but he relished this time to study her. He traced a finger over her button nose and her pink cheeks, and marveled at the luminescence of her skin. "My little pearl," he whispered as he bent to kiss her head.

He turned to the bed to find his wife watching him. "Hello, my Vivie. My love," he whispered. He kicked off his shoes and crawled into bed, pulling her close. "I've missed you."

She giggled. "You've only been away a few hours." She sighed with contentment as she relaxed into him. "I've never known such joy."

"That doesn't even begin to encompass the depth of my feelings," he whispered into her ear. "Thank you, Vivie. For Little Betsy. For loving me." He kissed her ear. "I can't imagine life without you."

She sniffled. "Nor can I," she whispered. "I want to remain in this room, cocooned in our happiness."

He chuckled. "Yes, as there is strife outside these walls." He frowned as her contentment seemed to fade. "What is it, my love?"

"Oh, Parthena and Savannah had an argument. It's as though I'm a prize, and they are fighting over who has the right to me." She tucked herself into his side. "Why can't they get along and understand I love them both?"

"Savannah will always mistrust your sister because of me, Vivie. Nothing will change that. And that will cause your sister to feel cornered and to attack Sav where she is most vulnerable." He shrugged. "I spoke with Parthena a few minutes ago."

When Genevieve tensed, he scooted down in the bed so they were face-to-face. "I needed to ensure she understood that, although I once held her in high regard, she was my past. That you and our baby are my present and my future. That I've loved you since almost the moment we eloped." He stroked her cheek. "I wanted there to be no doubt in her mind about how I felt."

She smiled, arching up to kiss him. "Thank you, Lucas. I imagine it was a difficult conversation."

He shook his head, gifting her with a wondrous smile. "Not in the least. It's the truth. I love you, and she needs to understand that."

"I'm thankful she feels the same for Morgan." She nuzzled the side of his neck.

"Does she? She spoke of them coming to an understanding and enjoying a companionship with each other today. That doesn't sound much like love to me," Lucas said.

Genevieve kissed him on his neck. "Trust me. A greater depth of emotion exists between them than she's admitted to." She kissed him again before drifting to sleep in his arms.

CHAPTER 3

Two weeks later, Morgan entered the room he'd been using as a makeshift office in Lucas and Genevieve's house, stopping when he saw Parthena sitting with her niece in the crook of her arm. She *coo*ed to her niece and kissed her nose, smiling with encouragement at her gurgling noises.

"Sounds more like she's spitting up than anything else," Morgan said as he teased Parthena. He closed the door behind him and approached the desk piled high with papers. He stopped as he beheld Parthena. Her straw-blond hair gleamed in the shaft of sunlight, and she appeared the picture of health. His breath caught as he watched her, fighting visions of her upon her release from the workhouse.

"You're a perfect darling, aren't you?" Parthena asked her two-week-old niece who had fallen asleep. Parthena rose, settling her inside a small crib near the edge of a settee and close to a heating grate. When her niece showed no signs of stirring, Parthena focused on her husband, finally noticing his intense regard of her. "Are you all right, Morgan?"

He nodded. "I like watching you with our niece."

She smiled. "I like that you consider her your niece," she teased.

His smile faded, and he turned toward his desk and sat at the chair behind it. "We are married, Parthena. I hoped you had come to believe your family was my family." He focused on the papers in front of him, although he failed to see them.

Parthena moved to stand beside him. She ran a hand down his arm before moving behind him to give him a shoulder rub.

"What are you doing, Hennie?" he snapped as he spun to confront her, the swivel chair squeaking as he moved.

Her hands fell away, and she backed up a step to avoid being thwacked by his chair before stilling her movements. "I don't know what I've done to upset you. I'll leave you to your work." She stifled a shriek as he grabbed her arm and yanked her to him. The baby continued her slumber as they spoke in low voices.

He exhaled twice before he spoke. "I'm in a wretched mood. Forgive me," he whispered.

She traced a finger over his eyebrows, going from one to the other with a featherlight caress. "Is it your business?"

His shoulders slumped. "If only it were that simple." He met her gaze, his filled with longing. "I entered this room and saw you holding a child, a baby, and ..." He closed his eyes. "And I yearn."

"Oh," she breathed. "I had no idea you desired to be a father."

He chuckled humorlessly. "I never did. Not after my childhood. But you make me believe again, Hennie. And that's a very dangerous thing for a man like me."

"Why?" she whispered, her fingers now stroking through his hair.

"Because I know you have no regard for me. Not truly. Nothing beyond passion anyway." When she began to protest, his glare silenced her. "I heard you speak with Lucas the other day. I didn't mean to, and I intended to back away when I heard you talking, but it was as though I were rooted in place." He cleared his throat. "I'm a fool because I thought we had so much more than *an understanding and companionship*, and I had hoped you desired more than my ... *support*."

"Morgan," Parthena pleaded but was cut off by her husband.

"Because I love you. I always have," he whispered. He watched as shock and disbelief flitted over her face, and her hands fell away from him. "And I should have known better than to yearn for more." The baby whimpered, and he nodded his agreement at her move toward the crib. "Yes, take care of your niece. I have pressing letters I must address."

"Morgan," she whispered again but was interrupted as her niece gave a low yowl. After ascertaining it was merely baby noises and she slept soundly, Parthena was unable to penetrate Morgan's intense focus as he concentrated on his business. She carefully lifted the cradle and left the room.

Upon her departure, Morgan threw down his pen and held his head in his hands. "Idiot," he berated himself.

~

Genevieve sat in the living room with baby Lizzie asleep against her shoulder. She had argued against putting her in her bassinette as she wanted to hold her, and Lucas had promised to take over when her arms tired. Morgan was in the makeshift office working while Parthena was in the back sitting room, playing morose songs on the piano.

"I would think Parthena would play uplifting music with the news that the United Kingdom has granted women over thirty the right to vote," Lucas said as he lowered his newspaper.

Genevieve shared a sardonic smile with him. "She would rejoice for a few moments and then sputter at the injustice for all the women who were excluded. And I think it frightens her to think that such a limited bill might be viewed as a gateway to the vote here."

"I think most agree that the only way forward is the amendment," Lucas said as he folded the afternoon paper. "Still, it seems that other countries are making more progress than we are."

At the soft tapping on the front door, Lucas answered it and beamed. He led his cousin Patrick Sullivan and his wife, Fiona, into the living room, before hauling their three-year-old daughter, Rose, up into his arms to prevent her from scampering over to see the baby and waking her.

"You must be quiet right now, Rosie," Lucas whispered. "Baby

Lizzie is sleeping, and we don't want to wake her. When she does, you can meet your cousin."

"She's tiny," Rose said.

"Yes, and you were that tiny once," Lucas teased. He sat on a chair and held her on his lap, quietly telling her stories to entertain her. She settled and eventually fell asleep.

"Only you have the ability to put her to sleep like that," Fiona complained. "I wish I had that magic power."

Lucas kissed Rose on her head. "I'm sure she was tired before you came over."

"No, you have an ability I will always envy," Fiona said, a gentle lilt to her voice that hinted of her native Ireland. "Forgive us for not coming sooner, but we have had terrible colds and did not want to share our illness." She smiled at Genevieve's grateful look.

"Isn't she gorgeous?" Genevieve asked, as proud as any mother could be.

"I thought you would call her Betsy," Patrick said as he sat on a chair near Lucas. He frowned at the somber music and then shrugged.

"Vivie wants her to know of our generous, kind-hearted aunt but wants our child to be her own person too. Thus, we will call her Lizzie while telling her about the woman she is named after."

Patrick nodded and then rose as Savannah entered. "Sav," he said as he pulled her into a close embrace. "I had thought you'd be in Missoula by now.

"I leave soon," she said with a smile. "Jeremy's letters are more insistent that I return, although he knows why I wanted to be here."

Her gaze softened as she saw Rose asleep in Lucas's arms. "You will be such a wonderful father, Lucas." She saw his pleased blush as he held the little girl he considered his niece. Savannah sobered at Patrick fighting a frown. "Is something wrong, Patrick?" Savannah asked. "Melinda is well, if you are concerned."

He smiled his thanks at her comment. "I know. We write weekly, and I find her letters more informative and joyful each week." His smile turned wistful. "You have done a wonderful job raising her."

Savannah nodded. "She is the daughter of my heart."

Patrick paused and shared a long look with his wife, Fiona, before answering Savannah's original question. "Mrs. Smythe has reappeared after her disappearance last fall."

Patrick's and Savannah's expressions became grim as the room fell silent. Every member of the extended family had at least one reason to loathe the manipulative Mrs. Smythe. For Patrick, it was complicated. Mrs. Smythe, as Patrick's stepmother, had married his father for the money she hoped to obtain from Sean Sullivan's successful black-smithing business. She had also tricked her half-asleep stepson into sleeping with her, resulting in the only child from her marriage with her husband, Sean. After Patrick was banished from the house and her husband died, Mrs. Smythe lost the generous inheritance due to her desire for a far grander lifestyle than she could afford. She sent her daughter, Melinda, to an orphanage, thankfully rescued by Patrick's brother, Colin, and adopted by Savannah and Jeremy.

After being banished from his father's house, Patrick had felt guilt and embarrassment, and had hid from his family after his letters to his siblings had gone unanswered. Years later he reunited with his siblings, and, even though Patrick was technically Melinda's father, he had had no desire to tear her from his cousin who had loved Melinda for years and had provided her with a stable home. He was content to love Melinda from afar.

Lucas glowered at the news, although his hold on Rose remained gentle. "Tell the authorities and have Mrs. Smythe arrested."

His cousin shrugged. "I wish it were that easy. According to the authorities, it is our word against hers, and she has a very powerful man championing her." His mouth turned down as Fiona pleated her skirt. "Samuel Sanders. It appears he is throwing around what clout he has to support Mrs. Smythe in an attempt to undermine me. To make Fiona out as a hysterical woman who staged her own attack to garner sympathy and malign a woman disliked by her family."

"But that's preposterous," Lucas stammered.

"It is, but it's exactly what I would expect from her. From him." He rubbed at his head. "Whenever Fee leaves the house, Mrs. Smythe seems to be nearby, as though mocking her. And, even when Mrs.

47

Smythe isn't there, Fee is always looking over her shoulder, in case she is around."

Savannah gripped his hand and then focused on Fiona. "Fee? What can we do?"

"'Tis little to do. The woman has broken no laws, at least not since she locked me in a closet and attempted to steal my child. But I fear what will occur again." Fiona fought a shudder as she remembered what she had suffered in October.

Genevieve frowned, her brows furrowed. "This woman, although mean, has always seemed rather devious. I would think she would tire of tormenting you and would want to take some action. Has she hinted at anything that she has planned?"

Patrick's gaze was bleak as he looked at his family. "She told me, when I confronted her one day as she loitered on a corner while I walked to work, that I might have escaped her plans, but that she would find a way to attack the least-suspecting one among us to pay for *his* duplicity."

Lucas shook his head as though he had just heard gibberish. "What in God's name does that mean?"

Fiona shrugged. "We've attempted to figure out what she meant, but it makes no sense, for none of us are deserving of her malice."

"Well, whether we are or we aren't, we will remain her focus until the day she dies," Savannah said. "I fear she will return to Missoula. She seems to enjoy playing cat-and-mouse games with you, but she has always focused more on Clarissa. Mrs. Smythe's hatred for Rissa knows no bounds."

Patrick nodded at the mention of his sister in Missoula. She had fled Boston seventeen years ago to escape Mrs. Smythe and an arranged marriage to Cameron Wright. "Will you warn her? Warn Gabriel? I fear we have not heard the last of Mrs. Smythe."

Savannah nodded. "We must all be on our guard. For, if there is one thing I know, that woman is unpredictable. And she has found a partner in crime who perfectly matches her for deviousness, spite and planning."

The conversation abruptly changed as Lizzie woke, her cry awakening Rose.

~

Parthena sat in the chair in the hotel room she shared with Morgan. Her bleary-eyed stare focused on the door, and she sat up as it creaked open. She met her husband's surprised gaze. "Where have you been?" she asked before wincing.

He half smiled. "You sound like a concerned wife." He moved to the closet near her chair and wrenched it open. He rifled inside, tossing clean clothes onto the made-up bed. He turned to pick up his clothes, but Parthena had risen to stand behind him, and he toppled into her, crushing her into the bed behind them.

"*Oof*," he grunted as he pushed up to lever himself off her. He stilled when she gripped his arms. She arched up, sniffing at his clothes. When she released him, he rose and motioned for her to roll to one side so he could gather the crushed garments beneath her.

"Morgan, where were you?" she asked as she propped herself on her elbows, remaining on top of his clothes. "I've been terribly worried."

He flushed. "I realized I'd been inconsiderate of your needs." He clenched his fists at his side but stared at her with a flat gaze and kept his voice emotionless. "I asked for another room here and slept there last night. You shouldn't have to suffer my presence in your bed every night."

Parthena's eyes filled with tears. "*Our* bed," she whispered. "It was our bed." She gripped his hand, holding fast when he attempted to free himself and move into the bathroom. "Please don't do this to us, Morgan."

Anguish seeped into his gaze as he beheld her. "Can't you understand that I'm not the one doing this to us?" He cleared his throat. "I'm not the one playing morose piano songs. I'm not the one hiding in back rooms, avoiding any contact with me." He sighed. "I'm sorry I said it. I'm sorry I said I loved you. I never meant to ruin what we had."

She nodded and tugged on his arm, pulling him to sit next to her. She moved to sit cross-legged so she faced him. After swiping at her cheeks in irritation at the tears that continued to fall, she took a deep, stuttering breath. "Do you know why I said what I did to Lucas?"

He watched her with fathomless eyes.

"I … What I feel for you is too new. Too private to share with anyone else. Why should I tell him how I feel when I haven't even told you?"

"Parthena, you don't have to fabricate feelings," he grumbled, his jaw ticking with irritation.

"No!" Parthena yelled, rising to her knees on the bed and clasping his face with her small hands. Her thumbs caressed his cheeks as she looked into his eyes. "I know it's taken me too long to tell you how I feel. But you need to know that I feel so much more than consideration. Than desire."

He arched away from her. "It doesn't matter, Parthena."

His cold dismissal acted as a fuse to her anger. She growled and climbed onto his lap. "It does matter. Please tell me that you'll believe me." She flushed at her beseeching tone.

He watched her with an arrested expression. "I've never known you to beg," he whispered in confusion. "Not with me."

She shook her head as though to clear her vision from unwanted tears. "Because nothing has ever mattered like this does. I love you, Morgan. I love you so much." Her breath shattered after she said it. A sob escaped when he held himself rigid and continued to watch her with wary indecision.

"When I woke in Washington and found you there, you cared for me as though I were beloved. You held me. You listened. You never judged. You never scolded me for my impetuous actions. You mourned what I had lived through and said you'd support me if I felt compelled to protest again." She bent forward and swiped her cheeks against his shirtfront. "I knew then I loved you," she whispered. "I think I had for quite some time."

"Why didn't you tell me?" he asked, his voice scratchy.

She continued to swipe her cheeks side to side against his shirt-front. "I know most people think I'm brave. And I am in certain instances. But when it comes to you …" She swallowed and met his gaze where hope fought disbelief. "If you didn't feel the same, I … I …" She shook her head as tears coursed out. "There are no words to describe how I'd feel."

"But I do love you, Parthena. What more did I have to do to show you?" he whispered against her ear, before backing away and meeting her gaze. "Why would you wait weeks to tell me after I admitted my feelings for you?"

"Only you, Morgan, have the ability to terrify me. What if you don't love me as much as I love you?" She shook her head, showing him that she needed him to remain quiet. "I realized, as I sat in that chair all night long and waited for you, that I had to overcome my fear. That I was hurting you as much as I hurt myself."

A tender smile bloomed, and he cupped her cheek.

She sobbed as she collapsed fully against his chest. "Don't spend another night in that room. Stay with me. You belong with me." She clung to him.

"*Shh,* … my little love, of course I'll stay with you." He kissed her head. "I thought you didn't want me here."

She pushed herself back, her tear-reddened gaze meeting his as she shook her head. "No, I want you. Even when I was too much of a fool to realize what I wanted, I wanted you." She traced his brows and pushed his hair back. "Please, Morgan. Please."

"Don't beg, my love. I believe you," he whispered, kissing her. "I love you and want no other." He tugged her close, sighing with contentment to hold her once again in his arms.

Later at the end of February, Morgan sat in the family parlor as Lucas tinkered on the piano with Parthena while Genevieve rocked baby Lizzie in her arms. Morgan swore as he read the head-lines, muttering his apologies.

"What has you so riled, Morgan?" Parthena asked as she turned on the stool to face her husband. Lucas nodded in agreement to the question but continued to play.

"Have you any idea what your state legislature has done?" He shook the paper at them. "They're idiots!"

Lucas slammed his fingers on the piano keys and rose, marching to each door leading into the family room and shutting them. "Careful what you say, Morgan. They might be idiots, but plenty agree with Montana's Extraordinary Session of the Legislature and what our legislature is trying to do."

Genevieve gave Lucas a long look.

He nodded, his lips quirked in an ironic smile. "And, yes, I under-stand why you were hesitant to have so many servants."

"They're all spies on us, Lucas," Genevieve murmured. "I hate that I can't talk freely in my own home."

Lucas approached a gramophone and set a record on it to play. "I know this will sound egotistical, but it's one of me playing with Perry Hawke."

Parthena waved away the music and focused on Morgan. "What does the paper say?" Her murmur was covered by Perry's booming voice filling the room as he sang of lost love.

"Your legislature has just passed a Sedition Law. It's a wordy law, as only government can make such things, but basically it states that, if you say or write anything against the government, any member of government, any action of government, you are acting in a treasonous manner and can be sent to jail for twenty years."

"What?" Lucas asked. "But that's insane. I know the Butte papers are in the pockets of the Company, but there is still the *Bulletin*. It says things all the time that are antigovernment and antiwar."

Morgan held up the edition of the *Anaconda Standard*. "Well, they'll risk being accused of sedition." He scanned the article. "According to this fine paper, it rather proudly proclaims, 'There is no freedom of speech any longer for the disloyal or pro-German. A man can talk all right if he talks right.'"

For a long moment, the only sound in the room was of Perry's soaring voice and Lucas's beautiful accompaniment.

"*Talks right? Talks right?*" Morgan growled as he dropped the paper onto a side table. "An essential aspect of living in this country has been the freedom to speak one's dissent. Forgive me if I'm showing my ignorance, but that's not the definition of freedom of speech I learned when I studied the Bill of Rights."

Parthena snorted. "If you think most Americans have given a thought to their rights, you're crazy. Most are so afraid of their shadows now that we're at war that they're willing to give up any and all of their rights for the mirage of security."

Genevieve kissed Lizzie's head. "I fear you are right, Parthena. We've lived among our German friends and neighbors for years, and now they are looked upon with suspicion. Too many allow fear to dictate how they act and what they will accept."

"Although I agree with all of you, the fact remains that, as of this moment, we must guard what we say." Lucas speared Genevieve and then Parthena with a quelling glance. "You are two outspoken sisters, and I do not wish to have either of you accused of sedition."

"Or sent to prison." Morgan watched his wife with blatant concern. "Perhaps now would be a good time to return to Massachusetts."

Lucas sighed, crossing his arms over his belly. "I fear you believe that, if you escape to Boston, you'll be spared living under such a law. However, you should be aware that Montana's two senators are attempting to pass such a law in Congress. I fear that the success of the law here will embolden them. Everyone in the United States might well be living under such a law soon."

CHAPTER 4

*Z*ylphia stood, staring out the window of her private study at the back of the house. She rarely spent time in her studio as she had tired of glaring at a blank canvas. She had painted little since her return from Washington in December, and her sketches were filled with disturbing images she did not care to bring to life. Her gaze distant, she wrapped her arms around her belly as she watched raindrops slide down the windowpane. After a moment, she closed her eyes, as though attempting to shut out the visions she saw. Heavy keys on a keychain rattled, and she shook, crumbling to the floor. She curled into herself and rocked, her arms wrapped tightly around her middle as she moaned.

Hands reached out, touching her back, and she shrieked. "No! I will not bend! You will not force me this time!" Her voice, muffled by her position, emerged determined yet panicked. When the hands persisted in coaxing her to rise, she struck out, earning an "*Oof*" in protest.

"*Shh*, love, no one is forcing you to do anything," Teddy soothed. He settled beside her on the floor and ran another hand over her quivering back. "You're here, with me, in our home in Boston. You're safe, Zee." He continued to croon and whisper to her, running warm hands over her as her panic abated. "*Shh*, my love."

Her shaking and crying continued, and he spoke to her throughout. "You're safe, darling," he chanted over and over. "Open your eyes, and see where you are." He kissed her cheeks, caressed her head and warmed her trembling body with his.

Many minutes later she raised her head and looked at him, lying beside her on the floor. "Teddy?" she whispered. She unfurled herself and pushed herself in an ungainly manner into his embrace. "Hold me. Hold me closer."

"Forever." His arms closed around her, pulling her tight. "No one will hurt you here, Zee." When her breathing had calmed, and it seemed she was so relaxed she was on the verge of falling asleep, Teddy stroked a hand over her head. "What frightened you?"

"I was standing at the window, unable to stop thinking about prison. About the workhouse. What happened there. The sounds. The smells. The treatment. And then I heard keys rattle." She fought a shudder as she pushed herself tighter into Teddy's embrace. "They always rattled the keys before they entered my cell to force-feed me."

"Oh, Zee," he sighed, kissing her head. "The maid must have rattled her keys by accident. I'll speak with her. She was terrified when she ran to get me."

"I'm sorry to be so feeble." She moved to push out of his arms but found his hold implacable. "I can't seem to get past these memories."

"You suffered a trauma, Zee, not only to your body but to your mind and spirit as well. Never be embarrassed for taking the time you need to recover from it." He caressed her cheek as she leaned away to meet his tender gaze. "You've helped me through my demons. Let me do the same for you."

She sighed and settled once more against his chest. He held her until she rose to go upstairs to rest.

~

Teddy returned to his office to find his father-in-law, Aidan, awaiting him.

"I thought you'd forgotten our appointment," Aidan said. He stilled when he noted Teddy's somber mood.

"No, I was detained." He sat and shook away an offer for a drink. "Zee was frightened, and I helped calm her."

"She had another attack?"

"*Another?*" Teddy's gaze sharpened.

"She had one a few days ago while visiting her mother. Delia was nearly hysterical at her inability to calm her. Thankfully Zee's panic abated before the doctor arrived."

"What provoked the one at your house?" He canted forward, his eyes gleaming with the need to better understand what tormented his wife.

"The cook decided to prepare bacon for a dish that evening, and the smell rose through one of the vents." Aidan shrugged.

"They cooked bacon at the workhouse to entice them to eat," Teddy whispered. He closed his eyes. "She told me a few days ago that she always feels guilty when she eats it now."

Aidan grunted in dismay and shook his head. "I don't know what to do for her, Teddy. The doctor wanted her to take laudanum, but Zee refuses."

"She's terrified of her dreams," Teddy murmured. "I think she doesn't want to spend any more time asleep than she already does." He scratched at his head, his fingers unconsciously tracing the scars he received when he fought in the Great War for England. He firmed his jaw and met Aidan's gaze. "She's not crazy." Teddy's tone was implacable. "I will not have her whispered about, with those of so-called good society saying she should be sent away."

Aidan nodded, his eyes flashing with anger at the suggestion. "I agree with you. Anyone with sense will understand she suffered a trauma while imprisoned."

Teddy shook his head and sat with shoulders stooped in his office. "I fear that has only emboldened some to say that she is accustomed to such treatment and would relish returning to such an environment." He met his father-in-law's irate gaze. "I know the staff gossips. I can't prevent their chatter. But I don't know how to protect her."

Aidan sighed, his business concerns forgotten as he considered his daughter. "The only way to help her through this is to continue to show her our love."

Teddy shook his head. "I think it's more than that for Zee. She must face her fears too." He paused a moment and then rose. "Will you excuse me?"

He marched from his front office and up the stairs to Zylphia's studio. Muted light entered through the tall windows on the rainy afternoon, and a blank canvas with a white palette sat ready for her, whenever she deigned to paint again. His gaze roamed the room, from the bookcase jammed full with trinkets and papers to the comfortable love seat and chair. He turned on a light as his gaze searched for a large black-covered book. He saw it on the floor by the love seat.

After he made himself comfortable, he opened it. The first pages of sketches were of Washington, DC, in the summer and fall. A father flying a kite with his young son. A man selling ices. A view of a memorial being built in the distance. He continued to flip through the pages, and his pace slowed as the tenor of the images transformed. Where those before had been light and whimsical, these were darker. "Demon dreams," he whispered. One was of a snake approaching her as she lay on the concrete floor, her leg shackled so she couldn't escape. He sat transfixed as he began to comprehend the depth of her fears.

"What are you doing?" Zylphia asked as she stood in the doorway to her studio.

"I'm snooping. I have no reason to hide what I'm doing." He watched her with concern. "Why don't you paint this?" He turned the book around to show her a specific drawing.

She shivered and held herself rigidly upright. "I have no need for the world to know of my inability to overcome what occurred."

"There is no shame in this, Zee." He flipped the page, sobering further at the image of her reaching for a baby but the infant always too far away from her for her to hold it. In the corner, a man sat with his arms crossed, glaring at her with contempt as he refused to render any aid. "Is this how you see me? How you still see me?"

Her eyes filled at his rasped question. "No." She swiped at her cheeks.

He waited for her to say more, and, when she remained quiet, he cleared his throat. "Is this man me?"

"Yes," she whispered. She blocked the doorway when he slammed the sketchbook shut and rose. "Teddy, please listen."

"You say that's not how you see me but that the man is me. It can't be both ways, Zee." He looked at a spot over her shoulder, crowding her in an attempt to push past her.

However, she stood her ground and wouldn't let him leave the room. "No, Teddy, it's how I think you should see me. Not how you do see me," she whispered.

His brows furrowed as he thought over her words, and then he shook his head. "What?"

"How can you forgive me when I can't forgive myself?" she wailed. "I lost our child out of pride and stubbornness."

He gripped her shoulders, his gray eyes lit with a deep passion. "Our baby died, Zee. We will never know why. I refuse to believe it was because you were in jail." He took a deep breath. "There is just as much likelihood our baby would have died had you been here, safe in our house, in my arms."

"If I'd eaten … If I'd not struggled …" she whispered. "I will never banish this guilt."

"Oh, my love." He pulled her into his arms, holding her close. "I don't know what to say to ease your torment." He held her as she shuddered. "I hate that you see me like that. That you believe I should perceive you like that."

She pushed away, meeting his gaze for a fleeting moment before ducking her head. "I don't know what to do, Teddy. I thought time would make things better." She swallowed as her throat seemed to thicken with tears. "But it's not."

He ran a hand over her head. "I would paint. Paint what you feel.

The good. The beautiful. That which you think is shameful." He met her gaze. "I would never think that of your art, but I think you need to express what you have inside, my darling."

"I fear …" She shook her head as he waited patiently for her to speak. "I fear that, if I paint what troubles me, I'll never be able to box away what I'm feeling."

He looked at her with his gaze filled with love and understanding. "You can't lock this away, Zee. You can see what this is doing to you. To us." He waited a moment before whispering, "Try." He kissed her on her forehead and slipped from the room.

～

Zylphia stood in front of the blank canvas, the brush in her hand immobile as she stared dazedly at it. She dipped the brush into the black oil paint on her palette and emptied her mind as her hand moved furiously, as though independent from the rest of her. She frowned as the image in her mind sprang to life on the canvas. Ignoring the paint that splattered her apron or the white sheet covering the floor, she maintained a ruthless focus.

Hours later she dropped her brush in diluted turpentine to clean it and scrubbed at her hands with a piece of clean linen. She studied the disjointed, troubling paintings that lined one wall of her studio. Each one a memory from her time in jail. "My fears brought to life," she whispered as she walked toward one of them, studying it with a critical eye.

A stark black chair sat in the middle of a room with the hint of a cell door in the distance. The background color was a gray-blue, with the only light shining in from the ajar door. She shivered as she examined it.

"Are you all right, Zee?" Teddy whispered.

She shrieked and then spun to face him. "What time is it? I'm sorry if I've neglected you." She scrubbed at her hands in earnest as he strode toward her and kissed her on her cheek.

"I'm not." His gaze flicked from one painting to the next. "You used your time well." He frowned at the one of her lying on a cot, curled in the corner of a cell. "How are you?"

"Exhausted," she whispered. Then she smiled. "But I feel a little better."

"Good," he said as he kissed her forehead. "Come. Sit and relax. I've saved dinner, and we can eat in here if you want."

After Zylphia washed her hands again at the sink and stripped off her soiled apron, he smiled as she collapsed onto her love seat. He called out to the maid to deliver their supper on trays to her studio. "I didn't think you could paint without more light," he murmured as he turned on another lamp.

"I found I didn't need the light this time. I just needed to set free what I needed to paint." She flushed as she looked at her drying paintings. "I don't want these shown, Teddy. These are for me only."

He frowned. "Of course. You are in control of who sees your art, Zee. I will never interfere."

She held out her hand and smiled as he clasped hers. "Except to encourage me to paint what I didn't want to."

He chuckled and agreed. After they ate their supper, she was on the verge of dozing on the settee. "Come, love. You should rest."

"Thank you, Teddy." She met his inquisitive stare. "Thank you for caring for me. For pushing me to improve. For not allowing me to wallow."

He stroked her cheek. "You are not a wallower, darling." His eyes glowed with deep emotions. "I know this will not heal all your pain, but I hope it will ease it."

~

A week later, Zylphia poked her head into Teddy's office. She smiled at him bent over a stack of papers, his hands raking through his disheveled hair as he considered a business venture. "May I disturb you?"

"Zee," he whispered. "Yes, of course." He motioned for her to enter, frowning as she paused before coming to sit in a chair before his desk.

"I've been painting a lot." She paused at the humor lighting his eyes at her statement. She had painted for hours every day for the past week. "I think I nearly bought out all of the gray and black oil paint here in Boston." She flushed as Teddy chuckled.

"You are doing what you need, Zee," he said.

"It saddens me that you don't have a painting for your office." She saw the remorse in his gaze at the destroyed cherry blossom painting. She had gifted him the painting before they were married, and he had demolished it the previous fall in a fit of rage after returning from seeing her in Washington. "I painted something new for behind your desk."

"Ah, Zee, that's … very considerate of you," he said as he failed to hide a wince. "I'm uncertain if your latest … masterpieces will match the decor of the room." He frowned as she giggled at him.

"Please, Teddy. I want you to be as proud of the art I am doing now as of that which I did before the War. Before Washington."

He sobered and nodded. "You know I am, darling. May I see the painting?"

She smiled. "Nothing can ever replace what was lost, but I hope you will find comfort in this." She hopped up and opened the office door, pulling in a large painting, the white back visible to Teddy.

"I hope I will receive my fair share of black and gray," he teased.

She flushed and shook her head. "No, my love. For you, I found inspiration in the Gardens." She spun the painting around and smiled with delight as he gasped at the scene of the Public Gardens in spring-time glory.

He moved around his desk, his eyes alit with joy. "Oh, Zee. It's stunning." He caressed her cheek before kissing her softly. "Thank you."

"I've found color again," she whispered. "I no longer see only black and gray." Tears seeped out as she whispered that truth.

"Oh, Zee," he murmured. He took the painting from her and set it at the foot of his desk. "I always knew you would."

He held her as she cried, giving silent thanks for her inner strength and perseverance.

~

"Florence, I can make a pot of tea," Zylphia said in exasperation as she gently pushed her very pregnant cousin and friend into a chair. She moved around Florence's kitchen in the home Florence shared with her husband, Zylphia's cousin, Richard McLeod, in Dorchester. They had a few hours before Florence's five boys returned home from school. After the tea was steeping, she sat beside Florence, slicing the crumb cake she had brought with her.

"Don't feel guilty about eating this," Zylphia said. "I brought two others for the boys and Richard."

Florence fought a smile as she took a bite of the cake.

"How are you feeling?"

Florence rubbed at her belly as she sat back in her chair, unable to hide an elated smile. "I am well. This is the worst part, besides the morning sickness in the beginning. But it's also the best. Because I know that I'll soon have my baby in my arms."

Zylphia smiled. "I pray, every night, that you have a healthy baby." She did not say "this time," but the look she shared with Florence expressed that sentiment. Florence and Richard had lost a baby daughter four years ago at birth. "Fate wouldn't be that cruel twice, Flo."

"I have dreams, Zee," she whispered. "I never tell Richard about them because I know he battles the same fears." She reached out and gripped Zylphia's hand. "But I see my daughter. So perfect. So still. With the cord wrapped around her neck again." She blinked. "I don't know if I could survive that a second time."

Zylphia blinked and lost her battle fighting tears. "I ... I ..." She shrugged.

"There's nothing to say to calm this type of fear, Zee. I know that. Only when I have my baby in my arms will I be fully at peace." Florence let go of Zee's hand and took a sip of tea.

"How is Richard?" Zylphia frowned as she thought about her second-oldest McLeod cousin who ran three blacksmith shops in

Boston. A dedicated father and family man, he seemed delighted at the prospect of another child.

"Apprehensive. He watches me with thinly veiled terror every day. I know he spoke with your father and that he is trying to fill these days with joy, but he is finding it difficult." She swiped at a tear on her cheek. "He remembers how much I mourned the last time."

Zylphia's frown turned into a glower. "He remembers how much he mourned, Flo. He was devastated at the loss of your daughter." She saw acknowledgment of that truth in Florence's gaze. "How much longer?"

Florence smiled as she tapped her belly. "Only another few weeks." She tilted her head and looked at Zylphia. "You seem better, Zee. What's changed?"

She flushed and played with the crumbs on her plate. "I … I painted." She continued to look at the plate and took a deep breath as she fought deep emotions. "I hadn't realized how much I needed to express what had happened to me. The fear. The rage. The sense of hopelessness. Of the powerlessness I felt every day I was in the workhouse or jail." She sniffled.

After a moment, she shrugged in embarrassment as she looked at Florence. "I never would have painted if it hadn't been for Teddy. Somehow he knew I needed to express myself in that way."

Florence smiled. "He loves you, Zee. He'll do what he needs to ensure you are healthy and happy again." When Zee frowned, Florence did too. "What is it, Zee?"

"I … I don't want to go back. To Washington," she whispered, torment plain in her eyes. "I want to remain here. But I hate being perceived as a coward. As unable or unwilling to continue to support the movement."

Florence's jaw firmed, and her eyes flashed. "Do you see me as unable or unwilling to support the cause because I am here in Boston and not in Washington? Do you think my belief, my dedication, any less than yours?" At Zylphia's instinctual shake of her head in denial, Florence nodded. "Exactly. Anyone who would believe that or would say such a thing is a fool and is attempting to manipulate you into doing what they want. Not what is best for you."

Florence gripped Zylphia's hand. "Zee, you could never be seen as a coward. Only you would ever think of yourself in those terms. No one else would. You lived through events I don't even want to contemplate." Her eyes filled as she unwittingly envisioned Zylphia's time while at the workhouse and jail. "Teddy will want you to stay."

"He has said he wants me here, but he hasn't said he loves me in so long," she whispered.

Florence frowned. "He's shown you his love in every way he knows how. His constancy. His belief that you will heal. His desire to see you paint again."

Zylphia nodded and swiped at her cheeks. "Yes, but I find I need the words too, Flo."

~

Teddy poked his head into Zylphia's studio, smiling as he saw her reading letters. Stacks of new artwork lined the walls of the room, and they were a mixture of what she called her *morose gray period* and her *joyful rebirth period*. "May I?" he asked as he nodded toward the paintings.

She smiled her agreement before focusing again on her correspondence.

He moved forward and pulled the paintings away from the wall, battling anger and guilt at the ones expressing her fears about her treatment in jail. He battled an equal measure of hope with her colorful paintings, worried this was a momentary stage. "They are remarkable as always, Zee."

"Perhaps, although I would like to see if we can visit friends in the country."

He frowned. "You've never shown much interest in leaving the city in spring before. Why would you desire to leave Boston in April?"

She flushed as she pulled a lap rug over her on the cool afternoon.

"I want to have a bonfire, and I do not believe that is appropriate for the alley behind our house."

He watched her, slack-jawed a moment. "Why do you wish to burn them, Zee?"

She shrugged and looked toward a somber painting that peeked out from behind a muted painting of a willow tree in blossom, its wispy branches fluttering in the wind. "I needed to paint them. To remove such darkness from me." Her gaze met his for a moment. "Some of it will always be there, Teddy. It isn't fully gone. But most of it is."

She glared at the black-and-gray paintings. "But I don't want to be reminded of it daily. I don't want this around me." Her jaw clenched shut for a moment. "I refuse to have others see such paintings."

"These could be your dark period. Like Goya's," Teddy mused. He gave her a chagrined look as she glared at him. "I do not mean to make light of what you desire." He clasped her hand. "But I don't want you to regret the destruction of your art."

"I won't. It will be a relief," she whispered. "Can you arrange for us to go somewhere? To have a private fire in the woods? It will need to be soon before the weather turns warm."

"Of course," he murmured, kissing her hand. "How was your visit with Florence today?"

"Good. She is impatient to hold her baby in her arms, which I think is normal." She saw the yearning in his gaze and forced a smile.

"Quite normal," he murmured. "Who has written you?" He motioned to the letters sitting forgotten on her lap.

"Alice and Rowena. They both write that they would like me to return to Washington. They are eager for my aid in persuading senators to change their positions so that the Anthony Amendment is passed and sent to the states for ratification." She frowned as he sobered further. "What is the matter, Teddy?"

"I enjoy our time together in Boston, and I will miss you when you are in Washington." He shrugged. "I shouldn't be selfish in hoping you would remain here."

"Well, my date for returning is undecided. First, we must have that bonfire." She frowned at his tepid smile and watched as he left her studio, deep in thought.

~

P arthena woke, her arms reaching for Morgan. She frowned to find his side of the bed cooled, and she sat up, her straw-blond hair cascading over her shoulders. "Morgan?" she called out. When she failed to hear him moving around in the adjacent bathroom or in his dressing room, she flopped backward with a sigh. She thought back to the two months of mornings she had spent with him in Butte, waking each day in his arms, and her heart ached at returning to a routine here in Boston. They had arrived home yesterday after the long trip across country. She smiled, thinking of the wondrous hours they had spent in their private train cabin.

"Serves me right," she muttered as she curled onto her side, unwilling to leave the warmth of the bedcovers just yet. She closed her eyes, refusing to cry.

"What serves you right, sleeping beauty?" Morgan asked as he slipped into the room with a tray.

"Morgan!" she said, sitting up on her knees before flushing as she had forgotten about her nakedness. After tugging the sheet around her, she beamed at him. "I thought you'd abandoned me for work."

He laughed, setting the tray on a table in the small sitting area in front of the fire. "I hope I'm astute enough to know when to postpone business. And I refused to have the staff bothering us, so I went for a tray."

She reached her arms out for him, tugging him to the bed. She pushed his robe off, running her hands over his shoulders and back. "I woke up and missed you terribly."

"Oh, Hennie," he whispered. He kissed her, rolling her to her back. After running fingers through her tangled blond hair, he smiled. "I will have to return to work, love. I never want you to doubt your choice in me."

She pushed at him until he toppled to his side so she could snuggle against him. "I will never doubt my choice of you. I thought such doubts were dispelled during our time in Butte."

He flushed. "I want to provide as well for you as he does for your sister." At her startled chuckle, he shrugged. "I don't know if it's something I can explain to you, but I know other men would understand." He met her intelligent, accepting gaze. "I want to be worthy of you, always."

"You are worthy simply because of who you are." She looked over her shoulder at the large room. "I love this mansion, but you could sell it tomorrow, and we could move into a much smaller place, and my love for you would not lessen. I am not your mother, Morgan. I will not abandon you if we have financial problems. My love for you does not depend on money." She gave a jaunty shrug. "I like to think, if we were in financial difficulties, that I'd find a way to help us earn money."

He pulled her to him, holding her close. "I know you would. You're intrepid and wonderful. I love you, darling Parthena."

"I hate that our life will return to how it's been now that we're back," she whispered against his shoulder, once she relaxed against him.

"It doesn't have to. There's no reason I must rush to meetings in the morning." He ran a hand over her back as he urged her even closer. "I used to schedule morning meetings so that I didn't feel like a fool for wanting to linger with you when you wanted nothing to do with me."

"Morgan!" She reared up, her gaze filled with shock and embarrassment. After staring at him a long moment, she blinked away tears. "I hate that we wasted so much time estranged. I don't want to go back to that. I want us to be like we were after I was jailed in Washington. How we were in Butte. I love you and want time with you."

"Life will intrude, Hennie. Yet I promise that I will make time for us. If you ever feel that I am neglecting you, you must promise me that you will tell me how you are feeling." He took a deep breath. "Are you returning to Washington?"

Parthena shivered. "No. I may return for a few short visits, but I will not return to work as I did last summer and fall. I have no need to be there."

His hands on her back stilled. "I know the cause is as important to you now as it ever was."

"Of course. But I refuse to suffer as I did." She met his concerned gaze with one filled with impassioned righteousness. "I am determined to take pride in what I did and to find other ways to continue to contribute to the cause."

She giggled as his stomach rumbled. "Come. Let's have breakfast." She paused from rising from the bed when he kept a firm hold on her hand.

"We are all right, Hennie?"

She balanced her hands on his shoulder and kissed him. "We're much better than all right, my love. We are married and in love. And we have a fleet of servants at our beck and call who can bring us trays of food if we so desire to postpone leaving our rooms for a few days." She smiled as he chuckled at her teasing.

*Z*ylphia sat in the private family sitting room at her parents' house, relaxing in front of the fire as her mother served tea. Her favorite room in her parents' mansion was the glass-enclosed conservatory, but one of the windows was leaking, and the room was too cold on this gray April day. "When will the conservatory be repaired?" she asked as she took a sip of tea and settled into the settee.

"Sometime next week. The new window pane had to be specially ordered." Delia shared a chagrined smile with her daughter. "Who would have thought, when we were living in cramped rooms in the back of the orphanage, that we would find this room not to our liking?" She and Zylphia had lived in the orphanage Delia ran in the North End until she had reunited with Aidan and then married him in 1903.

Zylphia laughed. "We are spoiled, but at least we know it. I'm accustomed to the light and beauty in that room in the afternoon." She sighed. "Did you read in the papers today that the Red Baron died yesterday?"

Delia nodded as she took a sip of her tea. "Hard to believe that the German flying ace has died. Hopefully this will mean our boys have more of a fighting chance."

Zylphia slumped into her chair. "I fear this war will never end. It seems like it's been going on forever."

"It seems longer to you because Teddy was involved from the beginning. For most here in America, the War just started for us last year."

Zylphia hugged a pillow to her chest. "For me, it's been almost four years now."

A long silence ensued in the room, only disturbed by the sound of the fire in the grate, the servants working in other rooms and birds chirping outside. As the minutes slowly passed, the tension eased from Zylphia, and she smiled at her mother.

"You seem better, Zee," her mother whispered. Delia, a striking woman at sixty-five, refused to dye her black hair mixed with gray as she celebrated her age. Her gaze roved over her daughter, who appeared more at peace and less brittle than during their last visit.

"I am. I think I will always be haunted by what happened to me. By what I lost and what I nearly lost." She shared a long look with her mother. "But I am finding my way back again." She smiled as her mother's gaze was tear-filled. "Thank you for always having faith in me."

"You are my daughter, Zee. I will always love you and support you in any way I can." At her daughter's nod, she asked, "Have you finally discussed with Teddy the reasons behind your separation?"

"He has forgiven me for my actions last fall. For what I have trouble forgiving myself for." She shuddered. "I still find it difficult accepting that the outcome wouldn't have been different had I not acted in a more sensible manner."

Her mother gripped her hand. "Zee, you will always have these doubts. But you must accept that you are human. That you make mistakes and learn from them." Her gaze became more somber. "I was referring to the initial reason behind your separation from Teddy."

Zylphia frowned and then nodded. "Oh, you mean his reluctance to apply for American citizenship so I can be an American again?" Her jaw clenched with residual anger. "I am not mad with him, but I will never forgive my government for stripping me of my birthright simply because I married the man I love."

Delia nodded. "You attempted to do what you could to sway their attitude when you spoke in front of Congress in December, Zee. None were persuaded."

Zylphia snorted. "I hate that there are always two standards. One for men and one for women. Why should I have to suffer the consequences of falling in love with a man who is not from this country, and yet men marry women from other countries with no concern of losing their rights as a citizen?" She wrapped her arms around her middle and took a deep breath before exhaling. "I haven't spoken with Teddy. I fear another argument."

Delia gave her a look of rapprochement. "That will only occur if you attack like a terrier and fail to listen." She softened her tone as her daughter frowned at her words. "*Listen*, Zee. Listen to Teddy. For once, determine why he doesn't want to pursue citizenship. When you do, I believe you will find peace. With him and with yourself."

A few evenings later Teddy entered his study, pausing to find Zylphia curled on the settee. A fire lit the grate, and a gentle warmth pervaded the room. She stared at the painting over his desk, a vibrant rendering of the Public Gardens in spring. "I like it almost as much as the first painting you gifted me."

Her lips lifted in the beginnings of a smile before she stretched out on the settee. She focused on him as he pulled a chair next to the settee and sat. He kicked off his shoes and propped his feet near her belly. He shivered as she stroked a hand down his feet and then up his calf, her hand moving with absentminded purpose. Sighing as he relaxed into his chair, his shoulders dropped and his head rolled back.

"Why continue the charade?" she whispered.

He stiffened and opened his eyes to study her. "Zee? What are you talking about?"

She shook her head in frustration. "I used to think Parthena a fool for continuing with her marriage as it was. For never demanding that things change." She met Teddy's shuttered gaze. "And here I am, doing the exact same thing."

He sat up, dropping his feet to the ground so he could lean forward, breaking contact with her. "Would you please cease speaking in riddles? I'm tired after a long day of work and entertaining family."

A flash of hurt sparked in her eyes, quickly replaced by indignation. "I used to be as important as your work."

His brows furrowed, and he rubbed at his temple. "I never said you weren't. Zee, you've been prickly for weeks. Tell me what the matter is."

She sat up, her face red and eyes drenched in pain. "Why won't you touch me? Why do you shy away from any intimacy with me?" Her breath hitched, and she batted away his hands when they reached for her. "No! Explain to me why you've acted like you have."

He outstretched his hand toward her as though approaching a potentially rabid animal and uncertain as to his touch's reception. When his featherlight caress on her hand elicited a shudder, he clasped it, raising it to his mouth to kiss it. "The doctor advised me that I needed to wait a few months before reinitiating any intimacy with you. That I needed to give you time to heal." He frowned as tears coursed down her cheeks.

He smiled at her with abject tenderness. "You'd never been shy about showing me what you desired in the past. I thought to give you the space and time you needed without compelling you to do something out of duty."

"Oh, Teddy," she whispered. "I thought you didn't want me anymore. That you were satisfied holding me in your arms every night after a kiss to my forehead."

He laughed and shook his head. "Never, my love. Not even when I'm ninety will that be enough." He sobered as he studied her. "I love you. I desire you. I cherish you." He waited a moment for her to subtly nod her acknowledgment of his words. "There isn't anything I wouldn't do or deny myself to ensure you had what you wanted."

She tugged on his hand, pulling him to the settee. She slid so she was flush against the back of the settee on her side.

Teddy settled next to her and pulled her into his arms.

"I love you, Teddy. I feared you no longer wanted me after … after what happened last fall."

"I will always regret what happened last fall. Not because I believe you could have done anything differently, but because I treated you terribly." He bowed his head and shuddered as she kissed it.

"We've had to forgive each other, my darling. And I have. I've cherished my time with you," Zylphia whispered. "After all those months of conflict, to have this time of harmony and peace …" She pushed herself further into his embrace, unable to speak as tears threatened.

He held her a few moments before easing her away. He leaned over, kissing her tenderly. "Although I love this settee and have many fond memories on it, will you come to bed with me, darling? I'd prefer our bed for what I've dreamed of doing with you."

He smiled as she giggled and held his hand out to her.

She rose, leaning on her toes to kiss him.

"God, Zee," he rasped as he broke from their impassioned embrace. "I'm trying to be chivalrous. To be gentle."

"To hell with that," she whispered. "I want you, Teddy. As you are. I want to know you missed me as much as I've missed you."

His hand shook as it swiped at a loose tendril of raven hair on her cheek. "We may be abed for a month," he whispered and then grabbed her hand and raced upstairs with her, exulting in her laughter.

"When are you returning to Washington?" Teddy whispered. Although he attempted to remain relaxed and calm with her in his arms, he stiffened after the question burst out.

She snuggled into his embrace and yawned. "When would you like me to go?"

He growled, the sound a rumbling in her ear as she had her cheek resting on his chest. "I never said I wanted you to go."

"What would you like me to do?"

He scooted down so that they were face-to-face with noses nearly touching. They shared the same pillow, and he stared deeply into her eyes. "I hate that I can't see you well with the long shadows in this room," he murmured, her face half in shadow with the only light on behind her. After another moment of stalling, he cleared his throat. "I want you to remain here. With me. To hold in my arms every night. To share silly stories with or inane jokes. To smell paints and turpentine, and to know you are creating art again. I want this house to continue to feel like a home because you are in it."

He swept a finger over one of her eyebrows. "And yet I know that is unfair of me. I have no right to ask you to remain here when your cause is precious to you." He closed his eyes when she continued to stare at him and remained silent. "Forgive me. I was too blunt."

She grabbed his injured hand and kissed it. She pushed until he lay beneath her, and she leaned over him, her face no longer hidden in shadows. She traced trembling fingers over his face, marveling that his eyes closed at her soft touch. "I love you," she whispered, smiling when she saw the pleasure those words invoked. "I never dared hope you wanted me here again. Not after last year's events." She blinked away tears. "Part of the reason I remained an invalid was so that you wouldn't expect me to leave."

He wrapped his arms around her, tugging her to him. "Never, my darling. Stay here with me forever, and I will be the happiest of men." He kissed her head. After a few moments, he sighed. "However, I know it's unfair of me to keep you from your pursuits."

"Now that President Wilson is backing full enfranchisement, I'm certain there will be work to do here in Massachusetts." She kissed his chest and smiled. "I'll make work for myself." She raised luminous eyes to meet Teddy's tender gaze. "I don't want to go back. I'm afraid to go back."

His arms tightened around her. "Returning to Washington doesn't mean we'd return to the animosity between us."

She attempted to nestle closer into him. "It feels like tempting fate." She kissed his chest again. "I loved my time there and what I accomplished. But the price was almost too high."

"We never talk about what initially drove us apart."

"Rowena advised me once that I would desire harmony more than anything else, and she was correct. I don't want to fight anymore, Teddy."

He moved so that her head rested on his arm and so they could look into each other's eyes. "Even though you feel cheated, every day, by me and by your government? How long will you be content?"

She traced the worry lines along his forehead and lost herself in his concerned gaze. "Will you tell me the truth? Why are you opposed to changing your citizenship?"

He flinched at her whispered words before closing his eyes.

"No matter what you say, my love, I'll not think less of you."

He sputtered out a mirthless laugh. "There's no need. I think less of myself already." At her soft caress on his cheek, he met her compassionate gaze and sighed. "I knew the United States would enter the War if it lasted long enough. It was only a matter of time." He let out a stuttering breath. "And I can't take the risk that they would deem me healthy enough to draft. I can't go back there, Zee." For a moment, she saw the terror and devastation the War had wrought before he blinked and hid it.

"Oh, Teddy," she whispered, pushing herself into his arms and holding him close. "I never suspected. Can you forgive me?"

He shook as he held her. "For what?"

"For never considering your fears and only focusing on myself and my anger." She pushed back and swiped at her cheeks, wet with silent tears. "Last year, my mother told me that I needed to listen to you and discover why you were opposed to changing your citizenship, but I was too stubborn. And I allowed the distance and animosity to grow between us for no reason."

"I didn't want you to see me as a coward."

She froze at his words and paused as she met his shuttered eyes. "*Coward?* How could you possibly believe I'd consider you a coward?" She sat up, straddling his lap and grasping his cheeks between her hands. "You are the bravest, most honorable man I know, Teddy Goff." His eyes shone with unshed tears at her words, and she gently stroked her fingers over his eyebrows. "You suffered horribly when you were on the Front, things I don't even want to contemplate. I would have died if you had to return there." She blinked, and tears coursed down her cheeks. "I would never have fought you if I'd known your fears. For they would have been my greatest fear as well."

She leaned forward and embraced him. "I can't lose you, Teddy. I love you." She gasped as his arms clamped around her and squeezed all the breath out of her.

After many minutes of holding each other, Teddy whispered, "When the War is over, I'll apply for citizenship. I want you to vote, my darling Zee."

She sobbed, burying her head in his shoulder.

CHAPTER 5

Missoula, Montana, May 1918

Clarissa McLeod worked the front desk of the library, laughing and chatting with a patron as she checked out books for a young mother and her children. Clarissa had worked at the library since she had first arrived in Missoula in 1901 before she married Gabriel. Then, the library had been above a storefront on Higgins Avenue, and she had had plenty of free time to exchange stories with Mr. A. J. Pickens, her friend and mentor who had died in 1914. Now, the two-story library was located one block off Higgins and always bustled with patrons.

Clarissa smoothed back a tendril of loose chestnut hair and sighed with contentment at the sight of mothers and children sitting in the reading room as they looked over books they had checked out. Her three eldest children were frequent visitors to the library, although they were often too energetic for a few of the patronesses. She tried to bring books home every few days for them to read and share. Her husband, Gabriel, enjoyed the ritual of reading them a bedtime story every night.

She focused on the head librarian, Hester Loken, who intently read a letter. "You look as though you've seen a ghost," Clarissa teased. When Hester raised confused eyes and motioned to follow her, Clarissa entered the back room and shut the door behind them. "We shouldn't leave the front unattended for long."

Hester waved away Clarissa's concerns and thrust the sheet of paper at Clarissa, whose brows furrowed as she read the missive. Hester waited, then spoke. "How can they do such a thing? We are to be an institution that fosters learning and tolerance!"

"*Shh*," Clarissa hissed. "You never know who's listening." She whispered in such a low voice that Hester had to lean in so that their foreheads nearly touched. "We can't get rid of these books."

"We can't get rid of *any* books! It's against everything the library stands for!" Hester's eyes were lit with passionate indignation. "Besides, they're all German books."

Clarissa nodded as she looked at them. "I fear, if we don't remove them, someone will come in to do a spot check, and we'll be in trouble." She shared a grimace with Hester. "You know Mrs. Vaughan would relish any opportunity to show that we are lax in our duties here." Mrs. Vaughan vied with her sister, Mrs. Bouchard, for town gossip, and the two were meddlesome busybodies who loathed Clarissa and her family. They were also patronesses of the library and would rejoice in any reason to see Clarissa dismissed from her duties.

"And she'd celebrate in calling us traitors because we refused to remove these books." Hester scrubbed at her face. "I've heard some towns in the state have gone a step further and burned those on the list."

Clarissa sighed, rubbing at her forehead. "For now, let's crate them and put them back here. I'll see if Colin or Gabriel can come by tonight, and we'll store them at one of our homes."

"That could prove dangerous, Rissa," Hester warned.

"I know. But ignorance and fear are worse." She gripped Hester's stooped shoulders a moment and moved to the front, forcing a smile at the patron waiting to check out a book. After waving goodbye to the customer, Clarissa pulled out the list of books to be banned and moved quietly through the library's stacks, extracting the books on the list. When she was finished, she pushed the cart to the back room. "Do we have a crate?" she asked Hester.

Hester nodded, pointing to an open crate next to her desk. She rose, aiding Clarissa in packing the books. "Aren't there more in German?"

"Yes, but they aren't on the list." Clarissa looked at the crate with satisfaction as it was only half full.

"I'd remove all of them. You know how some of our patronesses can be." She pinned Clarissa with an intense stare. "We both know this violates our beliefs, but we must act in such a way to protect the library and to ensure that our vision of the library endures during this time. Which means, we continue to work here. If we give the appearance we are complying with their mandate, we will be safe."

Clarissa shook her head as she knelt by the crate. "You're giving in, Hester. If they want more books banned, they should list them too. We shouldn't have to strip the entire library of anything to do with Germany or the German language."

Hester sighed. "Ideologically you're correct. Practically it's idiotic. Sometimes you have to act as though you're playing their game. This is one of those times." When Clarissa continued to glare at her mutinously, Hester pushed herself off the floor. "I'll determine what other books should be culled."

Clarissa sat next to the crate of books and closed her eyes. As though conjuring her old mentor and friend, Mr. Pickens, she heard his advice in her mind. *Ain't no use wishin for how things ain't, Missy. Ye gotta live with how things are. Quit yer bellyachin' an' dillydallyin and live fer today.* She smiled, squared her shoulders and rose, intent on aiding Hester.

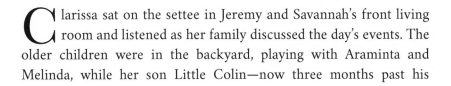

Clarissa sat on the settee in Jeremy and Savannah's front living room and listened as her family discussed the day's events. The older children were in the backyard, playing with Araminta and Melinda, while her son Little Colin—now three months past his second birthday—played on the floor at her feet with wooden toy animals his father had made. Jeremy and Savannah's house was a short distance from the home Clarissa shared with Gabriel.

"Can you believe that Mr. Caine tried to strong-arm me into selling my shop again?" her older brother Colin complained. He had moved to Missoula with her in 1901 and now owned his own black-smith shop. At forty-two, he remained unmarried, although many women in town had vied for his attention. However, he was content to spend his time with friends and family. "That man can't take no for an answer."

"How many times is it now that you've turned him down?" asked Gabriel.

"Must be close to six." Colin groaned as he stretched his arms overhead and then scratched his head. "I have no idea why he's so keen on purchasing it."

"You run a good business and make a tidy profit," Clarissa said. "Who wouldn't want a business like that?"

"Yes, but he'd buy it and beggar it within a year, like he did his own blacksmith shop." Colin sighed. "Thankfully he can't compel me to sell."

Gabriel, the eldest McLeod brother at forty-three, winked at his wife, Clarissa. More gray peppered his black hair, but he remained lean and strong from his work as a finish carpenter. Jeremy, the youngest McLeod brother, was married to Savannah, Clarissa's and Colin's cousin. The middle McLeod brother, Richard, lived in Boston with his wife, Florence, and their six children—the latest, a daughter, born just a week earlier.

When the conversation lulled, Jeremy asked, "What are those crates in my office? Are we stocking up already for next year?" He watched Savannah with a teasing glint in his eyes, but she sat next to Clarissa in a despondent haze and failed to respond.

Clarissa smiled and shook her head. "Why would we need to stock up?"

Gabriel laughed. "Because, at the end of the year, we can no longer purchase whiskey or any other alcohol in this fine state. You can't have forgotten that your temperance friends were successful."

"Of course not. I forgot the start date," she said with a light flush on her cheeks. "And I'm sorry to disappoint you, Jeremy. The crates are not filled with that sort of contraband."

"But it is contraband?" Colin said, perking up in his chair at the thought.

She laughed. "Of course not. Well, they're filled with banned books we had to remove from the library. A list was released from the Council of Defense of the books that could no longer be in circulation in schools or libraries. Order Number 3 from the COD."

Jeremy's brows flew up in surprise. "All those books were banned?"

Clarissa fisted her hand, tapping it on her thigh as she flushed in indignation. "No, not all of them. However, Hester thought it best to remove all books with a German author or theme as we have patronesses who can be overzealous. The council did recommend any books by a German, in German or about Germany to be removed."

"Bloody Mrs. Bouchard," Colin muttered.

"And vindictive Mrs. Vaughan," Gabriel muttered. "They'd love to find a reason to expel you again and to take over the running of the library." He bent down and picked up his young son named after his wife's brother, bouncing him on one knee and earning a giggle. "And the council likes to stick in its nose too. I still can't believe they passed a measure on March 15 outlawing parades."

Colin shook his head. "You know it was directed at Butte and their huge Saint Patrick's Day Parade." They all nodded and frowned as they considered the council and its growing power.

"We know you loathe the Bouchards for an entirely personal reason," Jeremy teased Colin as he changed the subject.

"How would you feel if another man were courting your woman?" Colin growled out.

"Considering you've never spoken to her about your feelings, I fail to see why you are so upset." Clarissa met Colin's irate glare, although concern and compassion filled her gaze. "As for the books, Jeremy, I was hoping we could store them somewhere here as your house is much larger than mine."

Jeremy looked at Savannah, who stared into space. "Savannah?" He frowned when she jerked at her name, finally focusing on her family surrounding her. "Would you object?"

She looked around the room at her family's inquisitive stares and shook her head. "No, I have no objection. If you would excuse me?" She rose, and her footsteps were heard ascending the stairs.

"What's wrong, Jeremy?" Clarissa asked. "She's been out of sorts for a few weeks."

Jeremy sighed and leaned forward, resting his elbows on his knees. "I have no idea. When I ask her, she acts affronted that I believe anything is amiss." He rubbed at his face. "I don't know what to do."

Clarissa looked toward the stairway and frowned. "Give her time. Well, a little time. And then, if she still won't speak about what is bothering her, push her. Savannah is too good at keeping her hurts buttoned up."

Excited voices and racing feet sounded down the long hallway from the kitchen, and the conversation turned to that of the children, their school day and their hopes for summer vacation.

When Araminta saw that the children were ensconced with their parents, she slipped out the back. She had arrived in Missoula in 1903 with Savannah, Jeremy and Melinda and remained with the McLeod family, working to care for their children. An orphan, Araminta had no family except for the McLeods, and, although she loved her role as an honorary aunt, she ached for something more. She walked as quickly as her lame leg allowed, making her way to her small rented rooms on the other side of the river near downtown Missoula. Upon arrival, she fought a smile to find Bartholomew Bouchard waiting on the porch.

Nephew to Mrs. Bouchard, Bartholomew had proven a steadfast friend in the past year. He also had a penchant for outlandishly colored suits, and tonight's was tame by recent standards. Rather than the puce or pumpkin-colored waistcoat worn the previous week, the cranberry tone seemed muted and dull.

"What a lovely sight, you walking with the evening sun casting its warming rays upon you!" Bartholomew called out as he jogged from the porch.

She rolled her eyes at his praise but was unable to fight a blush. "Hello, Mr. Bouchard. I hadn't expected to see you this evening."

"But you hoped you would," he said. "Come. Walk with me." At his coaxing, he led her away from her home on a slow walk around deserted side streets. "It's the dinner hour, and we have the town to ourselves."

She shook her head. "How you can make that sound illicit is beyond me."

"We've been friends for nearly a year now, Miss Araminta," Bartholomew said. "We've walked this same route more times than I can count. Even in the middle of winter, when we were bundled up like explorers to the South Pole." He sighed with relief when he saw her smile. "How was your day?"

"Wonderful. I spent it with the children, and it was filled with adventure and mishaps."

He shook his head in disbelief. "I can't imagine being content caring for other people's children. It's difficult enough when they're your own."

Araminta turned to study him intently. "Do you have your own that you are so familiar with the work and dedication that such care entails?"

He flushed. "I wouldn't be walking with you on this fine evening if I did, would I?"

She frowned at his ambiguous answer. "That's not an answer. Did you have a family?"

He smiled enigmatically and frowned. "My past isn't something I am proud of, Miss Araminta. Although I can assure you, there is nothing that would bring shame or ridicule upon you."

She frowned at his evasive and puzzling answer. "I would be

shocked if there were. You are a fine, upstanding member of our town."

He shrugged and allowed his attention to be drawn to the library. "I'm surprised the lights are still on. I thought it closed hours ago."

Araminta bit back further questions and focused on the library. "I believe a rearranging of the book catalog was undertaken today."

Bartholomew studied her a moment, his gaze intent. "You mean, they rid the library of the banned German books?" At Araminta's nod, he smiled. "Good. My aunts will be pleased such an important undertaking has been accomplished. Such dangerous material should not be allowed to circulate among the impressionable minds of our children nor our citizenry."

Araminta began to speak and then acted as though she had a slight cough. She waved away his words of concern.

"I'm certain you agree with me. The Council of Defense is acting in accordance with the desires of the state legislature and the governor. We must ensure that we are safe from any and all interference from Germany and its people."

"Of course," she murmured. "I'm certain the council has our best interests at heart."

He beamed at her ready agreement. "I like when we are in agreement on all things."

"No two people can be in agreement about all things," Araminta whispered.

"Perhaps not but, on the essential issues facing us as a country, I believe it is imperative there be agreement on what truly matters."

Araminta frowned as they approached her home. "Thank you for the lovely walk, Mr. Bouchard."

He raised her hand and kissed it. "I'd hoped by now you'd call me Bartholomew." He traced a finger over her cheek. "Or Bart." His eyes gleamed as he watched her luminous, yet shocked gaze. He kept his gaze locked with hers as he leaned forward and kissed her softly on her lips. "I hope you have a wonderful evening, Miss Araminta." He stroked her cheek again before backing away.

Araminta leaned against the wooden pillar holding up the porch roof and watched him as he strode toward downtown. When he faded from sight, she traced her lips, unable to fight a smile before turning to enter her rooms.

~

The following day, Araminta worked in Clarissa's kitchen while the older children were at school. She chopped vegetables and wrestled with the meal plan. Clarissa and Gabriel lived in a craftsman-style house with a living room, dining room and kitchen on the main floor, and the bedrooms upstairs. They had a wide front porch and a backyard for the children to play in.

"What has you glowering?" Clarissa asked.

"Did he go down for his nap?" Araminta asked.

Clarissa chuckled. "He's not at all like his namesake yet. Little Colin is a very docile boy, and he loves his naps. Colin, his uncle, is the exact opposite!" She watched as Araminta studiously avoided looking at Clarissa or reacting to any discussion about Colin. "Why are you glaring at the vegetables?"

"I'm sick of the dietary recommendations. Today's Wheatless Wednesday, and all I want to bake is bread." She pointed at the paltry vegetables and the bag of rice on the counter. "Wouldn't a loaf of bread be delicious with dinner?"

Clarissa laughed. "It would. But I refuse to have my neighbors informing the council or anyone else that they smelled bread or a cake or cookies being baked today in my house."

"I hardly believe baking bread could be construed as an act of sedition," Araminta whispered.

"Maybe not but they'd still find a reason to berate you in the papers and make you feel like a traitor for not following the 'recommendations.'" Clarissa smiled. "Besides, no matter what you make, it's delicious." She watched as Araminta continued to move around the kitchen, her agitation mounting. "What is truly bothering you, Minta?"

"I have a friend."

"Yes, Mr. Bouchard." At Araminta's shocked expression, Clarissa laughed. "You can't expect to have kept secret his attention, nor your frequent walks, in a town the size of Missoula. Besides, many in the family take an interest in your welfare, Minta."

Araminta sat on a chair across from Clarissa at the kitchen table. "We went for a walk last night and passed by the library. The lights were still on."

Clarissa frowned. "I wonder why Hester needed to work so late." She focused on Araminta. "But that's not what bothers you."

Araminta shook her head. "Ba—Mr. Bouchard approved of you removing those books. He expected me to agree with him."

Clarissa narrowed her eyes as Araminta fiddled with a carrot peel on the tabletop. "Do you agree with him?"

Araminta huffed out a breath and shrugged her shoulders. "A part of me does. I mean, if a German spy plane really was near Helena last fall, we must be cautious." She furrowed her brows as she finally met Clarissa's gaze. "And yet why would a German plane be in Montana? I fear that newspaper writer was simply trying to scare all of us and arouse our anti-German sentiment."

Clarissa smiled and nodded. "There is no reason for a German plane to be in Massachusetts, never mind Montana. However, I fear too few of our citizenry are willing to overcome their irrational fears and use logic during a time of war and uncertainty."

Araminta sighed. "That is what concerns me, Clarissa. The fear-mongering. The book-burning parties I read about in the *Daily Missoulian*. The joy people are taking in denying German pastors from speaking to their church members in their own language. It seems cruel." She bit her lip. "I was disappointed in myself for not speaking up last night. For allowing Mr. Bouchard to believe I agreed with him."

"Why didn't you?" Clarissa asked.

"I'm terrified of being seen as unpatriotic. You've read what they've done to those convicted of sedition."

Clarissa paused for a moment, her gaze distant and troubled. The stories of those who had been convicted and sent to jail for twenty years had made headlines in the state's newspapers. "Our politicians and leaders have failed us. They've silenced any possibility of civil discord with the threat of sedition and jail time, thus stripping us of our freedoms to openly discuss our concerns and disagreements. I've never believed in forced patriotism, and yet my silence is an implicit acknowledgment that I agree with the current law."

Araminta watched Clarissa with confusion. "You sound disappointed in yourself."

"If you must know, I am. I like to believe myself strong-willed and outspoken for what I believe in. And yet, the minute I am threatened with jail time, all I can think about is missing out on my children's lives." She smiled sadly at Araminta. "I'm not strong, like I envisioned, and that shames me."

~

Gabriel entered the bedroom he shared with Clarissa, smiling to find her sitting in her rocking chair, humming to herself. "Hello, my darling," he whispered. At her inquisitive stare, he nodded. "The children are abed, after three bedtime stories and a promise to play hide-and-seek tomorrow." He chuckled. "Little Billy should become a lawyer for his negotiating prowess."

He frowned when Clarissa failed to take her customary joy in his report about the bedtime routine for the children. He slipped off his shoes, then pulled down his suspenders. He perched on the edge of the bed and waited for Clarissa to speak. After many minutes, when she remained silent and in her own mind, he tugged at her arm and pulled her toward him.

"Come, love," he whispered, settling her on her side on the bed with him facing her. He traced a hand through her long brown hair, now shot with silver. "What bothers you?"

She shook her head and pushed herself into his chest, sighing with pleasure as his arms closed around her. The tension eased from her the longer he held her, his long fingers stroking her back.

"I know you are deserving of your sleep after a long day. But please share your worries with me, Rissa. I would support you in everything if I could." He kissed her head as she shuddered.

"I admitted to myself today that I'm a coward, and I find that hard to live with," she whispered against his shoulder.

He laughed, causing her to tense again. "How can you possibly consider yourself a coward? You've braved childbirth five times. You survived a horrible attack in Boston and demanded a full life with me, when others would have meekly accepted a half-life with Cameron. You champion a woman's right to vote and worked endlessly for success here in Montana in 1914." He swiped a palm over her wet cheeks. "Help me to understand how you could possibly consider yourself less than magnificent and strong and brave?"

A pent-up sob burst forth, and he pulled her closer, wrapping his arms around her and rocking her as her emotions flowed. "Don't cry so, my darling. I hate to see you this sad."

She talked in stutters, and he focused with intense concentration to understand her.

"I didn't have the courage to insist the banned books remain in the library. I haven't had the courage to speak out against the Sedition Law. I've remained quiet as those around us are accused and brought before the committee." She used his shirt to dry her face.

"Rissa, you know as well as I do that speaking out means, at bare minimum, a fine, or, at worst, twenty years in the state penitentiary. Twenty years! You saved the books so they weren't destroyed. Other schools and libraries across the state have taken pleasure in burning them." He moved so that he could meet her teary gaze. "We must continue with our quiet acts of defiance. We must help those we can."

"I'm ashamed because I think of myself first." She sniffled and took a deep breath as her sobs quieted. She traced a finger over his beloved jaw. "I think of you. Of our family. And I remain quiet."

"I think many of us feel the same. However, there is little we can do, Rissa," Gabriel murmured.

"Are you ashamed?" she whispered.

He kissed the top of her head. "I don't know if that is the appropriate word. I'm disappointed in myself every time I bite my tongue and don't speak up. Like when I read about another injustice in the paper and remain quiet, rather than discussing it with the children so they learn right from wrong."

He sighed, resting his forehead against hers and looking deeply into her eyes. "I made a promise, my darling. Once you escaped Cameron and were brave enough to share with me all you'd suffered in Boston after our separation, I promised I would do everything in my power so that we were never again separated." His callused thumb swept over her cheek, soothing her and clearing away tears. "I remind myself of that promise every day when I am tempted to speak out."

"Oh, Gabriel, what can we do?" she whispered.

He held her close. "I don't know what more we can do while the majority in the country are terrified of Germany and anyone who might threaten us. I think our resistance must be to raise our children free of hatred and fear."

CHAPTER 6

*M*ay had turned into a wet and dreary June, and low clouds hung over the mountains, hiding the distant peaks. The lilac bushes had faded, and now they waited for the columbine to bloom. Amelia Carlin took a deep breath as she stood on the porch, checking the address one more time before she raised her hand. She knocked on Clarissa's front door, her eldest son beside her. When the door burst open, she gave a tentative smile as she met Clarissa's shocked expression for a moment before being pulled into a full-body hug by Clarissa.

"Amelia! I can't believe you're here." Clarissa released Amelia and turned to Nicholas. "And I can't believe how big you've gotten." She gave him a quick hug and a kiss on his cheek. "How are you both? What brings you to Missoula?" She stepped back and motioned for them to enter. "You're very welcome."

She took their coats, hanging them on pegs by the front door and setting their cases near the stairs. "Please pardon the mess. I seem to live in a perpetual state of chaos, even with Araminta's help," Clarissa said with a smile. She tossed toys and a blanket in a box by the side of the settee. She glanced at a small playpen Gabriel had constructed for

Little Colin where he piled his toys, one on top of each other, most likely in an attempt to climb out of the confined space.

Clarissa laughed and picked him up, placing him on the carpet in front of the settee. She set paper and pencils on a small table for him to draw on, and he sat in contented silence as he fisted the pencil, working on a masterpiece. "Where are your other children?" Clarissa frowned as she thought of Amelia's six younger children.

"They are home with Sebastian. Anne is seventeen and old enough to oversee the younger children, for the most part. A neighbor watches out for them during the day when Sebastian is at work." Amelia fidgeted before sitting next to Nicholas on the settee. Amelia lived with her husband, Sebastian Carlin, in Darby, a town about sixty miles up the Bitterroot Valley where he ran the local sawmill. She and Clarissa had been best friends when Clarissa first came to Missoula, before Amelia married Sebastian and moved away.

"What brings you to Missoula? You haven't ventured down the valley since Mr. Pickens's funeral, nearly four years ago." Clarissa frowned as Amelia wrung her hands and shook her head, as though unable to speak.

"I've been drafted, Mrs. McLeod," Nicholas said in a deep voice. His previously russet-colored hair had darkened to a chestnut brown with red highlights, and his deep-brown eyes sparked with excitement. "They expanded the draft to include those who turned twenty-one after the draft last June. When I registered, it seems they were eager for a strong Montana man like me, and I was drafted right away."

Clarissa collapsed against the back of her settee as though she had had the air knocked out of her. "Oh my," she whispered. "How ... how patriotic," she murmured.

"Sebastian is proud Nicholas is to do his part," Amelia whispered. "I think he wishes *he* could be drafted."

"Not with his leg," Clarissa breathed, sharing a relieved look with her friend. Sebastian had been maimed in a sawmill accident fifteen years ago and would not be considered fit for duty. "Gabriel and the rest are too old. They won't draft men over age forty."

"Hard to imagine we'd be thankful for their advancing age," Amelia managed to joke as she clasped her hands together as though to prevent herself from grabbing Nicholas's leg or arm to ensure he remained near her.

"Why did you need to come to Missoula?" Clarissa snagged Little Colin as he rose and wandered the living room, approaching the fireplace and the metal poker. She pulled out toys hidden in a small basket by the couch, and he dropped to the floor to play with the trucks, occasionally running over his mother's feet.

"I leave from here tomorrow on the train." Nicholas's gaze was filled with a mixture of eager glee and trepidation.

"So soon? We must have a family gathering to celebrate your momentous departure. Let me speak with Araminta, and we'll arrange a party." She met Amelia's worried gaze. "We don't have much room here, but Colin has loads of room, as does Savannah. Would that work?" At Amelia's relieved smile, Clarissa waved at Amelia to remain seated. "Don't worry about a thing. Rest after your journey."

That evening Nicholas sat in the dining room and spoke with Colin, Gabriel, Jeremy and Ronan O'Bara about the War, the reports of the battles and the effect the American Expeditionary Force had on the Western Front. Ronan worked as a cobbler in Gabriel's and Jeremy's workshop. He had traveled to Missoula seventeen years ago from Butte with Gabriel, after a mining accident had crippled him. Ronan and Gabriel had been friends since Gabriel's first days in Butte, where Ronan had worked in the Butte mines with Amelia's first husband, Liam.

Jeremy shook his head at the eagerness glinting in Nicholas's eyes. "War will change you, Nicholas. It changed me and not for the better."

Nicholas frowned as he looked at Jeremy, sitting peacefully in Colin's dining room. "You seem fine to me."

"You will face your worst fears as you wait to meet your enemy and wonder if this day, this moment, is your day to die. As you wish it were your day," Jeremy said. "Now you are filled with the excitement and the romance of war. Soon you will know what war truly is."

"I don't understand. What do you know of war?" Nicholas asked as he stared at Jeremy in confusion.

"I was in the Philippines. And I fear what awaits you is worse than anything I can imagine." His green eyes were tormented as he looked at the young man. "You will do the unthinkable, more times than you knew you could. And then you will have to live with yourself." He pushed back from the table and rose, slipping out the front door.

"Was it truly that awful?" Nicholas asked as he stared at Gabriel.

"Worse, I fear," Gabriel said. "Jeremy rarely refers to the time he spent in the Philippines, and I wasn't in Boston when he returned. I only know of what he suffered from letters sent from my other brother, Richard." Gabriel sighed. "I understand your desire to meet your fate, Nicholas. Try to understand the sorrow of those you leave behind." His eyes glinted with anguish as he beheld Nicholas, as though recalling the boy who had charmed him all those years ago in Butte when his father, Liam, still lived. "We will worry about you until you come home to us."

Nicholas nodded, his gaze troubled as he stared at the closed kitchen door, his mother on the other side with Clarissa. "Yet I must go. I've been drafted."

"No one would want you to avoid what you've been called to do, Nickie," Colin said, calling him by his childhood nickname. Colin's eyes shone with pride and love as he beheld the boy he had played toy soldiers with those many years ago. "Heed Gabe. He knows what it is to watch someone he loves leave for the uncertainty of war."

"Remember those of us who have loved you since you were a lad," Ronan said, his voice roughened as he stared at the man but saw the impish boy who had crawled onto his lap after he was injured. The boy who never saw him as less because of his injury. "None of us will be happy until you are safely returned to us."

Nicholas looked at the three men, all of whom he considered his uncles, and nodded. "I know. I'll miss all of you, but I know I have your support."

"Always," Gabriel vowed as he clapped Nicholas on his shoulder. "Now, go soothe your mother. She battles her own demons." He gave Nicholas an encouraging nod as Nicholas took a deep breath and stood.

Nicholas neared the closed kitchen door. He nodded his thanks as Colin slapped him on the back and then joined Gabriel in the dining room, leaving Nicholas to approach his mother alone.

~

"Where was Savannah tonight?" Amelia asked. "I enjoyed seeing how much Melinda has grown, but I worry that Savannah was not present."

"That's why Melinda went home rather than remaining to help us with the dishes. She too was worried about her mother." Clarissa sighed. "Savannah went to Butte for a quick overnight trip and returned home today. Jeremy told me that she was too tired to come tonight." Clarissa shook her head in confusion. "I don't know what is wrong. Sav is withdrawn and sad but refuses to talk to any of us, including Jeremy."

Amelia frowned. "That doesn't sound like Savannah. Or the relationship she has with him."

Clarissa shrugged. "I know, but she won't open up." She bit her lip, and her pent-up question blurted from her. "Why didn't Sebastian come with you? I know I couldn't imagine doing what you are doing without Gabriel's support."

"Seb needed to work." She rubbed at her head, slapping the drying towel against the edge of the countertop a few times. "And I was a fool. Told him that I would be fine. That I wanted a little time with just Nicholas. That he was *my* son and that I needed private time with him." Her voice broke on the word *my*.

"You never," Clarissa breathed. "He's always treated Nicholas as though he were his own."

Amelia nodded, a hand over her eyes as she bowed her head. "I know. I could not have said anything more hurtful than that." She turned and looked at her friend. "It just popped out. The minute I said it, I wished for it back."

Clarissa heaved out a breath. "It's all right to be mad at the world for sending your son to war, Amelia. But don't hurt the man you love." She blinked as she thought of her estrangement from Gabriel after their son Rory's death nearly six years ago. "Not when you know you need his support as much as he needs yours."

Amelia nodded. "I've dreaded, for months, the day they extended the draft to include my Nickie." She bit her lip as tears spilled from her eyes. "It's like I'm losing Liam all over again."

Clarissa nodded. "I never knew your Liam. But, from how much Gabriel still misses him, I know he must have been a wonderful man."

Amelia sniffled and nodded again before scrubbing at her face. "But it's not fair to Sebastian. He's a magnificent father to all my children. He's never cared that Nicholas and Anne aren't his."

Clarissa squeezed her shoulders. "You were twice blessed, Amelia, to find two such men in one lifetime."

"I don't just feel sorrow," she whispered. "I'm filled with anger. How can fate be so cruel as to try to rip one of my last reminders of Liam from me?" She raised eyes filled with rage to meet Clarissa's somber gaze. Amelia's first husband and Nicholas's father, Liam, had died in a mining accident in Butte seventeen years ago. "I can't find it in me to calmly accept that fate."

"Nor would I want you to," Clarissa said. She tugged on Amelia's arm and led her to the backyard where they had a few chairs. "What does Sebastian say?" The rain had stopped, and it was a pleasant, cool evening.

"What can he say? Nicholas was called up, and he must report for duty. If he didn't, Sebastian's business would suffer. Nicholas would suffer for the rest of his life." She swiped at her cheeks. "But I can't bear to read about what is occurring in France. The battles they attempt to make sound glorious. The men who fight valiantly as they cross No Man's Land. The foolish decisions by generals who should have known better." Amelia shook her head. "It was bad enough when it was the neighbor's son who I dreaded reading about in the paper. I can't handle thinking about Nicholas."

Clarissa gripped her friend's hand and leaned forward. "I can't reassure you that you won't ever read such news. I can hope that you will not. I will pray that you'll never receive a telegram." She sighed. "But Nicholas needs you to be strong. He needs to see you smile as you wave him on his way tomorrow on the train. He may be proud of what he has been called to do, but he also needs to know you support him."

Amelia nodded and rubbed at her tear-stained cheeks. "You don't know what it is like, Rissa."

"That's true. And I don't know how you can be as strong as you are." She sniffled and glanced to the back door as it squeaked open. "Hello, Nickie."

He walked toward them in the backyard. "I had forgotten that nickname until it was spoken here tonight," he said in his deep voice. "I've been called Nicholas for so long." He smiled. "May I speak with my mother a moment?"

Clarissa and Amelia both rose, Clarissa giving Amelia a gentle squeeze on her shoulders.

"Clarissa and I wanted to enjoy a few moments free of the rain," Amelia said as she swiped at her cheeks again, her back turned.

"Mother," he rasped, spinning her to face him. "I'm sorry." He pulled her into his embrace, her head barely reaching his shoulders.

"I'm the foolish one, my Nickie," she whispered into his shoulder. "Forgive your mother her silliness."

He pushed away, his gaze meeting her watery eyes. "Do you know how much worse it would be if I left and you didn't care?" He gripped and ungripped his hands. "I'm scared, Ma," he whispered. "I don't want to leave."

"Oh, my darling boy," she murmured as she hugged him tight. "You will see places I've only dreamed about. New York City. Paris."

"The Front." He gripped her close as he firmed his jaw. "If I don't come back, please talk about me. Remember me."

She backed up and cupped his cheeks in her hands. "You are smart.

You are brave. You are resilient." She swiped away one of his tears. "I will always be proud of you." They shared a fierce look, filled with love and anguish at the parting that would come the next day. "Never forget that you are loved and that we will eagerly await your return. You will be a part of our family. Forever."

He dropped his head onto her shoulder again, holding her close for a few more moments.

∾

Jeremy paced behind his desk in his office, a glass of whiskey forgotten on his desk. He ran a hand through his black hair with streaks of silver, gripping strands of hair as his fingers shook. With a roar, he grabbed the crystal glass and heaved it at the brick fireplace.

"Father?" A knock sounded on the door, and then Melinda's head poked in. "I thought I heard a crash." She frowned as he panted, as though he had just run a few miles. Her frown deepened as he stared at her with glassy eyes. "What is it, Father?"

"Melly," he said, shaking his head and focusing on her. "It's nothing. I'm sorry to have bothered you."

She took a tentative step inside his office, and, when he did not protest her presence, she moved farther into his room. "What is it?" she asked again.

"We all have memories we wish we could banish, my darling." His smile was filled with regret. "You will too one day, I fear."

She reached forward with a trembling hand and gripped his hanging at his side. "Why are you angry that Nicholas is going to war? He has to. It is his duty."

He stared at her with a vast bleakness in his gaze and frowned as she shuddered at the hopelessness held within. "I fear how it will change him. War changes a man, Melly. No matter what he says or how he acts, he is irrevocably altered."

Her blond ringlets shook as her head tilted in confusion. "Nothing you could have done would shame me."

He squeezed her hand before tugging her close and wrapping her tight in his embrace. "Oh, Melly. How I wish that were true." He let out a stuttering breath as he held her tight for a few moments before releasing her. "Ignore your father. He's being foolish as he battles back his ghosts."

At the gentle knock, he looked to the door of his office. "Gabe," he whispered, his voice suddenly thicker as though fighting tears. "I wondered if you'd come."

Gabriel stood watching his youngest brother intently. "Melly, I need a few moments with your father."

Melinda nodded. She dropped her hands from around her father but leaned up on her toes and kissed him on his cheek. "No matter what, I love you," she whispered before she spun on her heel and bustled from the room. The door *click*ed shut after her.

Gabriel sniffed and frowned. "I didn't know you were opening a distillery."

Jeremy glared at him before he collapsed into his leather chair with a groan. "I threw a glass of whiskey at the fireplace. I'll have to pick it up before I go to bed."

"You scared Nicholas with your words earlier." Gabriel sat across from his brother, his relaxed posture failing to conceal the concern in his gaze.

"I wanted to." He glared at his brother in an attempt to mask his guilt. "He shouldn't go off to war believing it will be a lark."

Gabriel leaned forward. "Do you think he hasn't read the newspapers? That he didn't read about the one million men wounded or killed during the Battle of the Somme in 1916 or the devastating Spring Offensive on the Western Front this year by the Germans?" He shook his head in disbelief. "He knows what is going on over there. He knows what awaits him. At least in theory." Gabriel sighed with frustration as Jeremy remained mute, as though imprisoned by his memories. "I feel guilty too. I made Nicholas feel worse after you left."

"You can't know about war until you are there," Jeremy ground out, his fingers digging into his scalp. "And it will never leave him if he survives."

"Look at me, Jer," Gabriel commanded in a deep voice. He waited until his youngest brother met his gaze. Echoes of horror and regret mingled together there, and Gabriel clenched his jaw. "I would carry this burden for you if I could." His eyes shone with impotent fury at his inability to ease his brother's torment. "When Nicholas does return—and we must always have faith he returns to us—then you will be here to help him through that transition."

Jeremy scoffed as he dropped his head onto his desk with a *thud*. He spoke, as if to the desk. "Look at me. It's seventeen years later, and I'm still battling what happened." He jumped as his brother gripped his shoulder in an effort to offer some sort of comfort. "I still see their faces, their eyes as they realize they are going to die. That I would be the man who killed them." Jeremy closed his eyes and tapped his head against the desk a few times.

Gabriel pushed at him until his baby brother sat up. Gabe crouched, holding Jeremy by his nape. "You are brave and honorable. I know you did things you are ashamed of. But I am proud of you. And forever grateful you survived." He waited until Jeremy closed his eyes in understanding.

"Forgive me, Gabe. I can usually fight away these memories." He swiped a hand over his face. "I hate that I might have scared Melly."

"Your daughter is tougher than you give her credit for. She's worried about you." Gabriel looked around the room and then overhead, as though listening for footsteps on the second floor. "Where's Sav? Why isn't she here to comfort you?"

Jeremy shrugged. "We're having difficulties. Lately she doesn't want to spend much time with me. She even insisted on traveling to Butte to visit Lucas without me."

Gabriel frowned. "She should be here. She should know what you are suffering."

"She doesn't much care for me at the moment. I doubt she'd be bothered by my suffering." He let out a deep breath. "Our marriage has been in turmoil for months. I don't know what to do."

Gabriel's brows furrowed in confusion. "Go to her tonight. Tell her that you need her. That you need her strength." His eyes gleamed with memories. "For we need our wives just as much as they need us, Jer."

"She won't let me touch her." He frowned as the words burst forth. "She's moved to another bedroom. Doesn't want me anywhere near her."

"That's not like Savannah. She's always sought you out for comfort. Even after the cruelty she experienced from that bastard Jonas, she knew she could trust you." Gabriel frowned as he attempted to make sense of the nonsensical.

Jeremy sniffled. "I will be fine, Gabe."

Gabriel turned and left the library. After a moment he returned, carrying a rag, a dustpan and a broom. He swept up the broken glass and then wiped the area dry of whiskey. "You'll still want to wash it in the morning to clear out the smell." He turned to look at his brother, sitting in a dazed stupor behind his desk. "You will be fine, Jeremy. I know that because you are strong. But you would be better, with less anguish, were you to have her support." His eyes gleamed. "I find everything is better with Clarissa by my side."

Jeremy nodded. "Someday, brother. Someday." He rose and attempted a smile. "You should return home. And I will attempt to speak with Savannah."

Gabriel pulled Jeremy in for a fierce embrace before slipping out the office door. The front door *click*ed behind him. Rather than go upstairs, Jeremy sat again, his memories his companion for the night.

Amelia stood beside Nicholas on the cold, dreary morning as they waited for the train to arrive that would take him to Butte. He joined a group of other men awaiting the train that would travel across the state, picking up recruits as it made its way east. She ignored the other farewells occurring around them on the platform and focused on her son. They stood alone, a small island of misery, as a light drizzle fell. Amelia had declined Gabriel's and Clarissa's offer to join her at the station, wanting to have a last moment with Nicholas without worrying about anyone else.

"I will be careful, Mother. As careful as a soldier can be," Nicholas said. He saw other young men who would travel with him, their smiles and jovial attitudes bolstering his spirit. "How can such fine young men fail?"

"Oh, Nicholas," Amelia whispered as she pulled him close.

"Don't drown the young man," a man with a deep voice said behind her, and she spun to face the worried, supportive gaze of her husband. He stood tall, his lanky frame clothed in a chestnut-brown suit and his reddish hair windblown. He held his hat in one hand.

"Sebastian! What are you doing here?"

"I found myself unwilling to miss Nicholas's goodbye at the train station. I will miss you, son," he said as he held out his hand to Nicholas. After a short handshake, he pulled Nicholas into his strong, lean arms and gave him a few pats on his back. "Write often, or your mother will fret." He failed to hide the worry in his gaze. "As will I."

"Are my siblings with you?" Nicholas asked as he looked over his stepfather's shoulders. Sebastian had been as a father to him since Nicholas was a boy and had always treated him as a son, even after Sebastian and Amelia had children of their own.

"No, they are in Darby. Anne is nearly old enough to tend them all, and old Mrs. McVeigh was eager to help us." He rubbed at his dirty face. "I borrowed an automobile and drove a good portion of the night to ensure I would arrive here in time."

Amelia gripped his arm and leaned into his side. She fought a shudder as she saw the young men lining up as a plume of steam approached, heralding the arrival of the special train for the troops. "You have Araminta's food, and you will visit Lucas and Patrick if you have time?"

"Of course, Mother, but I doubt we will spend any time in Butte. I'm not going on holiday." He pulled her close one last time before picking up his rucksack and joining the line of men to board the train. He gave his name to a man with a clipboard and listened as the men around him laughed and joked.

Amelia sagged into Sebastian's side. "I don't know what I would have done had you not arrived," she whispered.

He kissed her head and watched as Nicholas gripped the grab bar to board the train. He waved as Nicholas paused a moment to look back one last time. "Our boy is brave. He's smart. He'll return to us, Amelia."

The train heaved into motion, a multitude of arms sticking out windows to wave and a cacophony of voices yelling as they were slowly propelled from view. When the last of the steam plume had faded in the distant canyon, Amelia turned into Sebastian's arms and sobbed.

"*Shh*, … love. My darling. He will be all right." He held her close as she cried. He curled over her as though to absorb some of her grief.

"You can't know that," she stammered. "Every mother is telling herself the same thing, but, for some of us, we'll never see our boys again."

"I know that is true. But you must believe he will come home." He rubbed tears away from her cheeks, unable to hide the sadness in his gaze.

"Thank you," she whispered, leaning on her toes to give him a fleeting kiss. "Thank you for knowing I would need you here. For loving him as though he were your own." A tear slid down her cheek. "For ignoring my false pride that I didn't need you." She watched as a flash of pain lit his gaze. "I'm sorry."

"I know you feel as though you are losing a part of Liam again. I would do anything to protect you from such pain, Amelia," he whispered as he kissed her brow. "But I can't."

She nodded and sniffled as a few more tears escaped. "I … Will you forgive me, Sebastian?" She gripped his hand and held it to her chest. "I know how much you love Nicholas and Anne."

He cupped her cheek with one palm, looking deep into her hazel eyes. "They are mine as much as the others. I cherish them as I cherish you." He took a deep breath. "Please don't hurt me like that again."

"I won't," she vowed. "I promise." She kissed his palms. "Your love for them only makes me love you more," she whispered as she hugged him close for a moment. "Must we return to Darby today?"

"No, love. We can return tomorrow. Have a mini-honeymoon after so many years. Besides, I'd like to see Gabe and Colin. It's been too long."

She smiled at him. "Good. I miss our children and will be eager to see them tomorrow. But I want time with you, Sebastian." She smiled as he held her close. "It's been too long since we've had time for just the two of us."

~

Sebastian sat on Colin's porch and relaxed into the comfortable rocking chair Gabriel had built. The rain had lifted, and now bright sunlight warmed the late afternoon. Everything—from the leaves on the trees to the grass to the flowers shooting green stalks out of the ground—sparkled in the bright light with the remaining raindrops. Sebastian smiled as a boy raced away from his mother on the sidewalk and jumped into a puddle, laughing with joy and ignoring his mother's scold.

Sebastian focused on the long-legged gait of his friend Gabriel as he walked down the sidewalk and raised his hand in welcome. After clapping him on the back, they settled side by side on Colin's front porch.

"I thought Ronan would come with you," Sebastian said.

Gabriel shook his head and settled on a chair beside his friend. "He's not feeling well. The doc says it's normal for someone who has suffered his type of spinal injury."

Sebastian frowned in confusion. "I don't understand."

"I don't really either, except that his kidneys aren't working as well as they should." He frowned with frustration. "He doesn't have the energy he used to and often leaves work early to head home to sleep. He was out last night and didn't have the energy for a second night out tonight."

Sebastian nodded. "I'll stop by the workshop before I leave to see him before I head home to Darby."

"Where's Amelia?" Gabriel asked.

"Resting. Today was one of the worst days of her life, and I doubt she slept much last night." Sebastian rocked and tapped his fingers on his leg. As a younger man, he had been in constant motion, rocking to and fro with an incessant energy. Now, in his late forties, he had a residual restlessness but was not as fidgety. "I'm glad I trusted my instincts and traveled to Missoula."

Gabriel studied his friend and frowned. Sebastian's hair was disheveled. and he had deep bags under his eyes. "I don't understand why you didn't travel with her yesterday rather than through part of the night and this morning."

Sebastian leaned forward and rested his elbows on his knees. "You know how much I love Nickie. I've never thought of him as anything but mine." His eyes shone with pain. "Amelia didn't want me here. Said she wanted time alone with Nickie. That I owed her that because he wasn't really mine, and she had the right to say goodbye to him the way she never had the ability to say goodbye to her Liam."

Gabriel sat back in the chair as though feeling the sucker punch that had been delivered to his friend. "Why would she say that to you?"

"She's terrified. I've not seen her like this since I was hurt in the fire. When she thought I might die. She hides it well, but the loss of Liam scarred her, and the threat of any further loss is almost more than she can bear."

Gabriel frowned and sat in silence with his friend a few moments. "She's a strong woman. She can handle anything."

Sebastian sniffled and shook his head. "She can survive, Gabe. I don't know if she would truly be the same woman if she loses Nickie." He shook his head. "I don't know what would happen to our children."

Gabriel cleared his throat. "When grief is shared, it is more bearable." He let out a long breath. "That doesn't mean it's any easier to endure, but the knowledge you aren't going through it alone ..." He let out a shaky breath.

"I can't imagine how hard it was for you and Clarissa, losing Rory," Sebastian whispered.

Gabriel nodded, and his eyes filled. "Don't let Amelia freeze you out. It's an ability we all have in an attempt to forestall any further pain. But, by doing that, we prevent any further joy or true feeling again."

Sebastian sat in quiet contemplation for a few moments. He looked out at the street scene as a couple walked by, waving as they passed. Birds chirped in the trees, and a soft breeze blew, sprinkling the remaining raindrops to the ground. "I promised myself I'd never pressure her."

"Sometimes we have to break our promises, Seb. When those we love most in this world need us to, we must break our vows." He leaned forward and rubbed at his head. "I hope to God you and Amelia do not have to suffer the loss of your Nickie. Our Nickie," he whispered as his voice thickened.

Sebastian stared at him as Gabriel's expression became distant. "I always forget you've known him longer than I have."

Gabriel nodded. "Yes. He was … He helped keep me sane when I was separated from Rissa—when I had little hope of a reconciliation with her while I lived in Butte." He dropped his head and rubbed at his nape. "I held him in my arms as they held a wake for his father. Nickie's presence was my greatest consolation." Gabriel cleared his throat. "I can't imagine a world where Nickie isn't in it." He nodded as Sebastian gripped his shoulder. "We all love your boy, Seb. We must continue to pray he comes home to us."

CHAPTER 7

Summer weather finally arrived in Missoula a few days after Nicholas left for the War. The mornings remained cool, but the afternoons and evenings were hot. The long evenings where the sun did not set until after nine were ideal for sitting on porches and telling tall tales. This afternoon Jeremy sat in his kitchen, listening as his daughter, Melinda, discussed her day at school. He attempted to appear stern but could not prevent the pride shining in his eyes as he beheld his only child.

He and Savannah had adopted Melinda when they had moved to Montana in 1903. She had been placed in an orphanage by her mother, Mrs. Smythe, after the death of her husband, Sean Sullivan. Although Jeremy suspected that Clarissa had intended to raise Melinda, as Clarissa was Melinda's sister, Clarissa had recognized Jeremy's and Savannah's love for Melinda and had rejoiced in their forming a family.

"And then," Melinda said in the middle of her story about one of the boys in her class, holding up a knife in the midst of chopping carrots, "he had the gall to tell me that I wasn't fit to attend university." She slapped the knife's edge to the cutting board and sliced the carrots into increasingly small pieces.

"What did you say to that?" He firmed his lips into a grim line, as he knew his daughter took after her mother and sister in her suffragist tendencies.

"I informed him that I was plenty smart to attend and that, if someone with the size of a baboon's brain couldn't see that, it wasn't my fault." She slapped the knife down in disgust once more, having finished mangling the carrots.

Jeremy coughed in an attempt to swallow a laugh. "I'm not certain that sort of language is accepted at school, Melly."

"I apologized for insulting the baboon," she said with a sniff.

Jeremy gave up and roared with laughter. He held out an arm for his daughter and pulled her into a one-armed embrace as she remained standing while he sat. "What did the teacher say?"

"Nothing. She seemed relieved it was the last week of school and that she'd soon have a reprieve for a few months." She leaned her head on his shoulder and sighed. "Why should boys be scared that I have a brain and that I'm not afraid to use it?"

"Ah, dearest, that's exactly why they're terrified. Because you aren't afraid of using it. And many are aware of, and embarrassed by, the fact that you are so much smarter than they are."

Melly tugged out a chair and collapsed onto it, her elbows on the table and her chin on the palms of her hands. "I like meeting someone smarter than me. Then I can learn. And have a really good discussion."

Jeremy ran a hand over her blond curls. "You're used to a family who discusses and debates constantly. Not every family is like that. You're also accustomed to people who value a woman's opinion."

"I'd think, after Montana gave women the vote and then voted Jeannette Rankin to Congress, that they'd be a bit more enlightened," she said with a roll of her eyes.

Jeremy laughed again at her exasperation. "At least you know the majority are," he teased. He rose, holding a hand out for her as he moved to help her with the meal. "Come. What is it you are attempting to make for supper? I'd like to help."

Melinda gave an exaggerated sigh. "It's Meatless Tuesday, so I'm trying to make a vegetable soup. However, most of the vegetables at the grocers were picked over and looked like they were from last year's crop." She held up a desiccated potato. "How is this appetizing?"

Jeremy chuckled and hugged her. "If we add enough of them all together, it won't be so bad." He pulled out a knife and a board, and aided her in chopping the remaining vegetables. "I haven't seen your mother today. How is she?"

Melinda shrugged. "Much the same as she usually is lately."

Jeremy frowned at his daughter's vague response and the thinly veiled criticism held within. "Well, I know she'll be delighted with your culinary expertise," Jeremy said with a broad smile to Melinda. When they'd put the pot on the stove to simmer for a few hours, he followed her to his study, where she sat at his desk to work on her homework, and he sat in a comfortable chair to read letters and the evening newspaper.

~

Savannah sat in her rocking chair in the bedroom she used to share with Jeremy, absently brushing out her long blond hair. She didn't acknowledge Jeremy's entrance into the room but continued to stare into space. She froze as he gripped the arms of the rocking chair and stopped her movement. Sitting back, she moved away from him as he leaned toward her.

"I need you to focus on me, Savannah. Tell me what is bothering you." His cheeks reddened with frustration as she remained silent. "Dammit, what did I do? Tell me, and I'll make it better. I'll change. I promise."

His whispered entreaty had her closing her eyes as tears trickled down her cheeks. She sniffled and then fell forward into his embrace.

After settling on the floor, he rocked her to and fro, cocooned in his arms, while she sobbed. "Tell me. I promise I'll fix whatever is wrong. I'm sorry for whatever I did," he whispered over and over into her hair as she continued to shudder into his shoulder.

"I wanted you to hate me," she whispered in a stuttering breath past her sobs.

He pushed her back, brushing her hair out of the way and smearing her tears in the process. "Why? I would never hate you. I couldn't."

"I'm so scared, Jeremy," she whispered. She shook her head and seemed to shrink into herself in front of him.

"This isn't like you, Sav. It's not like you to ignore all of us for the better part of three months. I've tried to reach you, but you've kept this hard barrier around you. I want to know why." He continued to rub his hands over her in an attempt to soothe her and himself.

"I have to tell you soon. You're bound to notice." She lowered her gaze, paling as she spoke. "I can't believe you haven't already suspected."

"Will you speak plainly and quit talking in riddles?" Jeremy demanded, the gentle entreaty giving way to a demand as his anxiety and anger over the past few months erupted.

"I'm pregnant," she whispered. "All of our precautions failed." She bit her trembling lip while tears continued to fall as his hands fell away from her. She pulled her arms around herself, hugging her middle. "The doctor I spoke with in Butte last week said there's a good chance …" Her voice broke.

"A good chance …"

"A good chance I will die this time. That nothing can be done to save me," Savannah whispered. She watched as Jeremy pushed away from her to roam the room.

He paused at the wardrobe, the muscles of his back tense as he propped himself on both arms. "God damn it to hell," he rasped. "I swear, Savannah, I never would have risked you." He slammed his hand against the wardrobe, then again to the point she thought he'd crack it.

"Jeremy, you'll frighten Melly," she reprimanded him.

"You think I worry about frightening Melly when you tell me there's a good chance you'll be dead in a few months?" He hissed, impotent fury rolling off him. "And you wasted some of the time we have left?" He shook his head in dismay and disappointment, his eyes devastated. "Why would you do that to me? This is my baby too. You're my wife. My life."

Savannah shrugged her shoulders, pushing herself up to sit again in the rocking chair, although she didn't rock in it. "I didn't want to believe it at first. And then I thought you wouldn't mourn me as much if there'd been a distance between us."

Jeremy reacted as though she'd stabbed him. He clutched a hand to his chest and leaned back against the wardrobe. "A distance? How can you not comprehend how much I love you after all these years? A distance would only hurt me more." He shook his head in incredulity. "You visited a doctor without me. You denied me the right to be beside you. You have to know I would support you. Do everything I could to protect you."

Faint trembling racked Savannah, and she stared into space again. "We've done what we could to prevent a baby. I knew you didn't want to try for another. I couldn't bear having you believe I intentionally became pregnant."

Jeremy slammed his palm against the wardrobe, earning a startled gaze from her. "Did you? Because that was the furthest thing from my mind until you said it."

"Of course not," she whispered. "I'm just so … I was just so…."

"Afraid? Of me? Of telling me, the man who loves you, who'll love our baby, the truth?" he asked, eyes brightened by tears. He ran his fingers through his hair and sniffled. "I have to get out of here."

"Jeremy, please stay and talk." She held out a hand to him in supplication.

"No, not now. You had months to talk with me, and you wouldn't. I can't right now. I won't." He spun for the door and wrenched it open, before slamming it shut behind him.

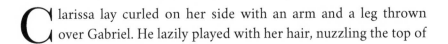

Clarissa lay curled on her side with an arm and a leg thrown over Gabriel. He lazily played with her hair, nuzzling the top of her head as she half dozed. He stiffened at a fist pounding on the downstairs door.

"Who would call at this hour?" Clarissa murmured, half asleep. "They'd better not wake the children."

Gabriel chuckled and kissed her head before slipping from bed and tugging on a pair of pants. He grabbed a shirt and closed the door behind him. When he entered the upstairs hallway, he lunged after his son Billy, pulling him into his arms. "Whoa, little buddy. You know you shouldn't go to the door without your mother or me," Gabriel said as he held him in his arms. He was almost too big to hold like this, but Gabriel relished moments when he was too sleepy to fight being held.

"They can't wake Little Colin," Billy said around a huge yawn, showing off his tonsils.

Gabriel set him down and gave him a pat on his bum, pushing him in the direction of his bedroom. "Let me answer the door so they don't," he said with a smile and a wink. He watched as Billy walked toward his bedroom door, tripping into the hall wall once before he safely maneuvered into his room.

Gabriel walked down the stairs and opened the door, his inquisitive stare turning to a frown of concern as he beheld his brother. "Jer," he murmured, pulling him inside.

Jeremy swayed, allowing himself to be tugged into the living room and pushed onto the sofa.

Gabriel sat on the chair across from him.

"I'm sorry to come so late. I'd forgotten the hour."

"You know you never need worry about that sort of thing with us. What's the matter, Jer?" Gabriel asked. His gaze roved over his youngest brother, and he frowned at the desperation he sensed. "Have you discovered what's wrong with Savannah?"

Jeremy nodded, raising terrified eyes to his brother.

Gabriel blanched as the panic made his brother's eyes shine a brighter green.

"She's pregnant. She believes she's going to die."

Gabriel stilled Jeremy's instinctive move to rise and pace with a firm clasp on his forearm. "All women have that irrational fear. As do most of the men who care for them. She will be fine."

Jeremy shook his head as desolation stole over him. "No, I've always known that, if she were to become pregnant again, she'd most likely die. You know what it was like the last time we lost a baby five years ago. How weak she was from the anemia. It took her weeks to recover." He sucked in a deep breath, clearing his throat in an attempt to speak without his voice breaking. "She visited a doctor. In Butte. And he confirmed her fears."

Gabriel frowned. "She's visited a doctor about your baby without even informing you that she was pregnant?"

Jeremy freed his arm from Gabriel's grasp, raising his palms to cover his face, scrubbing at his cheeks before rubbing his hands through his hair. He began to shake. "She said she was afraid."

"Of being pregnant? Of you?" Gabriel shook his head in confusion. "Because, no matter what, she had to know, at some point, you'd figure it out. A baby is pretty hard to hide."

"This isn't humorous, Gabe," Jeremy snapped.

"No, it's damn tragic that you two can't rejoice at the life you've created," Gabriel said, sorrow shining from his eyes as he watched his youngest brother suffer. "What can I do?"

Jeremy sank into the sofa's cushions. "Besides find a way for my wife to trust me? To not fear me?"

Gabriel scratched at his own head, sending his hair on end. "You know that's not true, Jer. She loves you."

Jeremy rose, pacing to the mantel. He stared at the painting Zylphia had created of the creek near the place where Clarissa and Gabriel's son Rory had died. Jeremy lost himself momentarily in the beauty of the scene with no hint of the tragedy that had occurred. "You've known loss. You know what it is to find yourself separated from Clarissa." Jeremy fisted his hand and slammed it down on the mantel top. "Do you know what it does to me to know that she didn't trust me? That she feared me?" He swiped at his face and sniffled but refused to face his brother. "After all this time, all the years since Jonas's death, she still doesn't trust me. Not completely."

"I know that's not true," Gabriel whispered.

"She thought it would be better if there was a distance between us, if I'd already started to resent her. So that, when she died, I wouldn't miss her as much." Jeremy attempted an incredulous snort but instead hiccupped out a sob. "As though I wouldn't mourn her forever."

"It sounds like the type of convoluted logic a terrified woman uses to protect those she loves most in the world." Gabriel placed a hand on his brother's shoulder. "She must be as afraid as you are."

"I hate that I was robbed of even one day with her due to her distancing herself from me," Jeremy said.

"And yet you've just robbed yourself of more time with your anger tonight," Gabriel murmured. "You must find a way to understand each other, Jer. Forgiveness might seem too great at this point. But I know you. You have the biggest heart of all us McLeod men." He reached forward and gripped his brother by the shoulders.

Jeremy allowed himself to be pulled into a bear hug before he eased himself away and rubbed at a tear that had leaked out. "I should go home. Speak with Savannah."

Gabriel nodded.

"I'll let you know how things are when I see you at the workshop."

"I'll tell Rissa that you're having problems. It's not a stretch, seeing how Sav's acted recently. Her news is hers to tell." He shared a long brotherly look with Jeremy before escorting him to the door.

When Jeremy returned home, he wandered into his downstairs study, rather than returning to his bedroom upstairs. He sat in his comfortable leather chair with a half-full tumbler of whiskey in front of him. It was largely untouched, but he enjoyed staring into its amber depths. He swirled the glass, watching it coat and then slide off the side of the glass. His eyes closed as the door creaked open.

"I thought I heard you come in," Savannah whispered as she entered in stockinged feet. "That was a few hours ago."

114

Jeremy turned to look out the side window, noting it was still pitch black out. "It seems this night will never end," he murmured.

Savannah flinched at his words.

"Why did you seek me out?"

She moved to a chair across from the desk. "I wanted to ensure you were all right. You weren't in any of the guest bedrooms."

Jeremy's shoulders hunched farther as he pinched the bridge between his nose. "What would you do to comfort me?"

"It's so ironic how I need you to comfort me too," she whispered. "I'm sorry. I'm sorry I acted like a witless idiot."

"You thought I'd react like Jonas," Jeremy said in a flat voice, a tone that hurt Savannah more than any raging or imploring could have.

"Oh, God, no!" Savannah cried out, rising from her chair and moving beside the desk. She pushed away the tumbler of whiskey, inadvertently thrusting it to the floor. She stood next to him, attempting to force him to look at her. "All I thought about was the pain I was causing you again. And I hate that."

"The only pain you've ever caused me is when you haven't trusted me," Jeremy whispered. "Every other moment with you I've known joy. Joy in sharing this life with you. Joy in raising Melinda together. Joy in facing hurdles together. Joy in comforting you when you are sad. Joy in sharing our sorrows together. I have only ever exulted in my love for you."

Tears dripped off her cheeks, landing on his head and shoulders. "Oh, Jeremy. I know. And I have no other way to say I'm sorry. I'm sorry, and I love you. I'm terrified of leaving you. Leaving Melly. Of not growing old with you. Not watching our grandchildren grow." She fought a sob.

He snaked an arm out and curled it around her side, moving his chair back enough that he could ease her onto his lap. "Don't cry, love," he murmured.

"I'm filled with such a rage! I don't want this threat hanging over us," she sobbed into his shoulder.

"I know," he whispered. "Instead of rejoicing at our good fortune, we are lamenting." He took a deep breath as she settled on his lap and cried. He rocked her to and fro, kissing her head, holding her tight as the storm of her grief broke.

"I know you'll care for our child even if I'm gone," she said into his ear. "But that makes me so sad. I want to be here too. Does that make me greedy?"

"No, my love," Jeremy said, kissing her forehead and continuing to rock her. "It makes you human. It makes me love you more."

She traced a hand over his arm and shoulder. "You don't hate me?"

"I could never hate you." He sighed. "I could be irate with you. I could wish things were different, but I could never hate you." He pushed her back and looked into her eyes. "I want you to know I'm not accepting that doctor's decree as though it were Gospel. I'll fight for you, for us, with everything I have."

"There's nothing we can do." She laid a hand over her slightly rounded belly as tears continued to seep out.

"I can't believe I didn't suspect. I never noticed," he whispered.

"I tried very hard for you not to," she said. "I had clothes made to hide my belly. And I don't tend to show the baby until the end of my pregnancy." His hand roved over her belly, and she bit back a sob as Jeremy bent over, kissing the bulge.

"Hello, little love," he whispered. "You will be cherished."

"Oh, Jeremy," she murmured as tears coursed down her cheek. She met his determined gaze and shrugged in resignation at her fate.

"We'll go to Boston, and Melly will come with us as school is soon out. We'll visit the best doctors in the city, and, if I don't like what they say, we'll go to New York City. I will not give up without exploring every avenue available to us. I will not readily accept any doctor's decree. We will fight against fate."

"The expense," she whispered.

"We have the money." He gave her an ironic smile. "I can think of no better way to spend his money than ensuring your safety during the birth of our child." His eyes were lit with a hint of revenge as he considered using her first husband's money to pay for her medical care.

He kissed her softly and then held her close as she fought tears. "We will rejoice at this news, Savannah. I promise you."

~

Araminta walked beside Bartholomew Bouchard on one of their customary evening walks. This evening they walked toward a neighborhood park and strolled the perimeter of it. When they were in an isolated corner of the park, far away from children playing in the late evening, he stopped and faced her.

"Araminta," he whispered in a low voice. "I believe you've come to understand my deep regard for you." He smiled as she stood stock-still and beheld him with wide stunned eyes. "I've been constant in my show of affection."

She nodded and attempted to back up a step but was held in place by his firm grip on her hands. "Forgive me if I've given you the wrong impression." His smile was sweet, although it did little to disarm or soothe her.

"I know you are intrigued by me. And I know you appreciate the time we spend together." His smile broadened at her blush. "Just as I hate to miss seeing you." He bent so his forehead nearly touched hers. "Marry me, Araminta."

Her breaths emerged in a gasp, and she stuttered incoherently before clamping her mouth shut. After a moment, she whispered, "Why would you want to marry me?"

His thumb traced a pattern over her hand. "You're clever and resourceful. You are loyal." He took a deep breath as his smile faded. He raised her hand and kissed the back of it. "I love you, Araminta. I want you as my wife."

She shook her head from side to side. "That's impossible."

"Why? Because someone else, who's had the opportunity to make his feelings known but hasn't because he's a feckless deceiver, has strung you along for years?" He gripped her shoulders. "I am not such a man. I will proclaim it to this town, to anyone who asks, that I am proud to have you as my wife."

She frowned. "Why?"

"Don't you want your own family? Your own children? Or do you want to live your life caring for those who will only ever see you as a glorified nursemaid? What happens when their children are grown? Will you start caring for their children too?" He gave her a slight shake. "Why don't you want more from your life?"

Confusion, despair and then determination filled her gaze. "Don't ever disparage me or my life again. Or the McLeod families," she demanded. "I have a wonderful life, and they have been very good to me."

He caressed her cheek. "Forgive me. I would never mean you disrespect. I want more for you, Araminta. I had hoped you wanted more too." He stared deeply into her eyes. "My greatest hope is that you envision me in your future."

She took a deep breath. "I never thought you'd offer marriage. I have enjoyed our friendship." She watched him as he tensed at her words. "I've enjoyed my time with you." She studied him further as she firmed her shoulders. "I will marry you, Bartholomew. Thank you."

She gasped as he swooped in for a quick kiss. He tugged her closer, deepening the kiss and only pulling back when the calls of children playing neared. He panted as he watched her with a triumphant light in his eyes and nodded. He patted her hand and looped her arm through his, tugging her away from the park and toward her house.

She kissed him again in the shadow of her porch before he walked off with a victorious spring to his step. As night fell, she sat on the porch rail and battled tears as she thought of announcing her decision to the family.

~

Clarissa opened the back door to Savannah's house and let herself into her kitchen. She grunted as Little Colin squirmed and set him down. "Sav?" she called out and then sighed as Little Colin raced toward the hall.

Savannah walked into the kitchen and picked up an exploring Little Colin. "How's my darling?" she whispered as she kissed his cheek. "He's so big," Savannah said as he rested his head on her shoulder a moment.

"Enjoy the cuddle. Soon he'll fidget and roam around like a wild man." She watched her cousin and son with fondness. "I can't believe he's already two."

Savannah kissed his head and nodded to the door. "Why don't we go outside and sit? We can watch him play in the yard, and you can enjoy a few moments without worrying he's getting into something."

"Oh, he'll find a worm to eat," Clarissa said with a sardonic smile. "Gabriel and I could not have given him a more fitting name. He's fast becoming just like his namesake. He does something outrageous and then smiles, as though he knows, if he is charming enough, he'll be forgiven everything."

Savannah smiled and followed Clarissa to the backyard. A portion of it had recently been fenced, and two chairs were set in the shade. She held Little Colin by his fingers as he got his balance, and then he ran away to explore the limits of his play area.

Clarissa sat with a sigh, setting a small bag beside her. "I brought toys for when he is bored wandering around the limits of his little kingdom." She took a few moments to enjoy the mild air, the gentle breeze and the soft birdsong. "Are you all right, Sav?"

"You know I'm not. Why would you ask me such a question?" Savannah held a hand over her middle, her gaze on her young cousin.

"Why would Jeremy need to visit Gabriel after we were all abed? Was he having more nightmares about the Philippines?"

Savannah turned startled eyes to Clarissa. "He hasn't dreamed of the Philippines in years. Why would you ask about that now?"

Her cousin frowned as she stared at the genuine confusion in Savannah's gaze. "How do you not know what he's been suffering?" Clarissa whispered. "He's been a wreck since he saw Nicholas the night before Nicholas left to go to the War."

Savannah paled, raising a hand to her head. She rubbed at her forehead, loosening a few strands of her blond hair from the knot tying her hair back. "I said last night how much I needed his comfort, and he wasn't there for me." She sniffled. "I wasn't there for him, was I?"

Clarissa shook her head with confusion. "Is there anything I can do to help you?"

Savannah blinked, but tears leaked out, forming a silent river down her cheeks. "I'm pregnant, Rissa." She nodded as her cousin failed to exult at the news. "The doctors say I will probably die with the baby's birth."

Clarissa's gaze sharpened as it roved over Savannah, focusing on her palms over her midriff. "How far along?"

"I'm due in October." She sniffled. "I never thought I'd hide it as long as I did."

Clarissa flushed. "I assumed you couldn't have a child. I thought … I thought you were merely gaining weight." She clasped one of Savannah's hands. "Did you speak with Jeremy last night?"

Savannah closed her eyes. "Yes. He's angry with me. For hiding my condition. For wanting to force a separation between us." She opened her eyes to battle the instinctive censure in her cousin's gaze. "If we were at odds, I had hoped he would not mourn me as much."

Clarissa snorted. "That's ludicrous. He'd mourn the time he lost with you." She glanced around the fenced-in area, smiling to see Little Colin sitting down as he played with a dandelion. "You hurt him."

"Yes. And I regret it," Savannah whispered. "But you don't know what it's like to love and hate the baby growing in you. To welcome and resent it at the same time." She swallowed a sob. "Why should I die? Why should I be separated from Melly and Jeremy? I love my life with them." She swiped at her cheeks. "It's so ironic. For years, all I wanted was another baby. Now that I am finally content with my life, I'm pregnant and desperately unhappy."

"You have to believe it will be different this time. You've already carried this pregnancy longer than the previous ones." Clarissa gripped her hand.

Savannah nodded. "Jeremy wants us to go to Boston. To see the doctors there." She pulled out a handkerchief and swiped at her face.

"He wants to ensure we are safe. That everything that can be done for us will be done."

Clarissa nodded. "Good." Her eyes filled. "I'll miss you, Sav. But I will eagerly await meeting your new baby as she is held in your arms."

~

olin's gaze stalked Araminta's loping movement through his living room. She paused to speak with Clarissa's children, laughed at one of Melly's jokes and then continued her somehow graceful movement into his kitchen. They had decided to meet at his house because Savannah and Jeremy claimed their house was in disarray with their packing for the trip east. Colin rose—bypassing Gabriel's attempt to sideline him and Ronan jutting his wheelchair out to impede Colin's movement—and followed Araminta into the kitchen.

He stood for a moment, watching as she hummed the tune *"If He Can Fight Like He Can Love (Good Night, Germany)"* while she cut bread and set out trays of food to bring to the table. He grinned at her song choice. "Do you ever tire of caring for us?" he asked.

"It's my job," she said, her humming ceasing at his words. "I care for those I choose."

"You are most diligent at it," he said, strolling forward to steal a piece of bread. He yowled as she slapped away his hand. "Ouch, Ari," he hissed, shaking his hand in pain.

"Don't call me that." She ignored him as he leaned against the counter next to her. He began to whistle the same song she'd been humming, and her expression soured.

"Why are you so angry with me?" he whispered.

She set down the knife with a *thud*, exhaling deeply. "Believe it or not, the world does not rotate around you. My every waking thought is not about you."

He laughed, nudging her with his shoulder. "I would hope not. Even I'm not that conceited." When she failed to comment at his attempt at a self-deprecating joke, he frowned. He watched as she prepared the food to be carried out to the dining room. He stood to his full height. "Let me help you take out the food." He gave her a look, suggesting that she had better not complain, and hefted two of the heavy platters she had just prepared.

He opened the swinging kitchen door with a kick of his foot and yelled "Dinner!" After plopping the trays onto the table, he returned to the kitchen to help with the rest of the food. "You may think we are done, but we have to talk."

"There's nothing to talk about. There hasn't been for years." She sailed past him with the bread and salad, smiling at his family as she sat between Melly and Geraldine.

Colin frowned as he watched her tactical evasion and vowed he'd find another way to speak with her.

He joined his family at the crowded dining room table and raised a glass. "To Jeremy, Sav and Melly. May you have a safe journey, and may you all continue with good health," Colin said, battling deep emotions. He reached a hand out to Savannah but refrained from saying anything more serious as Melinda had not been informed of the grave reason behind their trip to visit Aidan and Delia.

"Give our love to Richard, Florence and their boys," Gabriel said as he fed Little Colin so Clarissa could eat. Gabriel had his son perched on a modified high chair between himself and Clarissa, and Little Colin smiled, laughed and talked to himself while the adults visited. "Kiss baby Agnes for us."

"We will," Jeremy said. "It will be strange to return to Boston after so many years."

"I remember returning for my father's funeral," Clarissa said. "It was as though nothing and yet everything had changed, and a ghost seemed to be around every corner."

"It's hard to believe it's already been seven years since Aunt Betsy died. And over two years since my mother died," Savannah said, gripping Jeremy's hand.

Melinda bounced in her chair, making everyone laugh. "I hope Zee's there and not in Washington. She's so much fun, and I want to see her."

"She's a married woman now," Savannah said. "Besides, she's very dedicated to the cause."

"I could be dedicated," Melinda protested.

Clarissa laughed and shared a fond look with Melinda. "Yes, but her dedication means that she spends a lot of her time in Washington, DC. I'm uncertain she'll be at home while you are there." Clarissa pushed away her plate and held her hand out for the spoon to help Little Colin. He insisted he try to feed himself at most meals and had little pieces of food in front of him, but he preferred to play with his food rather than eat it.

Gabriel accepted a plate filled with a helping of everything and ate while everyone else sat around and chatted.

"Before we are separated, I have an announcement," Araminta said at the lull in the conversation. All eyes turned to her, and she flushed at their scrutiny. "I consider you my family, and I wanted to share my good news with you."

Colin tensed beside Gabriel, who set down his fork and lowered his arm to his side. Colin watched Araminta with a fierce intensity, as though willing her to stop talking.

"I've accepted a proposal of marriage," she said in a voice barely above a whisper. "To Mr. Bartholomew Bouchard."

As the rest of his family belatedly exclaimed their joy for her, Colin growled, "Like hell you have. You can't marry him!"

Araminta turned her disdainful gaze in Colin's direction. "I know some will say I am acting precipitously. However, this is what I desire, and I know I will be very happy."

"Like hell you will," Colin muttered again, his voice emerging as though he had been wounded.

Gabriel had a hard grip on Colin's leg underneath the table, preventing any movements and any actions Colin might later regret. "I'm happy for you Minta, although I can't say I envy you his aunts," Gabriel said in a jovial tone.

"Mrs. Bouchard," Savannah said as they shared a collective groan as they envisioned the busybody who was blessed with as passionate an opinion as her clothes were gaudy.

"Although I believe Mrs. Vaughan is worse," Clarissa said with a chuckle as she thought about the two sisters.

"Either are a nightmare, and I can't imagine wanting to align myself with such a family," Colin said.

"May you find the contentment you have always desired, Minta," Ronan said as he raised a glass. He sent a quelling glare in Colin's direction, and Colin knew he would have been kicked had Ronan had the ability.

Araminta sat straighter, pointedly ignoring Colin. She focused on Savannah, Jeremy and Melinda. "I hope you will be home in time for the wedding. We plan to wed in October."

Jeremy shared a long look with Savannah. "We will keep that in mind as we make travel plans."

"To Araminta!" Gabriel said as he raised his glass. "May she know as much happiness and joy as she has brought to us." He smiled at her as she fought tears.

Colin half raised a glass, his elbow propped on the table. He watched Araminta blossom under his family's praise and failed to drink the toast before he set his glass down with a *thunk*.

When his family was distracted telling stories in his living room, he snuck into the kitchen where Araminta washed the dishes. "Ari," he whispered. He stilled his move toward her when she froze at his voice. "What are you thinking?"

She shook her head and continued her work, her back to him. "I'm thinking it will be nice to be married. To be with a man who wants me. Who isn't afraid to admit what he feels."

"Ari, you know I—"

"Don't," she rasped in a low, intense voice. "Not now. Not when all of a sudden you feel as though you must act because your life might change, and you are terrified of it. You have no right to make me doubt my decisions." She spun and watched him with contempt. "He has only ever treated me with respect. He has only ever wanted what was best for me. He has seen me as more than …"

Colin stood stock-still, and the silence between them lengthened, only interrupted by soft laughs coming from the living room and a gentle drip from the faucet. "He sees you as more than what, Ari?"

She shook her head. "It doesn't matter. What does matter is that he admitted he loved me last night. I have agreed to marry him."

Colin swallowed. "A man will say whatever he needs to say in order to achieve what he wants."

She threw the dishtowel at him as her eyes filled with anger before they filled with tears. "How dare you? How dare you cheapen and demean the one good thing to happen to me in years?" She shook her head as she watched him in disappointed wonder. "How can you call me your friend and act this way?"

He moved, reaching out to hold her in his arms. "Ari, you have to know I—"

She hit him on his chest, pushing him away. "No! No! You will not speak your falsehoods to me simply because you're afraid I won't be here to act as cook and maid when you want to entertain your family. I want more, Colin. And I'll have it."

He stood, holding the damp dishtowel, bewildered and heartsore as she pushed past him and into the living room. When he heard her join in the conversation with his family, the discussion turning to her wedding plans, he sank to his haunches and shook with despair.

That evening Savannah rocked in her chair as she waited for Jeremy to come upstairs. She fell asleep, her dreams filled with tantalizing images of holding a baby in her arms, nestled in Jeremy's embrace. She woke with a start to realize that part of her dream was true, since she was no longer in the chair but on the bed, with Jeremy's strong arms around her.

"*Shh*, love. Go to sleep." He traced his fingers over her shoulder to her elbow and then back up again. "You were smart to change into your nightgown before falling asleep in your chair."

"Jeremy," she breathed before stretching and forcing herself awake. "Forgive me. I'm so tired all the time."

He caressed her cheeks as she had moved so she now faced him. "I understand. Our child is wearing you out." A pleased smile flitted over his mouth, and joy lit his eyes for a moment.

She kissed his palm and then held it to her belly. "She moves a lot. Can you feel her?"

He gazed into Savannah's eyes as he focused on his hand. After a moment, he gasped. "Was that her?"

"Yes," she whispered around tears as she watched the shock and wonder in his expression.

He leaned forward, kissing her softly. "Find joy in our baby, Savannah. I know you are scared. I'm terrified. But I'm also elated. I want to share the excitement and fear with you."

She nodded. "I hate having this hope," she whispered. "We've never made it this far before in a pregnancy. I wonder ..." Her voice broke off, and she resumed speaking after he gave her a gentle nod. "I wonder if it means this time all will be different for us."

"God, I hope so. I pray for it every day." He kissed her forehead and then backed away enough so that she could see his troubled gaze. "Do you believe I was happy with our life? That I never hoped, never planned for this to happen?"

"Oh, Jeremy," she said through a tear-thickened voice as she stroked her fingers through his ebony hair. "I never doubted, never, your dedication to me. To Melly. To the life we have. I know how much you love me." She swallowed. "I hope you can forgive me and try to understand that I acted as I did because I love you so much."

She leaned into him, allowing him to hold her tight. After a few minutes, she eased away. "I need you to forgive me for something else, darling." She traced a finger over the furrow in his brows as he watched her with guarded eyes. "I wasn't there to support you when you needed me."

He jerked back and shook his head. "It was nothing, Sav."

She held onto his shoulders and refused to allow him to roll away from her. "If you were dreaming of the Philippines again, I know it wasn't nothing." She fought tears. "I wish I had been there for you. To hold you. To make you understand how proud I am of you."

He let out a huff of air, as though in disgust or disbelief. "How? There are days I can barely look at myself in the mirror." He closed his eyes, as though in defeat, hiding the torment he concealed well in his green eyes.

"I know you find it difficult to face what you were ordered to do in the Philippines, my love. And I know you wish you had never done what you did." Her eyes filled as she remembered his agonizing account of his time as an interrogator while in the army and his use of water torture on the men he questioned. "But it does not diminish my love for you. The fact you feel such remorse only makes me love you more."

"Oh, love," he said, pulling her close. "I feared …" He shuddered as he clung to her. "I feared that you were reading about the atrocities in the War and imagining what I had done, and that you couldn't stand the sight of me." He buried his face in her shoulder.

"Never." She held him to her, cradling him in her arms. "Never." She sighed as his sobs quieted and then gave a small moan of pleasure as he kissed her neck.

"I got your nightgown all wet," he whispered.

"Then perhaps I should take it off," she teased, instinctively understanding he needed to focus on something other than his memories. "Make love with me, my darling."

He tugged her nightgown over her head, and his hands roved over her, pausing at her midriff to the subtle roundness there. "I know what can happen, Sav," he whispered, "but I can't rid myself of some hope."

"I know, love. I know." She tugged at his hair and kissed him, losing herself to his touch and their passion.

CHAPTER 8

Boston, July 1918

Savannah stood outside the door, her hand on the doorknob but unable to turn it. She noted the fresh coat of paint, where the "and Son" had been scraped away. She traced the faint outline of the letters a moment before taking a deep breath and pushing open the door. The tinkling of the bell evoked a multitude of memories: Her mother working behind the counter with her father. Lucas teasing her as he left for deliveries. Her father's careful cajoling of patrons to purchase more than intended and his wink in her direction when he was successful.

Savannah stood in the doorway a moment, expecting to see her father, but frowned when an unknown young man smiled at her as he nodded to the fine linens. When he opened his mouth to begin his sales pitch, Savannah murmured, "I beg your pardon. I was hoping to see Mr. Russell today."

"I'm sorry, ma'am, but he's detained and is unable to speak with patrons at this time." He held his arms out as though to showcase the displays of fine linen. "I'm certain I can be of service to you."

"I apologize. I'm not here to see linens but Mr. Russell." Savannah backed up a step as though to leave before moving with alacrity through the side door to the adjoining hallway. Her father's office door was ajar, and she pushed it open. Loud footsteps sounded behind her, and she bolted into the office, slamming the door shut behind her.

Seated at his desk, her father glared at the intruder. With a look of wonder on his face, he rose and walked toward Savannah, as though afraid he saw an apparition, rather than his daughter. "Savannah? Are you really here?"

"Yes, Father." Her voice broke before she could say anything further. She threw herself into his strong arms, shuddering when they closed around her.

When his young assistant then barged into the room, indignantly affronted at being outmaneuvered, Martin only waved him away.

When they were again alone, Savannah continued to cling to her father. "I never thought I'd see you again," she whispered.

"I never dared to hope," he murmured, kissing her head and stroking a hand down her back. "Why didn't you write and tell me you were returning to Boston?"

She eased away and swiped at her tears. After extracting a hand-kerchief from her handbag and scrubbing at her face, she shrugged. "I wanted to surprise you." She allowed herself to be settled into a chair, and he sat next to her. "There was too much to tell in a letter." She clasped her father's hand and squeezed it. "I'm to have a baby." Her voice broke on *baby*.

Martin beamed. "What wonderful news!" His smile faltered when Savannah took little joy in the announcement, and tears continued to course down her cheeks. "Why aren't you happier?"

"I was advised years ago that to have another baby would mean almost certain death for me. We tried to avoid pregnancy, but ..." She flushed and ducked her head at discussing such an intimate topic with her father.

"There must be something they can do for you, in this day and age," Martin argued. "I've read of all sorts of miraculous operations and medicines that are available now."

"I fear it will take a miracle to save both me and the baby," she whispered, clinging to her father's hand. "It's why Jeremy insisted we travel here. He wanted to ensure I saw the best physicians and didn't trust that the doctors in Montana would know the latest techniques." She took a deep breath.

"Whatever the reason that brought you home to me, I am delighted," he whispered. "You look beautiful, Savannah darling."

Her tremulous smile strengthened as he held her hand. "I can't wait for you to meet Melly. For you to know your granddaughter."

His eyes lit with joy. "I've read so much about her antics, I feel as though I already know her. But now, to laugh and to hear her tell her own tales will be a priceless treasure." He watched Savannah closely. "How is Lucas?"

"I've never seen him so happy," Savannah said, rubbing at her nose before putting her handkerchief in a pocket. "He's smitten with his Genevieve, and their daughter is beautiful." She shared a long look with her father. "They named her after Aunt Betsy, although they call her Lizzie."

He nodded before sighing deeply. "I hardly doubt your mother has earned the right to a namesake."

Her hand spasmed in his at the mention of her mother. "I'm sorry I wasn't here to support you when she died," she whispered.

He shook his head and smiled with infinite love in his gaze. "I hoped you would care for your family rather than rush home to me. Your mother and I had suffered from severe discontent for years before she died." He took a deep breath. "And I would never expect you to have forgiven her for the meddling that led to Jonas's presence here the night he died."

Savannah shuddered. "The night I killed him," she whispered.

Her father stroked a finger down her cheek. "He'd already shot me and Lucas. He showed no intention of leaving here without you, and I doubt you would have survived long at his mansion." His eyes glinted. "Never doubt my pride in you for protecting yourself and us." He traced a vein on the back of her hand before releasing it. "As for the time after your mother's death, I had Lucas for a few weeks before he ran away with Genevieve."

"You should have had more than that," Savannah protested. "You've had no one with you for too long."

He smiled at her. "I have friends, Savannah. I have letters from you and Melly and Lucas and Clarissa that fill me with joy. I'm not alone in this world."

Savannah looked around the cramped yet organized chaos of his office and shook her head. "Sell the store. Come to Montana with us. Live near me and Lucas and Melly. Rissa and Colin each live within blocks of me. We'd be a family again."

He chuckled. "We *are* a family, Savannah. Distance doesn't define what we are." He smiled at her. "Although I will consider your suggestion. I'm tired of linens and coaxing women into purchasing what they need but don't want to pay for." He glanced around in confusion. "Where are your husband and daughter?"

She blushed. "I had them wait in a nearby tea shop. I wanted time alone with you first. May we stay with you? I want to have time with you and for you to have time with Melly. If you prefer, we can stay with Aidan and Delia."

"No!" Martin said, gripping her arm. "Stay with me. I … I very much want time with you and your family, Savannah. It's been fifteen years since you left. I need new memories with you, my beloved daughter." He studied her for a long moment. "It does me good to see you happy. After all you suffered, you found happiness."

They rose, and he pulled her into his arms, holding her tight. "Welcome home, my Savannah. Welcome home."

~

Jeremy felt Savannah tremble next to him as they stood in front of the McLeod mansion. It was a large, imposing building on a corner lot on Marlborough Street in Boston's Back Bay. The roses in the front garden were in full bloom; the windows sparkled, and the mansard roof's black tiles gleamed in the sunlight. "Come, love," he urged.

"Give me a moment," she whispered as she stared at the large wooden door with its ornate hand knocker. She appeared as though in a daze, and he feared she envisioned scenes from her first marriage when she lived in this house with her abusive husband, Jonas Montgomery.

Melinda, impervious to the tension, ran forward and knocked on the door. She bounced with excitement as it opened, and a man in a formal suit answered. "Oh my!" she gasped. "It's like in a novel." She peered around him at the expansive front hall. "Is Uncle Aidan here?" she asked the young man.

"If you would be so kind as to inform me who is calling, I shall inquire," the man said in a clipped voice that brooked no argument.

"We're the McLeods from Montana," Melinda said. "Jeremy, Savannah and Melinda McLeod." She smiled with pride and then frowned as the door shut in her face. "He shut the door, Father."

Jeremy laughed. "He'll be back, once he determines that we are welcome." He raised his eyebrows at his daughter as the door was wrenched open. His uncle, with broad shoulders and barely a hint of black in his now nearly all gray hair, stood in front of them, delight sparkling in his eyes.

"Jeremy!" Aidan said as he rushed forward, pulling Jeremy and then Savannah and Melinda into his embrace. "Oh, it is grand to see you in Boston at last. Come in. Delia will be just as delighted to see you." He looped his arm through Melinda's and led them into the house.

"Come, love," Jeremy whispered to a recalcitrant Savannah. He gave her his arm as she inched toward the mansion's entrance. He paused as her breath hitched as she stepped over the threshold. "Is it much changed?"

She nodded. "It's familiar but so different," she whispered. She gave her light wrap to the butler, her gaze on the new wallpaper and the new carpets. "The staircase and the stained glass windows are the same, but everything else is different. It's much brighter."

Aidan watched her with concern. "It was terribly dark and fore-boding when I purchased it. Delia helped me to redecorate, and it feels much more like a home to us." He led them into the front formal parlor, pausing as Savannah gasped.

"The cherubs are still here," she whispered as she stared at the dancing cherubs on the ceiling.

Melinda giggled as she looked at them. "They are so cheerful. Why would you want to replace them?" Her attention was diverted by Aidan.

Jeremy stroked a hand down Savannah's arm. "Sav?" he whispered.

"I used to lay on the carpet, after he beat me. Or nearly strangled me. And glare at those cherubs as they seemed to mock me. They were content as I drowned in my misery." Her eyes flashed with loathing as she glared at the ceiling.

Jeremy stood in front of her, blocking her from their daughter's view. "I hate that you are suffering so. If you want to depart, we will leave. I believe Uncle Aidan would understand, and he will visit us at your father's."

She looked into her husband's eyes and focused on the love she saw within. "No. I will not run again. If I leave here, he will continue to control me, even from the grave. And I refuse to give him any victory."

Jeremy smiled as he traced a finger down her cheek. "There's my brave Savannah." He kissed her forehead. "I love you, darling."

Delia entered and embraced first Savannah and then Jeremy. She moved to Melinda, hugging her and keeping an arm wrapped around the young woman's waist. "I will not allow you to monopolize Melly's time," she said to her husband and gave Melinda a squeeze as the girl giggled. "Come. Please sit, and we'll have tea." She paused as she approached her chair, sensing Savannah's discomfort. She flicked a quick glance in Aidan's direction and turned. "I find I'd rather gather in the back sitting room. It's much more informal. And we are among family."

She gave Melinda a tug and led them from the room, down a long hallway to a room overflowing with palms and wicker furniture scattered throughout. "This is my favorite room in the house," Delia said. The entire back wall bowed out to floor-to-ceiling windows.

Soon iced tea had been delivered. "It's terribly hot, but that is to be expected in July," Delia said. "Now, what brings you to Boston?"

Jeremy gripped Savannah's hand. "We did not write to tell you as we wanted to inform you in person. We are to have a child. In October." He smiled as Aidan jumped up to pull him into a bear hug while Delia gave a delighted squeal before embracing Savannah and then Melinda.

After they had finished with their congratulations, Aidan sat next to Delia with her hand clasped in his, a bright smile on his face. "Why are you here, rather than in Montana?"

Savannah put an arm around Melinda's shoulders as she moved into her side. "There is a chance I will have a difficult delivery, and Jeremy wanted me to visit the doctors in Boston for a second opinion."

Aidan's smile dimmed as he noted the veiled tension between Jeremy and Savannah. "Very astute of him."

Delia nodded. "Yes. We have wonderful doctors, and I am certain they will help you." She smiled at Melinda. "And now that you are here in July, perhaps Melinda would be permitted to travel to Newport with us? I think she would enjoy seeing the cottage we rented for August."

Savannah relaxed next to Jeremy. "Oh, you rented a place? Is it large?" She flushed at the impertinent question. "Might we all come?"

"Delia chastised me for renting so large a place, but I thought perhaps Zee would fill it with her suffragists. Now we will fill it with family," Aidan said with a pleased smile. He shared a long look with Savannah. "I hope your father will join us."

She nodded and then laughed as Melinda bounced with excitement next to her.

"Will there be parties and *swearies*? Will I dance in a ballroom?" Her eyes gleamed at the prospect.

Delia giggled. "Soirees, darling, and I fear there aren't as many festivities now that we are at war. However, I'm certain you will have a full dance card."

"Will Richard come?" Jeremy asked.

"I'm attempting to convince him to take a vacation with his family. He worries that baby Agnes is too young." Aidan shared a look with Jeremy. "Perhaps you will have more luck than I did."

Jeremy left the linen shop early to avoid the midday heat. Rather than take the elevated train that ran down Washington Street, he decided to walk to his brother's forge. He remembered Clarissa's words, that everything and nothing seemed to have changed.

The trees in the Public Gardens were taller, and the Gardens seemed more ornate than he remembered. However, the people strolling through them seemed the same, only in different clothes. He continued past the Common, through a bustling Scollay Square and the steaming teakettle at one of the teashops and on toward the West End.

Rather than head directly to Richard's forge, Jeremy detoured down a side street and took a left. Rows of three- and four-story brick buildings, one after another, lined the street. He supposed they were called tenements. To him, it had been home.

His pace slowed as memories returned of a cold night and rushing from a burning building. Of standing on the street between Richard and Gabriel, waiting in vain for their parents to emerge. He paused, his gaze roving over the four-story brick building with sheets and linens hanging from the windows to dry. Passersby spoke in Italian, Russian and Yiddish, and he frowned as he didn't hear German. Children played with rocks and makeshift balls in the street, dodging the rare car that passed. Mothers sat on front steps with younger children on their laps for a momentary respite from the constant work of caring for a family, chatting with their neighbors and fanning themselves as the day warmed.

Little remained that reminded him of the place that had been home. No fruit peddler wandered the street. Horses were rare. He closed his eyes and inhaled. The scents of boiling cabbage mixed with anise and too many people living in close proximity provoked a smile. "Home," he whispered.

After a moment, he shook his head and walked at a brisker pace to Richard's nearby forge. Jeremy paused outside his destination and took a deep breath. After a moment, he pushed open the door and flinched at the sound of metal striking metal. He tugged at his neck cloth as a wave of heat enveloped him, as though he were in an inferno. A quick glance at the men working the forge showed none were his brother, and so he banged his fist on the closed office door.

Canting forward in an attempt to hear if he had been called to enter, he took a step back as the door wrenched open. "Rich," he breathed before pulling him into a bear hug.

"Jer!" Richard McLeod returned the hug and rocked side to side with him. After a moment he stepped back and shook his head "What are you doing in Boston? Is everyone all right? Savannah? Gabriel?"

He stopped his litany of names as Jeremy nodded and pushed him into his office. The relative silence was a relief, and Jeremy shook his head. "I don't know how you stand the racket." His middle brother shrugged, and a deep joy filled him at the sight. Gray peppered his black hair, and he had fine wrinkles at the corners of his expressive icy-blue eyes. He remained as strong and lean as ever, although, from his recent letters, Jeremy knew he rarely worked the forge. "Everyone is fine. I'm here with Savannah and Melinda."

"For a vacation?" Richard asked as he sat behind his desk, his brows furrowed. "Why wouldn't you write that you were coming?"

Jeremy shook his head. "I ... I wanted to surprise everyone. And tell you my news in person." He paused as Richard watched curiously. "Savannah is expecting."

"Oh, God," Richard rasped. "I'm sorry. Congratulations." He leaned forward, his elbows on the desk as his gaze sharpened to take in the worry and despair well hidden in his brother's eyes. He waited for Jeremy to speak, gifting him with his silent understanding.

"The doctor she visited in Montana, he thinks ... he thinks she'll die with the delivery," he whispered, the torment plainly visible in his gaze. "I couldn't accept that fate without a fight."

Richard nodded. "Of course not. It will be hard for her to be back in Boston. To face the past as she fears the future." He paused as Jeremy nodded.

"She went to her old house yesterday. Uncle Aidan's house." He shook his head. "I hadn't fully realized how difficult that would be for her. How many memories she would have to battle."

"We all have memories we must overcome, Jer. Although, if we are fortunate, they aren't as devastating as hers. Or yours." He raised an eyebrow as his brother flinched. "Gabe wrote and told me how you were affected after Nicholas's deployment."

Jeremy bowed his head. "This is not about me," Jeremy murmured. "This is about Savannah. About keeping her safe."

Richard tapped his fingers on the desk and frowned. "I love Savannah. She is a wonderful woman, and I know how much you love her. But you're my brother, Jer. I'll always worry about you. About how this affects you too." He cleared his throat. "When I realized Flo was pregnant with our last baby, I visited Uncle Aidan."

He paused, as though envisioning that scene last December. "I was terrified that we would lose the baby. That Flo would die. I didn't know how to find joy every day because I dreaded the future." His gaze was filled with a mixture of relief, anguish and hope. "I know what you and Savannah have faced is worse. What you fear is more profound than I can imagine. But, in a small way, I understand, Jer." He rose when Jeremy dropped his head in his hands as his shoulders shook. Richard sat in the other chair, next to his brother, and squeezed his shoulder.

"I don't know what I'll do if I lose her. And yet I don't want this time, the time before the baby comes, to be one of mourning. Of half joy." He swiped at his face and pulled out a handkerchief. "I hate that the joy I should feel at the birth of my child is missing."

"What does Melinda know?"

Jeremy took a deep breath and forestalled any more tears from falling. "That we are expecting a baby and that her mother needed to see a specialist. Not that Savannah is in any grave danger." He watched as his brother nodded in approval. "She's young enough that some of her innocence and naive optimism should be protected."

"If you believe you are hiding your true feelings from her, you're a fool. I thought I had hidden my fear from my boys, and even young Calvin knew something was wrong." Richard sighed. "What can I do, Jer?"

"What did you do?" he whispered. "How did you find joy in today and not worry about tomorrow?"

Richard shook his head. "I talked with Florence. I discovered she was as scared as I was and needed my support as much as I needed hers." He smiled. "And then I tried to focus on what I had—rather than what I feared I'd lose." He shrugged. "I won't lie and say I was always successful, but it helped."

"I don't want to frighten Savannah with the depth of my worry."

Richard laughed and leaned against the back of his chair. "If you think she isn't as worried as you are, you're an idiot, not a fool. She's the one who has to go through labor. She's the one who might die." He sobered as his brother paled. "Share the fear with her. It will make the burden lighter."

Jeremy nodded and let out a deep breath. "I have a favor to ask of you. It might not be fair, but ..." He paused as Richard nodded. "Come to Newport with Uncle. Let us all be together, in a house by the sea, with our families."

Richard glanced at the shop through a grimy window and then nodded. "Yes. I know Florence could use a break from the city, and it would do her good to be around family. I think the baby and the boys are running her ragged."

Jeremy smiled and tapped him on his shoulder. "I heard Aidan is inviting Sophronia too. Seems he rented a large place."

"I hope he took out insurance for its contents. When my boys are set loose, nothing will be safe." He shared a smile with his brother before rising and moving back behind his desk. "Come to dinner before we leave for Newport. I want you to finally meet them."

∽

*Z*ylphia embraced Savannah, holding her closer than usual for a long period of time. "I'm so happy for you," she whispered as she pulled back. "Mother couldn't keep the good news to herself."

"We are delighted but worried," Savannah said as she held Jeremy's arm.

Zylphia clasped Teddy's hand and smiled bravely at Savannah and Jeremy. "My mother explained the concerns, and I can imagine your fears, but Teddy has a friend who is a doctor at the Laying-In Hospital. I'm certain he'd be able to aid you." She moved with them into the sitting room, and they sat.

Savannah and Jeremy nodded their thanks. "I'd prefer to speak to a few doctors to determine who I trust with my wife's and child's welfare." Jeremy smiled at Savannah. "Some would say I'm overprotective."

"Then they're fools," Teddy murmured. He turned to his wife. "Don't you have a suffragist friend who is a doctor?"

Zylphia sat up excitedly. "Oh, you must meet Eliza! She's brilliant." At Savannah's curious look, Zylphia continued. "She's an osteopathic physician who learned a new technique in Germany before the war that helps women so they don't suffer so much pain during delivery. It's called Twilight Sleep."

"Twilight Sleep?" Savannah asked, her brows furrowed. "I don't know as I like the sound of that."

"Oh, it's absolutely brilliant. You don't feel a thing and will have no memory of the birth or pain." Zylphia nodded her head encouragingly and then frowned as Savannah paled.

Savannah shook her head, as though clearing it of old memories. "I already had a similar birth and lost my daughter due to that. I have no desire to be insensate again and lose another child."

Zylphia paled. "I'm so sorry. I had no idea." She looked to Teddy in a moment of panic, and he cleared his throat.

"I'm certain whatever you deem appropriate will aid you to have a healthy baby." He looked at his wife as she fought a giggle.

"You couldn't have sounded more formal, or British, if you had tried." She stroked a hand down his arm.

"Well, I am British, and we don't tend to discuss such matters in a drawing room."

Savannah sighed. "This is why I hate Boston Society. You never talk about anything of importance, but prattle on about so-and-so's dress or who danced with whom or who hopes to catch someone in marriage. It's all so pointless."

"I fear Melinda doesn't find it as boring or inane as you do," Jeremy said. "She can't wait for the dance parties in Newport."

Zylphia smiled as she sipped at her tea. "You may not enjoy them, but they are rather fun. Especially the ones held at the mansions on the coast. You can wander the lawns, listen to the waves, dance under the moonlight." She gave a flirtatious smile at Teddy. "And this year I have my dance partner with me."

"I'm surprised you'd want to go to Newport, rather than be in Washington, DC," Jeremy said. "I would have thought you would return to your suffragist activities."

Zylphia's bright smile dimmed. "I find I have no desire to return there. I want to remain here, with Teddy. I hope the bill in Congress will pass, and then I can work to ratify the amendment here in Massachusetts."

Savannah swallowed her bite of tea cake and chuckled. "The president can't say he is for the 'reign of law based on the consent of the governed' when half of those governed don't have a say in the matter." She shared an amused smile with her family. "I thought Rowena's commentary about the president's Fourth of July speech illuminating."

"Eviscerating, you mean," Teddy muttered. "The man is an idiot if he thinks he can say he supports the cause in January and then do nothing more to ensure the passage of the bill in Congress."

"Did you know that women from the NWP sat outside his office for weeks in May in an attempt to speak with him, and he ignored them?" Zylphia asked. "The president passed up his opportunity to speak with them for games of golf. His secretary wrote them a note, after they spent all those fruitless hours in vain, stating that they could say nothing more to increase the president's interest in the issue and that the president had already done all he could for the passage of the amendment." She shook her head in incredulity.

"Hogwash," Jeremy said with a twinkle in his eyes. "He's still a barrier to your success, even though he acts and speaks as though he's a proponent. It's as though he's worried about his public image."

"And that public image clearly clashes with his personal convictions," Savannah said. "For, if he were truly in favor of the amendment and universal suffrage, he would be more vocal."

Zylphia sighed. "Thank God for small mercies, and I didn't have to sit through weeks of pointless mornings waiting for an audience. Poor Ro."

Savannah bit her lip as she fought a giggle. She set down her teacup. "Will Rowena join us in Newport, or will she remain in Washington?"

Zylphia grimaced. "Her father, the overbearing tyrant that he is, insists that she leave Washington for a while and cease making such a spectacle of herself." She shook her head. "Although he seems to believe she is chaining herself to statues and wrapping her body in banners, she merely writes."

"You know the pen can have more power than anything, love," Teddy said with a sardonic smile. "And Rowena has a wonderful way of highlighting this administration's hypocrisy."

"I imagine her father merely wants to protect her," Jeremy said.

Zylphia did an impersonation of Sophronia's *harrumph*, earning a smile from Savannah. "No. He wants to protect his business dealings, and too many of the men he works with fear his daughter's radicalism will affect their profits."

"Be thankful Uncle Aidan doesn't feel the same," Jeremy said with a wink to his cousin.

Zylphia blushed with pride at the mention of her father and of his support for her causes. "Anyway, Ro will be with us for most of our stay in Newport. I imagine, after months of hard work in Washington, she will be looking forward to a break." She shuddered. "I can't imagine wanting to remain in that heat and humidity."

Savannah studied Zylphia. "Does Miss Paul accept that you wish to remain here? I can't imagine she is pleased with your absence."

Zylphia shrugged and pasted on a false smile. "She accepted my refusal to return ..."

"After three letters," Teddy muttered, his silver eyes flashing with annoyance.

"And I hope she understands my dedication to the cause has not waned, even though I remain geographically distant."

"The woman is worse than a damn terrier, the way she harassed you to return," Teddy said, his cheeks flushed with agitation. "And, yes, I understand that is her way of achieving goals and that tenacity should be esteemed. But she should also accept that you know your own mind." He heaved out a breath and calmed as his wife caressed a hand over his arm, lacing her fingers with his.

Melinda burst into the room. "Zee!" she shrieked, throwing herself into her cousin's arms, toppling both into the settee as Zylphia rose to embrace her. "Finally you are here to visit us."

Zylphia chuckled. "You could visit me at my house, Melly. I don't live here anymore." She tucked her cousin under an arm and held her to her side. "I've missed you."

"Are you coming to Newport? Will you teach me to dance? To speak properly?" She bit her lip as she shared her fears with her cousin, ignoring her parents in the room. "I don't want to look like a fool."

Zylphia let out a stuttering breath. "I fear, no matter what you do, you will be perceived as a country bumpkin. You don't have the snobbish shine or polish that these people have perfected over years of events." She gave Melly a gentle squeeze.

"But they'll gossip about me," Melly said.

"Either way they'll gossip," Savannah said. "These people don't live on food but gossip. And scandal."

Zylphia's gaze homed in on Savannah for a moment before focusing on Melinda again. "What you should know is that I never mastered the art of proper conversation either. I was too curious, showed too much interest and could never feign boredom."

"Why do you want to go through life bored?" Melinda asked, frowning as the adults in the room laughed.

"Exactly, dear cousin. Exactly." Zylphia paused at the lull in conversation and addressed Savannah. "Did you want to see your former sitting room? See what I did with it?" She smiled at Jeremy as he seemed interested in the offer. "I know I wrote you about it, but you might find it more interesting to see it."

"I would like to see that it is much altered from the last time we were here," Jeremy said. He shared a look with Savannah, recalling the day he and Florence had burst into Savannah's sitting room and rescued her from a beating at her husband's hands. "You left here with little more than the clothes on your back to live with Sophie."

Zylphia smiled at them. "Sophie will be delighted to have you in Boston again. Although I should warn you that she will attempt to have some society affair for you that will benefit the cause in some way."

"I will never enter Boston Society again. The murmurs of my return have already been more than I cared to contemplate." Savannah rose. "Come. Show me my old sitting room."

Melinda jumped up. "May I come too?" At her mother's nod, she gave a small *whoop* and looped her arm through Zylphia's. "What was it like before?"

"Dark. Gray. With heavy curtains and uncomfortable furniture," Zylphia said. She winked at Teddy as he remained behind in the conservatory.

"Sophie said it reminded her of an undertaker's office," Savannah said with a hint of a smile. She giggled as Melinda gaped at her. "My first husband was not known for his good taste."

"Except for marrying you, Mother," Melinda said with a smile. She frowned as the adults shifted uncomfortably. "Why is it that you react like that every time I speak about him in a favorable way?"

Savannah looked at Melinda, who now stood beside Zylphia in the upstairs hallway outside Savannah's old sitting room. "He was a mean man and took little pleasure in caring for me. He was nothing like your father," Savannah said. "The day I became a widow was one of the best days of my life." She smiled as her daughter's mouth fell open. "Which is shocking for a woman to say, but it is true."

Zylphia looked at Melinda. "When you marry, Melly, be wise in your choice. For it is hard to undo such a decision." She turned and opened the door, grinning as she heard the gasps from Savannah and Jeremy.

The room was bathed in late-afternoon light with no curtains adorning the windows. Painted a soft cream color, the walls and ceiling ricocheted the bright sunlight, giving the room an even brighter, airier feel. A settee and a chair were in the room, along with a blank palette. However, the room had a sense of disuse.

"What do you think?" Zylphia asked. She smiled as Savannah gaped at the room. The heavy dark furniture had disappeared, and a sense of openness enveloped them.

"I feel like I've never been here before," Savannah breathed. "There are no memories in this room."

Zylphia grinned at her. "I should think not. My father surprised me with this room for my first Christmas in the house, and he had already done the major alterations. I continued to trim away everything that distracted me from my painting, and I liked the bright light that flows into this room, allowing me to truly see my art."

"Is the room ever used now?" Jeremy asked.

Zylphia shook her head. "Not unless the servants have an interest in art, and they come here to doodle." She shrugged. "The house is immense. Once I moved out, my parents have had rooms they rarely enter."

Savannah nodded. "I never understood the need for such a monstrosity. But Jonas had a need to impress."

Melinda crinkled her nose. "That doesn't seem like Uncle Aidan. Who does he want to impress?"

Jeremy laughed. "No one, imp. He bought the house to help Savannah and me. And to protect us from any more gossip. He is generous and will do what he can to protect and aid his family."

Melinda smiled. "He's a McLeod."

Jeremy tugged her to his side. "Yes, thank God, he is."

~

Two days before departing for Newport, Melinda set out for a walk around Boston with her grandfather. She watched as he donned a hat and smiled as he looked dapper in a crisp beige linen suit.

He caught her smiling at him and grinned at her, winging his elbow out to her. "My father, your great-grandfather, always taught me that I was the best advertisement for the store when I walked around town in fine linens."

"And he was right," she said. She wore a simple blue day dress with a straw hat. "I fear my clothes are too plain."

"It's not just what you wear but how you wear them. Smile, have good posture and exude confidence. You could wear dun-colored sacks and still attract notice, if you were confident."

Melinda giggled. "That's silly, Gramps." She bit her lips as his jaw tightened at the nickname. "I'm sorry. I'll try to be more proper."

"No," he said with a shake of his head. "Please call me Gramps. You have no idea what it means to me to know you at last." He walked with her down a small residential street until they came to a block with brick bow-fronted homes lining a central park area. "Do you remember this at all?"

At the shake of her head, he led her to a specific home. "This was where you were born. Where Clarissa, Colin and Patrick were raised." He frowned at the peeling paint along the door and window frames, the dirty windows and the air of disrepair clinging to the building. "I hate to say this, but the area is in decline. At one time, this was one of the most fashionable neighborhoods in Boston."

He urged her to continue walking. "Now, where Aidan McLeod lives is where everyone desires to reside." Their stroll took them through the South End toward the Back Bay. They walked across Commonwealth Avenue with its grassy tree-lined middle parkway and on toward the Charles River.

Melinda sniffed. "It smells funny."

146

"That's the hint of the ocean. The salt from the sea. It has its own scent."

Melinda wrinkled her nose. "I think I'd rather smell a pine forest." She flushed as her grandfather roared with laughter. "Is that Boston too?" she asked as the pointed across the river. The river sparkled in the bright sunlight, and sailboats floated up and down the river.

"No, that's Cambridge. Harvard University and MIT are there."

Her wistful gaze wandered over the visible buildings. "Imagine going to school there."

"You could attend if you wanted to. You're smart enough."

She smiled and squeezed his arm. "Thank you, Gramps, but I think I'd miss my family too much. And Montana. I can't imagine not seeing mountains every day." She raised an eyebrow as Martin grinned. "Tall buildings do not suffice." She sniffed at the air again. "I've never seen the ocean. Can we see it today?"

"I'm afraid not, darling Melinda." He coaxed her along the promenade by the river. "I'm to deliver you to a friend's house for tea with your mother. However, you will see the ocean daily from the house your uncle has rented in Newport."

That mollified her, and they turned toward the Back Bay again. As they walked along Charles Street, the streets to the left were cobbled and steep as they climbed a hill. The brick homes had black shutters and polished door knockers. "What is this area called?"

"It's Beacon Hill," he said. "The State House is up there, along with big old homes owned by the oldest families in Massachusetts. Although some have been turned into residences for multiple families."

She stared at him and frowned at his poorly veiled disdain. "Who do you dislike who lives up there?" She watched in fascination as an automobile attempted to climb the hill and sputtered to a halt as it stalled. "If an automobile has that much trouble here, it will never function in Butte!"

"How often do you see your uncle Lucas?" Martin asked, adroitly sidestepping her question about who he did not like on Beacon Hill.

"Not nearly enough. I've only met their baby, Lizzie, once. We traveled there for the christening." Her eyes lit with delight. "Oh, you must come visit us so we can have a huge gathering and celebration! Now that I know you, I'll never be happy you are so far away."

He had turned them up Beacon Street and paused in front of an imposing bow-fronted home with green shutters. "Thank you, Melly," he whispered as he kissed her forehead before knocking for admittance.

～

Sophronia rose as the door opened. "At last, you are here," she said in a scratchy voice. She pulled Savannah into a long embrace. "I know you wanted time with your family, but I have been impatient to see you."

Savannah laughed and sat across from Sophie in a comfortable butter-yellow camelback settee. "I thought you had this room redone in blues."

Sophie waved away the comment. "Worse than a mortician's dream," she said. "I had it decorated again a few months ago, and it is finally light and airy, as I prefer." Zylphia's painting of waves crashing on the seashore hung over the mantel. "Now tell me. Are you traveling to Newport with the rest of the McLeods?"

Savannah nodded. "Yes. Jeremy and I have visited a few specialists, and there is no reason we should not travel. Besides, I think the break from the heat and humidity will do me good."

"Yes, and the ability to go on walks along the seashore. You must remain active for as long as you can." She shared a long look with Savannah. "Zylphia was here yesterday and explained to me the concerns you and Jeremy have."

Savannah sighed. "We are trying to take hope from the confidence displayed by the doctor we saw yesterday."

"Does he have reputable credentials?"

The younger woman smiled. "Yes, although he prefers to work with the poor and indigent. I find I admire him for that. He's also one of Teddy's few friends." Her smile broadened as Sophie *harrumph*ed. "I can't believe I have missed that noise."

Sophie laughed. "Well, if Teddy likes him and has sought out his advice, then I would have more confidence in him." Her aquamarine eyes shone with curiosity. "What was he like when you spoke with him?"

"Courteous, as I would expect from a doctor." She paused. "What I appreciated was that he spoke to me. Listened to my fears. Didn't ignore me for Jeremy." She sobered. "He recommends I have a surgery rather than risk a birth."

Her friend frowned. "Seems a risky proposition."

"Birth is a risky proposition," Savannah whispered. "However, I believe I will follow his recommendation as I want the greatest chance at surviving. Jeremy agrees, although he is as terrified as I am."

"I'm glad to hear you are both being sensible. Zylphia mentioned that you were to meet with Dr. Eliza Taylor Ransom. Did you speak with her?"

Savannah nodded. "Yes. However, Jeremy understands my fears about not remembering another birth. I liked her, and I trust in her competence, but I don't want Twilight Sleep."

"I see. It sounds like you have found a doctor you have confidence in." When Savannah nodded, Sophie said, "If you ever need anything, all you must do is ask." She paused as Savannah nodded again and then asked, "How is Clarissa?"

"Very well. She delights in her children and greatly enjoys her work at the library." Savannah smiled at Sophie as she thought about her cousin who was more like a sister.

"I have read in her letters that she and Gabriel are doing well. Is that true? The last time I saw them, they could barely mutter a civil syllable to each other."

Savannah sighed. "Sophie, you are overprotective of us. That was five years ago when we met in Washington for Alice's march!" She sobered. "I think the death of their son Rory will always haunt them, but they have found peace and the comfort of having the love and support of each other to survive such a difficult time."

"I'm glad they are showing sense again." Sophie tapped her cane on the floor. "I blame you Montanans for this abominable law we are all living under now. It was bad enough imagining one state living under such an edict, but for the entire country to be subjected to a Sedition Act?" She *harrumph*ed her displeasure.

"Sophie, you really shouldn't speak in such a loud voice," Savannah whispered. "They might arrest you."

She squinted as Savannah fidgeted on the settee. "Is the law that fiercely implemented in Montana that you are in fear while speaking in your own home?" At Savannah's nod, Sophie's gaze turned mournful. "To think this is what our country has come to. We have a president who spouts his 'Making the world safe for democracy' speech, and then he condones such treatment of citizens here in the United States. To strip us of our rights to freedom of speech and press is not democracy!" She *thunk*ed her cane down in agitation. "And, if they want to arrest me for speaking my truth, I dare them to come."

Savannah's eyes shone with admiration. "I'm afraid we have allowed our fear to silence us. Jeremy has told me how upset Gabriel is by what he sees but that he keeps quiet because he dreads a twenty-year prison sentence. That he bites his tongue so that he will not be separated from Clarissa and the children."

Sophronia's gaze became mournful. "That's dreadful. What a horrible dilemma."

Savannah nodded and sniffled.

Sophronia looked to the door. "Now, when am I to see Melinda? It's been too long since I saw her." At that the door open, and the butler intoned her arrival.

Melinda entered, her cheeks rosy and blond hair slipping from pins as she kissed her mother and plopped down next to her. "Hello," she said with a friendly grin. "I'm Melinda McLeod. You have a nice home." She stared around the newly refurbished room with blatant curiosity.

Sophronia's eyes sparkled with delight as she beheld Savannah's daughter. "Oh, you are a wonder, child." She poured her a cup of tea and handed it to her. "I met you when you were only a few years old. You've grown into a fine young woman."

Melinda made a face. "At least you didn't say pretty or beautiful. It's as though that's the only thing valued. I'm as intelligent as I am pretty." She smiled as Sophie stared at her a moment before cackling with laughter.

"Oh, you are a joy, child. Tell me. What did you think about your short walk around town with your grandfather?"

She shrugged. "I've never been to a big city before. I guess it's nice, although there are too many people, and it's always noisy." She trained her curious gaze on the older woman. "Doesn't it make you agitated, all those people rushing around, and the automobiles and streetcars zooming by? I'd want to escape it as often as I could."

Sophie smiled. "This is the life I am accustomed to. I rather like it." She tilted her head as she heard the distance noise of the front door opening. "I was informed that you hoped to dance at a ball in Newport. I spoke with a dance instructor, and he agreed to come here and meet with you. You'll have to spend most of tomorrow trying to learn how to dance properly. Even then, you will be little more than a novice."

Melinda sat up eagerly, her tea forgotten. "How wonderful!"

Sophronia shared a smile with Savannah. "These are the sorts of contacts Aidan wouldn't have." She smiled as the door opened and then glowered at the woman who marched inside. "I'm uncertain as to why you believed that you would be welcomed in my drawing room." Sophie's warm tone had transformed to glacially cold in an instant. Sophronia waved away the affronted butler who stood behind the interloper.

Savannah froze next to her daughter at the sight of the woman, and gripped her daughter's hand.

The woman, now rail thin and leaning heavily on a cane, ignored Sophronia and cast her gaze over Savannah and Melinda. "I thought we'd raised you better, Savannah. You should rise to greet your grandmother."

Savannah shook her head. "I have nothing to say to you, and I will never rejoice in seeing you. If you have any sense, you will leave now."

Instead, Margaret Thompson, one of Boston's elderly elite who shared a home with her husband in Louisburg Square on Beacon Hill, collapsed into a chair. "No, I will join this tea party. I will meet my great-granddaughter."

Savannah glared at her. "You have wanted nothing to do with me or Clarissa since we left Boston years ago. Why are you here now?"

"You are family. Family must always come first." Her avaricious gaze traveled to Melinda. "There is a new generation to mold."

Savannah shook fiercely. "Stay away from my daughter. You did enough damage to me. To Clarissa. You won't have the opportunity to wreak your influence on the next generation."

Sophronia's eyes flashed with malice. "I find it interesting you only have an interest when you believe you can exert your influence. Not when they needed your support. Not when they needed your love."

Mrs. Thompson flitted her hand in the air. "*Bah*, love. Highly over-rated and an unnecessary addition to any worthwhile marriage."

"For a harpy who has no heart!" Sophie snapped. "You should know by now that we do not share your sentiments."

Mrs. Thompson ignored her granddaughter and great-grand-daughter to focus on Sophronia. "Why should one such as I be concerned with what you believe? You are not a member of my family, nor will you ever be."

Savannah spoke, her voice cold. "Sophie is more a part of my family than you have been in fifteen years. She supports me and takes pride in what I have done. She does not sit in her mansion with an imaginary abacus, tallying up my faults to determine if I am worthy of support, money or affection."

Her grandmother sniffed with distaste. "I see you continue to be without sense, Savannah. I had hoped your time away from society had shown you what you had missed. Your uncouth, classless husband will never be anything more than a boor."

"How dare you speak about my father in such a way?" Melinda asked, her eyes round. "He's never done anything to you!"

"Except entice my granddaughter away from a respectable man." Mrs. Thompson's lips turned down in a grimace. "You will never be accepted back into society."

"You no longer know me if you believe that is my concern," Savannah said. "I had hoped never to see you again." Her eyes shone with sadness and disappointment as she looked at her grandmother. "I had hoped my daughter would never have the misfortune of meeting you. For I have always tried to instill in her that generosity of spirit, kindness and love are the values to be emulated and celebrated. Characteristics lacking in everything you do." She looked to the door. "Please leave."

Her grandmother's hands shook as she looked from Savannah to Melinda. "I will not attempt to aid you again. I will not help your daughter."

Savannah's eyes sparkled with bitterness. "If only you had shone me such consideration before I married Jonas." She watched as her grandmother frowned and then heaved herself up, exiting the sitting room.

After a long moment's silence, Sophie said, "That is not how I had planned this afternoon." She stared at Savannah, whose hands shook as she attempted to raise her teacup. "You did marvelously, and I would not fear that she bothers you ever again."

Melinda looked from her mother to Sophie and then back again. "Am I really related to her?"

Savannah gave a mirthless snort of laughter. "Unfortunately, yes. She is your great-grandmother, and she believes that social standing is more important than anything else."

Melinda gripped her mother's hand. "Then I feel sorry for her. She missed out on a wonderful life."

Savannah blinked back tears as she squeezed her daughter's hand and shared a thankful smile with Sophronia.

CHAPTER 9

*P*erry Hawke stood in a secluded alcove in one of the mansions off Bellevue Avenue in Newport, Rhode Island. Although hidden from prying eyes, he still had a vantage point of the ballroom. He leaned against a pillar, sipping a glass of champagne as he watched guests gossip, flirt, dance and ignore those they considered beneath their notice. Although Zylphia and Teddy Goff were too important to directly snub, the guests showed their disdain for the couple by ignoring their cousins from Montana. He watched as the young girl, who had entered the mansion with a vivacious sparkle, stood on the side of the ballroom with a brittle smile as another dance started without being asked to join in. He had heard snippets of conversation that she was distantly related to Lucas Russell.

He sighed and set down his glass, abandoning his hideaway with great reluctance. Ignoring the calls of those around him, he headed straight for the young woman with blond ringlets in a demure mauve dress. "Might I have this dance, miss?" He paused as she gaped at him. "Unless your card is full?"

"Oh, no, and thank you, sir." She placed her hand in his, her brows furrowing as though trying to remember all the proper steps of etiquette.

"Just follow my lead and smile," he whispered as he placed a hand on her waist and whisked her into the opening strands of a waltz. He grinned at her as she tripped over his feet. "One, two, three," he murmured into her ear. After a moment, she relaxed and followed his movements around the dance floor.

"I tried to master these steps, but I always fumbled the beginning." She bit her lip. "I beg your pardon."

He frowned. "Why? You're blunt and honest, like your cousin Lucas." He smiled as her eyes lit with joy at the mention of Lucas. "He is a good friend of mine, although I haven't seen him for far too long. I hear he is content in his mining town with his wife and child."

She lost any timidity and spoke in hushed tones as she had been instructed. "I'm his niece, Melinda McLeod. My mother is his sister. Did you know he has a daughter, Lizzie?"

Perry smiled. "I know. We write frequently. He likes to tease me about my constant touring—I am a singer—and tempts me with invites to stay with him."

Her eyes lit with joy. "Oh, you should! That way we could see you too. Maybe you could put on a performance together."

He chuckled at her innocent comment as he realized she did not know who he was. "Perhaps," he said. "Are you enjoying the ball?"

She shrugged, some of her youthful vivacity dimming. "It's not what I expected."

He raised an eyebrow as though mocking her. "You thought those who have more money than sense would welcome a young woman from the wilds of Montana with open arms? They are not so forward-thinking, Miss McLeod. However, I'll let you in on a secret." He leaned forward, his smile widening as the murmuring in the room escalated. "You are a delight and not what *they* expected."

Her eyes shone with happiness.

"Never allow these jaded men and women to make you feel inferior."

Their dance came to an end, and he led her to the side of the ballroom where her father waited. Perry smiled at him as her father battled a glower. Perry released her and held out his hand. "Hello, I'm

Perry Hawke, and I'm a friend of Lucas's." His grin broadened as Melinda's mouth dropped open at his name.

Jeremy beamed and gipped his hand. "A pleasure. I'm Jeremy McLeod, and, as you know, this is my daughter, Melinda." He looked around. "I'm uncertain where my wife has gone."

"I'm sure she's off with Zylphia and her suffragist friends, plotting to have me perform again to raise money for their cause."

Jeremy watched him in confusion.

"I'm a singer, and I performed for them in January in Boston. I presumed you were related to Mrs. Zylphia Goff."

"Oh," Jeremy said, understanding dawning. "You're *that* Perry Hawke. It's nice to meet you." Jeremy watched as a few men approached Melinda and gave Perry a quick smile before striding over to stand beside her.

Perry's gaze moved around the room, and he walked with purpose, smiling impersonally to those he passed as he approached the alcove again. "Blast," he muttered when he found it occupied.

"I'm willing to share," a woman with a soft voice said.

He focused on the alcove's occupant and smiled. "Miss Clement, I had thought you unable to attend tonight." He frowned at her. "Why are you always hiding?"

"I could ask the same of you," she said with one eyebrow raised. "Even when you're mingling, you have an impenetrable mask on." She flushed as she bit her lip after her rash words.

He chuckled. "You see more than you let on, don't you? Which, I imagine, makes you a wonderful reporter."

He paused as she remained quiet, and then he said, "I was disappointed to not see you when I visited the NWP headquarters in May."

She sighed. "I was informed of your visit after you had departed. While you were at Lafayette Square, I was sitting outside the president's office, attempting to speak with him." She shook her head. "I should have known he would never meet with us, but we had to try."

He smirked. "A man like Wilson won't concede more than he has to." His smile became genuine as he looked at her. "I've greatly enjoyed your articles."

"You're reading *The Suffragist?*" she asked.

He moved to the edge of the alcove and snagged two glasses of champagne from a passing waiter and then hid again in the alcove with her. "Of course. I had to see if the woman who wanted to blend in with the wallpaper was as successful as she thought she was."

Her jaw clenched at his words. "And?" Her eyes shone with challenge.

"And I think you are wrong." He saw her fight disappointment as she pasted on a smile. "I think you are a brilliant reporter, and there is no need to hide in the shadows. These people are too foolish to watch what they say around you because they'll always underestimate you."

She gaped at him, her disappointment replaced by incredulity. "I … I don't know what to say."

"Quite an achievement to make a journalist speechless," he said with a chuckle. He motioned for her to be silent as a small group of women paused near them, not realizing the alcove was occupied. He and Rowena instinctively moved farther into the shadows.

"I tell you, that woman should have known better than to return to society. She should have remained in that godless country with her penniless carpenter," one woman said in a strident voice.

Another *tsk*ed her agreement. "How he has had the courage to remain married to her is beyond me. I would worry she'd stab me while I slept."

The third woman tittered at the thought. "Although they are quite rich due to her actions. I should wonder how the authorities allowed her to carry out such an act without suffering any jail time. It sends a dangerous precedent."

The first spoke again in her authoritative voice. "Well, the McLeods were wrong to believe they could bring her here and have us accept her. She will never be respectable company again." She sniffed in disgust, and the three women moved away.

"Oh my," Rowena murmured. "It's worse than Savannah feared."

"Who is Savannah? What were they talking about?" Perry asked as he sipped his champagne.

"How can you walk around a roomful of people gossiping about one topic and have no idea what they are discussing?" She shook her head in wonder. "Savannah, the mother of that young girl you were dancing with, killed her first husband. She's your friend Lucas's sister."

He choked on his champagne and gaped at her. "This isn't some figment of your imagination?"

Rowena nodded to where the three women had stood. "No. It happened. From what Zylphia has told me, Jonas Montgomery was an abusive, horrible man, and Savannah fled his home. Preferred to live in sin with Jeremy than with her husband. Jonas surprised her one night at her parents' house and tried to force her home. In his attempt to persuade her, Jonas shot her brother and father, who almost died."

"Lucas was shot? He almost died?" he asked.

Rowena raised her eyebrows and nodded. "Yes. Savannah attacked Jonas with a letter opener, and he died instead. The authorities deemed it self-defense, and she was set free."

His shocked gaze roved over the crowd, once again seeing Melinda standing by her father in an ostracized circle along the wall. "They'll never accept her daughter." He saw mothers berating their sons and recognized them as the young men who had approached Melinda after Perry's dance with her.

"No, never," Rowena said. "I would have thought it better to forego the balls and entertainments and merely enjoy being by the seaside." She shrugged. "But Mr. McLeod can be a determined man, and he is irate at how Savannah is punished for protecting herself."

"I would think her husband would protect her from such censure," Perry said with confusion as he watched her husband glare at the crowd.

"No, not Jeremy. Aidan McLeod. You remember him? Few would dare to defy one of his wishes, but I fear he cannot control public sentiment on this occasion."

Perry watched the crowd, their mild disinterest in his presence now making sense as they were too busy reviving ancient gossip. "Would they have preferred her to die?"

Rowena snorted. "For some, it would have been the most advantageous outcome. A woman who believes she deserves more than the back of her husband's hand is a dangerous woman."

Perry's focus shifted from the crowd to the woman standing next to him in a demure gold dress. "You miscalculated in your attire. Not every room has gold wallpaper." He saw her smirk and then focused on what she had said. "I should think they would celebrate such a woman."

"Then you are a singular singer," she said as she moved past him to join Zylphia, who now stood by Melinda. "Good evening, Mr. Hawke."

He gripped her hand as she was about to slip out of the alcove. "Dance with me," he whispered, his brown eyes lit with a passionate intensity.

"I have no more desire to be the focus of this crowd's interest than Savannah does," she murmured, freeing her arm from his grip. "Good evening." She moved effortlessly through the crowd until she stood beside her friend.

He watched the quiet misery enveloping the small group on the side of the ballroom as Zylphia, at turns, attempted a show of gaiety and then glared at those in the ballroom. He snickered as Rowena rebuffed another man's attempt to dance with her, and then Perry snuck out a side door, breathing in the fresh night air as he headed back to his modest rented rooms.

Zylphia stood next to Melinda, attempting to smile at the ball guests as they gossiped about her and her family. Zylphia played a game with herself where she looked a guest in the eye and counted the number of seconds before the guest broke eye contact. "Four," she murmured. "Spineless fool."

"Who's a spineless fool?" Rowena asked.

"Oh, are you done hiding?" Zylphia asked with a bright smile. "I'm seeing how long it takes for guests to break eye contact with me. So far, the most stalwart has taken seven seconds."

"You don't expect those here to be courageous, do you? They

bolster each other up in their small-mindedness, but, if they were alone, they'd fall to the ground in a spineless heap." Rowena raised her eyebrows as Zylphia smirked at her.

"They should be thankful your pen is aimed at those against suffrage." She took a sip of champagne as she eyed the restive crowd.

"Yes, but we will win the passage of the amendment, and then I will still need something to do. Evenings like this make me think I'd enjoy writing accounts for newspapers."

Zylphia watched her curiously. "After the first report, you'd never be allowed into another ball."

"Who's to say I'd use my real name? And none here are astute enough to think mousy little Rowena Clement could string two sentences together, never mind an article condemning them for their narrow-mindedness." She frowned as her friend stiffened. Zylphia's expression had blanked, and her eyes were glacial in their lack of warmth.

"Hello, Mr. Hubbard," Zylphia said. She looked at the preening woman in peacock blue next to him. "Mrs. Hubbard."

His smile was ingratiating and condescending at the same time. "*Miss McLeod*, always a pleasure to see you. Not dancing this evening?" He looked at the wide expanse of open floor around her family and smirked. He seemed to enjoy his attempt to remind Zylphia that she was undesirable, even though he knew she had chosen to marry Teddy over him. "Seems the men are intelligent enough to keep their distance from women like you."

"Yes, they fear that they might have to think if they were to speak with us," Rowena snapped. "Such a dreadful outcome."

Owen Hubbard, a man who had vied for Zylphia's hand before she had married Teddy, had perfectly styled blond hair and an air of debonair ennui about him. However, his primped and manicured fingers gripped his glass of champagne at Rowena's comment. "Always disappointing to see they continue to allow you admittance."

"Some of us don't have to profit from a war to maintain our standing in society," Rowena said. "Or marry to curry favor for more kickbacks." She met Eudora's surprised gaze at the comment as she was Parthena's sister. However, Eudora had never been close to Parthena's friends and was always disdainful of the suffragist cause.

Eudora Hubbard glared at Rowena and then Zylphia. "You are abominable women." She made a pointed glance around the room. "Only tolerated because of your fathers."

Zylphia smiled. "If you believe it is any different for you, Eudora, you're a fool." She relaxed as a hand stroked down her arm and then linked with hers. "I believe you remember my husband, Mr. Goff."

Owen and Teddy shared a loathing-filled look. "I had hoped that your English upbringing had taught you a sense of honor, but it seems your penchant for poaching my clients continues."

Teddy's eyes glinted with amusement. "As long as you continue to mismanage their funds." His lips quirked in a smile intended to rouse Owen's ire. "Mr. Hawke has not complained of our aid."

"He was thriving under our tutelage!" Owen hissed.

"Yes, and you were profiting handsomely from his commission. Tell me. Do you bleed all your customers dry, or do you leave them with just enough blood so they can crawl away to die out of your sight?" Teddy's voice, although soft, was lethal with its hatred.

Owen's eyes flashed with anger, and he glanced around to ensure no one was listening in on their conversation. He glared at Zylphia's and Rowena's amused expressions. "I had hoped you'd finally been sent to an asylum, Teddy. Everyone knows you are hardly sane since your return from England. Although, by the accounts I hear, they should have a suite of rooms set up for you and your wife."

Zylphia smiled, refusing to flinch under his insinuation that she and Teddy needed to be in an insane asylum, him for his time spent at the Front and her after her jail time in DC. "You've always been a singularly unpleasant man. Even when you courted me, you only cared about prestige, money and my father's influence." She looked at Eudora. "I hope that will be enough for you."

Eudora gave a stilted smile and turned away from Zylphia, Teddy and Rowena. Owen glared at them. "You have no right to upset my bride."

Rowena shook her head and glared at him. "But you have a right to attempt to put us in what you consider *our place?*" She raised her eyebrows at him as she called him on his hypocrisy. "You are a fraud and a weasel, and, one day, you will wish you had people like us to support you."

Zylphia watched him leave and then shared a look with Rowena. "Bravo," Zylphia said. "I never thought you'd speak to him in such a way."

"I loathe him, and I hate that he believes himself superior simply because he is a man."

Teddy choked on a laugh. "I believe it's more than that." His silver gaze glinted with malice as it followed Owen's progression around the ballroom.

Zylphia leaned into Teddy's side. "He'll always resent that you are a brilliant financier and that he has to pick up the scraps left by others."

"Did you really steal away Mr. Hawke's business from him?" Rowena asked.

Teddy shook his head, relaxing with Zylphia nestled into his side. "No. Mr. Hawke approached Aidan about the prospect of us looking at his portfolio when he sang at Aidan's mansion in January. He visited us the following day, and it was shocking to see the risks being taken with his investments." Teddy shook his head and glared at Owen as he mingled with guests across the ballroom. "Thankfully Mr. Hawke has good instincts and knew something was not right."

"So you and my father have been helping him?" Zylphia asked.

"Yes. Mr. Hawke is intelligent and curious. From all I have learned, he's worked hard for his money and doesn't want it squandered. I rather like him." He took a sip of his champagne, kissed his wife's forehead and moved to speak with Jeremy.

"Well, that's as much of an endorsement as Teddy will ever give, but I'm glad he likes Mr. Hawke." Zylphia shared a look with Rowena, who then stared at the crowd with bland impassivity. "Come. Let's try to raise Melinda's spirits a bit before we head home."

They joined the young woman and soon had her giggling and animated as they discussed the dresses, the food and the stately home.

~

Sophronia sat on the back veranda of the mansion Aidan had rented for his family's use for the season in Newport. The gentle roar of waves sounded in the distance, and she glared at the steady stream of people as they walked along the Cliff Walk at the far edge of the lawn by the coast. Before today a mere trickle of society members had been eager to take a stroll. However, after Savannah's reappearance at the ball the previous evening, the back of their rented home seemed to be of greater interest. Tall hedges on either side of the lawn afforded privacy from their neighbors.

"What do they hope to see? A reenactment of that fateful night as we sip our tea?" Savannah muttered as she turned her back on the beautiful water view and focused on the veranda and hydrangea bushes that formed a hedge on one side of the house.

Sophie tapped her cane down and would have waved it about had it done any good. "Insufferable fools," she muttered. "Didn't have the good sense to speak with you last night, and now they want to peer at you while you relax at home."

Savannah held a hand over her growing belly and fought tears. "I was the fool. I should never have agreed to reenter society."

Sophronia *harrumph*ed and then focused on the young women joining them, a wide smile bursting forth. "I never thought to see you here." She embraced Parthena and watched as she sat beside Rowena while Zylphia sat on a wicker love seat with Melinda.

Melinda watched the conversation with wide-eyed interest, content to listen and rarely speak.

"I convinced Morgan that we should escape the city and join our friends. When he realized he could work with Teddy and Mr. McLeod here, he wasn't as reluctant to leave Boston." She sighed with contentment as she took a deep breath of the ocean air.

Sophronia watched her with eagle-eyed alertness. "Weren't you just along the coast, but north of Boston instead of here in Newport?"

Parthena gripped a day pillow as though protecting herself. "Yes, but it was horrible. The only person who desired my company,

164

besides my husband, was my youngest sister, Isabel, and even she was banned from speaking with me by my mother."

Zylphia grimaced. "Rowena and I had the unfortunate pleasure of speaking with Eudora and her husband last night at the ball. She is delusional in her belief that she has made a brilliant match."

Parthena fought tears, but a few leaked out. "She lorded over me the fact that she was not being forced into marrying a wealthy man. That she had been successful in choosing an affluent man our father approved of while I had been forced into my marriage with Morgan. She relished taunting me with the indiscretions of my past."

Rowena made a *tsk*ing noise. "Does it matter what nonsense she spouts? She has to know, on some level, what a scoundrel and loathsome man she has married. She was quite uncomfortable last night when Zee and I criticized her husband. I think she has more doubts than she cares to admit." Her expression was filled with compassion and loyalty as she beheld her friend. "You've always only seen the best in your sisters, and you thought you made a sacrifice for the good of your family when you married Morgan. Thankfully you've found happiness with him. However, your two youngest sisters are selfish, and often cruel, something you don't like to admit."

Parthena sniffled. "I hated being at the estate my father rented in Manchester-by-the-Sea. I was seen as nothing more than a decorative object to dangle from my husband's arm. I couldn't escape soon enough."

Zylphia patted her hand. "Well, you're here now, and we've always loved you better than your family." She winked at Parthena as her friend grinned.

Parthena focused on Savannah. "I wish I could have been here last night to offer my support."

"It was a hopeless endeavor," Zylphia said as she collapsed against the back of the settee. "That crowd was only too eager for something else to talk about other than Marty Higgenbothem's scandalous affair with the opera singer." She flushed as Melinda giggled next to her. "Sorry, Sav," Zylphia whispered as she shot a chagrined look in Savannah's direction.

"No, Melly needs to learn about the realities of life, and this seems the perfect time." Savannah met her daughter's worried gaze with a tepid smile. "Not everyone is kind, and too many relish cruelty."

"Would it really be that awful for Mr. Higgenbothem to wed a singer?" Rowena asked.

"Only if he wishes to eat," Sophie muttered.

Zylphia gaped at Rowena as Parthena choked on a biscuit, swallowed, then spoke. "Of course it would! That particular opera singer has had dozens of lovers already and is rumored to have three children from three different fathers," Parthena said. "No man of society could marry such a woman."

"But your sister married a musician and is quite happy," Rowena said to Parthena. She flushed as though remembering Parthena had been involved with Lucas before he fled Massachusetts with Genevieve. She mumbled an apology that Parthena waved away.

Parthena nodded and smiled. "To my great delight, they are as happy as I am with Morgan. I was too blind to see how happy Morgan and I would be together, and I'm thankful I have discovered how much I love him."

Zylphia beamed at her friend. "Oh, how wonderful! I'd always hoped you'd come to discover how well suited Morgan and you are."

Savannah spoke up. "As for Genevieve, she was wise to marry Lucas as he adores her as much as she adores him." Savannah's smile was sardonic as she looked at Rowena. "And I like to believe my brother is slightly more respectable than this opera singer in question."

"The fact is that Mr. Higgenbothem's finances are in shambles, and he needs an heiress to remain part of good society," Sophronia said with a lift of one brow. "The opera singer, I fear, would prove a fickle companion should he suddenly be beggared."

"Doesn't she have a name?" Melinda asked. "It seems so odd to refer to her only as 'the opera singer.'"

"Quite right," Sophie said. "But we never refer to her by name. Because then she becomes a real person. And then we'd have to acknowledge her, which is the last thing we want to do." She raised her eyebrows as she looked at Melinda, nodding with satisfaction as Melinda appeared to understand, even if she did not agree. "As for Lucas, he's from a respectable family, and he's a man. Men are allowed to have their ... transgressions."

Zylphia sighed and rolled her eyes. "It's so unfair! It's 1918. Women should not continue to be held to a different standard than men."

"Dearest, you will go to your grave fighting that battle. It would be better to find one that you can win," Sophie said. "Now, Rowena, why are you here rather than in Washington? I thought you were impervious to your father's mandates by now."

Rowena shrugged. "I was hot and tired, and I knew Alice planned another round of picketing. I didn't have it in me to explain to her once more why I couldn't and didn't want to picket." She shared a look with Zylphia and Parthena, whose gazes had clouded over at the mention of picketing. "I know those who picket will be arrested yet again."

"No, Ro, you shouldn't want that," Parthena said. She cleared her throat. "Although I suppose I should be braver and take pride in what they are willing to do."

Sophronia *thunk*ed her cane down with such force that all the women jumped and the china rattled on the table. "I want to hear none of that nonsense again, Parthena. You and Zylphia did more than almost anyone else last fall, and you suffered horribly for it. You should never feel guilty because you have no desire to be jailed and abused again."

"It's hard not to feel guilty when I lie in my husband's arms and give thanks that I am here rather than in a cold cell with nothing to eat," Zylphia said.

"You shouldn't feel guilt. You should feel pride that you have sense," Sophie snapped. "When Alice writes you, asking for money, do you donate? Do you write letters in support of what she is doing in Washington? Do you attempt to persuade the recalcitrant senators of their erroneous beliefs?" At their nods of agreement to all of her questions, she gave a small *humph*. "You are doing more than almost all the women in this country to obtain the vote. You don't have to do more."

After a few moments of silence, Savannah said, "What do you think I should do?" She pointed to the busybodies on the Cliff Walk.

Parthena looked around at the concerned faces on the veranda and let out a deep breath. "I know this won't be the popular answer, but I would enjoy my family and friends and not bother with society. Why should you put yourself through another evening like last night just so you can give them something to talk about? You don't owe them anything."

Savannah frowned and bit at her lower lip. "Won't I be seen as a coward?"

Melinda squirmed in her seat. "Why do you care what they think, Mother? You know you aren't. Father knows you aren't." Her eyes shone with pride as she looked at her. "I wanted to dance a Mr. Pickens's jig when I heard what you had done last night. How brave you were!"

"I wasn't brave, Melly. I did what I had to do to survive and to protect those I love." Savannah swiped at her cheek. "I pray you never have to suffer the same."

Her daughter smiled at her. "I won't. Because you and Father would never expect me to remain with a man who hurt me. And I'd be sure to tell him who my mother was so that he was afraid to harm me." She smiled at her mother with pride as her mother stifled a sob.

After a moment of silence, Zylphia spoke with a glint of mischief in her gaze. "I'd enjoy the peace while we can. Richard, Florence and their brood arrive tomorrow."

Melinda squealed with pleasure. "We'll play on the lawn and have all sorts of adventures!"

Zylphia laughed. "Yes, we will. For now, I'll enjoy the quiet." She shared a look with her friends and rose. They followed her move to rest and then to dress for a casual dinner.

"Rowena, will you sit with me a moment?" Sophie asked, although it was understood as a command.

Rowena shared a look with Parthena and Zylphia as she sat near

Sophie and stared across the lawn, ignoring the chatter of the other women as they entered the house. "Mr. McLeod couldn't have chosen a better home to rent."

"No, he couldn't have, and we should remain thankful he was willing to share it with his daughter's friends as well as his family." She paused, waiting until Rowena looked at her. "What is it that I hear about you hiding in alcoves with a singer of questionable reputation?"

Rowena let out a deep sigh and shook her head. "Did we not just say that men are able to weather such gossip better than women?"

"When they are from a good family, yes. He is from the slums of Albany. It is hard to imagine he would be acceptable to your father."

Rowena firmed her jaw. "My father might not approve, but he is no longer in control of my inheritance." She blushed as Sophie raised an eyebrow at that information. "I don't want it to be common knowledge, but, when I turned thirty nearly two years ago, my mother's money became my money."

"No longer under your father's control?" At Rowena's shake of her head, Sophie smiled. "Good. Then you can cease acting like a demure half-wit, hiding in alcoves when in society, concealing your intelligence no matter the setting, and begin dressing with more elegance."

"There are other reasons I have no interest in attracting a man's attention," Rowena murmured.

Sophronia clasped her young friend's hand and gripped it. "Do not be ashamed of your mother, Rowena. Many from fine families have German blood." She waited as Rowena battled tears. "Your father knows exactly what to do to continue to manipulate you."

Rowena looked upward as though studying the striped pattern of the canvas awning, rather than trying to prevent tears from coursing down her cheeks. "I fear few are as liberal as you, Sophie. You've seen what the CPI prints. How it rouses suspicion and fear." She sniffled as she thought about the Committee on Public Information. "Since the War started, we've changed the names of so many things that used to show German pride. Streets in Chicago are no longer Frankfort and Hanover Streets but Charleston and Shakespeare. Hospitals in New York City have changed their names. Germania Life Insurance

Company changed theirs to Guardian Life Insurance Company of America." She rubbed at her head. "The Red Cross won't allow those with a German last name to enlist because they fear they will sabotage the effort." She stopped talking and met her friend's worried gaze.

"The CPI is a propaganda machine like any other. It wouldn't like to be referred to in that way, but that is what it is." Sophronia paused. "I recall recent pictures plastered on street corners of a large hulking ape, with the words *Beat Back the Hun with Liberty Bonds* in bright letters emblazoned over it. The CPI is doing an effective job in shaping public sentiment." After a moment, Sophie looked at her friend. "However, what I don't understand is why you continue to speak with and seek out Mr. Hawke. I heard a rumor that you saw him while you were in Washington."

She flushed. "I did. He had a performance, and I was invited to attend by a fellow activist. I wanted to hear him sing again, and we spoke at the party after his performance." She shrugged. "He came by the new headquarters, too, but I did not see him."

Sophronia's aquamarine eyes flashed with concern. "I'm uncertain his interest is appropriate."

"Do you know I'm not sure I care?" A smile flit over her lips, one that caused her older friend to frown. "He sees me, even when I do my best to blend into the wallpaper. He's the only one who's ever accused me of that. Besides you."

"And he's not wrong," Sophie said with a huff. "There has to be more to it than that."

"He reads my articles. Says I underestimate myself. That I'm a better reporter than I give myself credit for." She shrugged. "It's nice to have an attractive man notice me for once. I've lived in Zylphia's and Parthena's shadows long enough."

"You've pined long enough," Sophie snapped, earning a fierce blush from her fidgety young friend. "He seems like a good man, and I appreciate that he is friends with Lucas. However, his dalliance with that singer makes me concerned that he is not as steadfast as I would want him to be for you, Rowena."

"I do not presume to know him well enough to confirm whether or not he is steadfast," Rowena murmured.

"What do you hope will come of it?"

Rowena shrugged. "Nothing will come of it. He would hate the scandal of a half-German bride and its effect on his career, and I would hate the life he lives. I simply enjoy the few moments of subtle flirtation."

"There is little subtlety in a man like Mr. Hawke."

The following afternoon Richard and his family had arrived and were settled in. Florence was upstairs resting; a competent nanny had been hired by Aidan to help with the baby, and the boys were outside frolicking on the wide lawn. Richard, Aidan and Jeremy had gathered in the room Aidan had taken over as his Newport study. Dark paneling on all the walls was offset by floor-to-ceiling windows that bracketed a large desk. Bright sunlight streamed in on the warm August afternoon, although the room would be dark and dreary come winter. To one side of the room, comfortable chairs formed a conversation area, and the men sat there.

Parthena played the piano in a nearby room, and the soft sounds reverberated into the study.

"What is she playing?" Richard asked as he tilted his head to one side and listened.

Aidan chuckled. "'*Oui, Oui, Marie.*'" He waved at a gramophone in the corner. "I have a recording of it. We should play it tonight and have Parthena accompany it. I think she would add to the song."

Jeremy chuckled. "I think it is interesting how they are trying to find humor in the war."

Richard shrugged. "Not all can be like '*After You've Gone.*'" He shivered. "Every time I hear that song, I want to shut it off or run away from the place playing it. Florence cries."

Aidan sighed. "Imagine how someone who has a loved one in the

War would feel. Like Amelia." He saw Jeremy nod. "I give thanks every day that you boys are too old to be drafted."

Jeremy shook his head. "I don't need something else to worry about."

Richard frowned.

"I'm trying, Rich."

Aidan watched the two men. "I'm glad you have time together. I wish Gabriel were here too. You three have spent little time together since Jeremy left for the Philippines twenty years ago."

"Only those days in Washington for the parade at Wilson's inauguration in 1913." Richard yawned hugely. "Sorry." He outstretched his long legs and rested his hands on his belly. "I'd forgotten how exhausting a baby can be."

Jeremy watched him with envy. "Why won't Florence accept help?"

Richard shook his head in frustration. "She believes that, because she stays at home, she should be able to do it all." His light-blue eyes clouded. "It's running her ragged, and I fear she will wear herself out if she doesn't accept some aid."

Aidan smiled. "It's why I hired the nurse and nanny without speaking with you. I know Florence was annoyed, but I'm certain I saw relief in her eyes as she handed the baby over before she went to your room to collapse."

"And she knows that Melly and Zee will run the boys ragged today, so they'll sleep well tonight," Jeremy said with a chuckle. "I don't know as I've ever seen Zee so excited as when the boys arrived."

"She adores her cousins," Aidan said with a soft smile as he thought about his daughter. "I hope she has coaxed Teddy outside too. It would do him good to frolic in the sun."

Richard snorted. "I heard him muttering something to her about only liking to play cricket."

Aidan laughed. "If I know Zee, she'll have him outside, playing with them, before the afternoon is over."

~

Teddy stood on the side of the lawn, watching as Richard McLeod's five boys raced around. At first they tagged each other, but soon their antics gave way to basic wrestling matches. He watched as eleven-year-old Thomas and ten-year-old Gideon rolled around on the grass while their eldest brother, Ian, egged them on. "Don't you think your father would rather you prevented them from coming to harm?"

Ian laughed and shook his head. "No, he always said a good tumble and pummeling with a brother lets off steam." He shrugged. "As long as we have no bruises Mum can easily see."

Teddy chuckled. "I'm sure she'll see them at bath time."

The second-eldest brother at thirteen, Victor, said, "Oh, we don't have to worry about baths with Mum watching anymore." He shared a relieved look with his eldest brother as Teddy chuckled again.

"Why must you always act like savages?" Zylphia asked. She shrieked as Ian lunged for her, and Victor grabbed one of her arms. Soon they were tickling her until she squealed with laughter and tears coursed down her cheeks. When they finished tickling her, she rested on the lawn and caught her breath. "You were no help," she said to her husband.

"Why should I come to your rescue? You were enjoying yourself," he sat next to her and saw the brothers running between the hedges that separated their property from the neighbors. "I can't remember ever having as much energy as they do."

"Sophie always says it's wasted on the young." Zylphia shared a rueful smile with her husband. "I imagine you were worse with Lawrence."

His smile turned wistful as he thought about his twin who had died years ago. "Yes. We were true hellions." He nodded at the McLeod brothers. "They're novices."

"Well, don't give them ideas, or Florence will never forgive you." She nudged him and stood. "Come. Let's play baseball." She headed to a wicker basket full of items she had left on the edge of the lawn before joining them. "Come on, boys! You too, Calvin!" She yelled to Richard and Florence's youngest son, who was eight.

They ran to her and peered into the basket. "Baseball!" their young voices said in excitement.

"Now, as I see it, we can have two teams of three with an umpire, or we can have one team with three players and another with four." She looked at the brothers. "What do you think?"

"No umpire. None of us will be impartial," Ian said and sent Teddy a challenging look. "Not even you, Uncle Teddy. You'll always side with Zee."

Teddy shrugged as though that were an obvious assessment. "Fine, then we need two captains." He looked over the McLeod boys, and they stood tall. "I choose Calvin as a captain."

Zylphia smiled. "Fine choice. I choose Thomas." As the two brothers moved to stand in front of them, she said. "Now, you have to decide who is on your team, and Calvin has the team with four players."

When they were divided up, Calvin, Ian, Zylphia and Gideon were on one side, while Thomas, Victor and Teddy were on the other. Morgan had wandered outside with the commotion, and, rather than be added to a team, he was given the role of catcher for both teams.

They used cushions from furniture on the veranda to mark the bases. Because the teams were so small, their basic strategy was to hit a home run, strike the opponent out or have them called out at home.

After they had played for an hour, Zylphia stood on the pitcher's mound. "Okay, Teddy, let's see if you can hit this!" she taunted as she wound up to pitch. She slung her arm back and threw with all her might. Teddy swung but missed hitting the ball dead on. Instead it careened upward and backward.

Their heads tracked the trajectory of the ball and a collective "Oh, no," sounded as it crashed into an upstairs bedroom, shattering the glass.

Zylphia winced as a shriek sounded from inside the house. "Whose bedroom?" she asked to no one in particular.

Teddy shrugged and then waved as Sophronia thrust her head out.

"If you insist on breaking my window, you could have at least insisted that I keep score!" She waved to the boys and smiled away their attempts at an apology.

"I think that's enough for today," Zylphia said as the boys groaned. "Your uncle will be mad enough as it is. Be thankful Teddy has to explain what he did." She winked at her cousins whom she considered nephews. "Do you think he'll be sent to his room with no supper?" She ruffled Calvin's hair as he giggled.

Teddy rolled his eyes and walked toward her. "Only if you are confined to your room too. You did pitch that ball to me."

She shrugged and grinned flirtatiously at him. "But then it wouldn't be a punishment." She laughed as he kissed her cheek, and they helped the boys pick up the equipment and cushions. She herded them inside to drink lemonade and to rest, passing her father standing on the veranda with an inquiring expression.

"Care to explain?"

"You know what happens when you play baseball," Zee said.

He chuckled. "Next time, ask me to play. We should have a huge game, with all of us. I think the boys would like it." He ran a hand down his daughter's arm. "I'll have a new window ordered tomorrow." He shook his head as he looked at Teddy. "Although I thought a man raised playing cricket would be a better batter."

"I blame it on the pitcher," Teddy said with a laugh. The adults followed the boys inside, listening as they regaled their father and uncle with their antics.

Florence McLeod groaned at the gentle knock on the door and heaved out a weak, "Come in." She lifted her head off her pillow and leaned up on her elbows. "Delia," she said and then fell back onto the comfortable bed.

"Oh my," Delia breathed. "I knew you were tired, but I never realized you were this exhausted." She walked to Florence and ran a hand over her forehead, nodding with satisfaction to find it cool to her touch. "Do you feel well?"

Florence opened an eye and shared a rueful smile with her friend and the woman she considered as a mother-in-law. "I haven't truly slept in months. To finally have a few hours without worry …" She yawned hugely. "How is the baby? Where is the baby?" She sat upright, her blue eyes filled with panic that her three-month-old daughter was not in the room with her.

Delia pushed on her shoulders until she lay against a pillow. "She's well. She's with the nurse and sleeping soundly. I just looked in, and everything is fine."

"I hate how relieved I am that Aidan ignored my wishes and arranged for a nurse and nanny." She flushed as she settled against a pillow. "I should be able to take care of my own children."

Delia shook her head and sat near the bed. The windows were open, allowing a soft breeze to enter, along with the sounds of Florence's boys playing outside on the lawn and the distant melody of waves crashing on rocks. "You must learn to accept help when it is offered. I think Richard was at his wit's end with worry over you."

Florence curled onto her side. "I am competent, Delia. I have no other work. I should be able to do this."

Delia smiled and gripped her hand. "No one will ever doubt your competence as a devoted mother. As a wonderful wife. But you must take care of yourself too."

Florence nodded. "It's only now that I've stopped that I realize how tired I am. Thank you," she whispered as Delia tucked a throw blanket over her. "Are we having a quiet family dinner tonight? I will be terrible company if we are having a formal affair."

"We won't be having any formal parties here, although there are those who'd wish we would. Savannah was quite the talk of the ball we attended, and too many would like any chance to stare at her."

"To gossip and smear her, you mean," Florence said with a frown. "It's unfortunate you and Aidan move in such society. It's much more pleasant among the working class." She smiled at Delia's laugh.

Delia gave her hand a pat. "As for dinner tonight, it is a quiet affair, although Sophie did invite a friend. A singer who is Lucas's friend."

Florence smiled. "Savannah will enjoy speaking with him." She yawned again. "I beg your pardon."

"No, I should beg yours for intruding on your time to relax. Rest assured that all your children are well looked after, Florence. Please catch up on much-needed sleep while you are here." Delia stroked a hand over Florence's curly black hair as Florence already slipped back into sleep.

CHAPTER 10

Savannah poked her head into Aidan's study, letting out a sigh of relief to find Aidan alone. She wore a new dress as her older dresses were too tight with her expanding waistline. The pale green highlighted her golden hair and blue eyes. "Hello, Uncle," she whispered.

He looked up from papers he read and smiled at her. "Darling Savannah, you look marvelous." He rose and gave her a quick hug before helping her to a chair. Rather than sitting behind his desk again, he sat beside her. "What is the matter?"

She let out a small laugh. "I should have known better than to think I could hide any distress from you." She paused and then firmed her shoulders. "I know you mean to help Jeremy and me. That you want the best for us." She gripped her hands together on her lap. "But I don't want to go into society again."

Aidan leaned back in his chair and watched her. "I believe they would come to accept you, Savannah. They have a perverse need to make you suffer before they will welcome you again."

She flushed, and her eyes flashed with anger. "Why should I waste my time trying to obtain approval from people I don't even like? I might be dead in a few months' time, Uncle. I don't want to waste it with them. I want to spend it with my family. With my friends." She sniffled. "I know I used to believe I wanted to be a part of that world. I don't. Not anymore. And I don't want my daughter to live in it either."

Aidan smiled softly at her, the lines at his eyes crinkling. "Delia said much the same to me. Said I was a fool to have subjected you to a moment's worth of misery at that ball." He sighed. "Forgive me, Savannah. I never meant to cause you to suffer."

She gripped his hand. "I didn't refuse to attend. I should have. I knew it would be a disaster." Her eyes shone with anger. "But I didn't want to disappoint Melinda. She was desperate to attend."

"At least she had her one dance," Aidan said. "I fear none were eager to dance with her once they learned who her mother was."

"Why would Mr. Hawke dance with my young daughter?" Savannah nibbled at her lip.

Aidan shook his head and rose, helping Savannah to stand. "As a friend of your brother's, I imagine he thought he was aiding her and doing his duty as a friend. He's been invited to dinner tonight, and you should ask him. Sophie thought his presence would be welcome."

Savannah took Aiden's hand and linked her arm through his elbow. "Thank you for understanding."

He shook his head. "No, Savannah. Thank you for forgiving me for subjecting you to such a trial." He ushered her out to the sitting room, where the adults had gathered before dinner was announced.

Savannah sat near Delia, who gripped her hand a moment. "When does your father arrive, Savannah?"

"He wrote that he should be here tomorrow. Rather than hope his assistant remains competent and doesn't rob him blind, he'll close the shop for a few weeks and take a holiday." Her eyes lit with pleasure. "It will be wonderful to see him free of his cares."

Delia smiled. "You should use your time with him to convince him to sell. He would then have the freedom to travel to Montana to see you and Lucas. To meet his newest granddaughter."

"I don't want to pressure him." Savannah shared a hopeful smile with Delia. "But that is one of my greatest wishes."

"Then I will be sure to make the same recommendation." She

looked up as Perry Hawke entered, dressed in a formal evening suit. "Oh dear," Delia breathed. "Sophie forgot to mention we don't change into formal clothes for dinner."

"Not when it is only family," Savannah said. She bit her lip as she looked at Perry, splendid in white tie, while the rest of the men wore day suits.

Delia rose and approached him, her smile gracious and contrite.

Rowena sat next to Savannah and shared a chagrined smile with her. "I suppose Sophie didn't bother to inform him that we are a casual group?"

Savannah nodded to Sophie, whose expression of innocence was not to be believed. "If Jeremy had to wear such clothes on a regular basis, he would return to Montana on the next available train."

Rowena giggled as she looked at Jeremy and Richard. The McLeod brothers were handsome in a rugged way, whereas Perry looked polished and urbane. She watched Perry move around the room to speak with all present as she ran her hands over her skirts.

When he approached the settee, Savannah smiled at him. "I was informed you are a good friend to my brother, Lucas. It is nice to finally meet you."

"I am, Mrs. McLeod. I'm unsuccessful in my attempt to lure him on tour with me. The beauty of Montana has kept him content."

Savannah laughed. "You wouldn't say that if you saw Butte! It's an ugly city, Mr. Hawke. I believe he is satisfied because he is with Genevieve, and he can do what he pleases."

He smiled. "I'm certain you are correct." He gave a slight bow. "Miss Clement." His impersonal smile failed to light his eyes with joy, and he turned away to join Aidan for a drink.

"Well, he is as charming as he is handsome," Savannah said, her hands resting over her curved belly. "I've read that women fall at his feet in every city he visits."

"And I'm sure he loves the attention," Rowena muttered, and then rose to follow Savannah into the dining room.

~

Rowena slipped outside, escaping the stifling sitting room as the men chatted about politics and finances. She had no desire to speak further about the recent arrest of the NWP suffragists for picketing at Lafayette Square and their expected imprisonment. She took a gulp of cooler air as she emerged onto the veranda, walking along it and then down to the lawn. A half moon shone, partially illuminating her steps as she approached the rocky coastline.

She stood, staring into the waves, their song timeless and soothing, as she thought over dinner. Perry—"Mr. Hawke," she told herself with a scold—had been aloof and distant during the entire meal. He failed to comment on her brighter aquamarine dress and had ignored her to speak with Savannah about Lucas. Rowena shivered and wrapped her arms around herself, reluctant to return to the house.

She stifled a shriek as a jacket was slung over her shoulders. Raising large shocked eyes, she watched as Perry stood beside her. "Why are you here?"

He shrugged. "I worried when you left the room." Then he half smiled. "My jacket is quite large on you. You are swimming in it."

"I should get back," she whispered, moving to slip the jacket off her shoulders.

"No," he whispered. "Dance with me."

She frowned at him, finally accepting his jacket and stuffing her arms through the sleeves. She rolled them up three times so that her hands were free. "Dance with you? Why should I after you've spent the better part of the evening ignoring me?"

His charming smile faded, and his gaze turned from a light flirtation into one of fierce concentration. He cupped her face, his callused fingers eliciting a gasp as they roved over the soft skin of her cheek. "How could I pay attention to you with all those curious eyes? I want you to have the chance to know me without them backing you into a corner. Or pushing me away."

She blinked as tears rose. "It doesn't matter. It's an impossibility." Yet she turned her head into his touch as his thumb swiped away a tear.

He leaned forward and whispered in her ear, "Nothing is impossible. For, if it were, I would never be here, in an evening suit, with you in my arms in Newport." He frowned as she cast a furtive glance toward the illuminated house. "Come." Gripping her hand, he tugged her a few paces until they stood in the next-door-neighbor's backyard.

"We shouldn't be here," she protested, yet she moved into his outstretched arms.

"They have yet to arrive for the season. Sophie told me that just before I slipped out to find you." Perry tugged her close until her chest met his. He lowered his head to breathe in her subtle lemon and lilac scent. "I thought women of elegant breeding always wore fancy scents."

"My mother liked simple things," Rowena murmured, her hands on his shoulders. "I take after her. Not my father."

He made a sound that could have been approval as he spun her into a dance. He chuckled as she stifled another squeal, and then he sighed with pleasure as her hands inched their way up until they were around his neck. When she rested on his shoulder, he kissed her head.

"There's no music, and yet we are dancing," she murmured.

"Don't you hear it?" he whispered. "The waves against the rocks. The insects buzzing. Even the heavy night air has its own sound." He continued to move with her. "With you in my arms, it's better than any symphony I've ever heard."

"Mr. Hawke," she said as she moved back to look into his partially shadowed face. "I don't know why I'm doing this."

"Don't you?" he asked as he leaned forward and kissed her. The kiss was at first a gentle meeting of their lips, but he soon gripped her to him, holding her close as his mouth opened over hers. When she gasped in surprise, he surged within, holding her head between his hands.

She gripped his shoulders, standing on tiptoe to kiss him back. When one of his hands released her head and wandered over her fully clothed body, coming to rest over her breast, she gasped again but did not break their kiss. She arched into his touch and then backed away at the reverberating sound of a loud wave crashing. She tried to break free of his hold, and he released her, although he continued to caress her shoulders.

"That was..." She shook her head as a tear streaked down her cheek.

"Extraordinary," he murmured as he attempted to catch his breath. He frowned as she battled tears. "I had hoped I had more finesse than to move you to tears."

"There's no hope. No reason for this," she said.

He nodded. "I know that I am little more than a singer who pawns his talents in the expectation of being paid. But I had hoped, with your penchant for eccentric friends and scandalous causes, that you would consider me someone worth knowing."

She bit her lip as she met his sincere gaze. A light breeze blew, ruffling his blond hair. Her hands itched, and she gave into temptation, swiping the locks from his forehead. "Silky," she murmured. She blushed and dropped her hand, backing up a step again. "I fear I would bring you more problems than you would like."

He frowned as he looked at her. "Don't you believe that is for me to decide?"

"You say I have a penchant for eccentric friends. From what I have heard, you have a penchant for exotic women. Something I will never be accused of." She blushed fiercely as he stared at her.

"You hide your intelligence and independence well, don't you, Rowena?" He stepped forward, cupping his hands around the back of her head so his fingers met at her nape and his thumbs caressed her cheeks. "I had an affair with an opera singer. I think it has been well chronicled that Miss Woodward left me for what she hoped would be a more generous benefactor." He let out a deep breath. "I won't lie, Rowena. Her defection hurt me. I had thought to marry her."

Rowena nodded, her expression frozen and becoming more remote as he spoke. However, she could not hide a shiver as his thumbs moved over her cheeks.

"I realize now that she did me the greatest of favors." He leaned forward until their foreheads were touching. "She never truly cared for me, and I want more from life than a woman who merely desires my money. Or esteem from the fame that I have earned."

She swallowed and felt her cheeks reddening under his intense stare. "What do you want, Mr. Hawke?"

He smiled, tenderness lighting his eyes. "I want you to start calling me Perry. I want to have permission to write to you. I want your friends to know that I have an honorable interest in you."

She frowned as she gazed deep into his eyes. "What else?"

He broke his gaze free of hers and dropped his hands. He took a step away and shook his head. "I beg your pardon."

She leaped forward, grabbing his strong arms and grunting in frustration as her hands tangled in his long coat sleeves. "No," she demanded as she pulled at him. She moved until she stood, blocking his path. She shrugged out of his jacket, letting it drop to the ground, and reached up, cupping his face. "Tell me. You've come this far, and it's only fair."

He chuckled, but it did not sound humorous. "I should have known a suffragist would be determined."

He stood so that the moon shone on his face, and she could easily read the frustration and longing in his expression.

"I want you to see me as a worthy man," he whispered. "Not as gutter scum."

She recoiled from his words, and he gave a sardonic laugh. "I should have known it was too much to hope for that my past didn't precede me. Not in your world."

She pushed at his chest as he attempted to depart and stumbled a step as she tripped on his jacket on the ground. "Stop." She raised irate, defiant eyes to his. "It's my turn."

He stilled, although his breath emerged more quickly than normal, nearly a pant. He nodded, and his eyes gleamed with appreciation as she stood her ground, even though she was nearly a foot shorter than he was.

"I ... There are things I'm not ready to tell you yet. Things that might change how you feel about me. If you can accept that unknown,

I would like us to write. To see each other when we can." She bit her lip. "I want to know you, Perry."

"Why?" he whispered, his hand rising of its own volition to play in her loosened auburn hair.

"You don't look at me as *pathetic Rowena, still single at nearly thirty-two.*" She blinked as she attempted to clear her tears. "You see me."

He grinned and lowered his head until their foreheads touched again. "I see you, darling." After a moment he whispered, "Are you afraid to tell me about a fierce passion in your past?" He watched her closely as she flushed. "That would not matter to me."

She swallowed. "That's not what it is. It's not something I'll discuss tonight." She paused as he watched her with curiosity. She smiled and leaned upward, kissing him again.

After another long, drugging kiss, he eased her away. "No more, love. Not unless you want me to become your passionate secret you must conceal." He smiled as she giggled. He held his hand out to her and linked their fingers together as they walked around the hedge to the water's edge again.

"You will write me?" she whispered.

"As often as I can." He raised her hand and kissed her palm, evoking a shiver. "Write me about your day. Your frustrations. Your dreams. I want to know you, Rowena. Not the facade that everyone can see, but the woman underneath."

She nodded and sniffled. "I want the same. Not the man who wears the mask, but the man who dances with me and hears a symphony on a quiet night." She paused. "When will I see you again?"

He leaned forward and kissed her softly and then backed away. "Forgive me. I shouldn't have done that in sight of the house." He stroked her cheek. "I leave Newport soon, and then I am touring for a few months. Letters will be all we have for now."

She nodded and bit her lip. "I'll understand if ..."

"Rowena, look at me," he whispered. "I promise to be honest with you. I promise to not deceive you. I promise to cherish what is growing between us." He took a deep breath. "I'm old enough, and jaded enough, to know these sorts of feelings are not common. I will not risk them for a meaningless flirtation." He paused. "I will need you to ignore the incessant drivel written about me in the papers. They love to print half-truths to scintillate their readership."

She nodded. "I will believe you before any gossip article." She glanced toward the house. "I should go in first. I ..."

He nodded his understanding. "I shall retrieve my jacket, and then I will follow. That should give you plenty of time to enter alone. There's every reason to believe I went in the opposite direction as you and that you've been strolling the grounds alone."

Rowena shook her head in frustration. "Except for the fact that Sophie has eyes as sharp as an eagle." She squeezed his hand and walked up the long lawn toward the mansion. She glanced over her shoulder as she was about to step onto the veranda and saw him standing there, watching her, as though mesmerized. She gave him a small wave and then turned into the house.

~

Parthena half dozed on Rowena's bed while Zylphia sprawled on the chaise longue. "How long do you think they'll remain outside? Should we send Morgan or Teddy out?"

Zylphia snorted. "Are you insane? It's the first time Rowena has had the chance to know any passion. I'm not about to ruin it for her. With any luck, they've found a comfortable cranny under the hedges."

The door creaked open, and Rowena tiptoed in. Her eyes widened at the presence of her two best friends, and she blushed fiercely as their gazes roved over her disheveled state.

"No cranny," Zylphia said with a hint of sadness in her voice.

"What are you referring to?" Rowena said as she attempted to infuse her voice with an upper-class hauteur.

Parthena rolled her eyes and pushed herself up to a sitting position while yawning hugely. "That you hadn't found a comfortable place to explore your passion with Perry." She smiled as Rowena flushed. "And we were sorry for it."

"How do you know I was with him?" She frowned when she

looked in her dressing glass mirror. Her hair had tumbled from its pins; her dress was wrinkled and had a palm print on her hip, and she had a burn mark on her neck from his whiskers. She slipped pins from her hair, shaking loose her long auburn tresses so that they fell nearly to her bottom.

"You have such beautiful hair," Zylphia murmured as she rose. "I know you hate the natural curl and thick waves, but you should be thankful for it." She grabbed the brush out of Rowena's hand. "Here. Let me act as your maid tonight. We sent them all to bed in case you didn't want them to be a witness to …" She raised her eyebrows and smiled. "So, what happened?" she asked with a wicked smile as she brushed Rowena's hair. She stilled her movements when Rowena spun to face her and Parthena.

"He wants to get to know me. To prove to me that he is a man worthy of my time. Of my consideration."

Parthena smiled. "Lucas always spoke highly of him. And I enjoyed my time with Mr. Hawke in Minneapolis. Even Morgan believes he's a decent man, although a musician." She smiled at her friend. "Now you have three of your friends speaking for him on his behalf, and I'd consider that all the recommendation you need."

Rowena frowned and pursed her lips. "My father will hate him."

Zylphia scoffed as she eased Rowena from her confining shoes. "Your father hates everyone. I shouldn't worry about that. Besides, you have money now. You needn't worry ever again about what your father wants."

"He's my only family," she protested.

"Perhaps, but I like to think we are family too," Zylphia said as she pointed to Parthena. She smiled as Rowena rose and moved behind the modesty barrier to change into her nightgown.

When she emerged, she frowned at Zylphia's disgruntled expression. "What?"

"Is that all you did? Talk?" She grunted as Parthena hit her on her arm. "You know you're as curious as I am." Her smile bloomed as Rowena blushed. "Oh, good, it was worth waiting up for. I had hoped the whisker burn on your neck was from something other than a chaste discussion of the beautiful moonlight." Her eyes danced with humor. "Do tell."

Rowena perched on the edge of the chaise longue while Zylphia and Parthena sat on the side of her bed. "He wanted to dance with me." She closed her eyes. "It was magical. I never knew a man could smell so good." She opened her eyes at her friends' giggles. "And then he kissed me."

When she paused, Parthena made a motion with her hand. "And? What did you feel?"

"Like I finally knew what all the fuss was about," Rowena whispered.

"Oh my," Zylphia murmured with a grin. "Then you'll be even more elated when you learn exactly what all the fuss is truly about." She laughed when Parthena hit her with a pillow. "So, what now?"

"He leaves to go on tour, and I don't know when I'll see him again. He wants to write me. But, if he writes me at my father's house in Boston, my father will have a fit." She tilted her head. "I never thought of that when I agreed to his request."

"He can send his letters to one of us. We'll make sure you get them the same day." Zylphia and Parthena shared a look and nodded. "I don't mind deceiving your father."

"Zee," Rowena said with a sigh, "you make it sound like it's for a noble cause."

"Because it is, you goose. You've found a man who's interested in you and who, by all accounts, is a good man. Why would you pass him up?"

She firmed her lips into a grimace. "I didn't tell him about my mother."

Parthena frowned. "Why would you? She died years ago. He doesn't need to know about the trust she left you. Not yet."

"No, P.T.," Zylphia said, calling Parthena by her old nickname before she married, when she was Parthena Tyler, "that her mother was German. That Rowena's half German."

Parthena sighed and flopped back onto the bed. "I wish I could say it doesn't matter. But it will to some." She leaned up on her elbows. "Do you think it will to him?"

Rowena shrugged. "I don't know. He depends on commissions and his reputation. What would be said if he were to be linked to me? To a woman whose mother was from an aristocratic family in Germany? Too many believe that all such families were friendly with the Kaiser."

"Wasn't yours?" Zylphia asked.

"Remotely," Rowena said. "The way Teddy's family was friendly with the Royal Family in England."

Zylphia shrugged. "All that should matter is that you're an American citizen," Zylphia said. "Which is more than can be said of me. Why should anyone care where your mother was born? Or who her family was? You've proven your loyalty to this country over and over."

"Those with a pea-size intellect will believe that Ro's support of the suffrage cause might be her way of attempting to sabotage the war effort," Parthena murmured.

Zylphia rolled her eyes. "They aren't even worth mentioning."

Rowena sat for a long moment in silence and then shook her head. "I don't like deceit, and I already fear that my lack of full honesty will bring me sorrow." She firmed her jaw. "If Perry and I are to write, then he will write me at my father's."

Parthena beamed at her. "Bravo."

Parthena slipped into the room she shared with her husband and moved behind the privacy curtain to change into her nightgown. She emerged, flicking off the lamp and crawled under the covers.

"Are you finally to bed?" Morgan said as he curled an arm around her waist and pulled her close.

"Yes," she said as she stroked a hand over his arm. After several moments, she felt him stir behind her, and she turned to find him attempting to wake up. "What are you doing?"

"Something is the matter, and I don't want to be too sleepy to understand what you say."

She smiled and crawled onto his chest, kissing him. "I love you, Morgan. I'm sorry for worrying you." She frowned. "Although I fail to see why Mr. Hawke's presence tonight should concern you."

"Did he harm Rowena?" his voice had chilled, and Parthena shivered at the tone.

She stroked his forehead, attempting to rub away the worry lines. "No. In fact, I think he might be intelligent enough to see how remarkable she is."

He smiled. "Good. She needs to get over her infatuation …" He shook his head and shrugged. "She deserves to be happy." He caressed his wife's face and frowned. "What aren't you telling me? I have a sense you are keeping secrets, Parthena."

She stroked a hand over his cheek and then at his neck to his chest. "Did you mean it?" When he stared at her blankly, she admitted on a rush, "I didn't mean to listen in on your private conversation, but I heard you speaking with Jeremy today. I listened as he talked about his fears." She raised her worried gaze to his. "Did you mean it when you said that you would prefer me to never have a child than to suffer such worry?"

He nodded. "Of course. I hate imagining you in such pain. I hate considering you suffering." He shrugged. "I'm happy as we are, Hennie, with or without children." He frowned as tears coursed down her cheeks. "What is it?"

"Do you not want children?" she whispered around a sob.

He pushed her until she lay down, and he leaned over her, stroking her cheeks. "I want you. Nothing else. If we are blessed, then I will find a way to survive a fear that I worry will be nearly insurmountable. But I will try to do anything for you."

"But do you want them?"

He closed his eyes and exhaled. "Yes," he rasped. "I feel selfish saying it, as I hate that you must suffer to give me this desire. But I want a daughter. A son. As many as we can have." He raised haunted eyes to her. "I want our house to be filled with laughter and joy and chaos, the way mine never was. I want to know that there will always be love."

"Oh, Morgan," she whispered as she pulled him to her and held him, rolling with him as he held her on his chest. "I have been keeping secrets." She kissed his palm and pressed it to her belly. "We are to have a child, darling."

"What?"

"I thought … I thought when I heard you speaking with Jeremy today that it meant you didn't want one, and my heart nearly broke. I want a baby, our baby, so much." She sniveled inelegantly and laughed as he gave out a *whoop* that could awaken the house. "*Shh*, love."

"God, how I love you, Parthena," he whispered. "I promise I always will."

She kissed his lips and then his head as he leaned down and kissed her belly. "Oh, Morgan," she whispered, her fingers playing in his hair. "Thank you."

He looked up at her with an expression she had never seen before: one of absolute peace and contentment. "There's nothing more that I want on this earth than to have you, and our child, with me. Everything else is a boon."

"Never leave me," she whispered. "Promise me."

He frowned. "I think I should be the one demanding that of you. You're the one who will be going through the travails of motherhood." His fingers intertwined with hers. "I have one dream left, Hennie."

"Only one?" she asked with a frown.

"Only one that matters," he said with a smile as he scooted up to steal a kiss. He settled on the bed with her head cradled on his shoulder. "I want to grow old with you. To retell our stories to each other as we remember these youthful adventures. That is what I want, more than anything else."

She kissed his shoulder. "That is my dream too."

Savannah burst into the sitting room facing the sea, the doors open to allow the breeze and gentle sound of the waves to enter. "Father! Oh, I'm so glad you're finally here."

He set aside the newspaper and pulled her close. "My darling girl," he smiled as he looked at her. "The house has been too quiet without you, Jeremy and Melinda."

"Please say you'll stay until September. Until we return to Boston."

He tugged her to sit next to him on a comfortable settee facing the back lawn and ocean. He smiled absently at the sight of Zylphia playing tag with her husband and Richard's children. "I've been here an hour, and I'm more relaxed that I've been in years. Of course I'll stay."

She gave a small squeal of delight, sounding more like her daughter than a forty-one-year-old woman. She sobered after a moment and said, "But what about the store? You've never taken more than a day or two off since I was born."

He smiled mischievously, reminding her of Lucas. "I wasn't able to join you when you first arrived here because I was negotiating the sale of it. I will run it for another month or two after I return in September as I train the owner's new staff. It will give me the opportunity to reassure my loyal customers that the same high-quality service and products they have come to rely on will continue. Then I will be a free man."

She gripped his hand. "Where will you live? I assume they will take possession of your home over the shop."

He nodded. "They will. I'll find a new home." He smiled. "Or I will finally travel to Montana with you."

She battled tears as she leaned into his side. "Yes, please," she whispered through her tears. "I want my baby to know you, and Lucas has missed you too."

They sat in companionable silence for a few moments. "How have you liked Newport?" he asked.

She grimaced. "I love this house and being so close to the ocean. Early morning and evening walks are enjoyable." She sighed. "But I had a disastrous reentry into society. They gossiped about me and were cruel to Jeremy and Melinda."

"I doubt that bothered your husband. He never seemed the sort of man to yearn for a ballroom." He grinned as she giggled. "Although I am sorry for Melinda. I know she looked forward to dancing at a ball."

"Oh, she danced once. With the singer, Perry Hawke. He seems impervious to concerns about his reputation."

"I'm altogether certain it is improper for such a man to woo a woman of Melinda's age."

Savannah shifted so she could meet her father's glower. "I believe he danced with her as a favor to Lucas. His interest appears to lie with a friend of Zee's. Rowena Clement."

Martin Russell let out a deep breath. "I can only hope he is more steadfast in his dalliances than most artists I've been acquainted with."

Savannah frowned. "Father? Lucas isn't like that."

He smiled as he thought about his son. "No, and I'm thankful he isn't." He closed his eyes a moment. "It's no great secret that your mother and I had trouble in our marriage. That she wished I were more successful."

"Grander," Savannah said.

He nodded. "You know how her parents were—are—overbearing and determined to bludgeon everyone around them into the pattern or mold of their choosing. Ironically only your aunt Betsy followed their dictates." His eyes were unfocused a moment. "Before we wed, an attractive performer from Scollay Square ruined her reputation. I wed her to save the family store and to save her from social condemnation."

He focused on Savannah. "You don't seem surprised." Shock glint in his gaze.

"Aunt Betsy told me all about Mother's wild youth after I left Jonas. I believe she wanted me to better understand my mother." She shrugged. "However, I'll never understand her or forgive her." After a moment she asked, "Why do you fear Mr. Hawke is like that man?"

"I've read quite a bit about him in the papers," Martin said with a wry lift of his eyebrows.

"Yes, but then we read a lot of rumors about Lucas that aren't true."

Her father's eyes gleamed with pride as he beheld his daughter.

"Then I will hope Mr. Hawke is not as feckless as I fear. For Miss Clement's sake."

~

Martin wandered outside and found Melinda sitting on the steps leading to the yard. "How are you, my darling grand-daughter?" He smiled as she leaped up and hugged him. "I have missed you."

"Oh, I've missed you so much, Gramps," she said as she sniffled.

He frowned as he traced away a tear. "What's this? Why are you crying?" She was fidgety, so he motioned for her to walk with him. "This is a beautiful time of day, and few will deign to walk now. They are resting or preparing for their evening out, so we should have the Cliff Walk to ourselves." His frown deepened as his words eased her anxiety.

He waited for her to speak, but she remained uncharacteristically quiet. "Your mother informed me that your foray into society didn't go as you had hoped."

"Oh, Gramps, it was a disaster. I was too loud. My dress was too simple, and I know I'll never perfect that look of boredom that everyone wears."

He laughed. "Why should you?"

She shook her head as her natural exuberance returned. "But how can they be bored here? Are they that accustomed to being in a room with gold gilded mirrors and crystal chandeliers with fifty lights and doors spilling out to a lawn that leads to an ocean?"

This time he sighed. "I'm afraid most of them think that such an environment is their due and find nothing special in such an occa-sion." He paused with her as they reached a promontory overlooking the coast at the large homes up and down it. "It boggles my mind, but they have so much money that they don't know what to do with it."

She bit her lip. "I did have the sense that some of them were panicked. Why would that be?"

Martin shrugged. "Well, until 1913, none of them had to pay an income tax. That changed with the Sixteenth Amendment. Now the majority of those in that ballroom have to pay 7 percent each year to the federal government." He watched as she crinkled her nose as though attempting to figure out a puzzle. "It doesn't sound like much," he continued, "but many of them don't like letting go of a dime."

She tilted her head to one side as she looked at her grandfather. "But they already have so much. Why can't they share some of it?"

He laughed. "That is the question, dearest. You should have been a Populist." He encouraged her to sit on a low rock and sat beside her. "I'm sorry you were unable to dance more at the ball."

"The boys were rude and seemed to believe I didn't know they thought me inferior." Her confused gaze met her grandfather's. "I don't understand why Mother liked society."

He laughed. "Oh, you are a joy. I can't say I understand why she did either. However, after she met your father, she's had little desire to be a part of it."

She paused, staring at her grandfather before she spoke again. "I met my great-grandmother."

He stiffened next to her. "The old bat?" He flushed. "I beg your pardon. I should never refer to her in such a manner to you."

Melinda looked at her grandfather and studied him in his well-cut suit and fashionable hat. "I don't understand why she believes her daughter married beneath her. My grandmother married a successful businessman. Shouldn't that please her mother?"

He heaved out a breath. "Darling Melinda, among your grandparents' people, it's not acceptable to work. At least not how I work. If they dabble at business—which I imagine is what they believe Teddy does—that is tolerable, although rarely commented upon. I sell goods to make a living. I am a tradesman. That is seen as lower class. That is how they perceive your father too."

"Snobs," she muttered. "Why can't they see you have the ability to make something beautiful from nothing? Like Father and Uncle Gabriel from wood?"

His eyes glistened as he looked at her. "Not all are as singular as you, Melly."

She took a deep breath, closing her eyes, relaxing in his presence and the pleasant afternoon.

"How do you like the scent of the sea now?" he asked, watching her with curiosity.

"In Boston, it was a mixed-up jumble of scents. But here"—she sniffed—"it's glorious. I wish I could bottle the scent and bring it home with me to Montana to remember the seaside."

"We will have to collect shells so you can bring those home." He smiled as her eyes danced with joy at the prospect. He rose with reluctance. "Come. We must prepare for supper."

She rose and walked beside him. "How long can you stay?"

He nudged her with his shoulder. "I'll let you in on a secret. I'll be here until you leave, and then, when you return to Montana, I'll travel with you." He gasped as she threw herself in his arms.

"Oh, that's wonderful. I hoped and hoped that's what you'd say. Mother will be delighted."

He beamed at her. "She already knows. I'll inform everyone tonight at dinner. I can't wait to see what your life in Montana is like, Melly."

CHAPTER 11

Butte, Montana, July 1918

Colin knocked on the door and waited for the sound of approaching footsteps but heard none. He knocked again, louder this time, and turned to stare down the street. Rows of similar homes with small front porches and narrow walkways leading to the sidewalk lined the block. He sighed as the door remained unanswered and moved to a chair set to one side of the door. After propping his feet on the porch railing, he closed his eyes and willed himself to relax.

Savannah and Jeremy had left for Boston the previous week. He had seen them off, hugging Savannah too long and too tightly for it to go unnoticed by Melinda. Clarissa had been unable to forestall crying, and Gabriel's eyes had shone brightly. Colin did not doubt Jeremy's decision to travel to Boston in an attempt to alter the feared outcome. "I just want to see Savannah again," he whispered. "I want to hold their baby in my arms."

He opened his eyes and focused on the clouds passing overhead. Today they were big white fluffy clouds, visible even through the thick haze of soot. The type of clouds he loved to stare at and try to find shapes in. After a few minutes, he groaned and sat up, rubbing at his hair. He leaned his elbows on his knees and shook his head at his inability to relax and to enjoy the few days off he had allotted himself from the smithy.

When he heard a soft lilting voice as someone sang along the sidewalk, approaching him, he canted forward. He beamed when he saw his sister-in-law, Fiona, walking slowly with her young daughter, Rose, now three, holding on to one hand. Fiona carried a bag of groceries in her other hand. He hopped up and trotted down the steps to greet them. "Fee!" he called out, grabbing the bag and leaning in to give her a kiss on the cheek.

"Oh, Colin, what a wonderful surprise!" she exclaimed. She smiled as he knelt in front of Rose and tickled her nose.

"There's my darling girl, my little Rosebud," he said. He laughed when she threw her arms around his neck and called him "Cowen." He shrugged apologetically, handing the bag of groceries back to Fiona and lifted Rose into his arms. Rose leaned away from him and jabbered about their walk into town. He listened appreciatively and earned a high-pitched squeal when he nuzzled her neck.

Walking with Fiona up the porch steps, he waited as she unlocked the door and let them in.

He sat Rose down in the living room, and she scampered over to her play area to the right of the entryway while Fiona moved to the kitchen. After retrieving his travel bag from the porch, he left it near the front door before joining Rose on the living room floor. A hallway off the entryway to the right led to three bedrooms. Fiona joined him after a few minutes, smiling with gratitude to see him watching Rose. He nodded his thanks as she handed him a glass of cold water.

"How are things, Fee?" He took a long sip of water as he studied her. She wore her red-gold hair in a loose knot at her nape, and her eyes shone with contentment when she beheld her daughter.

"Lovely," she replied. "And quite the same as the last time you visited." Her gaze signaled she had little interest in answering further questions. "And you?"

"Lovely," Colin quipped and laughed as Rose made a pile of blocks and then knocked them over. "I wanted a few days off, so I thought I'd come for a surprise visit." He flushed at Fiona's knowing gaze but refused to explain further.

"I should have thought it difficult to leave your smithy on a Wednesday."

He shrugged. "I have a good man working for me who'll keep an eye on things. I'll be back by Monday."

As the front door opened, Colin turned, and his brother, Patrick, walked through. "Hi, Pat," Colin said with an endearing smile.

"Look who's come to call," Fiona said with a raised eyebrow. She rose, kissed Patrick on the cheek and then moved toward the kitchen. "Dinner will be ready in about an hour. I'll prepare Colin's room."

Rose ran to her father for a hug and a kiss, and then continued to play. Patrick watched her with absentminded affection; then he turned toward Colin. "Why are you here? Why didn't you let us know you were coming? Is everyone all right?"

"Everyone's fine. I'm the one who needed to get away, and so I did." He focused on Rose and ignored his brother's intense stare.

Patrick glanced up with a smile as Fiona walked into the living room and held out a hand to her. He kissed it, and a contented joy filled his gaze as he beheld his wife.

"Your bedroom's ready, Colin, if you want to freshen up before dinner," Fiona said, before she kissed her husband on his head and returned to the kitchen.

"I'm glad to see you and Fee are still on good terms," Colin said. "I'm also happy that I don't have to worry about kicking you out of your old bedroom."

Patrick laughed and shook his head. "No, thankfully that's no longer an issue. Not since last June." He shook his head at Colin's reference to the time he and Fiona had been estranged and he had slept in a different bedroom.

Colin smiled. "At least one of us is no longer acting a fool." He waved at Patrick to remain with Rose and moved into his bedroom to wash up and prepare for a quiet family dinner.

After dinner, Patrick sat outside on the porch with Colin. Fiona tended to little Rose, giving her a bath and readying her for bed. Patrick would give her a good-night kiss before she fell asleep. He sat with his back to one of the porch's posts, his legs in front of him on the concrete rail while Colin sat in the uncomfortable chair. "Why are you really here?" Patrick asked softly.

Colin closed his eyes, leaning his head back and stretching his legs out to the side so he could act as though relaxed. "I'm a fool. And I have no one to blame but myself." He cracked an eye open to see Patrick waiting patiently for him to continue. "Ari's to marry another."

"I know. Rissa wrote me. She also wrote you acted like a jealous idiot when Araminta made her announcement." Patrick frowned. "That's not like you, Col. You're always happy for everyone."

"But that's just it, Pat. Ari and me, we were always supposed to end up together." He leaned forward, his elbows now on his knees and his head in his hands.

"How was that to happen? Were you waiting for her to propose to you?" At Colin's offended sputter, Patrick looked nonplussed. "For you certainly never gave any indication that you were truly serious about her." He sobered further as he saw how his words hurt his brother. "You've known her for nearly sixteen years—"

"Fifteen last month," Colin interjected.

"Fine, fifteen years. What in God's name has taken you so long to ask her if you were really interested in her?" Patrick shook his head in disbelief. "You're not a young man anymore, Col. You're forty-two years old. You must want more from life than a bachelor's existence."

"At first I didn't want to rush her because she was so young. And then I thought she didn't like me, well, not like that." Colin closed his eyes. "And then I almost kissed her."

"When?" Patrick asked.

"Four years ago. When Lucas was in Missoula for a concert to support the suffragists. She's hated me ever since." He ran a hand through his hair. "I could never convince her afterward that I wasn't simply playing a game. That I was seriously interested in her."

"Did you ask her, in plain English, 'Will you marry me?' Did you say, 'I love you' so there was no way she could misunderstand your feelings?" At Colin's blank stare, Patrick shook his head. "Col, women need us to act without prevarication when we are proclaiming ourselves. It's really rather simple. When you were trying to demonstrate you weren't playing a game, you showed her you still were because you refused to declare how you felt." He paused as his younger brother took in his words. "How do you think that made her feel?"

"Like I was leading her on. Lying to her." Colin's shoulders sagged in defeat. "Like she couldn't trust me anymore."

Patrick watched his brother with fond exasperation. "You've lived a charmed life where your quick smile and glib wit have gotten you out of quite a few binds. She's seen that. That's not what she wants."

Colin sat back in his chair, his arms crossed over his chest. "Clearly she wants boring bloody Bartholomew Bouchard. A banker."

Patrick burst out laughing. "I don't know if you could conjure up any more *B*s to describe him."

"Give me a few minutes," Colin growled.

Patrick chuckled again and relaxed against the railing. "Have you spoken with her?"

Colin shuddered. "Yes. She despises me, and I fear that, no matter what I say now, it will always be seen as a ruse so that she won't marry him." He closed his eyes. "I'm such an idiot. I could have married her years ago and been happily living with her at my house and our numerous children by now. Instead I live alone as the only woman I've ever loved plans to marry another."

"Have you told her that? In those exact words?" Patrick kicked his brother with a foot. "It's hell declaring how we feel, but we must, Col. Some things in life are worth taking a risk for." After a few moments of silent companionship, Patrick whispered, "Is there really a chance Sav will die?"

Colin raised frightened eyes to Patrick and nodded. "I almost couldn't let her out of my arms at the train station, and I fear I squeezed her so tight I hurt the baby," Colin murmured. "I don't know what I'll do, what Rissa will do, if she doesn't come back."

"Jeremy will be ..." Patrick shook his head, unable to finish the sentence.

"There are no words for what he'll be. I fear he'd never recover."

Patrick watched his brother with dismay. "It makes me realize just how much of a bloody idiot you've been, as Fee would say." At Colin's glare, Patrick nodded. "Why won't you take a risk for Araminta and your relationship with her? I don't understand why you won't take such a chance."

"I like harmony, Pat," Colin murmured.

"We all do, but it's unrealistic to think you'll never have strife in your life. There will always be a time when you have to stand up for what you want. For what you believe. For who you love." He speared Colin with a glare. "You've stood by Rissa and Sav and me. I don't understand why you won't do the same for you and Araminta."

Colin shook his head. "It's easy to be brave when it doesn't have the ability to rip out your heart."

Patrick choked on a laugh. "That may be true, but the reward is a lot less." They sat in silence a moment, the sounds of neighbors' conversations, a fiddle playing and a baby crying carrying on the wind. "You had faith in me as I faced my deepest fears. Now you need to have faith in yourself."

Patrick waited in bed that evening for his wife to enter after checking on Rose. "How is she?"

"Clinging to the wee bear Colin brought her and sound asleep." She slipped from her dress and donned a nightgown.

"I don't know why you put one on," he teased. "It only ends up on the floor."

She flushed, the slight redness enhancing her beauty. "I want one nearby in case Rose calls out in the middle of the night." She raised a teasing eyebrow as she played with the lace collar of the voluminous white nightgown. "Although I could leave it on the chair." She pulled it off her head and tossed it to the chair, meeting her husband's startled, delighted gaze with an embarrassed smile. "I did say I'd try to be more daring."

He held up the sheets for her, and she crawled into bed. He sighed with pleasure as she rested her head on his shoulder. "Are you all right, Fee?" When she pushed her face against his chest, he said, "It seemed that Savannah and Jeremy's news upset you."

"I worry about them. About how she will fare," she whispered. She played with his chest hair and remained silent.

"*But ...*" he murmured. "Tell me, Fee." He ran a hand through her thick red-gold hair.

"But I envy them," she said. "Not the worry. The doubt. The fear." She sighed and refused to meet his gaze. "They have a baby on the way."

He rolled until she was caged underneath him. "Can you imagine the fear Jeremy is living with? The agony that he has to hide, every day, from the woman he loves, because he might lose her?" He shook his head. "I won't lie and say I don't want a baby with you, Fee. A little brother or sister for Rose. But, if we never have a child, I will always feel blessed."

She blinked as a tear snaked down her cheek. "Truly? You don't blame me?"

He kissed away the tear and chuckled. "Why would I blame you?" He smiled at her as his hold on her eased. "Besides, it could easily be because of me that you don't find yourself with child." He kissed along her neck.

"I want your child," she said as she arched into his touch.

"Rose *is* mine," he said in a voice that brooked no argument.

She blinked and nodded. "She is. In every way that matters." She kissed him, running her hands through the hair at his nape.

He met her gaze and cupped her cheek. "I promise you, Fee. If we have ten more children, or none, what we have now is more than I ever dreamed I'd have. This is paradise for me." He teased her with soft kisses before losing himself to the passion that flared between them.

~

Patrick, Colin and Lucas sat in Lucas's study. The curtains shivered from an anemic wind, barely stirring the still and hot summer air. Lucas stretched out his legs, giving Colin's foot a kick. "I never thought to see you midweek."

Colin shrugged. "I have a good foreman, and I wanted to see my brother." He slunk farther in his chair as Lucas watched him with patient eyes. "I needed to escape Missoula for a few days."

"Running away won't solve your problem, Col. You need to speak with her." Lucas tapped his fingers on his belly as though playing a requiem on the piano.

Colin huffed out an exasperated breath. "Does everyone know about Ari?"

Lucas raised an eyebrow and shared an amused glance with Patrick. "Ari? I always thought you should have acted on your inclination four years ago, when I made a stop in Missoula on my tour across the country." He frowned as he saw how miserable his cousin was. "How does she not understand how much you care? You're the only one who calls her Ari."

Colin ran a hand over his head. "She thinks I'm not really serious about her. That I'm only offended now because she won't be available to see after my house the way she always has." He shared a miserable look with his brother and cousin. "And, yes, I know I've been a fool."

Lucas shrugged. "I can't say I would have had the good fortune to marry Genevieve if we hadn't been forced together by circumstances. I would have nursed my resentment toward her sister for years." He steepled his fingers. "Sometimes we need something to give us a nudge to force us to act."

Patrick snorted. "Col needed a nudge ten years ago." He chuckled as Colin batted him on his arm. "Go home tomorrow, Col. See your Araminta."

Colin shrugged. "I'll return by tomorrow night. I was a fool to leave, but I couldn't stay there and imagine her happy, planning her wedding. Not when I'm miserable."

Patrick's gaze held a shadow for a moment. "I've found that women are more pragmatic than we expect. Speak with her, and I have a feeling you'll learn that she acted for reasons that would surprise you."

They sat in silence for a few moments, an infant's cry sounding and almost instantly soothed. "Genevieve is with Lizzie," Lucas said. "I'm sorry you might not see her this trip, but she was already in her crib for the evening when you came over."

Colin smiled. "I'll visit tomorrow, before I catch the late train to Missoula. I have to see my young cousin and bring a report back to Missoula about how she fares, or Clarissa would skin me alive." He looked from his brother to his cousin. "How are things with Smythe and Sanders?"

Lucas shook his head in frustration. "Too calm, wouldn't you agree, Patrick?"

Patrick nodded. "Yes. We rarely see Mrs. Smythe lingering on a nearby street corner any longer, although I know she is still here because I see her infrequently as I walk through Uptown." He scratched at his head. "I should be satisfied that she hasn't attempted anything, but I know she is plotting something."

"She's always plotting something," Colin murmured.

"Exactly," Lucas said. "I've hired no new servants, and the ones who work here are loyal to us. They know they will be dismissed from a well-paying job if they attempt to cross us." His jaw clenched as he thought about Joseph Rigionneri, the young man he'd offered work to last summer. He had also worked for Samuel Sanders in an attempt to steal Rose away from Patrick and Fiona.

"Does Sanders still want Rose?" Colin asked.

Patrick shrugged and then ran a hand through his hair. "I don't know. It's Fiona's worst fear, having Rose stolen from us. But we don't know what Sanders and Mrs. Smythe will do next."

Colin shook his head in confusion. "It makes no sense to me. He intentionally used Fiona for information about our family and then left her with child, with no intention of providing for her or her baby. Why would he now want that child?"

Lucas's jaw tightened. "Power. He'll do anything he can to harm Gabriel or someone from his family. And we are an extension of Gabriel's family."

Patrick fisted his hands. "I agree with Colin. It still makes no sense. However, we are vigilant, and we will be until he is either far from Butte or dead."

"I'd be vigilant until he's dead and I've spat on his grave," Colin muttered. He shared a remorseless look with his brother. "He is not a man to be mourned."

Patrick nodded. "I know. I hate that I ever befriended him." He let out a long breath as he fought his guilt at his short-lived friendship with Gabriel's cousin when Patrick had first arrived in Butte. He'd had no idea at the time that Samuel Sanders and Henry Masterson were the same person and that Patrick was being used to get to Gabriel. "However, I have a sense that their focus has changed." He looked at Colin. "I don't know why, but I'd be careful, brother."

Bartholomew Bouchard followed the attractive secretary down the long hallway to a large office on the top floor of the Hennessy building in Uptown Butte. The view from the windows over Uptown Butte to the flats was impressive and also gave the momentary sensation that the onlooker was in the clouds. A quick glance around the office showed artwork of landmarks in Butte and a few paintings of Boston. He focused on the man behind the desk and held out his hand. "Samuel," he said, his smile broad and friendly.

"Bart," Samuel said, motioning for him to sit on one of the chairs across from him. "It's about time you visited me. You've been in Montana for over a year now." Samuel exuded a determination of purpose that belied his slim frame that made him appear otherwise weak.

Bart sighed and unbuttoned his jacket, relaxing into his chair. "You knew it would take time to establish myself in Missoula. My uncle is loyal to family, but he isn't a fool."

Samuel nodded. "I presume you've proven to him your financial prowess." At Bart's nod, he grunted with satisfaction. "Good." He tapped a newspaper in front of him. "I was pleased to finally read of your engagement."

"As with all things, it took longer than expected."

Samuel snorted, his hands crossed over his belly as he studied Bart. "I thought you were the man for this job. I assured my associate you were. However, it's taken much longer than we would have liked for this announcement." He tapped the article again, smudging his fingers with black ink. "I will be very disappointed if you allow the cripple to escape your net."

Bartholomew flushed. "She's not a cripple, Sam." He glared at the man he had met over a decade ago in New York City before the financial crisis in 1907. "And she has accepted me. There is no reason to believe she will renege."

Samuel shook his head. "Of course there is. She's a woman, and they never keep their word. Besides, she's besotted with that Sullivan fool, and, if he were to crook his finger at her, she'd run to him." He leaned forward, and his soft voice became rapier precise. "You've already been played a fool twice, Bart. Don't be that man again."

Bartholomew's cheeks glowed with shame. "I never expected to be on the receiving end of a con."

Samuel laughed. "Not when you had always been the one pulling off the scheme!" He cleared his throat. "Now I will be at your wedding. And I want to be assured it will occur."

Bartholomew sat back and watched the man who was as much an adversary as a friend. "What more reassurance do you want?"

"If it doesn't happen, then she'll have an unfortunate fatal accident. That family must continue to suffer, and the only one who hasn't yet is Colin." He shrugged. "Personally I wouldn't spend much time on him as he seems a charming buffoon, and I'd rather focus on my cousins, but my ... colleague wants his aim on Colin."

Bartholomew paled and glared at Samuel. "I want nothing to happen to Miss Araminta."

Samuel's laughter grated like nails on a chalkboard. "Don't tell me that you've developed feelings for the pathetic woman who doesn't even have a last name? She's a nobody who no one would miss."

Bartholomew furrowed his brows and shook his head. "That's where I'm afraid you are wrong. Too many people in Missoula like and respect her. She isn't unknown, and there would be an inquest. After what happened here in Butte last October with Patrick Sullivan's daughter, I think you should be cautious before rousing any more interest from the police." Bartholomew's eyes glowed, and he shared a nefarious smile with Samuel. "If your target is truly Colin, then a threat of sedition, from a respectable man such as myself, generally quiets everyone down."

Samuel's expression was serenely doubtful. He watched Bartholomew for long minutes before finally nodding. "So be it. Don't make me act."

～

Colin sat on the settee in Genevieve's small sitting room, holding his nearly six-month-old niece on his lap. He held up a shiny object and laughed when she attempted to grab it. "She's very smart, Genevieve."

Genevieve beamed with pride. "She is. Every day she does something new. I never knew how much I would love being a mother."

Colin smiled at her, noting her rosy cheeks, shiny brown hair and glowing brown eyes. "You were made for it," he teased as he picked up Lizzie and held her high a moment before lowering her. He did that a few times before tucking her into his side. Faint piano notes sounded from the nearby music room.

"Lucas will join us soon," Genevieve said.

"Oh, I'm not worried. I saw him already on this trip. This visit was to see you and my darling niece." He rubbed his nose against Lizzie's. "Yes, darling girl, I consider you my niece, as does Clarissa. You will have your fair share of us loving and protecting you. Which is only right, considering who you're named after. A marvelous woman who loved and protected all she held dear."

Genevieve's eyes filled. "I wish I could have met your aunt Betsy."

Colin nodded. "It's still hard to believe she's been gone for seven years. But her legacy to us was one of love and understanding." He rose and wandered the well-lit room, pausing as he approached a side window that overlooked a tiny side yard and their neighbor's house. "I don't remember this."

Genevieve rose, laughing. "That's because Lucas just had it commissioned six weeks ago, and they finished it last week. With our neighbors' permission of course." Tickling her daughter's foot, she stared out the window with Colin. Their neighbor's wall, devoid of windows, had previously been a plain, boring brick wall. Now a mural of an English rose garden was painted on it. "It is rather whimsical."

Colin kissed Lizzie's head. "He learned Aunt Betsy's lessons well, Genevieve. I imagine growing a real rose garden would be rather difficult in Butte." He shared a smile with the woman he considered cousin.

"It's impossible. I've already tried and failed twice." She became teary eyed as she stared at the mural. "The only thing I'll miss is the beautiful smell of fresh roses in my garden, although Lucas buys them often for me to enjoy inside."

Colin grunted and walked around the room. "Lucas is lucky to have you."

Genevieve sat and watched Colin's restless wanderings around the room with her daughter in his arms. "Why aren't you in Missoula? I've never heard of you leaving your smithy in the middle of the week before. Unless it's a holiday."

He eyed her for any deceit and then asked, "Haven't you heard the news?" At her shrug, he said, "Araminta is to marry another."

Her eyes rounded, and she frowned. "You must stop her. She wants you, Colin. She always has."

"She might have a few years ago, but she hasn't lately. She's besotted with Bartholomew Bouchard, banker and businessman." He speared her with a dour look. "I have plenty of other words that begin with *B* for him." He fought a smile as she giggled.

"Every time we are together, she always knows where you are. She is deeply attuned to you." She bit her lip as her words seemed to cause him distress.

"If she is, it's because she wants to avoid any possible interaction with me." He sighed. "I'm sorry, Genevieve, but I'm rotten company." He kissed baby Lizzie again and handed her to her mother.

Genevieve accepted her daughter but then clung to his hand. "Colin, I know what it is to fear that the person I love can never truly love me. I was wrong, as Araminta is wrong about you. Help her overcome that fear, and you will be happy. More than you ever could have imagined."

~

Bartholomew wandered into one of the over two hundred bars in Butte and paid for a glass of beer. He moved to the side of the small room, leaning against a wall as he sipped his drink. Although a cool wind blew outside, breaking the heat wave, a fine sweat lined his brow.

"Are ye comin' down with somethin' lad?" an Irish miner asked. When Bartholomew shook his head and smiled his thanks at his concern, the man joined his friends and left Bartholomew to his thoughts.

He closed his eyes and fought a fine tremor. The summons to come to Butte had arrived yesterday, and his uncle had believed Bart's yarn about attending to a private commission with an old client. He was adept enough to bluff his way out of having to showcase any newly acquired account from this trip when he returned to Missoula.

The tremor turned into a shiver as he thought about Samuel Sanders. They had met in the early 1900s when the economy was on a roll and when everything they touched seemed to turn to profits. Then it all had tumbled to dust around them, and they had scurried out of New York as fast as possible. Bartholomew to San Francisco and Samuel to God-knows-where. After a few years, Bart had resurrected his reputation and career, masterly portraying himself as the victim in his loss of wealth in 1907, rather than the advisor to clients who lost entire fortunes. After two schemes failed to produce their desired outcome in San Francisco, he had agreed to an exile in Montana at his uncle's bank.

"Goddamn Samuel," he muttered. "He would be in Montana." He took a sip of his drink and then frowned at finding it empty. He had hoped to never see him again after New York and had hoped the announcement of his appointment to his uncle's bank in Missoula had remained local news and beneath Samuel's notice. However, soon after his arrival, he had received a letter, advising him of what was expected of him if he were to continue to have his secrets remain just that.

He jolted as a hand slapped him on his shoulder.

"Bouchard."

He stiffened and stood tall. "Sullivan." He met the irate, wounded blue eyes of Araminta's most ardent admirer. And Samuel's latest target. "What brings you to Butte?"

Colin tilted his head to the side as he studied him. "The same could be asked of you. I have family here, and I wanted to see how my cousin and his baby are. How my brother and his family are." He took in Bartholomew's slightly disheveled state, the frustration glinting in his gaze that he was unable to conceal and his empty glass. "Seems your business isn't to your liking."

"They are quite satisfactory. It just proves how little you know about anything of importance, blacksmith. Perhaps you've spent too long near an anvil."

Colin squinted at him. "I'm not quite sure what you're trying to say with that, but I'm still of sound hearing, sound mind and even sounder judgment, banker."

Bartholomew stood to his full height and met Colin's glare. "Then, if you are, you'll understand that Miss Araminta has made her decision. I hope you are astute enough to respect her choice."

Colin's eyes flashed with pain before he could hide his reaction. "I will never accept that you are good enough for her."

"You will have to because we will marry in October. With or without your blessing." He shared a long stare with Colin for a moment before he pushed past him and out the door, only belatedly realizing he held the bar's glass. He handed it to a man entering the establishment and headed to his hotel, unable to shake the sense that his future was on the verge of unraveling.

CHAPTER 12

a soft insistent knocking on her door roused Araminta out of a daydream. She smiled ruefully. *Or a night dream,* she thought to herself. She rose, opening the door a few inches to determine who visited on a Friday evening. Bartholomew was in Butte on business, and she did not expect to see him until she joined him for Sunday dinner with his family. She glared at the person on the other side of her threshold. "Why are you here?" she whispered, hating the defeated tone of her voice. "I thought you were in Butte."

"Let me in, Ari." A push on the door caused it to creak open, and Colin eased inside. He shut it behind him and paused to look around the room. A comfortable, worn settee was against one wall while two stuffed chairs flanked it. A small table on the opposite wall with wooden chairs formed the tiny dining area while a miniscule kitchen area at the far wall made up the kitchen. A single door led to a tiny bedroom while the bathroom was down the hall.

"You being here doesn't help anything," she said in a low voice. "If someone saw you enter …" Her voice trailed off as she shook her head in resignation.

"If they did, it would only aid my cause." He roamed around, smiling at the small mementos on tabletops. He recognized a colorful rock Rory had so proudly brought home after an afternoon's adventure, a piece of gnarled wood Myrtle had insisted Araminta keep and a photograph of all of them from a few summers ago.

"And what would that be? To completely disgrace me in front of the townspeople?"

He spun to face her, shock and dismay replacing his joy at her eclectic collection. "Never, Ari. I'd never want to cause you pain."

She rolled her eyes at him as she plopped onto a chair. "I'll ask again, Colin. Why are you here?"

His gaze roved over her, taking in her casual dress, a few buttons opened at the collar, with sleeves rolled to her elbows. She'd kicked off her shoes and stockings, and he grinned at seeing her so at home. "I've never seen you this relaxed before. You've always been busy. Taking care of us."

"I saved enough money to afford my own place last year and my privacy," she whispered. "And it's hot tonight."

"Yes. I remember you calling it your refuge." His gaze sharpened as he watched her flush. "I can see why you wanted a place that was wholly yours and had nothing to do with us."

"You make me sound ungrateful for what your family did for me since I left Boston and the orphanage fifteen years ago. I'm not."

Colin sat on the sofa, facing her, his expression earnest as he attempted to conceal his desperation. "I'm not criticizing, Ari. I'm saying, I understand. You wanted a place of your own. As I did. As most people do. And you finally have it. I couldn't be prouder of you." He frowned as his words evoked tears. "What have I done to upset you now?"

He reached a hand out to stroke her cheek, but she leaned away from him. "No, Colin. You had your chance. You need to leave me alone."

"I can't," he whispered, his voice cracking. "Don't ask me to stop caring for you."

She glared at him, her eyes filled with unshed tears as she breathed heavily. "How dare you come to my home and ruin the one place that has always brought me peace?"

He blanched at the sincerity of her words.

"You had your chance. You never took it."

"Ari—"

"You're worse than your nieces and nephews. At least they apologize. At least they acknowledge when they misbehave." She waved her hand at him as she choked back a sob. "But you, you simply act like whatever you want is your right. With no regard to how that hurts those around you."

Colin flushed with anger. "That's patently unfair. And unjust." He paused as he swallowed, his throat working as though he had trouble speaking. "And I pray you don't really mean what you say." He leaned forward, grasping her restless hands. "Ari, I've always loved you. At first, I thought it was like how I loved Rissa. Then I convinced myself it was the way I loved Sav because I knew I didn't love you like a sister. I knew how you viewed yourself, and I never wanted you to think I was taking advantage of you." He played with her fingers. "You became one of my dearest friends, and I dreaded harming that relationship if you didn't feel like I did. Then, that night Lucas performed here in Missoula four years ago, and I held you in my arms ..."

He sighed with absolute contentment. "It was heaven. And then I almost kissed you and ruined everything. You wouldn't talk to me, wouldn't answer any of my questions and wouldn't come to my house unless forced to. I thought you hated me and that I'd destroyed our friendship and any chance I had with you." He paused, staring at her a long moment. "I couldn't stand to see that look in your eyes."

She sniffled. "What look?" she whispered as tears tracked down her cheeks unchecked.

"Every time after I almost kissed you, you looked at me with disdain. Distrust." He sighed as he closed his eyes. "Disgust." He paused. "I should have tried harder to make you see I was sincere. That I wasn't toying with you. That I esteem you above all others." He frowned when he saw her tears soaking the front of her dress. "Even now, even in your distress, you are silent. Why won't you wail? Scream? Beat at me and demand better?" He cupped her cheeks. "Why don't you believe you deserve better? Why don't you believe you deserve *me?*"

She attempted to free herself from his implacable hold but eventually settled and allowed him to scrub at her cheeks and accepted his handkerchief. She swiped at her face and blew her nose. "You're only here now because another is threatening to take away what you think is yours."

His gaze transformed from tenderness to irate in an instant. "Dammit, you know that's not true. I don't see you as an object I own. As something to control or have power over. I see you as ..." His voice faltered. "As my Ari. As the woman I want to grow old with. In a way, I thought we were conducting a long-term courtship."

She wrenched a hand free and punched him lightly in the chest. "No courtship takes fifteen years."

"It does if you're an idiot like me," he murmured. "Don't marry him, Ari." His eyes bored into hers. "Do you want me to beg?" He tucked a strand of hair behind her ear. "Because I will. Please, don't marry him."

She began to cry again and leaned forward, resting her head on his shoulder. He *coo*ed meaningless words in her ear as he stroked his strong hands over her back, shoulder and head, pulling her tighter to him with every caress. She moved to get even closer to him until she sat in a very unladylike manner with her legs wrapped around him in a full-bodied hug. "I can't bear to let you go," she whispered through her tears.

"Then don't," he said into her ear. "I very much want to be snared."

She laughed at his comment before crying some more.

"Why does my love devastate you?"

"You're too late. It's too late," she whispered. She ran her hands over his back as though attempting to memorize the feel of him in her arms and then eased away.

He groaned and clung to her, refusing to release her from his embrace. "I don't care, Ari. I don't care if you've been with him."

She pushed with her head to put space between them, glaring at him. "Why would you think I'd disgrace myself in such a manner? Do you think because of who I am that I have no honor?"

"Ari, arriving to one's marriage untouched is not an indication of whether or not you have honor," he said with a tender smile. He leaned forward and kissed her nose. "It means you've known passion and allowed yourself to act on it."

He frowned when he felt her shudder in his arms, the subtle revulsion she attempted to hide from him. He traced a finger around her eyes, easing her tense expression. "You are honorable, Ari. The actions of others, specifically your parents, have no bearing on you."

She burrowed into his embrace, seeking comfort but also preventing him from seeing her expression. "I've never wanted to be in a position where I'd act like them," she whispered.

He laughed as he ran soothing hands down her back in a modified massage. "You would never be. First, because you would have the fortitude to keep your child. And, second, because all of us would stand by you to support you, to aid you." He kissed her head when she clasped him tighter around the waist. "We'd never allow you to suffer."

She raised wondrous eyes to him and moved forward a fraction, kissing him. Her touch was gentle, barely more than a soft caress of two lips, but he instantly groaned and clasped her even tighter to him.

"Ari," he rasped as he kissed her eyebrows and cheeks. "Careful what you're asking for."

"I know what I want. In this moment, it's you," she whispered. She smiled as he groaned and eased her even closer to him on his lap. "You have no idea how good you feel."

"Oh, I think I do," he teased. "Let me love you, my Ari, as I should have years ago." He paused his fervent kisses to meet her gaze. He let out a deep sigh as she watched him with fathomless light-brown eyes. He closed his eyes and leaned his forehead against hers. "Forgive me for presuming too much. Let me rise and leave you to your evening."

She clung to him like a burr and shook her head. "No, don't leave me. Stay with me. Show me."

"Everything changes, Ari, if I do," Colin said.

"Everything already has changed," she said as she leaned forward for a kiss, this one deeper and more passionate. She arched into his touch, gasping as he eased callused fingers under her light cotton dress. "I never knew ..." she whispered as she broke from his kiss and tilted her head to the side as he kissed her along her neck.

"Never knew what?" he whispered as his hands worked to free her upper body from her clothes.

"I never knew how a touch could feel so good and so inadequate, all at once." She bit back a shriek as he dropped his head and nibbled along her shoulder and then her collarbone.

"Don't hide from me, Ari," he murmured, his breaths emerging in deep pants. "Show me what pleases you."

She pushed at his shoulders, and he eased away, his light-blue eyes lit with a fire for her. She ran fingers over his cheeks and then up again into his hair. "I never..." She swallowed and fought tears. "I never thought to have this with you. I thought you'd want a woman of standing in town."

His expression changed to one of incredulity. "*You* are a woman of standing. You are everything I have ever wanted." He pushed her away and stood, holding his arms out to his side for a moment. "I'm going about this all wrong." He took a deep breath and let it out, but the passion in his gaze remained. "Show me what you want." When she remained in a disheveled state on the sofa, he murmured again, "Show me."

She rose on trembling legs, her hands shooting to the hem of her dress. When she saw the veiled disappointment in his gaze, she dropped her hands, allowing her dress to hang at her waist. Only a thin chemise covered her as she had foregone a corset on this hot evening.

His fingers twitched, as though wanting to caress her, but he kept his hands at his sides.

"You'll think me brazen."

He smiled. "I want you bold and shameless." His gaze roved over her, as loving as any caress. "I want you to feel as free to express what you feel for me as I want to show you how much I love you." He saw her eyes flash at his declaration. "Be brave, my Ari."

"Do you truly not care that I have no last name? That my parents discarded me like rubbish on the orphanage doorstep?"

His jaw ticked at how she described herself. "You are not rubbish," he declared. "You are cherished. Your parents acted in such a way as to provide you with the best life they knew how for you. And they gave me the greatest gift. You." He took a step forward and then froze. "I'm on the verge of breaking my vow, Ari."

A wondrous smile spread as she saw Colin, a strong, independent, intelligent man standing in front of her as he waited for her to act. "I want you," she whispered.

She gasped as he grabbed her and yanked her to him. He held her in a fierce grip, nearly squeezing all the air out of her.

"*Shh*, love," she whispered as he shook in her arms. "I'm here. I'll always be here."

"Don't marry him, Ari. Please," he begged. "Not when we love each other."

She took his head between her hands and stood on her toes, kissing him deeply. As they kissed, her hands worked to slip his buttons loose, and soon he shucked off his waistcoat and shirt. She gasped and backed up a step as her fingers played in his chest hair. "I never imagined," she whispered as she ran her hands over his chest, watching his reaction as he jerked at her soft caresses. "Does my touch hurt you?"

"No, it feels too good," he whispered. "Ari, may I … may I remove your shift?" He met her momentarily startled look before she backed up a step.

She wriggled out of the bottom half of her dress and then stood in front of him in only her shift.

"If I remove this, there's no going back," he said, his fingers moving up and down the valley between her breasts.

"I don't want to go back. Be mine, Colin," she said as Colin leaned forward to kiss her breasts through the thin linen. She held her arms up as he tugged the fine cotton off her, revealing her fully to his gaze.

He dropped the shift and grabbed her hands before she could cover herself. "You are a man's fantasy." He raised covetous eyes to hers and tugged her closer to him. "You're my fantasy." He groaned as she rubbed against his chest. "Come, love. Let me love you."

"Yes, and teach me how to love you in equal measure," she said, and she lost herself in his kiss as they backed toward her bedroom.

~

Colin lay with a slumbering Araminta in his arms. He felt her stir, and he kissed her head. "*Shh*, love," he murmured as she stiffened in his arms. "It wasn't a dream."

"Colin?" she asked, her head bumping his as she raised hers to meet his loving, amused gaze. "I thought … I thought it must have been."

"When's the last time you went to bed without a stitch of clothing on?" he teased and then laughed when she hit him on his arm.

"*Shh*, you can't make much noise, or the neighbors will know you are here. I don't want to be evicted." Araminta settled her head on his chest, her fingers playing with his chest hair.

"It won't matter. Soon enough you will live with me." He felt her stiffen in his arms, and he tilted his head down in an attempt to see her expression. "Ari? What did I say?"

"Why would I live with you?" Her voice was breathless, and she shied away from his caress to her cheek.

"I want my wife to live with me. I refuse to sneak over to your house, when I have a perfectly good home for us to share."

"Your wife?" She perched herself on his chest, and he saw her luminous wide eyes in a shaft of light.

"Of course. What do you think this was all about?" He ran his knuckles over her cheeks. "I want to marry you. To build a life with you. To have children with you. As we should have done years ago. Will you marry me?"

A delighted smile bloomed, but she shook her head. "I can't agree to marry you when I'm still engaged to another man. You'll have to ask me again." She swallowed a shriek of laughter as he tickled her and rolled her over.

"I never knew you were such a flirt. Do you know how hard it is for a man to ask a woman to marry him?" He saw absolute joy in her eyes and smiled. "I'd ask you a hundred times, as long as you became my wife, Ari."

She leaned up and kissed him. "Love me again, Colin."

He growled as he kissed her, his hands roving over her. When she fought, and failed, to hide a grimace at one of his caresses, he rolled away. "No, I refuse to hurt you, Ari. It's too soon. There will be plenty of time for us for future lovemaking." He smiled as he saw the disappointment in her gaze. "For now, let me hold you. That will be enough."

"As long as I know our nights to come will be filled with passion," she whispered, kissing his shoulder.

He chuckled. "My bold Ari. You are my fantasy come to life."

Araminta stood outside Bartholomew Bouchard's office and clasped her shaking hands together. She frowned at her inability to conceal her emotions. Before Colin's visit last night, she had had no difficulty hiding her deepest desires and feelings. She took a deep breath before knocking on the door.

"Enter," his low-pitched voice intoned. He looked up from a stack of papers in front of him as she opened the door, and he smiled when he saw her. He rose at her entrance and motioned for her to sit. "It does me good to see you eager to visit me on my return from Butte. I hadn't hoped to see you until tomorrow. Alas, the deal did not go as planned, but I made a good contact."

His engaging smile faded as he belatedly noted her desire to put distance between them and her reticence to kiss his cheek. His smile faltered further when she shook her head and remained standing and away from him.

"Araminta, why are you here?" He frowned as she took in a deep breath. "Are you all right? What's happened? Nothing can be as bad as all this." His attempt at cajoling a smile from her failed, and his frown deepened.

"I wanted to thank you for the honor you gave me by asking me to be your wife. However, after further consideration, I've come to realize that it would not be a good decision for me. I believe we are not well suited."

He moved around to stand in front of his desk, less than an arm's-reach from her. "Why are you filled with fear now, Araminta? We are suited. We share the same beliefs and dreams." He glowered when she flinched away from his touch.

She shook her head, shuddering slightly. "I was mistaken to accept your offer. I should have had faith and said no."

He glared at her with anger, his concern evaporating with her insistence they not wed. "Are you telling me that you are to receive a better offer than the one I'm giving you?"

She stiffened and stood her ground. "Yes." She met his irate gaze and refused to cower even as his expression darkened.

"So it doesn't matter to you that I love you?"

She softened at his quiet, plaintive words. "Bartholomew, I will always be honored that you care for me. But it wouldn't be right to marry you. It would be deceitful."

He took a deep breath and shook his head. "I'm afraid you don't understand, Araminta. You will marry me in October." He snagged her hand, tethering her in place. "For many reasons, we will wed." He tugged her to him, cradling her in his arms even though she stood as stiff as a board. He whispered in her ear the varied reasons for their marriage to occur. When he'd finished, he stroked her cheek and met her devastated gaze. "So you see? We *will* marry."

"I ... I ..." A tear slipped out of one eye and cascaded down her cheek. She stood immobile as he caressed it away. "We will be miserable."

"Only until you forget the blacksmith. It won't take long. I can be very persuasive," he soothed. His severe expression met hers. "Don't defy me, Araminta. Marry me come October 5, or I cannot make any promises about protecting you and those you claim to care for."

She took in a stuttering breath. "You've told me what you require. I need you to promise me that you won't do anything to harm him," Araminta said. "Promise me you won't hurt Colin. Or any of the McLeods."

Bartholomew's grip of her jaw was just shy of bruising in its intensity. "I want your vow that you will endeavor to love me."

She blinked, but her tears poured out. "I will try."

He nodded, releasing her. "As long as you stay true to your word, I see no reason to use the knowledge I have." He pushed her toward the door, and she lurched before she caught her balance. "Go. I have important matters to attend to."

Araminta's fingers slipped from the doorknob before she finally grasped it and yanked it open, fleeing the room. She stood outside, her back against the door, shaking at the realization of the bargain she had just struck.

~

Araminta remained frozen outside Colin's house, her basket on one arm and the other raised to knock. She shook her head and used the key in her pocket as she always did when she came to his house to clean or to prepare for a gathering with the family. She slipped inside and moved to the kitchen. After opening a window, she prepared a simple meal. She sniffled as she battled tears. When long arms snaked around her middle, she shrieked and dropped her paring knife into the sink, barely missing cutting herself. "Colin!"

She wriggled until she'd freed herself from his embrace and spun to face him. Before she could speak, he'd lowered his head and kissed her. She groaned and attempted to not react to his touch. However, his gentle kiss coaxed a response, and she flung her arms around his neck, pulling him tighter.

He growled as he broke the kiss, peppering her neck with kisses as he spun her around and backed her away from the sink and toward his bedroom. She arched into him, bowing back even further when his mouth momentarily covered her corseted and cloth-covered breast. "Colin!" she cried out, tangling her fingers in his hair.

He grunted as he pushed her onto his freshly made bed. "I need you, Ari," he whispered into her neck. "Tell me you need me too." He raised luminous eyes and stilled as he studied her. "Ari?" he asked, his fingers suddenly shaking as he stroked her tear-drenched cheeks. "I'd never mean to scare you."

He pushed himself off her and moved to her side. He continued to run a soothing hand over her shoulder and arm, and watched her with confusion. "Forgive me. After last night I want you more than ever." His gaze was tender and loving as he watched her attempt to compose herself. "I promised myself I wouldn't jump on you like a ravening beast, and yet that's exactly what I did."

Her tears continued to pour, and he frowned. "Ari?" He brushed hair away from her forehead. "Talk to me."

She sighed and leaned into his touch a moment, curling onto her side to move into his embrace. She froze when she realized what she was doing. She slid away from him and kept her gaze downcast.

He gripped her elbow, stalling her slow slide away from him and out of the bed. "Ari. Please don't cry. Your tears, your pain devastates me." He whispered on a broken breath, "I never meant to hurt you, my love."

She raised her eyes to see his concerned gaze, his eyes shimmering in tears. "I can't do this, Colin. Last night was … a mistake." His hand on her arm tightened as though he'd been physically harmed and needed to hold on to an anchor to prevent losing his place in the world.

He scooted closer to her, raising his hands to cup her face. "How can you say that, Ari? Finally we were honest with each other." He searched her gaze, his eyes roving desperately for some sign of hope. "You know how much I love you. I showed you how much I love you. Don't do this!"

"That's the problem, Colin," she whispered, refusing to meet his gaze. "I don't love you. I thought I did, but I was caught up in the moment, the novelty of what I was feeling. I never have loved you, and I never will." She gasped as he gripped her face and forced her to look at him. She bit her lip at his incredulous stare. "I thought I felt more for you than I would a kind brother or cousin, but last night showed me I was mistaken."

"Ari, I know I caused you pain, but that's because it was your first time. Let me show you …"

She covered his mouth with both her hands, her fingers twitching as though they wanted to caress his cheeks and swipe at a tear that had fallen. "No, Colin. I desire nothing more from you than to be allowed to leave this bed and to make supper for the horde that will descend in a few hours."

He released her, any joy in his eyes replaced by disdain. "Get out of my bed. Get out of my house. Go to Rissa's. Have the gathering there. I don't want you here. I never want you here again."

"Colin, nothing has to change between us," Araminta protested as she pushed herself upright.

"Everything has changed." He glared at her before sitting with stooped shoulders and bowed head on his bed. "And nothing will make it right again."

~

Clarissa heard the clattering of pots and pans in her kitchen and frowned. She looked to Geraldine to watch her siblings and poked her head into the kitchen. "Minta! What are you doing here? I thought we were to have the gathering at Colin's." She frowned when she saw Araminta's shoulders shake.

She moved into the kitchen, the swinging door closing behind her. "Minta?" she whispered, touching her friend lightly on the shoulder. She put gentle pressure on Araminta so that she turned to face her. "Oh my," she breathed as the tears poured down Araminta's face at the sorrow she was unable to contain. "What happened?"

"Colin. … he … he … I didn't want …" Her words came out in stuttered fragments. "And then, on his bed, … and he …" She could say no more, her words drowned out by her sobs.

Clarissa froze, her mind returning to a long-distant sitting room. A sunny room in late afternoon with a yellow settee and the overwhelming scent of bay rum. The terror and torment, the devastating hopelessness as she was overpowered. She shook her head to clear her mind of her memories and focused on Araminta. "Are you harmed?"

"I just want to forget," Araminta cried, her tears soaking Clarissa's shoulder.

"I promise you that things will get better. Gabriel and I will endeavor to keep you safe," Clarissa soothed. She rocked Araminta in her arms until she calmed.

Araminta pushed away, flushing. "You are the last person I should complain to. You will always take Colin's side." At Colin's name, a few tears poured out. "I should continue to work on dinner."

"Minta, consider this dinner canceled. Go home." Clarissa took a deep breath. "Do you want me to have the doctor called?"

Confusion clouded Araminta's gaze, but she declined with a shake of her head.

"If you are certain, then go home and rest. I'll be by to see you later." She pulled Araminta into a tight embrace a moment before forcing herself to release her.

After Araminta had left and Gabriel returned home for the evening, Clarissa stormed over to Colin's nearby house. Gabriel's kiss goodbye with the whispered, "Guard your temper," only added fuel to her anger. "*Guard my temper*," she hissed. "As though he'll ever understand ..."

She burst through Colin's unlocked door, slamming it shut behind her. Moving through the living and dining rooms, to the kitchen and back bedrooms, she paused to find him lying on his bed, a hand over his heart. He stared morosely at the ceiling. "How could you?" she shrieked. "How could you?" she asked again, her voice breaking.

Colin raised his head, studying his sister in confusion. "How could I not? It's been coming for fifteen years, Rissa." He took a deep breath. "She's just scared now because she doesn't know what to do with her feelings."

"You saw how I suffered. You saw what it took me to get over ... get over ... and yet you ..." She shook her head as tears poured out.

Colin frowned, his dull grief momentarily replaced by incredulity and then anger. "What?" He pushed himself up and faced his sister. "What do you think I did?" When she sputtered at him, he shook her shoulders. "Tell me."

She pushed on his chest with both of her palms, propelling him back a step. "You forced her! How could you?"

An irate flush rose on his cheeks. "How could you ever imagine I would act in such a way?" He watched her with scorn masking his deep disappointment and hurt. "Why would you even think it?"

Clarissa's chin rose in defiance. "Araminta was sobbing in my arms this afternoon, babbling incoherently about being forced into your bed. About only wanting to forget." She glared at him. "Tell me that you didn't touch her."

"I can't," Colin rasped. "I did touch her. But I can swear she desired my touch." He paled when Clarissa shied away from him when he attempted to clasp her hand. "Jesus. You don't believe me. Me! Your brother who raced across the country with you so you wouldn't have to bind yourself to that monster." He took another step back from Clarissa. "I remember what you went through. I saw you suffer." He closed his eyes a moment. "How can you, Rissa?"

The heartbreak in his voice caused Rissa to throw back her shoulders in defiance. "I saw Minta, Colin. She was devastated." Her haunted gaze met his.

"Not every devastation is due to cruelty," he snapped. "Think, Rissa. Do you truly believe I would do such a thing? Me, Colin?" At her persistent glare, he backed away from her until he bumped into a wall. "I can't believe you."

"Stay away from my house and my children," she ordered.

Colin groaned and fell to sit on the edge of his bed as she spun and ran out of his house.

~

That evening, a soft light shone from the bedside table lamp, casting long shadows and a gentle glow on the room. Clarissa sat at her vanity, stroking her long chestnut-colored hair.

Gabriel sat in the window seat he had constructed a few years ago, his gaze speculative. "What did you do?" When Clarissa started at his question, he sighed. "I know you did something, or you wouldn't attempt to brush your hair a thousand times to avoid talking with me."

"I fought with Colin." She set down her brush and turned to face Gabriel. At his patient silence, she sighed. "And I acted a fool."

Gabriel chuckled. "I was the fool to encourage you to hold your temper. Should have known it would only make you more irate." He sobered. "Apologize tomorrow. He'll forgive you."

Clarissa shook her head. "I said unforgivable things. Made such horrid accusations."

Gabriel frowned. "He knows you, Rissa. He'll give you a hard time, but I know he won't want to endanger his close relationship with you." When she shook her head, her gaze filled with doubt, his brows furrowed. "What did you say?"

She flushed with embarrassment. "I accused him of forcing Araminta." At Gabriel's incredulous stare, she shrugged. "She cried incoherently in my arms, and all I could think of was that room. Of being overpowered by Cameron. Of having no choice." She shuddered as she focused on Gabriel and allowed his loving gaze to ground her in the present. "I was irrational and terrified, and lashed out in fear."

"That's not something you falsely accuse a man of, Rissa," Gabriel said, rubbing at his temple.

Clarissa swiped at her cheeks. "I know. And I know Colin didn't hurt her. After I returned home, I thought through my conversation with Minta. She seemed confused that I'd think she needed a doctor." She bent forward and covered her face with her hands, her hair sweeping down to brush against the floor. "Colin's heartbroken. Araminta has broken with him, and now I've destroyed my relationship with my brother."

"All in a matter of one day," Gabriel breathed. "Make at least one thing right again. Talk with Colin, Rissa."

~

C larissa stood outside Colin's door the next day and knocked. She knew he'd be home, as it was Sunday, but there was no answer. She tried the door, but it was locked. She sighed, pulling out her key but then frowned when her key no longer fit the lock. She banged on the front door. "Colin!"

When he didn't answer, she leaned her head against the wood a moment before spinning to return home. Gabriel played with the children in the living room and would soon venture to a nearby park with them. She shook her head at his worried expression, and she saw him frown. "I need to speak with Araminta." At his nod, she kissed him on his forehead and departed for downtown Missoula.

She crossed the bridge, with the large Clark Fork River separating downtown from her neighborhood. She glanced up, the peaks of the Rattlesnake Mountains visible over the haze of smog that clung to the city and hid the low-lying hills on this still day. The large brick Missoula Mercantile did a bustling business on the street corner of Front and Higgins. She nodded to acquaintances and smiled at patrons she recognized from the library. The streets were crowded with wagons, carts, streetcars and automobiles. When she reached Pine Street, she turned right and walked a few more blocks.

She knocked on Araminta's door, attempting a confident smile when Araminta answered and motioned for her to enter. She wandered around, smiling at the small mementos. "I love your home, Minta. I'm sorry it's taken me a year to finally visit you here."

"Thank you. We're always at your home, and you're busy with the library and your children." She stared at Clarissa for a long moment. "Why are you here? I don't have long before I must meet Mr. Bouchard."

Clarissa watched her closely for a long moment. "I'm surprised you are going to marry him." When Araminta remained silent and studied Clarissa, she plopped onto a chair with a sigh. "I tried to speak with Colin today. I fear he'll never forgive me."

Araminta frowned with confusion. "Why wouldn't he forgive you? You've never been at odds."

Clarissa's laugh lacked humor. "I'm afraid that's where you are wrong. I accused him of hurting you, Minta. Of forcing you to be with him. When I calmed down from my rage and fear, I knew I'd been wrong. But, by then, it was too late."

"What did he say when you spoke with him?" Araminta whispered, sinking onto a chair facing Clarissa.

"He said he'd never forced you." She paused, seeing Araminta's agreement with that statement. "He said you were afraid of how you feel and that you needed time to overcome your fear." Clarissa rubbed at her head. "However, he's changed his lock and won't answer the door. I'll have to wait until tomorrow to inform him I was wrong and that he's not barred from my house."

"You barred him from your house? From seeing the children?" Araminta's eyes widened at that. She lowered her head a moment as she remained lost in thought. "I would appreciate it, if for my sake alone, if you'd ensure he's not allowed at your house until I'm married."

Clarissa gasped and shook her head. "You don't know what you're asking me to do. Being estranged from Colin for a day is too long. I can't imagine a few months."

Araminta swallowed. "I know what I ask. I ask that you grant me this boon after years of service to your family. I can't see him. I can't speak with him. If I know I can come and go from your house without the worry of running into him, I can continue to work for you. If not, I'll have to find another position." She raised determined eyes to Clarissa. "I will marry Bartholomew Bouchard, and seeing Colin will only make things more difficult. For him. And for me."

Clarissa sank against the back of the chair, deflated at the request. "I must discuss this with Gabriel, as it also affects him." She ran a hand over her hair. "Why were you with Colin when you knew you'd marry Mr. Bouchard? It makes no sense to me."

Araminta rose, grabbing her purse. "Not everything in life must make sense. I will do what I have to." She bit her lip and shook her head. "I must go. I'm sorry we can't have a longer discussion."

Clarissa rose, reaching out to grab Araminta's hand before she could storm from her own home. "Minta, I will try to do what you ask." Her eyes filled with tears. "With Savannah gone to Boston and now Colin lost to me, I don't know what I'll do." She took a steadying breath and focused on Araminta. "But what worries me as well is why you're acting like you are. You have the love of a good man in Colin. He'll support you in anything and everything, something few women are fortunate to have. Why would you spurn him?"

Araminta wrenched her hand from Clarissa's gentle hold and bolted for the door. "You'd never understand," she said and burst through the door, leaving Clarissa behind in her living area.

After a few moments, Clarissa departed for home, lost in thought. When she arrived, she encouraged Geraldine, Myrtle and Billy to play outside in the fresh air. Little Colin was asleep upstairs for his afternoon nap. Gabriel watched her as she sat in quiet contemplation.

"What is it, love?" Gabriel murmured.

"Minta wanted me to promise that we'd not welcome Colin into our home until after her wedding to Mr. Bouchard." She raised tormented eyes to Gabriel. "I don't know how I can agree to her demand."

Gabriel sighed, kicking out his legs in front of him. "We want Minta to feel comfortable here. If that is what she requests, I'm afraid we must honor it. However, that doesn't mean you can't attempt to make peace with Colin before the wedding."

"He changed the locks." She shook her head. "He doesn't want anything to do with me."

At her mystified expression he sighed. "You accused him of a horrible act, Rissa. He's angry and hurt, like a wounded bear. You might want to wait a few days before you approach him again."

~

Araminta sat at the dining room table next to Bartholomew as Mrs. Bouchard, Mrs. Vaughan, their spouses, children and friends gossiped over Sunday dinner. She smiled at Mrs. Bouchard, who beamed at her before passing her a bowl of roasted potatoes. After taking a few and passing the bowl to Bartholomew, she picked at the food on her plate. It was underseasoned while the meat had been boiled to the point it was as tough as leather.

She flinched when Mrs. Vaughan spoke in a booming voice. "It's appalling, reading about those who refuse to support the war effort. It's bad enough there are those who don't support food conservation. Can you imagine the stories we have to read every week about the cafés and restaurants who are in defiance of Meatless Tuesday and Wheatless Wednesday?" She shook her head. Her ensemble today was nearly fashionable, had in not been for the bright sheen on the turquoise fabric that caused any light to ricochet off it and blind those who beheld her.

"It makes one want to keep a list and to boycott those establishments," Mrs. Bouchard said.

Araminta watched them with curiosity at their hypocrisy as she'd been at their homes and seen them in defiance of both suggestions in the past weeks. She looked around the table to see if anyone would remark on it and remained silent when she saw only nods of agreement.

"I should think they'd be brought in front of the council," Bartholomew said. "Although it's only a suggestion and not a formal ration rule." He shook his head in disappointment. "It's unfortunate they're only intent on prosecuting those who are guilty of sedition. Many more are just as guilty."

Araminta choked on her small bite of food. "Those poor people have done little to earn such censure and convictions." She tensed when Bartholomew frowned at her.

One of Bartholomew's friends guffawed. "I imagine their neighbors are thankful they've been convicted."

Araminta stilled as she watched his friend in horror. "No one would be so cruel as to accuse someone merely to gain their property."

He shrugged nonchalantly. "I would, especially if they had a successful farm or ranch. It would save a lot of time, money and lawyer fees."

Araminta gaped at him and those around the table who nodded at his reasoning. "But you're ruining someone's life."

Mrs. Bouchard snickered. "They shouldn't have been stupid enough to speak out against the war effort. We don't need those with treasonous thoughts in this country."

"Everyone must be a patriot," Araminta murmured, her brows furrowing.

Mrs. Bouchard beamed at her. "Exactly. I'm delighted our Bartholomew has found such an intelligent woman who is a hard worker."

"I'd do it for a good business," said Vernon Vaughan, Bartholomew's cousin. "It would reduce startup costs, and the business would already have a good reputation in the community."

Araminta watched as Bartholomew nodded, a calculating look in his eyes. She gripped his hand on his lap and whispered, "Remember your promise."

He looked down at her and nodded. "As long as you remember yours."

She paled and broke away from his penetrating gaze, looking at her plate of unpalatable food. She feigned a smile when his aunts prattled about the wedding in October and the important out-of-state guests coming for the event.

"Of course those wretched McLeods must be invited as they are perceived as important members of Missoula society," Mrs. Vaughan muttered. "If I had my way, they wouldn't be allowed near a church after what they did to my darling daughter, Veronica."

"Now, sister, you know Veronica is doing quite well for herself in Seattle," Mrs. Bouchard soothed.

"She should be married with a gaggle of children," Mrs. Vaughan boomed. "Those meddling McLeods ruined everything for her." She pointed her fork in Bartholomew's and Araminta's direction. "I won't countenance them interfering in your nuptials."

"Of course not," Araminta murmured. "There's no reason for them to."

Her soothing voice went unheard by the mostly deaf Mrs. Vaughan, and her complaints about the McLeods continued until Mrs. Bouchard turned the topic to the wedding feast. Araminta allowed the conversation to flow over her as she conceded all decisions to Bartholomew and his aunts.

After dinner, Bartholomew walked her home. She attempted a brisk pace, but he held her back with his slower gait. "Araminta, I need you to ensure that everything will go as planned for the wedding."

She fought a grimace and smiled. "Of course it will. I will meet you at the altar and bind myself to you."

He growled and pushed her into a shadowed alley. "You don't have to sound so eager," he said, pressing against her. "What have I done to earn such animosity from you? I'm willing to provide you with my name, my home, my future." He raked his gaze over her forlorn expression. "My love."

She blinked as she fought tears. "I have given you my word, Bartholomew. Don't ask for more than that." She stilled as he kissed her, accepting his kiss but not reacting to it.

"Why will you no longer respond to me? What must I do to earn your passion?" He looked into her eyes before stepping away. "Will he always be between us?"

"You know the answer to that question," she said, pushing past him and onto the main street. She reluctantly linked her arm through his as he matched her rapid pace through town. "You knew the price of my agreement to your bargain."

He shook his head. "I never realized it would be so severe."

CHAPTER 13

With the hint of autumn in the air in early September, Gabriel and Clarissa opted to warm themselves by a fire in their living room rather than sit on their front porch. Gabriel relaxed in his comfortable chair in the living room with Clarissa near him on the settee while the children sat at the dining room table working on their ledgers. A sweet silence pervaded after the children's grumbling about wasting precious daylight had abated, and Gabriel glanced in their direction to see them focused on their homework. He winked at Clarissa, who smiled as though they were coconspirators. Their youngest had just gone to sleep upstairs.

He knew Clarissa feigned contentment, but her ongoing conflict with Colin was wearing her out. Colin refused any overtures from her, did not answer his front door and turned his back on her when she visited his blacksmith shop. Although Gabriel understood Colin's initial right to his anger, his ire at his brother-in-law steadily grew as his wife's silent suffering increased.

Gabriel focused on the newspaper again. He stilled, his momentary contentedness dissipating. "Damn," he whispered. He glanced in his children's direction and sighed with relief that it appeared they had not heard him.

Clarissa set aside her book and focused on him. "What is it?"

"Have you read this evening's paper?"

"If you mean, have I seen that Jeanette Rankin is running for the Senate, yes, I have." She smiled at her husband. "I hope she wins. I'll have to see what I can do to canvass for her here in Missoula."

"I wouldn't think winning in Missoula would be her greatest concern." He shook his head and lowered his voice further. "They're expanding the draft."

She stilled, and her breath caught.

"To include men up to age forty-five."

"No, … I … Not you." She blinked rapidly and grabbed his hand. "You can't register. I can't lose you."

"And I can't be accused of being a slacker or of being in favor of sedition. I won't go to jail, Rissa." His eyes wild with anger, fear and remorse met hers. "I have to register." He traced her cheek and waited until she nodded.

"All of you, all who I thought safe because you were too old to be drafted, are now in danger," she whispered.

"Patrick and Sebastian are safe. They're old enough." He raised her hand and kissed it. "I just turned forty-four, so I'm considered young enough. I'll be considered in Class II with a temporary deferment because I have dependents under age sixteen. But, if they need me, they will draft me."

"*Colin*," she choked. "They'll draft him right away."

His eyes mirrored her sorrow. "Yes." He cleared his throat. "Registration day is September 14. The Council of Defense has issued Order Number 14, stating that the saloons can be closed that day to ease the burden of registration."

Clarissa attempted a laugh, but it came out as a stifled sob. "I'd think they'd open more bars, so that men could have a drink before and after registering."

"*Shh*, love. You wouldn't want anyone to hear such talk," Gabriel whispered.

"I hate that all I can do is pray that this horrible war ends. That there's nothing more I can do." She turned her head and kissed his palm cupping her cheek.

"I hope simply a show of strength will cause the Germans to realize we are only just beginning to send men over to France. That this will provoke them to want a cease-fire." He sighed. "I know that sounds idealistic, but I have to hope, after four years of war, they're tired of it."

"Men seem to relish it," Clarissa said, unable to hide the bitterness in her voice.

"Not all men, darling," Gabriel murmured. "What did you learn in your letters today?"

"Savannah enjoyed Newport after they shunned society there. And I had a long letter from Zee. She and Teddy appear to be fully reconciled, and she sounds happy for the first time in over a year. Did you know that one of the main reasons Teddy was reluctant to become an American citizen was that he was afraid the Americans would draft him? Even with his injuries?"

Gabriel raised his eyebrows at that. "I doubt we would have, but I can see why he wouldn't want to make a drastic change until the war was over."

Clarissa nodded. "Amelia wrote and attempted to be her usual cheerful self." She frowned as she met her husband's worried gaze. "She hasn't had word from Nicholas in weeks, and she's terrified something's happened to him." Clarissa glanced at her children. "I feel so guilty to be thankful they're too young to be involved in this war."

"I don't. I'm damned grateful." He leaned forward and gave her a soft kiss before rising. "Who needs help?" he called out as he approached their eldest children. He laughed at something Billy said before pulling up a chair and tugging Billy onto his lap. At eight, Billy was almost too big to sit on his lap, but Gabriel relished these moments with his children. Generally Clarissa helped them with their homework, but tonight he would do what he could.

"No, Billy, love, the Pythagorean theorem is not related to the extinction of the dinosaurs." He winked at his eldest, Geraldine, who was attempting to use the theorem.

"But, Papa, it sounds like a dinosaur name." Billy squirmed on Gabriel's lap and turned frustrated eyes up to his father.

Gabriel bit his lip and furrowed his brows to hide a laugh and smile, as he knew this was important to his son. "I know it does, Billy, but not everything has to do with dinosaurs."

"Can we visit Uncle Colin? He told the best stories about dinosaurs and the beasts that roam the forests." Billy's eyes shone with anticipation, as though he were about to hop down and don his shoes for the short trip to his uncle's house.

"No more talk of beasts, Billy, or your sisters won't sleep tonight," Clarissa called out from the living room. She shared an amused glance with Gabriel as Billy was the one who suffered from nightmares, not his sisters. "And your uncle remains too occupied for a visit."

Billy stared at his parents, and his shoulders stooped as he curled into his father's hold. "I hate not seeing Uncle Colin."

Gabriel kissed his head. "I know, Billy. I know."

∼

G abriel joined the line of men who waited to register for the draft, or the Selective Service, as President Wilson liked to call it. Gabriel peered around the stout man in front of him and saw four tables set up against a wall with women seated behind them, filling out a card full of information for each man seated across the desk from her. An American flag hung on one wall, while Montana's state flag hung on the other. Bright sunlight shone in through the bank of windows behind the women at the desks.

He inched forward, his hat in his hands. Most men smiled and appeared excited to be called up to register. He wondered how much of that was an act to assuage the eagle eyes of all watching the steady flow of men in and out of the room. No one wanted to be accused of not fully supporting the war effort.

Finally it was his turn. He rattled off his full name, date of birth and permanent address.

The woman ticked the White box for his race. "Where were you born?" the woman asked as she peered at him over her glasses.

"Boston, Massachusetts." He frowned as she *X*'d the Native-Born US Citizen box.

"Your occupation and employer?"

"Cabinetmaker. Self-employed." He gave her his business address on Main Street.

"Name your two nearest relatives and where they live."

He paused as he momentarily envisioned Clarissa and Jeremy receiving word of his demise and then shook his head as he gave their names and addresses. He frowned as the form was thrust at him to sign. He glanced at the other half of the form that the registrar had to fill out about him, pausing before he signed his side. He saw he'd been declared tall, with a medium build and gray hair and brown eyes. "I beg your pardon, ma'am, but I have blue eyes."

She glowered at him, yanking the form back to correct that detail. "If you believe eye color will determine if you are drafted, you're crazy." She nodded at him to sign, and he did.

"Thank you, ma'am," he murmured as he rose. He stilled when he saw Colin in the line. Gabriel's jaw clenched as he moved past the waiting men. Rather than returning to his workshop, he leaned against the building outside. A few cars rumbled by on the street, although the majority of the traffic remained horse-and-buggy and horse-drawn wagons.

After nearly twenty minutes, Colin emerged.

"Colin." Gabriel frowned as Colin stiffened at his voice. "Wait."

"There's nothing for us to say," Colin said with his back to him.

Gabriel grabbed his arm and spun Colin to face him. He flushed as curious men eyed them as they entered and exited the building. "Come to my workshop, so we can talk privately."

After a long moment, Colin nodded and walked beside Gabriel. Once at the workshop, Gabriel waved to Ronan, who worked on a pair of shoes. Gabriel shut the front door behind him and faced the man he considered his brother. He watched as Colin stood with aloof detachment, ignoring Ronan.

Gabriel had owned and worked in this workshop since his arrival in Missoula in 1901. Along Main Street, the shop had a large door with a window on either side. Upon entering the shop, Ronan's cobbling business was to the right with a staircase along the back end of that wall that led to a storage area over the workshop. Before it was a storage area, Gabriel had lived there with Clarissa for the first years of their marriage. Throughout the workshop, there were workbenches, small stacks of lumber and pieces of furniture in varying stages of completion. Gabriel ignored everything around him and focused on his brother-in-law.

"Why are you acting like this?" Gabriel demanded. He saw a momentary glint of anger in Colin's eyes before he stared at Gabriel impassively. "Do you not care what your silence is doing to your sister?"

"I write Melinda. I enjoy hearing about her adventures in Newport and Boston."

Gabriel growled and took a menacing step toward Colin. "Dammit, you know I meant Rissa."

Colin's icy gaze bore into Gabriel. "Why should I care how she feels? How she fares? I already know the depths of her disdain."

Gabriel sighed and gripped the back of his neck. "Who did you put on your form?" He saw understanding glint in Colin's gaze.

"Patrick and Lucas."

The fight left Gabriel as suddenly as it had erupted, and he collapsed onto a chair. "Why won't you speak with her? Allow her to apologize?"

Colin's eyes glowed with anger, and his icy disregard cracked as he stared at his beloved brother-in-law. "Forgive her? Forgive her for thinking I would ever harm Ari? Or any woman? Or should I suddenly forget that she thought I'd be a danger to her children too?" His breath emerged in agitated pants. "Am I still barred from your house?"

"Colin, it's not that simple," Gabriel said, his tone world-weary. "Minta ..."

Colin waved at Gabriel to quiet him as he was about to say more.

242

"And even if I were inclined to forgive, how could I ever pardon the fact that Clarissa has worked to keep me separated from Ari? I can't visit Ari at her home. I can't speak with Ari at your home because you've barred me. You've formed a little oasis to keep me out. You tell me, Gabe, how you'd feel if someone had come between you and Clarissa the way my own sister has come between me and Ari?" His jaw ticked. "You'd hate her as you hate Mrs. Smythe."

Gabriel blanched. "You can't, … not like that." He shook his head. "You don't understand, Col. Our hands are tied. Araminta …"

Colin's eyes flashed with an agonizingly deep pain at her full name. "She will be lost to me soon. Because her fear is stronger than her courage. And I will always resent you and Clarissa for not challenging her. For allowing her to feed that fear. For granting her a safe harbor rather than forcing her to face me." He spun and stormed out of the workshop, slamming the wooden door behind him.

Gabriel sat with his head in his hands. "I wish I had Old Man Pickens here for advice."

Ronan's wheelchair squeaked as it rolled toward Gabriel. He stopped when he sat in front of his despondent friend. "He doesn't understand the half of it, does he?"

Gabriel shook his head. "I know what Rissa accused him of was despicable. And she regretted it almost immediately." He gripped his hands together and took a deep breath, his voice emerging graveled and tear-thickened. "But no one, no *man*, can ever understand the depths of her terror. And that she can be thrust back into her memories at any moment." He raised tormented eyes to meet Ronan's concerned gaze. "I would ease her of that burden if I could. But I can't." He let out a deep breath. "And I hate that Cameron's attack continues to affect her, even now."

Ronan nodded and shifted forward to pat Gabriel on the knee. "Colin will come to understand. You must believe that."

Gabriel shook his head. "For that to happen, she needs to do something for him and Araminta. Only then will there be any hope for a reconciliation."

~

D ear Clarissa and Gabe,
         Thank you for your recent letter. It helps to know that you are sending letters and prayers for Nickie too. I hear from him infrequently, although I received three letters in two days. It seems there was a mix-up in France, and his letters home were delayed. Thankfully he is doing well and has yet to see any real fighting.

The general he is under has recognized his talent as a logger and has sent him to work in forests near the Front. He says he is working hard to ensure that there is enough lumber and materials for those fighting on the Front, and doesn't have time to be bored, unlike the men who spend long hours on the Front, whiling away time. I can sense a yearning in him to do more for the war effort, but I will continue to pray that his work in the forest will keep him out of any battles and that the War will end soon.

I can only imagine how difficult it was for you when Gabriel registered for the draft. I never thought I would be thankful that Sebastian is no longer such a young man as he nears fifty. Let us hope this was a mere formality and that there is no reason for Gabriel, Colin or any of the other men to head to that horrible conflict.

I wish we could attend Araminta's wedding, but it is too difficult to leave the sawmill right now. We hope to travel to Missoula sometime soon, and we shall celebrate her marriage then.

Your friend,
Amelia

CHAPTER 14

Boston, September 1918

Room 712 at the PHH, 7:00 p.m.

P

owena scrunched up the note in her hand and fought the
urge to look furtively around to see if any of the servants
were staring at her. However, the servant who had delivered the
message had already left the room, discreetly shutting the door
behind him. She sat in the informal living room of her father's
mansion on a lumpy lady's chair. Mahogany wainscoting and deep red
wallpaper gave the room a dark feel that no amount of lighting or
windows could brighten. When she was younger, she had spent hours
envisioning how she would redecorate the room, but her father had
insisted the room showcased their wealth and importance, and was
not to be altered. Rowena let out a deep breath as she battled a blush
and rose, exiting the living room to prepare for her rendezvous, only
to come to a stumbling halt as her father exited his study.

He cast a quick glance over her and frowned. "I had hoped by now
you had more grace than a three-legged cat." He glowered at her flush.

"And I forbid you to come down with that so-called influenza that is circulating through the city. I don't have time to care for an invalid." He stormed up the stairs and down the hall, the door to his room slamming shut. She knew he would change for dinner, attend a function with a business associate and return home late.

She walked on silent feet to her suite of rooms, on the opposite side of the house as her father's, shutting and locking the door behind her. As she approached the mirror on her dressing room door with halting steps, her critical gaze took in the trepidation in her amber-colored eyes. She raised a hand to her auburn hair, wishing for the millionth time it was blond and that she was beautiful. "Stop pining for what will never be." She closed her eyes and breathed deeply a few times before opening them and firming her shoulders.

After yanking open her large closet door, she searched for an attractive yet demure dress. After donning the dress, fixing her hair, and placing scent on her neck and wrists, she flopped onto her bed as she listened for the sounds of her father's departure. Her mind wandered, thinking about Perry's letters from the past six weeks. They had been frequent and varying in length. When he had time, like when he was bored on a long train ride, he wrote pages of details and thoughts to her. She treasured the insights into his life as he lost his inhibitions the longer he wrote without interruption. She sighed as a contented smile spread. She adored his short missives too. The hastily scratched-out messages conveying his desire to see her. His frustration at their separation. His need to kiss her again.

She closed her eyes, straining to hear the sounds of the house. Soon her father left. She waited another ten minutes before she rose, donning an even plainer jacket and hat, then wearing a mask of boredom as she approached the front door. The staff, accustomed to her outings without a chaperone or car, largely ignored her departure. She slipped outside and walked to a nearby subway station. With her nondescript jacket, she blended into the crowd.

Scollay Square bustled with life as people hurried to meet friends, to attend a show or to rush home after a day of work. She skirted around a cart, its owner pushing it through the crowd as he peddled pickles. Her step faltered as she approached the large hotel, jostled by the crowd. She nodded to the doorman as he opened the front door for her and slipped inside.

Mahogany wood shone as though just polished, and chandeliers illuminated the long hallway leading to a bank of elevators. She firmed her shoulders and acted as though she were a guest. She strolled to the elevators and instructed the elevator man to bring her to the seventh floor. Once there, her courage faltered, but she disembarked and walked with slow, purposeful steps until she stood in front of room 712. She raised her hand, but it was as though she were frozen, and her hand would not fall to rap on the door.

A laugh from someone exiting a room down the hall propelled her into motion, and she knocked on the door. She waited as she heard footsteps approaching, and then the door was flung open. Her breath caught at the sight of Perry, standing in front of her with his white shirt undone at the collar.

"Ro," he whispered, before he tugged on her hand and dragged her into the room. He slammed the door shut behind her and pulled her into his arms. "God, you smell exactly as I dreamed you did. Forgive me, but let me hold you a few minutes."

His tight grip slowly eased until his hands caressed up and down her back. "I worried you'd forever remain out of reach. Like a fever dream." He stepped back, keeping her head between his hands. "Why are you crying?" he whispered as he frowned.

"I ... I thought our time in Newport wasn't real. That I'd have to live off those memories forever." She sniffled and then smiled, her eyes lit with a transcendent joy. "I never thought to be in your arms again."

"Oh, love," he murmured as he pulled her closer. "I had hoped my letters would help ease your doubts."

"They did. But they only made me yearn for you more." She kissed his cheek and stepped away. "And they made it that much harder to ignore the newspapers who spoke about your latest lovers." She flushed at her hasty words.

"I have no one but you, Rowena. I need you to trust me." He

relaxed as she nodded. "I hate that I am a constant item in the gossip columns, but I also need them to spark interest in my career." He brushed his fingers over her silky cheek.

"I know I can't compare to the women you meet every night." She failed to hide the doubt in her gaze.

He smiled and nodded. "You're right. You don't compare." He saw her shock, and his grip firmed as she attempted to step away from him. "You are far superior in every regard. You are intelligent. Determined. Loyal. You are beautiful, but it is not your beauty that makes you irresistible, Rowena. It is everything else about you."

"Perry," she whispered, stepping forward and wrapping her arms around him. "I've missed you so much. How is that possible when I barely know you?"

He let out a stuttering breath. "I recognized you, Ro." His eyes flashed with hope as he tilted his head down to search her gaze. "Please tell me that you felt the same."

She nodded and stood on her toes to kiss him. "Yes," she breathed. She sighed as he deepened the kiss. Her fingers tangled in his blond hair, tugging him closer, and she giggled, breaking their kiss as his fingers knotted in her coat.

"Why are you wearing such a wretchedly ugly garment?" he muttered as he struggled with her light outer coat. He grinned as he pushed it off her shoulders and then frowned at her plain amber-colored dress. His fingertips traced the satiny fabric, eliciting a shiver.

"I didn't want to alert anyone that I was meeting someone other than my friends." She dropped her head back as he kissed along her neck and nibbled at her ear. "That … that I was meeting you rather than attending another boring function."

"So I rate over a boring function?" he teased as he breathed deeply, inhaling her lilac and lemon scent. "God, I'm dizzy already."

She ran her fingers over his whiskered cheeks. "Yes. You'll always rate over any function." She watched as a deep emotion flared in his gaze. "But I shouldn't stay long."

He lowered his head so his forehead rested against hers. "I won't lie to you, Rowena. I will never lie to you." He met her gaze, content when she nodded. "You can always ask me anything, and I will tell you the truth." He let out a breath. "I want you. In my bed. To love, over and over, all night long." He smiled as her breath caught at his declaration. "But I fear that may be too much, too fast."

He took a step back, smiling as she clung to his hand, unwilling to break contact with him. "Come. Sit with me on the comfortable sofa by the fire. Let me hold you." He raised her hand and kissed it before easing her the few short steps to the sofa.

"How did you arrive here tonight?" He stroked a hand over her shoulder and down her arm. After she settled, with her back against his front, he slung his arm over her belly and held her close.

"I rode the subway." She frowned as she felt him stiffen beneath her. "I always take public transportation when I can."

"Don't, Ro. Not now. Not when so many are sickened every day from an illness we don't understand. Hire a cab or take one of your father's automobiles."

"I don't want to rouse his suspicion," she said, turning to face him. "And I like my freedom."

His hold on her tightened. "Please, darling. I couldn't bear it if something happened to you." He relaxed when she nodded her agreement.

"I know this isn't enough for you," she whispered.

He encouraged her to turn so that she rested with her elbows on his chest and so they could stare into each other's eyes. "That's where you're wrong. Do you know what I miss when I am touring?" He saw confusion in her gaze and traced a finger over her silky cheek. "I miss the quiet. Time to reflect. Time to be alone. With nobody clamoring for a moment with me." He sighed as she rested her head on his chest. "Moments like this."

His nimble fingers freed her hair, and he massaged her head and upper shoulders. "Holding you, like this, is a dream come true."

"You'd miss the charming smiles and the adoration of your fans," she murmured.

"I'd miss the applause when I finished a song. I would never miss the boring after-parties. The incessant chatter from mindless idiots as they spouted on about things they thought I cared about." He sighed.

"It's part of your life, Perry. It's what you must do to have the adoration," she said as she relaxed into his embrace.

"I know." He paused, and she felt his deep inhalation as his chest moved underneath her. "It would be more bearable if I had someone to share it with."

Her head rose, and she stared at him, her mouth dropping open. "I'm sure I'm not hearing you correctly."

"I want to see where this goes between us, Ro. But I hate being separated from you." He flushed. "I never meant to be such a fool as to speak so rashly." -

She shook her head. "You don't know me."

His eyes flashed with anger. "I know you are loyal and patient and trustworthy. I know you try, and fail, to earn your father's esteem. You are dedicated to your cause and a brilliant journalist. You try to hide your intelligence because you believe that isn't esteemed in a woman. You have a sharp, biting wit that emerges in your writing, and yet you are kind to those you believe are in need of kindness. You love nature, as every letter remarked upon something to do with the time of day, the light, the smell." He frowned as she battled tears. "Your friends adore you, and yet you are surprised they do."

"Perry," she whispered.

"Tell me, Rowena, tell me what I don't know about you. Tell me what shame it is that keeps you apart from me."

She pushed on his chest, glaring at him as he held her wrists and would not let her rise.

"You know I've had love affairs. You know I am far from perfect." His voice dropped as he fought regret at the pain his words evoked. "Share yourself with me."

"I don't want to risk your career," she whispered. "I know how much it means to you."

He froze and released her arms. "You think my career means more to me? That it should?"

"I know how hard you've worked for it," she said. "It's yours. Something you've earned. Not something given to you."

He slipped out from under her on the settee and rose. "I thought people of your class didn't believe a man should work for anything. That, if he were worth being esteemed, it would all be given to him."

She shrugged. "Some believe that. Although, as you know, many work. Look at Teddy and Morgan."

He stared into the empty fire grate, one hand gripped in a fist at his side. "Teddy and Morgan," he whispered. "Which one was it?" He spun to look at her and saw her panicked expression before she could hide it. "Which one was your lover before he married your friend?"

She sputtered out a laugh and then stifled a sob, brushing away a tear. "Neither. I was never lover to either of them." She sniffled and took a deep breath. "Although I had hoped Teddy would notice me, I realized that was a vain desire once he met Zee."

"And you've pined all this time?" He raised an eyebrow. "Until you decided to mingle with the singers and the gutter scum?"

She rose and grabbed his arm. "Don't speak like that!" Her eyes flashed with anger. "You are not gutter scum."

"Oh, that's exactly what I am, Rowena. I was born in the slums of Albany, and there is little I didn't do to get out of it. I'm surprised your friends didn't warn you away from a man like me." His caustic laugh evoked a shiver. "If you knew who I truly was, you'd want to scrub yourself clean with bleach for ever having allowed me to touch you."

She flinched at the derision in his voice and backed away. Fighting tears, she spun, looking for her jacket and hat. As she fumbled with her coat, her motions stilled, and his words echoed in her mind. "I know you," she whispered through a tear-thickened voice. "You're arrogant and proud and terrified of being hurt again. You're loyal and patient and persistent. You're compassionate and giving and kind." She turned to face him, her brows furrowed as she saw him standing in silent agony across the room from her. "I had hoped you were a man brave enough to be mine." She spun, wrenching open the door and fleeing into the hallway.

∾

The following evening, Perry sat in a quiet corner of the Parker House Hotel lounge, nursing a whiskey. He ignored the men sitting in small clusters nearby, his gaze dark and foreboding as he reenacted in his mind the scene from the previous evening with Rowena. "What an ass," he whispered, taking a long sip of whiskey. He hissed as the liquor burned and closed his eyes.

"Hawke," a man said as he sat beside him. He carried himself with the self-assurance of a man of the upper class, exuding wealth and power.

"Sir?" Perry said as he nodded. "I'm afraid I have yet to make your acquaintance."

"Isn't that curious? You seem to know so many of my associates. And some of them quite intimately." The older man, with gray mixed in his chestnut hair, glared at Perry. "How long are you to remain in Boston?"

Perry tilted his head and shrugged. "I'm uncertain it is any concern of yours, but I have no fixed plans as of now." He jerked as the man grabbed his arm, sloshing the whiskey from his tumbler.

"Fix them," the older man said. "I want you out of Boston by tomorrow evening."

Perry's brown eyes darkened with restrained anger. "Who are you to advise me?"

"The father of the woman you defiled last night," he uttered in a voice only audible to Perry. "I am Reginald Clement, and I have the influence and power to bury you."

Perry infused humor into his gaze. "Many have made such claims in the past and failed. Why should I fear you?"

"I know who your investments are with. I will ensure you lose everything."

Perry froze, unable to hide the terror in his gaze.

"And then I will ensure you never sing again, except for in a two-bit cantina on the Mexican border."

"Why?" he asked.

"My daughter is worth more than some fortune hunter. Have you no shame?" Reginald's eyes glowed with animosity as he beheld his foe.

"I have no need of whatever meager dowry you intend to bestow upon her," Perry said, flushing as he realized too late he had tipped his hand. He shivered at the man's laugh.

"You thought to marry my daughter? To align yourself with the Clements of Boston?" Reginald shook his head. "You are a fool. But then I expected no better than that from someone from Albany. What do you think Rowena would say if she knew about your past?"

"She knows already," Perry whispered.

"All of your past?" Reginald said, smiling with satisfaction as Perry paled further. "You are not worthy of being in the same room as her, never mind speaking with her." He rose. "Stay away from my daughter, Hawke, and do yourself a favor. Leave town."

~

Rowena joined her friends in Parthena's opulent mansion on Commonwealth Avenue. The large white-stoned mansion on a corner lot had many gables and a large conservatory in the back. Parthena's sitting room was paneled in black walnut wood and had a piano in one corner. Ornate molding decorated the ceiling, and a large crystal chandelier hung from the center of the room's ceiling. A thick Aubusson rug covered the wood floors, and an intimate sitting area near a window had a settee, two chairs and a table. Although somewhat formal, the room had a lived-in feel to it and was a welcoming place for Parthena's friends.

Rowena attempted a bright smile but failed as tears threatened. She gave silent thanks as both Parthena and Zylphia appeared preoccupied. "What was so urgent that you felt we needed to meet?" Rowena asked.

Zylphia held up a letter and frowned at Rowena. "I thought Alice wrote you too. She is determined that we return to Washington. The vote for the Anthony Amendment will soon occur in the Senate, and she wants us there to help in the final weeks to persuade the recalcitrant senators."

Rowena sighed and tugged a pillow to her chest. "They will vote as they want to, not as they should. Besides, I'm not returning to Washington anytime soon. My father has forbidden me from traveling there as he believes I am in violation of the Sedition Act if I continue to work toward full enfranchisement."

Parthena snorted. "Women have every right to highlight the hypocrisy of the man who spouts nonsense about bringing democracy to the free world but then denies it to half of his own citizenry." She shared a look with Zylphia. "I know Sophie says that repeatedly, and I agree. I feel like we should have banners waving from our homes with those sentiments."

Zylphia laughed. "Oh, to see Teddy's face. He might agree with my sentiments, but he'd be upset with the disruption to his business and his quiet life."

"Besides," Parthena said, addressing Rowena's concern, "I haven't heard much talk about charging suffragists with sedition."

Rowena sighed. "There are more murmurs than I'd like in Washington." She shared a rueful look with her friends. "There are always those who are sticklers, wanting to keep to the letter of the law. And then there are those who will look for any excuse to find a reason to discredit the movement. The Sedition Act seems ready made for them, but, so far, we've managed to evade being a target."

"They're too busy rounding up the Wobblies of the IWW and other progressives," Zylphia muttered. "Never mind harmless German immigrants." She sighed as she looked at Rowena. "You look awful, Ro. You mustn't let fear deter you from what you want to do."

Parthena nodded. "And you have to stand up to your father and show him that you will do what is right for you, not continue to cower to his ultimatums."

Rowena shrugged. "I see no reason to go back right now. I write the same article, twenty different ways, and I'm rather fatigued by it all." She sagged against the settee back. "Which makes me feel rather weak-willed for admitting that, but it is the truth."

"You've been working hard for years," Parthena said, sharing a worried glance with Zylphia. "I'm glad you are taking a break."

After a few moments of silence as they fixed cups of tea, Zylphia said, "Do you know who I saw entering Teddy's office as I was leaving to come here today?" She smiled broadly at her friends. "Perry Hawke. I'm sure you will see him in person rather than depending on a letter." Her mischievous smile faded as Rowena's face crumpled into tears. "Ro?"

Rowena shook her head and then raised her hands to cover her face as a sob escaped.

Zylphia moved to sit on one side of her on the settee and Parthena on the other. "What happened?" Parthena whispered.

"I saw him. Two nights ago. And we fought. It was horrible." She looked at her friends as she tried to speak through her tears. "Wonderful at first. To be in his arms again. And then it all changed. I don't know what I said." She quickly summarized what happened for her friends, who sat in silence a few moments after she stopped talking. Her breaths emerged in stuttering gasps as she attempted to catch her breath after her crying jag.

Zylphia sighed. "From what you said, I think he fears he doesn't belong in your world. And that you deserve someone better than him." She shook her head. "We like to think our backgrounds don't matter, but they always affect us."

Rowena stared at her friend and bit her lip before blurting out, "How did you get past having grown up in an orphanage? I know you weren't an orphan, as you were raised with your mother who ran it, but ..." Her voice trailed away.

"I had many moments where I didn't believe myself worthy. Only with time, and the constancy of my father's and Teddy's love, did I come to accept that my beginning did not have to determine my future." She frowned as she thought of her early life, growing up in an orphanage, believing herself fatherless. "I don't know if that makes sense."

"I think it does," Parthena whispered. "What will you do, Ro?"

She sighed as a few more tears streaked out. "I don't know. I worry I'll never see him again."

"Would that be terrible?" Parthena asked.

Rowena nodded. "I think I love him. But I wonder if I know what love really is."

Zylphia took one of Rowena's hands. "You know what it is, Ro. Your mother showed you." She met her friend's devastated gaze. "I know you argued with Perry, and you think that means you can't really love him. But, if you didn't care for him so much, you wouldn't hurt like this now, would you?"

Rowena nodded, tears leaking out. "What will I do if I never see him again?"

Savannah sat in the upstairs living room over her father's linen shop. She listened for her daughter's return, growing restless at the late hour. "Where can she be?"

"She's with Delia. She's fine," Jeremy said, clasping her hand.

"I hate that she went out with all this illness affecting Boston," Savannah said. "She should have stayed home."

Jeremy rolled his eyes. "You know as well as I do that Melly was going crazy, feeling cooped up here. A small outing with Delia won't hurt her." He winked at her as he focused on the paper.

She smiled at her father as he entered the living room. Where Lucas's piano had stood was now another settee and chair. "How was your day, Father?"

"Oh, good enough, although I had hoped my days as a linen shop owner were behind me." He shared a chagrined smile with Savannah. "When I was in Newport, I couldn't wait for September, so I could begin training the new owner and his small staff. Now, having to wait until mid-October seems too long."

She frowned. "Well, it seems the poor man suffered terribly with that dreadful influenza. It makes sense he would want to be stronger before taking over a new business." She rubbed her belly and smiled at her father. "I'm certain he will be well soon and that you will be free to travel with us when we return to Montana."

He beamed at her. "I am counting on it. Now, how are you feeling, my dear?"

She patted her stomach and looked at her bulging stomach with fondness. "We are well. The doctor said that we should consider the operation in a week or two."

Martin frowned as he looked at his only daughter. "I fear that there is too much risk with that surgery."

Jeremy grunted and set aside the paper. "There is risk either way, sir." He clasped her hand over her belly, smiling as he felt the baby kick against their hands. "I would spare her the pain and uncertainty if I could, but I can't."

Martin nodded. "I know, son." He sighed. "Promise me that you will do everything this doctor recommends. I want to hold you and the baby in my arms."

"I will, Father, as that is my dream too," she whispered. She leaned into Jeremy's side and fought tears.

$\sim$

R owena stood on Teddy and Zylphia's doorstep, waiting for the butler to answer the door. She had hoped for a quiet evening at home to think through her conversation with her friends and to puzzle through her fight with Perry in a rational manner. However, she had found a summons from Teddy when she had returned from a solitary stroll after tea with Parthena and Zylphia. After being shown into Teddy's study, she wandered behind his desk to better examine the painting over his chair.

"It is rather fine, isn't it?" Teddy said from behind her. He wore a blue suit with white shirt and collar. His alert silver eyes took in her plain green day dress with no adornment and the sadness in her gaze that she was unable to mask.

"Yes. I haven't had enough time in Boston lately to visit her study and see what else she has painted. Are they all like this?" she asked as she met Teddy's contemplative gaze.

"More so now than before. She had to experience her *dark period* before returning to what she calls *the light*." He smiled as Rowena moved from behind his desk, and he motioned for her to sit in a chair by a dormant fire. He sat beside her in another high-back chair.

"Why did you need to see me, Teddy?" she whispered.

He sighed. "I want you to know that I was honored when you asked me to look into your finances and to confirm they were sound. Your mother left you quite a legacy, and I want to help ensure it remains just that for you." He paused as his jaw ticked a moment while he fought a deep emotion. "I hope you know I am honorable and will only act on your behalf when it comes to your accounts."

She reached forward and gripped his hand for a moment. "Of course I know that. It's why I wanted you to help me."

"Your father ..." Teddy paused. "Your father visited me early this morning. He exerted a considerable amount of pressure to change the financial investments I had made for you." He met her shocked gaze. "I want you to know that I did not bow to his pressure."

"Why?" she whispered.

"Because of me," Perry said from the doorway.

"Perry?" Her gaze flitted from him to Teddy and then back again. "What are you doing here?"

Teddy continued. "Your father also wanted me to ruin Mr. Hawke, in no unequivocal terms." Teddy's cheeks flushed with anger. "It was all I could do not to throw him out bodily onto the street."

"I don't understand," Rowena said as she sat with stooped shoulders.

Perry inched into the room, shutting the door behind him. He stood in front of Rowena, an arm's-length away from her.

Teddy said, "If you are financially ruined, and Mr. Hawke has no money, there can be no hope for you as a couple."

Rowena shook her head and gave a bark of humorless laughter. "There's no hope for us as it is," she whispered. "My father didn't need to do anything."

"That's not true, Ro, and you know it," Perry said, remorse etched on his face. "We had our first fight. We will overcome it." He crouched in front of her and traced his fingers over her hand. "He wanted to take any chance of reconciliation away from us."

"How did he know?" she whispered. "How did he know about us?"

Perry shrugged. "I don't know. But I wasn't secretive about the letters I sent you. Or the frequency of them. He had to have noted them, especially since you only spent a few weeks in Washington when you left Newport and then returned here." He squeezed her hand. "But it doesn't matter, Ro. He knows." He glanced at Teddy who rose and exited the office, leaving them alone. "He thinks I ... I debased you when you visited me in my hotel room."

She shook her head and cupped his jaw. "No, never." A small amount of her sorrow lifted as he turned his face into her palm. "If he only knew what did happen."

"To my regret, nothing. Except an idiotic argument." He let out a deep breath. "I'm supposed to leave Boston tonight, or he threatens I will never perform again."

She smiled. "He likes to believe he wields that much influence, but it doesn't extend much farther than the Charles River. He resents men like Aidan and Teddy because what they say is actually followed." She ran her fingers through Perry's hair. "I shouldn't worry overmuch about my father."

Perry sobered as he stared at her, now on his knees in front of her. "But I do. Because you care for him, and I do not want to come between you and your father."

She shook her head. "You can't. Already so much animosity exists between my father and me that you could do little to worsen the chasm." She leaned forward and kissed his forehead. "He married my mother for her money and because he was caught with his pants down by her father." She flushed as Perry chuckled. "He resented her from the moment she had me and was informed by the doctor that she could have no more children. He hated her for denying him his coveted son. Then she died."

259

He chucked her under her chin when she ducked her head. "What? Why the reticence to speak about your mother?"

"She was German. Well-born. A cousin to the Kaiser," she blurted out. "If it were known ..." She blinked. "It could affect your career."

He laughed and leaned back on his heels. "This is the great secret? That you mother is *German?*" He shook his head incredulously. "I thought you had a child hidden away or ten lovers or had been a member of a circus." He laughed as she shushed him, covering his lips with her fingers.

"It matters to me," she said as she battled tears. "It matters that I was forbidden from speaking about her. From writing my family in Germany. From knowing how they fare."

He sobered and caressed her cheek. "I'm sorry, love. I can see that he tried to shame you for who you are, but it doesn't matter to me. I can only imagine how you feel, but it's a relief to know I'm not battling the ghost of your past lover."

She looked at him, her gaze somber. "No, I'm battling yours."

He sighed and closed his eyes. "Your father ... Your father also promised to tell you all the salacious details of my past if I didn't leave town tonight." He rose and tugged on her hand. "Will you sit with me on the settee and listen?"

He sat with her in his arms and spoke, his deep voice low and powerful as he began. "You know I was born in Albany. To a woman who fell in love with a fickle man. He married her and then ran off when he found out she was pregnant." He sighed, his fingers playing with hers. "I'm not even certain they were truly married. I'm most likely a bastard, although I was given his name."

He paused for a long moment. "When I was six, she died from consumption. I had no family, and none were concerned about me. There might have been an orphanage I could go to, but I didn't know what that was. From that moment on, I had to live by my wits. Doing whatever I could to survive."

"What did you do that shames you?" she whispered as she raised his hand and kissed his palm.

"Life is not kind if you are poor. And it can be cruel if you are a

260

handsome boy with no one to protect you." He let out a deep breath. "I did things I regret, just so I wouldn't go to bed hungry."

"No one would blame you," she whispered. "Tell me. ... Tell me so that you never have to fear again."

He closed his eyes as a tear trickled out. "I ... ended up in a brothel. At first I was an errand boy, and the girls doted on me because I always managed to steal a treat for them. A toffee here. A piece of chocolate there. A ribbon." His gaze became distant and glazed. "The woman in charge of the brothel was a good woman. Cared for her girls. Wouldn't let anyone hurt them and hired a good-size thug to scare away brutes. Dominic." He let out a deep breath.

"Who hurt you, Perry?" she whispered.

He paused for a long moment as though battling with himself, and then he shook his head. "*Almost* hurt me," he murmured. "I was almost hurt, but Dominic was sharp and fast, and knew when things weren't right. He knew I had no interest in bartering myself. To men." He stared at her without guile as he waited for her to understand what he was saying.

She frowned at his words, and then her eyes widened in shock. "Oh, God." She ran her hands over his chest. "Please tell me you weren't ... hurt like that. You were just a little boy."

He grimaced at her reaction. "Yes, but I had long lost my innocence, living in a whorehouse." He frowned as she stiffened in his arms. "I might have still been sexually inexperienced, but I'd seen things that were shocking." He shook his head.

"Oh, Perry," she whispered as a tear leaked out. "I hate that you had such a terrible childhood."

He shrugged. "I didn't know differently. I did my best to learn all I could so that I could escape someday. I knew I didn't want to spend all my days at a brothel."

"How did you start singing?" She traced a soothing pattern on his chest.

He gazed distantly over her shoulder. "I loved to sing. I sang while I worked, and eventually the mistress turned me into a show. By the time I was eighteen, I had my own stage in downtown Albany. By my mid-twenties, I was in New York City." He closed his eyes. "There are those who believe the mistress is my mother because I sent her money for years."

"Why?" she asked.

"She was good to me. Protected me as she could from the harsh world. Recognized my talent and then let me go. Taught me how to recognize a con." He shrugged. "She was as much a mother to me, in her way, as the woman who gave birth to me."

Rowena murmured her understanding and ran a hand over his chest. "I'd like to meet her."

He gave an incredulous chuckle and tugged her closer. "God, Ro, you are astounding." After a moment, when he had calmed, he whispered, "She died a few years ago."

"Oh, Perry, I'm so sorry."

He tipped his head onto her shoulder. "Anyone else would say, *Good riddance*," he whispered as he held her close. "Thank you."

She backed away and held his head between her hands. "Having loved her does not shame you, Perry. That others would try to harm you with such knowledge is reprehensible."

"Your father believes I'm the son of a whore. That is worse than gutter scum, Ro. He wants you far away from me."

"I do not care what others think. What others want. I only care about us, Perry. I trust what you tell me is the truth." After an intense stare, she smiled and tried to lighten the mood. She spoke in a prim tone as she looked at him. "*Mr. Hawke is from Albany. His parents are deceased. This is his fourth album.*" She smiled as he recognized her mocking the bare-bones information on the jackets of his records. "Nothing you could say would cause me to turn away from you."

He sobered. "Polite society doesn't want a man like me around their womenfolk. A man who stole and bartered whatever he had to."

She moved so that she sat astride him on his lap, any concern about propriety forgotten as she reacted to the agony in his voice. "I couldn't give a damn what society thinks. I know what I see. A good man. A man who cares for me and for others. Don't let your past shadow your future."

He wrapped his arms around her. "Forgive me for the other night, Ro. I thought ... I thought it would be better if you left. If you could find a man worthy of you."

She shook her head and gripped his cheeks between her palms. "I have, and I'm looking at him. You, Perry. I want you."

"Oh, God, love," he rasped, kissing her with pent-up passion. His arms banded around her back, and he pulled her even tighter to him.

At the slight tap on the door, their kiss broke apart, but Rowena remained on his lap in his arms, her head tucked into his neck. "Yes?" Perry called out.

Zylphia poked her head in, and an impish smile spread as she saw them together. "I wanted to inform you that we have readied rooms for you both for the night. And that dinner will be ready in twenty minutes."

"Zee, I can't stay here," Rowena said. "What would my father say?"

"Oh, I sent him a note informing him that you were not feeling well, and the doctor insisted you not be moved tonight. He won't argue, and I doubt he relishes any further disagreement with Teddy today." She winked at them and backed out of the room before poking her head in again. "Unless you'd rather have dinner on a tray in here?"

Rowena smiled and nodded. Zylphia grinned and backed out again, closing the door behind her.

"You have wonderful friends," he whispered, peppering kisses down her neck.

"So do you. They consider you a friend, or they never would have readied a room for you or encouraged me to spend more time with you."

He gave a small growl of discontent. "I hate that we are expected to be in two rooms." He looked at her quizzically as she giggled.

"If I know Zee, they connect somehow or are next door to each other. She'd never expect me to sleep alone tonight if I didn't want to." She kissed him, arching into his touch. "She was disappointed we didn't have more of an interlude in Newport."

"And do you?" He met her confused look. "Want to be alone tonight?"

"No, God, no," she murmured as he kissed his way down her neck, relishing their time together until dinner arrived.

After a hastily devoured dinner where she and Perry tasted little but ate an appropriate amount to prevent gossip in the kitchen, Rowena and Perry were shown to their rooms. Although not connecting, they were side by side. Zylphia blithely remarked that they were their only guests in the house and the only ones on that floor for the evening. Rowena shared a hidden smile with Perry as she entered her room to prepare for bed.

She answered the soft knock at her door, opening it a crack. She found Perry standing there in a robe and pants and let him slip inside. She heard the door *click* and then the lock turn. Her cotton nightdress hung on her as it was on loan from Zylphia who was much taller than she was. "I look a fool," she whispered, flushing.

"No," he rasped. "You look gorgeous." He reached forward and snagged a strand of her auburn hair, running it through his fingers. "Like silk." He took a step forward, pausing when her breath caught. "We don't have to do anything more than we've done. Kiss and hold each other."

She shook her head. "No, Perry. I want more." She took a deep breath and stepped forward until her cotton-clad chest brushed against his robe. "I want you."

He shuddered and lashed his arms around her, pulling her closer. He watched her with a quizzical expression but didn't speak as he stuttered out a breath.

Standing on her toes, she kissed the underside of his jaw, whispering in his ear. "I love that my words affect you."

"God, Ro." He lowered his mouth, capturing her lips in a deep kiss. His hands moved over her shoulders, her back, and he broke their kiss, chuckling as she squealed when he picked her up and placed her on the bed. He leaned over her, soft fingers tracing a path from her temple to her collarbone and back again. "I want to go slow and to be gentle and to show you how much you are treasured."

She smiled tremulously. "I know I am treasured because I am here with you." She kissed him and then followed his muttered command

264

to lift her bottom. Soon her nightgown had been tossed to the floor. She closed her eyes as he stilled over her. "I'm sorry." His breath at her shoulder made her shiver, and she turned her head away, battling tears.

"No, my love, don't turn away from me. Don't shut me out," he coaxed. He eased from her, resting beside her rather than braced over her on his elbows. "Why are you sorry?"

She kept her eyes closed as a tear trickled out. "I know you are accustomed to beautiful women in your bed. I'm … I'm just me."

"Look at me, Rowena." His voice harsh, he frowned as his tone caused her to jolt.

After a moment, she opened her eyes and met his intense gaze.

He grasped her hand and held it to his cheek. "You are more beautiful, and more precious, than any woman I have ever known."

"Perry," she croaked out, "you promised never to lie."

He nodded and met her gaze. "Exactly." He waited for her to nod. He then rolled over, onto his back, his robe open to his waist. He still wore his black pants. "Show me what you want. I will not rush you."

"I don't know what to do." Her whispered words were plaintive.

"You do, my love, if only you followed your instincts." He tapped her forehead. "Stop thinking. *Feel*. Touch me. Whatever you like, I will like. I promise you."

"You want me to touch you?" Her brows furrowed as she watched his chest rise and fall more rapidly than it should if he were simply lying on a bed.

"God, yes." His brown eyes were filled with desire as he looked at her. He smiled as she bit her lip and then scooted over, her small hands tracing a pattern over his chest. He gasped at her touch, soft as gossamer. He arched up when she kissed his chest.

She leaned closer, kissing his lips as her hands continued to form patterns over him, at times soft, other times firmer.

He tugged at her until she straddled him, and he lost the battle with himself to keep his hands at his sides as they roved over her as well. When she leaned forward, pressing her naked chest to his, he yanked his mouth from hers and growled. "God, I want you, Ro."

She smiled down at him, tracing the small lines around his eyes and then his mouth. "Good, because I want you too." She swallowed a shriek as he rolled her over.

He rose up, tugging off his pants until he was as naked as she was. He paused, searching for any doubt in her gaze, but was soon lost to their kisses and her novice touch.

~

He stirred at the sound of Rowena moving beside him and reached out for her as she slipped from bed. A soft lamp lent a gentle glow to the room. "Where are you going? It's the middle of the night."

She searched the floor, finding and tugging on the voluminous nightgown over her head. "I ... I thought I should go to the other room. It wouldn't be seemly for us to be found together in the morning."

He groaned and sat up, scratching at his head and sending his blond hair on edge. "Ro, what are you doing? This is your room. It would be even more remarked upon if you were suddenly in my bed and bedroom." He saw her standing with stooped shoulders, swaying as though with indecision. Holding out a hand to her, he murmured, "Come here, darling."

"I don't know what to do," she whispered. "I hate this!" She swiped at her cheek and then took his hand, climbing back into bed to lie beside him. "After ... afterward, I thought one of us snuck out."

He sighed and rubbed her nose with his. "That's only when there is no affection between the two people." He cupped her cheek. "I want to hold you in my arms all night long. I doubt we will scandalize Teddy or Zee if I am seen scurrying to my room around dawn."

She lowered her head, breaking eye contact. "I don't want you to feel trapped."

He stiffened. "Or is it that you don't want to feel trapped?" He waited as she raised confused eyes to meet his frustrated gaze. "What do you believe just happened between us?" When she remained quiet, her eyes luminous, he whispered, "What do you think it meant?"

She shook her head. "That's the problem. I don't know what it meant to you!"

"What did it mean to you, Ro, my love?" he asked, scooting down so he could see her eyes.

"Everything." She flushed. "But I don't want you to feel obligated."

He frowned. "*Obligated. Trapped.* Odd choice of words you have after glorious lovemaking."

"Oh, Perry, please," she breathed. "My father was forced to marry my mother due to an indiscretion, and they were miserable."

"You mean, he made her miserable." He saw the truth in Rowena's eyes. "Have you ever considered that your father is a miserable man and that anything or anyone around him naturally suffers?" He dug his hand into her hair, massaging her scalp. "I would never feel as though you trapped me. As though you were an obligation. You are the greatest treasure I could ever be fortunate enough to have."

"What happens when the novelty wears off?" She flushed. "You'd still be stuck with plain, old, boring me."

His jaw tightened as he fought anger. "You are beautiful, young and brilliant. You are far from boring. It's just that few have the ability to see beyond your facade, darling." He closed his eyes. "I fear you want me to speak plainly, and that terrifies me."

He looked into her eyes and took a deep breath. "I never thought I'd feel like this, Rowena. I never thought I could love again. But somehow I do. I love you more, with a greater passion, than I have loved anyone or anything in my entire life." His eyes glowed with sincerity. "I never dreamed you would be receptive to a man like me. I thought I would have to make do with the crumbs of your affection." He smiled as she frowned at that remark. "But I want you. I want children with you. I want a life and home with you, even if that is in hotel rooms across the country and world as I sing. I want you by my side, always."

"Perry," she whispered, her hands rising to cup his face. She leaned forward to rest her forehead against his as tears leaked out. "I never dreamed."

"Will you, Rowena? Will you take a chance on me?" He waited as she watched him wide-eyed.

"Yes, I will." She backed away a moment to prevent him from kissing her, her soft touch easing the sting of what he interpreted as a rebuke. "I love you too, Perry."

He groaned, kissing her deeply. "God, Rowena, I never thought to have a woman like you love me," he said between kisses. He tugged on the borrowed cotton gown, earning a gasp and a laugh as he tore it in his haste to free her from it. "Let me love you again."

"Yes, Perry. Please," she moaned as she arched into his touch.

S ophronia stood in the doorway to the Russell living room and gave a small *harrumph* to herald her arrival. Although a bright day, lamps were lit in the sitting room as the elevated train running down Washington Street blocked much of the room's natural light. Every few minutes, the room rumbled and shook from the trains that passed. Savannah looked up from reading the afternoon newspaper and rose with as much haste as was possible for a woman approaching the birth of her baby. "Sophie!"

"I had thought to invite you to my house for tea but then thought it might be wiser to visit you," Sophie said as she moved into the room. "I hope you don't mind, but I informed the maid loitering in the hall that we wanted refreshments."

Savannah smiled and nodded. "That's fine. She doesn't have enough to do and spends her time near the doorway in hopes that I'll play the gramophone." She motioned for Sophie to sit. "How did you arrive?"

"I came in my automobile, and your husband pointed me in the direction of the sitting room. He is a joy, although rather informal." She raised an eyebrow as Savannah laughed.

"I'm surprised he was here to tell you where to find me. He has been spending most of his time with Richard." She smiled at the thought of her husband catching up on lost time with his brother.

"How are you, my dear?" Sophie asked.

"I am well, although I am a bit more nervous as each day passes." She bit her lip. "I know that there will be pain with childbirth, but I don't know what to expect with a surgery. I worry I will be a terrible ninny."

Sophie *thump*ed her cane down. "None of that talk. You will do wonderfully well and will hold your baby in your arms. We will have another generation to raise in favor of our causes." She smiled with delight as Savannah laughed.

"Your own daughters don't support your cause, Sophie. Why should you think mine will?" Savannah smiled at the maid and motioned for her to leave the tea tray on the table.

"I am an optimist. I have to be to believe what I do." Sophie poured the tea as it was difficult for Savannah with her protruding belly. "Now, where is that darling daughter of yours?"

"She has been spending time with Delia and Aidan. They are showing her universities around the region, although she should be home today or tomorrow."

"Would you want her to study so far away from you?"

"No, but, if that is what she desired, I would not want to deny her." Savannah sighed as she linked her hands over her abdomen. "I want her near me, but that is selfish. When I think of what my father has sacrificed, with Lucas and me living so far away from him, I realize I must be as generous of spirit as he has been."

Sophie nodded. "Very noble of you. Few would be as brave."

Savannah gave a wry smile. "I speak bravely now, but, if Melinda were to leave Montana, I'd cry like a blubbering baby." She took a sip of tea and rested the cup on her belly. "Tell me. What news of Washington? The cause?"

Sophronia cleared her throat and glowered. "I'm afraid it is not going as well as we had hoped. The House passed the Anthony Amendment in January, but the Senate is slow to see to their duty. I believe there will be a vote soon, but I fear that it will not go as it should. Too many senators are unconvinced that a female electorate will be to their benefit."

Savannah snorted. "One way or another, the tide is changing, and they will rue the day they tried to thwart us." She smiled at Sophie. "Do you remember when I lived with you after I … left my home? How unwilling I was to believe in universal suffrage?" Her smile grew. "It's astounding how time changes a person."

Sophie's gaze filled with deep love as she beheld Savannah. "You learned to think and to feel for yourself. You learned that a good man would still want and love you, even if you were perceived as radical. And you knew, after you had been in jail for protecting yourself, what a precarious position you were in simply because you were a woman."

Savannah shivered. "If I'd had to go to trial, I would have been tried by a jury made up of men. They aren't my peers." She shared a glower with Sophie and then smiled. "I hope that Melinda lives in a more just and equal world."

Sophie sobered. "It will be more just than what you or I experienced. But it will still have its injustices and struggles. I would count on that."

CHAPTER 15

*Z*ylphia joined Sophronia for tea in Sophie's redecorated front sitting room. Light yellow paint had replaced the dour gray-blue hues, giving the room an airy, bright feel. Three front windows overlooked Beacon Street and the Common, letting in plenty of sunlight. A new painting by Zylphia of the dawn's light over the Charles River hung over the fireplace.

"Teddy did not want me to come here today," Zylphia said. She took a bite of cake and then a sip of tea. "I think, if he could, he'd lock me in my studio."

Sophie looked at her young friend. "I am glad you are here, although I can understand his concern. The reports in the paper of the number of people who are sick and dying from this dreaded influenza are shocking."

"I agreed to take the automobile," Zylphia said. "It was the only way Teddy would allow me to visit. Although I think it is hypocritical, as he still meets with his associates for business concerns."

Sophronia *harrumph*ed. "I should think you'd appreciate your husband worrying about your welfare. I know I should have waited for this influenza to ease, but it feels like it never will. The city has suffered from this epidemic for nearly a month."

271

Zylphia sighed. "They've closed schools, theaters and bars. Now we are discouraged from attending church on Sundays." She shook her head in dismay.

"No one should be encouraged to congregate with others *en masse* at this time," Sophie said. "Although, if that were the case, they should shut down the subway and the elevated railroad. Too many are in close contact while riding public transportation."

"People have to get to work in order to make a living." Zylphia raised an eyebrow as she watched her friend.

"They also need to be alive to arrive at work," Sophie said with a tap of her cane on the floor. "Did you know over two hundred died yesterday in Boston alone?" She saw Zylphia pale. "I hope that our small get-together will not jeopardize your health."

"Why did you want to meet today?" Zylphia asked.

Sophie held up a yellow piece of paper. "I presume you heard the news yesterday from Washington?" When Zylphia nodded, Sophie tapped her cane down with more force. "Rowena was good enough to send me a telegram last night as I had requested."

"I can't believe, after all their hard work, that the measure still failed," Zylphia whispered. "And Parthena traveled there to be with Rowena to celebrate with her. How can the senators be so short-sighted?"

"I'm still surprised Rowena returned to Washington. I had thought she had a reason to remain here," Sophie said with a raised eyebrow.

Zylphia met her friend's curious and challenging look. "That reason might have traveled south too."

"*Hmmph,*" Sophie said and then grinned. "Good for her. As for her being in Washington, I am thankful she returned, as I enjoy her reporting. I look forward to her criticism of the senators who voted no."

"I can't believe we were only two votes short!" Zylphia said as she slapped her hands on the arms of her chair in frustration. "What more could we have done?"

Sophie shook her head. "Nothing. If the president had spoken up and encouraged the members of his party to follow his lead, this would have been very different. We could have passed this months ago." She shared an exasperated look with her friend. "However, you know as well as I that the president likes to make grand speeches and then do very little except golf."

Zylphia choked on a laugh. "I'm not sure that is true, Soph."

"In the case of universal suffrage, I believe it is." Sophronia once more tapped her cane down with added force.

"Have you heard what Alice is planning now that the amendment has failed?" Zylphia asked.

"She is considering targeting the senators who were against the Anthony Amendment, especially that wily man from Idaho. She has women there who are willing to work against his reelection."

"Senator Borah will say whatever he needs to in order to be reelected," Zylphia said. "He excelled at evasive tactics when I was in Washington."

"I imagine he is like many of his cohorts. As for the amendment, I refuse to think of it as dead. It's merely postponed. I must hope the new Congress will take up this challenge once again next year."

Zylphia relaxed against the back of the settee. "I hope so too. Somehow the senators need to understand the reckoning they will face if they do not vote for passage of the amendment."

~

Parthena burst from the automobile, failing to wait for the driver to open her door for her. She barreled past people walking by her on the street and ran up the steps to her home, heedless of the spectacle she made. She pushed on the door, screaming in frustration to find it locked. She pounded on it, swaying from foot to foot as she waited for it to open. When the butler finally cracked open the door, she pushed on it with all her weight, thrusting it open and gaining entrance.

She flung her travel coat to the floor, dropped her purse on top of it and ran to the stairs. "Don't tell me I'm too late," she yelled as she ran. She ascended the stairs and raced to the bedroom she shared with

Morgan. At the door, she paused, her gasping breath rising as wisps of steam in front of her.

After a momentary attempt to compose herself, she pushed open the door and entered the room. The nurse rose and bustled toward her, arms outstretched as though to propel her from the room. Parthena skirted around her and moved to Morgan's side. "I'm his wife," she hissed at the nurse. "You will not keep me from him."

"It's not safe for you here. You too could become gravely ill," the nurse argued.

Parthena shook her head and clasped Morgan's hand as she sat on a chair next to him. She frowned as he shook with a fever. "What can I do for him?" she whispered, raising terrified eyes to the nurse.

"There's nothing to do but wait and hope," the nurse said. She frowned as she watched Parthena wipe at his brow. "If you are intent on remaining, you should wear this." She thrust a flimsy cloth mask at Parthena.

Parthena grimaced at it before donning it. "Thank you. You look as though you could use a respite. Please go to the kitchens and have some tea and a snack." The nurse departed after being effectively dismissed.

Parthena studied Morgan, weakened by the fever, coughing and illness. In a short time, it appeared he had lost weight, had dark circles under his eyes and was covered in a fine sweat from the fever. His natural vitality had been replaced by an air of fragility. She washed his forehead, cheeks and neck, rising to replace the soiled cloth with a new one and to find fresh water.

"Drink this, my love," she whispered. She groaned with frustration when it dribbled out of his mouth and down his neck. Even with coaxing and tickling of his neck, she failed to induce him to swallow any water.

"Please, Morgan. Please," she murmured. "I can't ..." She fought tears, and they soon tracked down her cheeks. "I can't lose you."

～

ours later she returned to his room after she had rested in another bedroom. She sat beside Morgan, her mask on and her hand clinging to his. The doctor had just left, looking haggard as he made his rounds, with plans to return in the morning. He had told her that, if Morgan lived through the night, he had a good chance of surviving. She watched as he coughed and struggled to breathe, and tears coursed down her cheeks. "Please fight, Morgan. Fight for me. For us. For our baby." She gripped his hand, lacing her fingers through his.

"Do you remember the first time we met?" she whispered. "We were children, and I was five or six. I thought you would help me build my tree house and have adventures with me." She sniffled. "But you never seemed to like me or my desire to do the unconventional. I hate that I thought you boring." She swallowed a sob. "You were always there, my love. Whenever I needed a hand or an adversary to bolster my courage, you were there." Her eyes shone as she looked at him. "Do you remember our argument at the New Year's Eve Dance?" She smiled through her tears and traced a finger over his unshaven jaw. "When I pushed you into the fountain?"

She lowered her head and fought a sob. "I was too stubborn to realize you loved me, even then. I hate all the time we lost."

She rested her head next to his arm a moment. "Oh, I wish I'd known, all those years ago, about how you suffered. But I know now, darling. And I love you. So much. Please, fight this illness. Be with me as we have our baby."

She stopped speaking for a few moments as she fought a sob. "I know you wanted me out of Boston as the influenza worsened. But it was coming to Washington too. And I couldn't stay away when I received the telegram you were ill." She frowned and continued to babble to her insensate husband, wiping at his brow as he began to sweat again rather than shake from cold.

"Besides, the amendment failed, darling. After all the work Alice and Ro and all the other women did, the amendment failed. There is still so much to be done, and I want you beside me as we work to achieve this goal." She reached for a dry cloth and wiped at his brow again. "I want you beside me as I vote for the first time."

"Please, Morgan. Fight." She continued to speak to him, her anxious gaze tracking the rise and fall of his chest, taking comfort in each breath.

~

Savannah rubbed her belly as she sat in a chair in her father's parlor. She listened to one of Lucas's songs play on the gramophone, her eyes closing with pleasure at the beautiful music. When the door opened, she smiled in expectation of welcoming Jeremy and Melinda. She had not seen Melinda for days and was eager to see her daughter. When she beheld only Jeremy, she frowned. "Where is Melly? I want her here with us."

Jeremy ran a hand through his hair and leaned against the door. "She's decided to remain with Aidan and Delia."

"Why? I know she is fond of them, but I want her here with us. She's spent enough time with them, traveling to see universities. I know you thought it sensible for her to leave Boston, but I want her here now. I want her to have time with my father." She rubbed at her belly again, smiling as the baby kicked against her hand.

Jeremy wandered the sitting room as though in a trance. His silence was profound as the gramophone had ceased playing.

"Jeremy?" Savannah heaved herself up and waddled toward him. "What is going on? I've known for a few days something is wrong. Is it Richard?"

Jeremy clenched and unclenched his fists on his thighs, although he refused to look at her. "I haven't spent any time with Richard." He met her confused look. "Melly hasn't been traveling around the state, looking at universities." He met her gaze, his filled with panic and dread. "Melly is ill. Delia is caring for her."

Savannah gasped and collapsed into a chair near him. "How could you have kept such a thing from me?" She took a deep breath as her heart raced with abject terror. The daily papers were filled with tales of those who'd died from the Spanish Influenza. Just recently she'd read about a young woman who had improved only for her mother to find her dead the next morning. "How could you?"

Jeremy spun and glared at her. "Do you have any idea how much I've wanted you beside me? What it's like to watch someone I love …" He wiped at a tear on his cheek as he met her devastated gaze.

"No," she whispered. "Don't tell me that." She rose with an unexpected alacrity for a heavily pregnant woman and would have hit him on his chest, but he grabbed her arm.

"She's not dead." He tensed as Savannah's anxiety eased. "But she's ailing." He pulled her to him against her protestations, holding her close as she squirmed and kicked and cried. "Forgive me."

Pushing with all her might, she stepped back a pace, freeing herself from her husband's embrace. "I'll only forgive you if you allow me to see her." Tears poured down her cheeks. "I can't believe you'd make me beg to see my own daughter."

Jeremy's voice emerged strangled. "Savannah, you and our babe could die if you catch her illness. I can't risk you. It's why you've been cooped up here in your father's house for days. Weeks. We agreed to minimize the risk to you and our babe."

Shaking her head, she stiffened her shoulders. "This is a risk I have to take. I'm her mother." They shared an anguished look. "Will you travel there with me?"

Jeremy's gaze was wild. "You don't know what you're asking of me."

She raised a hand to his cheek. "I'm asking that you allow me to live my life as I need. I must see her, hold her, soothe her as I can. Please don't deny me that."

Jeremy pulled Savannah against him, holding her tight as he fought a sob. "Perhaps your father would like to travel with us," he said, when he released her, scrubbing at his cheeks. "We should travel in an automobile. I don't want you exposed to public transportation."

She nodded mutely as he left the room. Soon she was eased into a car, and they rushed to Aidan and Delia's mansion a short distance away in the Back Bay. She heaved herself from the car and pushed on the heavy wooden front door, refusing to wait for the butler. She moved with as much speed as possible, meeting Aidan's worried gaze as he walked down the stairs.

"Show me to her," she demanded, her voice ringing out with the authority of one who had been wronged.

As they approached a room, Aidan's pace slowed. He placed a hand on her shoulder and waited until she met his gaze. "She struggles, Savannah." He waited for her to nod and then handed her a mask.

The door creaked open, and she crept inside, sniffing at the smell of camphor and illness that pervaded the room. She battled tears as she saw her daughter lying in the middle of a double bed, her cheeks reddened and forehead sweat-streaked. After sitting on a chair beside the bed, she gripped Melinda's hand. "Fight, my darling girl. Fight," she whispered. "Your mother is here."

Melinda gave no evidence of recognition that her mother was present. Melinda continued to gasp for breath, her body shaking subtly from the fever. Savannah swiped a cloth over her forehead and looked around for something useful to do to aid her.

Delia entered the room, closing the door behind her. "Oh, Savannah," she whispered. "We are doing the best we can."

"Would it be better for her at a hospital?" Savannah croaked out through a tear-thickened throat.

Delia ran a hand along the bedspread beside Melinda. "We've had the doctor in numerous times. He told us the hospitals are overrun with those suffering from the influenza and that she would have a better ... better ..." Delia stalled.

"Better chance to survive," Savannah whispered.

"Yes, if she stayed here." Delia met Savannah's anguished, accusatory gaze. "I wanted to inform you from the first instant that we suspected she was ill. Aidan wouldn't go against Jeremy's wishes. I'm sorry, Savannah."

A tear trickled down Savannah's cheek as she watched Melinda battle for breath. "She's my daughter. I should be with her, caring for her."

Delia made a conciliatory noise. "I understand how you feel, as I'd react the same way if Zylphia were ill. However, you are expecting a child soon. Jeremy is already fearful of the birth."

Savannah glared at Delia. "In all of this, do any of you consider how I am doing? How I feel? All I hear about is how worried you are about Jeremy and his concern for me. What about how afraid I am? For me and now for Melinda?" She flushed at her outburst and focused on her daughter, wiping away sweat from her brow with a cloth from a side table. She made soothing noises when Melinda stirred, and then Savannah sighed with relief as Melinda appeared to calm.

"You're right, Savannah. I know it has appeared we were only concerned about Jeremy. However, you will discover that's not true. Aidan telegrammed Lucas, and he will arrive tonight."

Savannah's composure cracked further. "Lucas is coming?"

"Yes. We thought it imperative he come to be with you." She patted Savannah on her shoulder. "Genevieve is to remain in Montana with baby Lizzie. From what I learned, she will have the support of Patrick and Fiona."

Savannah gripped her daughter's hand and battled a sob. "If Lucas is coming, you fear the worst." She met Delia's somber gaze and buried her face in the bedding. "I can't lose her! I can't."

Jeremy slipped into the room and stood behind Delia. Savannah raised anguished eyes to Jeremy. "Don't ask me to return to my father's. Please, don't keep me away from her. Not now."

"*Shh*, … love, it's not good for you or the baby," he soothed, kissing her forehead and using a handkerchief to rub at her tears. "We'll stay here, as will your father. We'll be right by Melinda. However, I need you to get some rest. For your sake and mine." He helped her to her feet and watched as she bent to whisper her love into Melinda's ear.

She followed Jeremy into a room two doors down the hallway and eased onto the bed. She moved like a rag doll, allowing him to undress her. When he pushed on her shoulders gently and tucked her into bed, she latched onto his hand, tugging him down with her. "Stay with me. For a little while."

He curled around her, placing a protective arm over her belly. He

279

sighed with pleasure when the baby kicked against his hand. "Hello, little love," he crooned, leaning over to kiss her belly. He stilled when his actions caused her to sob. "Savannah?" he crawled over her so he faced her and brushed her loosened hair off her face. "What is it?"

"How could you?" she whispered in a broken voice. "How could you keep me from Melly?"

He clasped her head between his hands and held her tightly to meet his gaze. "You are my life. I won't survive without you," he rasped. "I can't lose you, Savannah."

"But Melly," she whispered.

He nodded, tears leaking out. "Our beloved Melly," he said, his voice cracking on *beloved*. "I've been with her almost every moment. She knows how much we love her." He buried his face in his wife's shoulder. "I can bear almost anything but losing you or our baby or Melly."

"What will we do?" she whispered as she clutched him to her, his shoulders shaking with sobs.

"She's young. She'll survive. The influenza doesn't kill the young," he said with forced confidence. "You know they make up sensational stories in the paper."

"Hold me, Jeremy," she whispered.

He pulled her tight. "Do you forgive me for trying to protect you?"

"Yes," she breathed into his ear. "But I won't forgive you if you become ill. For I won't survive without you either." He tugged her closer, his long arms reaching around to encircle her and cocoon her as they attempted to soothe each other.

A few hours later an urgent rapping on their door woke them. A haggard Delia poked her head in the room. "Come. Now," she barked before spinning out of the doorway.

Her harsh command galvanized Savannah and Jeremy. He leaped from the bed and pulled Savannah up. She rubbed at her belly as she threw on her dress, and they donned masks before they reentered Melinda's room. Rather than the darkened sick room, barely lit for the overnight hours, the room was as bright as midday. Aidan and her father were at the foot of the bed, while Delia was on the other side of the bed.

Savannah rushed to her daughter's side and sat on the empty chair by her bedside. Melinda lay on the bed, tugging at the sheet, arching her back, holding her chest as though attempting to force air into her lungs. Dark spots had appeared on her cheeks. Each subsequent breath was more labored than the last.

"Fight, Melly," Savannah urged. "Fight, my darling daughter. I love you so much." She clutched her hand, squeezing it as she watched her daughter struggle to take a breath.

As each breath was more labored than the last, the skin on her neck and face took on a slight blue tinge. Savannah stilled when she noticed the subtle change and reached forward to stroke Melinda's cheek. "No, Melly. No!"

As Melinda's chest stopped its laborious rising and falling, and the last air left her lips on a long hiss, Savannah shrieked. She shook off Jeremy's hands on her shoulders and ran her fingers over Melinda's chest, pushing on her chest as though to restart her breathing. "Try," she sobbed. "Try."

"Savannah," Jeremy whispered, wrapping an arm around her upper chest and hefting her away from their daughter. "She's gone. Our Melly is gone."

"No!" She screamed as she kicked and fought him. "No," she cried again as Jeremy toppled to the floor with her. She keened and wailed, lost to her grief. His gentle caresses went unacknowledged. Only when she had cried herself to a near stupor did she allow Jeremy to coax her to stand and to move from the room.

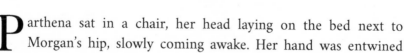

Parthena sat in a chair, her head laying on the bed next to Morgan's hip, slowly coming awake. Her hand was entwined with his, and she blinked a few times as she attempted to recognize her surroundings. Her head jerked up when she remembered she was at Morgan's side. Her mask had slipped off in the night, and she rubbed at her face as she ran an assessing gaze over her husband before she righted it. Her frantic heartbeat calmed when she saw his chest rising and falling with shallow breaths.

She raised his hand and kissed it. "Come back to me, my love. Fight for us," she whispered. She lay her head down again as fatigue overwhelmed her. When the fingers she gripped gave her a small squeeze, she gasped.

"Come lie next to me, Hennie," he croaked out.

"Morgan!" She crawled up the bed to perch on her knees next to his side and to clasp his whiskered face between her hands. He opened weary eyes to her and attempted a smile. Reaching for a glass half-filled with water on the side table, she scooted an arm around his shoulders and eased him to a sitting position.

After he took a deep sip of water, he lay back against the sheets and sighed. "Come," he said, holding his arm up for a moment. "I want to feel you next to me."

"You are not going to die," she commanded, biting her lower lip as it wobbled with the word *die*. She scooted so she rested her head against his shoulder, her arm over his chest.

"Not today," he sighed. "Not today, my love." He kissed her forehead and drifted back to sleep. When he awoke, Parthena remained in his arms, fast asleep. He moved, his arm having long since become a dead weight underneath her head.

His subtle movement woke her, and she patted his face.

"I have no fever. I think I am finally better."

"You are far from better, but I believe you will recover." She stroked a hand over his whiskered cheeks. "When I received word you were ill, I didn't know what to do."

He laughed soundlessly. "Of course you did. You raced here and never left my side." His gaze was filled with love and fear. "I only hate that you put yourself in harm's way due to me."

"I love you, Morgan. I know you would have done the same for me." When he sighed his agreement, she smiled. "I know it's stupid, but I had this belief, if you knew I was with you, if you could somehow sense my presence, that you wouldn't die. I couldn't leave you."

He traced a hand over her eyebrow. "I wish that were the case. Then we'd have no need of medicines, and there wouldn't be all these senseless deaths from this horrible disease." He turned his face and kissed her palm cupping his cheek. "I knew, somehow I knew you were with me, Hennie. And you gave me the strength to struggle back." He flushed.

"I love that you are as whimsical as I am in my love for you," she said as she tightened her grip of her arms around his waist. "Don't scare me like this again, Morgan."

He sighed as he held her close. "I'll try not to, my love."

～

Three days later, Savannah sat in a back parlor room in Aidan and Delia's large house. Although she had wanted to return to her father's home, Jeremy insisted they remain with his uncle. She had not had the energy to spare on an argument. The echo of the front door opening and closing resonated through the house, and she imagined the few guests leaving who had braved entering a home of sickness due to deference to Aidan.

She stared into space as she envisioned the sunny morning filled with such promise. The birds' cheerful calls from the nearby trees, the well-tended front garden, the faint scent of the sea carried on a gentle breeze. She closed her eyes as she remembered the low incantations from the priest as they had lowered her beloved Melinda into the ground, Savannah's inability to cry, her insistence that she stand stoically without support from anyone. She ignored the door to the small room opening and closing, her mind reliving the events of the past few days.

Lucas sat in front of Savannah, frowning when she failed to notice his presence. She sat with a stupefied look, and his jaw clenched. He moved to sit next to her on the settee and grabbed her hand. He squeezed it to the point of pain, finally earning a reaction from her.

"Lucas," she murmured. "Why are you here?"

"I received an urgent telegram to come at once. Of course I came," he said. He watched her quizzically. "I've been here for over two days now, and yet, every time you see me, you are surprised at my presence."

"I don't know why they should have seen fit to disturb you when they couldn't be bothered to inform me of my own daughter's illness." She clamped her jaw shut and glared out the window.

Lucas canted his body so he faced her before gripping one of her shoulders so she was forced to meet his gaze. "Do you have any idea what Melly's death has done to Jeremy? To Aidan and Delia? To our father?"

"Why should I be concerned about them?" She glared at her brother. "They lied to me. They kept me from her. I could have had more time with her." Her voice broke, but she fought her tears.

Lucas shook his head and growled at his sister's stubbornness. "Do you believe that you could have cared for Melinda better than Delia, Aidan and their horde of servants? Do you believe you could have found more professional doctors, in the midst of a doctor shortage, than Aidan?" Lucas breathed heavily with his agitation. "They did everything in their power to save your daughter. Their beloved great-niece. You have no right to disparage their attempts to aid her or to protect you."

She slapped at his shoulders twice before he gripped her hands. "How dare you agree with them! You're my brother. They weren't protecting me. They were coddling me!"

"Look at you, Sav," Lucas said, unable to hide the pleading tone in his voice. "You're about to give birth. In the midst of an influenza outbreak. How can you blame Jeremy for doing everything in his power to keep you healthy? It's why you came to Boston."

"And that's why Melly died!" she yelled. Her eyes rounded, and she ripped one of her hands free from Lucas's hold to cover her mouth. She shook her head from side to side as though appalled at herself.

"You can't blame him," Lucas whispered. "Not truly. He did what he needed to do to help you and the baby. Nor did he want to be separated from Melly all that time. You can't blame him." His whispered words provoked deep racking sobs in Savannah. He pulled her close, holding her as she cried.

Jeremy poked his head into the sitting room to see Lucas holding a sobbing Savannah. He waited until Lucas noticed him and then raised an eyebrow. When Lucas motioned for him to enter, he shut the door behind him and pulled a chair closer to the settee where she sat.

"Savannah," he whispered.

Her head jerked up at his voice, and her sobs intensified. "I wanted to hate you," she whispered.

He jerked backward as though she had slapped him, and his wounded eyes became more tortured. "I failed you. I don't know how to ask you for forgiveness."

Savannah let go of her brother and reached out to Jeremy. "You didn't," she stammered. She barely acknowledged her brother rising and slipping from the room. "I needed someone to be angry with. To hate." She closed her eyes as tears continued to pour down her cheeks.

"I hate myself enough for the both of us."

At his words, she tugged at him until he sat on Lucas's spot on the settee.

"If I hadn't insisted we come to Boston ... If we had remained in Montana, Melly would be ..." He choked on a sob. "She would be ..."

"No," she whispered, gripping his hand, her eyes widening at the depths of his grief. "Oh, my darling," she breathed as she leaned into him. "You have only ever acted to protect those you love." She sniffled and swallowed a sob. "You can't blame yourself for coming here. You could never have known that such a tragedy would strike."

She clung to him as he pulled her tightly to him, his tears soaking her hair as he silently wept. "I'm so sorry," she whispered.

He kissed her head and whispered in her ear, "Why, my love?"

"Because, when I sat there and watched Melly, ... watched us lose her, all I could think about was myself. My loss. My despair. My anguish at losing another daughter." She trembled. "I never thought about you. About how you suffered too." She kissed his cheek. "I was selfish in my grief. I wasn't there when you needed me."

"You are. You're here now," he whispered. "I feared you doubted …"

"What?" She stroked a hand over his back.

"I feared you doubted how much I loved her. Cherished her."

She pushed at him until she met his eyes, bloodshot and shattered after the loss of their daughter. "Never. No one could have loved her more than you did. Than we did."

He tugged her close again, the agony slightly more bearable as they shared the burden.

The following day, Savannah sat on a settee in the small sitting room in Delia and Aidan's house. She stared with unseeing eyes at the window, failing to note the soft rain falling outside. A book open to the same page for the past three hours sat on her lap. She jolted as a man spoke, breaking the silence in the room.

"How are you, Savannah?" her father asked. He wore a mourning suit, and the black coat matched the dour mood of the house.

"Surviving," she whispered. "I try, Father. I am to have the baby soon, and I try. But I find it hard to kindle much joy."

He held her hand. "Of course you do, my darling daughter. And I fear that you will suffer by postponing your procedure."

She looked at her father, her expression dazed and deadened to any deep emotion except sorrow. "I appreciate the doctor's caution. He does not want me to go to a hospital overrun with influenza victims to have my surgery. Besides, he is run off his feet caring for those sick with this illness."

"You can't remain pregnant forever," her father said with a sardonic smile. "The baby may decide not to keep to your time frame."

She nodded and sniffled. "I know. And if that happens …" She shrugged. "I know I won't survive a normal birth."

Her father frowned and gripped her hand. "You can't know that, Savannah. You are strong and healthy. You must believe you will hold your baby in your arms."

She blinked away tears. "Melly was strong and healthy. Look what happened to her," she whispered. "None of that matters."

Her father moved from his seat to sit beside her on the settee, tugging her into his arms. "I would take away this sorrow for you, for our family, if I could." He cleared his throat as he fought tears. "I miss her dreadfully, even though I only knew her a few short months. She was such a bright, inspiring young woman."

Savannah nodded. "She was. And I was fortunate enough to be able to call her my daughter." She rested her head on her father's shoulder. "How long are we to stay here? Shouldn't we return to your home, Father?"

He sighed. "I've spoken with Delia and Aidan, and they have generously agreed for us to remain here as guests." He kissed her head. "The linen business will be sold soon, and I will have no home here in Boston. I'd prefer not to buy anything, and I'd rather not be out searching for rooms to rent just now."

Savannah nodded. "We could stay here forever, and I doubt Aidan and Delia would mind."

Her father chuckled. "They are very generous. And delighted to have family in their home again."

She fell silent as she rested in her father's arms.

After many moments, he whispered, "There are no words to ease your pain, Savannah. Mourn our darling Melly. But don't live with her ghost. Live with us. Live for the future, not the past." He kissed her head again and rose, leaving her to her thoughts.

Jeremy knocked on the door and waited entrance. He looked at the brick building with bow-fronted windows and the small front garden, equal in splendor to neighboring houses. When the butler opened the door, he was shown into the family sitting room.

"Jeremy!" Zylphia exclaimed. "What a lovely surprise." She pulled him into a hug and motioned for him to sit.

"You smell like turpentine," he said as he sniffed at her.

She blushed and waved a hand as though pointing upstairs. "I was painting." She sobered at his grim expression. "Are you well? Is it Savannah or the baby?"

"No," he said with a quick shake of his head. "We are all well. Except for the loss of ..." He cleared his throat. "We are finding it difficult to overcome Melinda's loss."

She gripped his hand and sat beside him. "Of course you are. How is Savannah? I tried to see her yesterday, but she refused my visit."

Frustration glinted in his eyes. "Hurting. Devastated." He sighed. "I think, over and over again, if I would have done something else ... Could have done ..." He looked at his cousin, searching her gaze for censure or judgment and saw none. "I am riddled with guilt that I kept Savannah away from Melly those last days."

Zylphia's eyes filled. "I can only imagine how you feel. I wish I'd seen her, but Teddy begged me not to go." She sniffled. "I ... I was angry with my husband too, Jeremy." Her grip on his hand tightened. "But I see the wisdom of his thinking. So many have fallen ill, and too many have died."

Jeremy frowned as he looked at her. "Who else?"

"Morgan was very ill, and Parthena feared he would die. But he survived. Three of Florence and Richard's boys were ill, but they've come through it. Parthena's youngest sister, Isabel, died yesterday."

"I feel so selfish. I've only thought of myself, and Richard must have been terrified. For himself. For Flo." He shook his head as a tear escaped. "I can't believe Uncle Aidan didn't tell me."

"You have a right to focus on your own grief, Jeremy. We can only cope with so much at a time." She stroked a hand down his arm. "And you must know that any anger Savannah feels is an attempt to not feel so much anguish."

He closed his eyes. "The agony will never go away." He sniffled. "And I pity this poor baby who will be born in the midst of such sorrow."

She shook her head, and her smile was luminous. "No, Jeremy. Rejoice at the birth of your child. Rejoice that you and Savannah will have a baby together. Tell her stories about her big sister Melinda. About how she would have played with her and taught her all sorts of things that you would rather have kept secret." She squeezed his arm. "Talk about Melly. Don't turn her into a ghost member of the family due to your grief."

He nodded. "I know it is a lot to ask, Zee. And I know you don't paint such subjects." He firmed his jaw as he looked at his cousin. "Will you paint a portrait of Savannah and the baby?"

She beamed at him. "I'd be honored to, although you'll find I'm not that good at capturing people on canvas." She pulled him close for a hug. "You will survive this, Jeremy," she whispered as he let out a deep breath on her shoulder. "And we are all here to support you."

He leaned away and met her worried gaze. "I will survive. But I'll never be the same again."

~

After visiting with Zylphia, Jeremy walked to the Public Gardens and sat on a bench for a few hours. The rain had stopped during his visit with Zylphia, and he wanted to spend a little time outside. He sat alone on the bench, his gaze unseeing as he thought about Melinda. Her wide smile when he taught her to fish. Her clomping down the hallway in his oversized shoes, upset that she would never have feet as big as his, nor be as tall as he was. Her shrieks of laughter when she attempted something and failed spectacularly. His breath caught as he fought a sob.

He sniffled and blinked a few times, focusing on the Gardens. A few of the trees had lost leaves in the recent rainstorm, and scattered leaves floated on the pond in the middle of the Gardens. A gust of wind blew, and he shivered. He realized how late it was and rose to walk back to his uncle's house.

When he arrived, Aidan ran from the front sitting room. "Jeremy! Where have you been?"

"Out. I saw Zee and then went to the Gardens." He noted his

uncle's panicked expression. "Savannah!" He attempted to push past Aidan, but Aidan caught him.

"No, she's not here. Her pains started, and Delia, Lucas and her father took her to the hospital. She's there now."

"I have to … I have to be with her," Jeremy said, his gaze frantic.

"Of course. I have an automobile awaiting us outside. Come." He pushed Jeremy out the door and into the waiting car. When they arrived at the hospital, Aidan gave him a mask and donned one before they raced inside. They were shown to the maternity ward and stopped in the waiting area. Once inside the ward, they took off their masks as they were told it was an area free of the influenza.

"Delia!" Jeremy called out in a breathless pant. "How is she? I need to see her."

Delia shook her head. "You're too late, Jeremy." She gripped his hand as he paled and swayed in front of her. "They've taken her back for her operation. We should know soon how she did. She was healthy and fine, although a bit scared."

"I should have been here for her," he whispered.

Her father patted Jeremy on his shoulder and tugged him to a seat. "It's all right, son. I know what it is to mourn, and you needed a little time."

Lucas slung an arm over Jeremy's shoulder. "The waiting is the worst part, but soon you'll have a baby to spoil."

Jeremy bent forward with his head in his hands as the time ticked by at a slow pace. After a few hours of relative silence, where his family realized he was in no mood for mindless chatter, the doors swung open. Jeremy shot up and met the doctor's guarded gaze.

"She is recovering well," the doctor said.

"And?" Jeremy asked.

"And you have a healthy son," he said with a broad smile.

"A son," he whispered as he collapsed backward onto a chair. He looked at the doctor. "You're sure Savannah is well? That she will be fine?"

"She is currently healthy and recovering well. I can say no more than that." He turned to leave, but Delia grabbed his arm.

"When can we see her? The baby?" Her eyes were lit with joy.

"The nurse will inform you when you are allowed to see them." He nodded at their thanks and left.

Aidan hauled Jeremy up and pulled him into a bear hug. "Congratulations, my dearest nephew," he whispered. "I'm so happy for you."

Delia pushed aside her husband and hugged Jeremy before kissing his cheek. "Oh, what wonderful news."

Lucas clapped him on the back, and Savannah's father pulled him close. "Thank you," he whispered in Jeremy's ear. "Thank you for ensuring she was safe."

Jeremy shuddered, and his eyes were filled with tears as he backed away from his father-in-law. He saw understanding and compassion in Martin's gaze and nodded.

After what felt like an eternity to him, the nurse approached their group, and he was granted permission to see Savannah. He followed the nurse down a brightly lit hallway that smelled of antiseptic. His footsteps echoed off the walls, enhancing the sense of forced quiet in that part of the hospital.

The nurse opened a door, and he entered. Three other women were in the room, although Savannah had a bed by the window. She rested with her eyes closed.

"My love," he whispered, tracing his fingers over her hand. Her eyes opened, and he smiled at her. "Oh, my love." A tear leaked down his cheek as he saw her, healthy after the operation.

"I'm sorry," she whispered, her gaze remote.

"For what?" he asked, raising her hand to kiss it. "You are alive and well. I could ask for no more." He saw her battling tears and frowned. "We have a healthy son, Savannah. I'm sure they will bring him to us soon."

Her gaze flew to his, filled with a fearful hope.

He nodded as he stroked her cheek. "The doctor told me that we have a beautiful baby boy." His breath hitched as she let out a sob, her hand clutching her waist.

"I couldn't remember," she whispered. "When I saw you there, ... I thought I'd, we'd, lost our baby."

He rested his forehead against hers. "No, my precious darling. No," he said as he kissed her and then dropped his head by her neck. "God, I want to hold you in my arms and never let you go."

She ran her arms over his shaking back. "I love you, Jeremy," she whispered. "So much."

"And I you. Thank you for being brave. For risking everything for our child." He sniffled and cleared his throat as the nurse gave an "*Ahem.*"

"Your son," the nurse said with a broad smile, picking up the sleeping baby from the bassinette and placing him in Savannah's waiting arms.

Savannah lost her battle with tears, and they streamed down her cheeks. She kissed his forehead, his cheeks, his nose and then played with his hand that had come free of the swaddling. "Our son," she said as she met Jeremy's dazzling smile. "Our son."

He wrapped an arm about her shoulders and pulled her close, his head against hers as they gazed at their baby, his hand over hers as they held their child to her chest. "Our son."

CHAPTER 16

Missoula, Montana, October 1918

"*W*hat happened between you and Rissa?" Patrick asked. He sat on Colin's porch the night before Araminta's wedding in early October, his feet balanced on the railing. "I never thought I'd arrive to find the two of you fighting."

Colin closed his eyes as he leaned his head against the back of his rocking chair. "I love nights like this. The weather is still mild enough to enjoy being outside, even though there is the promise of the changing seasons." He jolted when Patrick belted him on his shoulder.

"I'm serious, Col. What happened to cause such disharmony between the two of you?" He watched his brother with confused brown eyes. "You've always been close to Rissa."

"Ha, that's what I thought." Colin shook his head in disgust as he surveyed the street with unseeing eyes.

Patrick frowned further at the rancor in Colin's voice. "When I saw her today, it was evident she's as upset with you as you are with her. This can't continue."

Colin opened blue eyes filled with a steely determination. "I will never apologize to her. *I* did nothing wrong." Soon the only sounds enveloping them were those of the soft evening. The sounds of a squirrel scurrying as it prepared for winter. A soft breeze, the creak of a rocking chair. "She believes I attacked Ari. That I did to Ari what was done to her by Cameron."

Boots hit the wooden porch boards as Patrick sat upright. "What?" He stared at his brother with incredulity. "How could she ever think that?" He ran a hand through his thinning brown hair. "Why would she ever think that?"

Colin looked at his brother, a deep sadness in his gaze. "I can't say I didn't touch Ari. That I didn't try to convince her to be my wife, rather than that bastard's." He leaned forward and clasped his hands. "But I swear to you, I never forced her."

Patrick stared at him for many moments, his gaze distant before he met Colin's gaze. "Of course you didn't. That's a preposterous accusation. The question is, why does Rissa believe it? That's what I'm trying to figure out."

Colin shook his head. "I guess Ari went to Rissa's house after she spurned me and said unintelligible things as she cried in Rissa's arms."

Patrick sat in silence for a few moments. "I know you supported Rissa after her attack. That you helped her escape Boston." He sighed as he ran a hand through his hair again. "But, after living with Fee and seeing how she fights her demons every day, I don't know if you can understand what seeing Ari so distressed could have done to Rissa." Patrick paused as he met his brother's hurt gaze. "You know she counts on you. You know she trusts you. You know she loves you."

Colin's eyes flashed with pain.

"But some terrors are nearly impossible to put behind us. And I would guess that Rissa lost her balance with that battle for a moment."

"How could she think that of me, Pat?" He shook his head, unable to hide the hurt in his voice.

"I doubt she truly did, not after she thought it through. By that time you were too stubborn and pigheaded to listen to anything she had to say to you. This is as much your fault as hers."

Colin sat in silence for many moments and then nodded. "I've rebuffed every attempt she's made to reconcile with me. I've treated her abominably."

Patrick kicked Colin in the foot in a brotherly way. "Then you must hope she'll forgive you as you must forgive her. Do you think that is possible?"

Colin shrugged his shoulders. "I don't know." He took a stuttering breath. "And tomorrow I lose Ari."

～

Araminta stood in front of the mirror in Clarissa's bedroom, her gaze somber and mouth unsmiling as she watched Clarissa fuss with her veil. Araminta ran a hand over the simple cream-colored dress, having resisted pressure from Bartholomew's family to buy a more elaborate gown. Her future aunt-in-law Mrs. Vaughan had protested at the plain design of her wedding ensemble but had grudgingly admitted she had to agree with Araminta's sense of style. As Araminta beheld herself in the looking glass, she nodded with approval. Nothing too fancy for a woman from an orphanage.

Sunlight streamed in on this bright Saturday morning in October. Although fall, the crisp morning air would give way to a warm afternoon. However, no wedding festivities would occur outside, even though Araminta had argued for a gathering in the park she and Bartholomew had circled innumerable times during their courtship. She dreaded feeling caged inside during the wedding celebration. As she glanced outside, the sunlight seemed to mock her false serenity and her overruled desire.

"You look beautiful, Minta," Clarissa murmured. She gripped her friend's fingers and shook her hands in the space between them, as though preventing herself from shaking sense into her friend. "I'm so happy for you."

Araminta watched Clarissa with an impassive expression, as though all emotion in her had been frozen. "I hope Bartholomew is correct and that the guests will know to arrive at the church early."

Clarissa eyed her with concern. "It seemed rather inconsiderate of the priest to change the time at the last possible minute."

Araminta took a deep breath. "In the end, all that matters is that the two marrying are there."

The knock at the door had Clarissa giving a disgruntled grunt as she dropped her fluttering hands and moved to open the door. She wore a blue dress that matched the color of her eyes and a hat at a jaunty angle. "Gabriel," she said with a broad smile tinged with relief.

"I'm here to see the blushing bride to the church." He stepped into the room and shut the door behind him. "I wouldn't want any others to get a sneak peek of you." He winked at Araminta.

"Has everyone gone ahead to the church?" Araminta asked. She watched as Gabriel and Clarissa shared a long look.

"Hester, Patrick and Fiona have taken the older children to the church, while I'll arrive with Little Colin," Clarissa said.

Araminta nodded her understanding at what they didn't say. She took a deep breath and approached Gabriel. "I'm ready."

Gabriel smiled at Clarissa as she slipped from the room, closing the door softly behind her, and then he stepped in front of Araminta, preventing her from rushing from the room to her future. He held her by her shoulders and bent his knees to meet her eyes. "Are you sure?" When she remained silent, he squeezed her shoulders. "I don't want you to make a mistake."

"I'm not. This is what I want." Her voice cracked on *want*, but she maintained her composure and met Gabriel's gaze with a calm serenity.

"Well, if you're sure," he murmured, holding his elbow out for her. After he opened the door for her, he flushed. "I have a surprise for you." On the table in the hallway, a small bouquet of yellow and white roses was perched precariously in a pitcher. "Here. A bride should have flowers on her wedding day."

Araminta bit her lip as she fought tears. "You shouldn't have, Gabriel." She met his worried but proud gaze. "Thank you."

"I think of you as my little sister, Minta. I hope you know you can always come to me, no matter the time of day or the cause of your distress." He patted her hand when it tightened on his arm. "It's to church for the two of us."

Upon arrival, Araminta looked around, but no one was outside on the sun-drenched steps to the church. She smiled at Gabriel and walked up the steps with him. However, upon entering the church, she yanked on Gabriel's arm and paused at the back of the church, near the door. For a moment it appeared she would run, but then she firmed her shoulders and gave a nod.

Araminta smiled bravely at Gabriel a moment before they walked down the aisle, her subtle trembling more pronounced the closer she came to the altar. Gabriel kissed her forehead, placed her hand in Bartholomew's with a glower for him and then moved to take a seat beside Clarissa.

When the priest finished his lengthy sermon about the sanctity of marriage, the organ player blasted out an off-tune piece, more appropriate for a funeral than a wedding. After a few moments, those gathered murmured and chuckled at the ominous notes. When the priest was about to begin the exchange of vows, the door at the rear of the church *clang*ed open. "Stop. This wedding cannot proceed," a man's irate voice sounded.

"Oh, no," Araminta breathed.

Clarissa turned and gasped as she saw Colin striding down the aisle, ignoring the hissing from Mrs. Vaughan. Mrs. Bouchard belted him with her hefty eggplant-hued purse. He grunted as the purse made contact with his stomach, but he continued moving forward.

"She should have aimed lower," Gabriel muttered to Clarissa, earning a tap on his arm. His son Billy jumped with excitement on the pew, and Gabriel corralled him with an arm to prevent him from joining Colin as he made his way down the aisle.

Araminta stood stock-still, her hand in Bartholomew's. Colin came to a stuttering stop on her other side. "What are you doing here?" she whispered.

"You know damn well and good what I'm doing here. Stopping you from making a terrible mistake." He looked at Bartholomew. "I'm sorry it's come to this, but she refused to see sense."

"I believe she knew what she was doing, choosing one such as I am rather than a lowly blacksmith." Bartholomew looked Colin up and down with disdain at his disheveled clothes. "If you will please cease with the dramatics and allow us to continue? We are getting married today."

"You are correct. This is no better than a play, and I've yet to determine if this one is a comedy or a tragedy." Colin gripped Araminta's free hand. "Ari, please come with me. Cease this lunacy."

"Colin, I've given my word."

"And that means more than ..." He broke off as he looked at the priest watching them with avid interest. "May we talk in the apse over there?"

As Bartholomew opened his mouth to protest, the priest speared him with a fierce stare. "I think you should, young man. I will not marry you unless I know there is full consent from both parties."

Bartholomew snarled at Colin and dragged Araminta to the side of the church, with Colin following. Araminta tripped as her weak leg was not strong enough for such fast, erratic movements, and Colin caught her. "It's all right. I've got you."

"Get your hands off my bride this instant," Bartholomew barked, reddening as Colin held Araminta.

"If you treated her with any sort of regard, you'd know you can't tow her around like a prized mare," Colin snapped. He ran a hand down Araminta's back before releasing her. They stepped into the apse and away from curious eyes.

"Why do you believe you have the right to disrupt my wedding?" Bartholomew demanded, tugging Araminta to his side.

Colin frowned at Bartholomew's possessive treatment of her. "Ari made a promise to me, and I would like her to keep it," Colin murmured.

"Colin, no," she whispered.

He met her pleading gaze with his wounded, wild gaze filled with desperation. "You've left me no choice." He held up his battered hands from his work at the smithy. "I know of no other way, Ari."

Bartholomew watched the two of them and sneered. "She made a promise to me first," he boasted. "And I plan to ensure she keeps that promise." He pointed toward the filled pews. "That church is filled with my family. With the most important businessmen of this town and state. With my friends. I will not allow your family to humiliate us Bouchards again."

"You're delusional if you think that my aim in all of this was to, in any way, affect your family or your perceived esteem among the community," Colin snapped. "My sole aim is to protect Ari from a man such as you."

"Oh, a man who is successful? A man who has prospects? A man who knows how to treat his wife?" Bartholomew yanked on Araminta's arm, provoking a small shriek of pain.

Colin took in a slow breath and watched him with a deep, calculating look in his eye. He ignored Araminta's pleading gaze. "Would you still want her if you knew she'd already been mine?"

Colin had no chance to catch Araminta as she was thrust to the floor. He was too busy fending off Bartholomew's vicious uppercut. Colin barely danced out of the way as Bartholomew screamed, "You defiler!" Colin absently heard Araminta's moan of distress and the murmur of titillation from the gathered wedding crowd. Colin landed a punch to Bartholomew's midsection, and soon they were kicking and grappling with each other in an ungainly, undignified scrapple. He tripped Bartholomew but was pulled down with him as Bartholomew held on tightly to his shirt.

A loud rending sound was heard as Colin was yanked off Bartholomew. Patrick wrapped strong arms around his middle while Gabriel held a hand to Bartholomew's chest, a warning gleam in his eyes daring Bartholomew to take him on. With heaving breaths, Bartholomew wrenched himself from Gabriel and spun to glare at Araminta. "Harlot," he hissed as he stormed from the apse.

The word "Off!" was yelled a few times, and then excited voices were heard in the central area of the church. Gabriel and Patrick patted Colin on the shoulder and moved toward the entrance of the apse in an attempt to give Colin privacy with Araminta. She sat, crumpled on the floor in her fine wedding dress, her bouquet clutched in both hands. A stream of tears poured down her cheeks.

"Ari," he whispered. He held up his arms as she pummeled him with her bouquet of flowers. He grunted as the thorns bit into him but did nothing to prevent her from venting her anger. When she lowered her arms, he lifted and dropped his hands twice, uncertain if he should touch her.

"How could you do that to me, Colin?" she breathed in a broken voice. "All I've ever wanted was to belong."

"How could you do that to *us*?" he demanded. "Do you think I relished prancing down the aisle to stop you from marrying him?"

She glared at him, her air of fragility fading as anger replaced despair. She refrained from belting him again with her flowers. "You could have come by the house this morning. You could have asked to speak with me like an adult."

Colin gripped her ankle, keeping her from moving away from him. "I was barred from Rissa's house, or don't you recall that?" He removed his hand and looked at the floor but not quickly enough to hide the hurt flashing in his eyes. "The only reason I came in when I did was because I was tired of waiting outside. I was told the wedding started at one, not eleven."

"Oh, dear," she whispered, her mouth falling open.

"I'd hoped to catch you outside when you arrived. I finally heard the organ, and I realized you were already in here. I had no desire to become this month's—this decade's—gossip." He shook his head ruefully.

"The time was changed at the last minute," Araminta breathed, her eyes rounded and her tears falling again.

His eyes flared. "Either that or you were misled because he was afraid I'd do something like this." He ripped a piece of linen from his torn shirt to swipe at her eyes. "I forgot a handkerchief."

She gripped his hand to her cheek, sobs bursting forth at the contact. "How did you know the original time? Clarissa?" she whispered.

He scooted forward and gathered her into his arms, pulling the pins from her hair which held the veil in place before stroking a hand over her head. "Yes, she sent me the invitation. Said in her note that, if I wasn't a complete idiot, I'd know what to do." He shuddered in her arms. "I never got word the time had changed."

"We didn't know until this morning."

A deep voice cleared from a few feet away. "Sorry to interrupt, but I'd suggest continuing this in a more private locale," Patrick said. "We have an automobile waiting out front for you."

Colin leaned away to look at Araminta, sitting in a dazed stupor. "Will you come home with me so I can explain? So you can explain to me?" He sighed at her hesitation, looking at his brother in frustration.

Patrick smiled. "Fiona and I were talking about how we're concerned that Savannah's house has been empty all these months. Gabriel agrees that we should stay there a few nights, so no one thinks it's abandoned. You'll be ensured privacy at your home."

Colin flashed him a grateful smile and waited for Araminta to nod her agreement. He rose and held a hand out to heave her upward. He gave her time to gain her balance, then followed Patrick and Gabriel outside, noting Clarissa had already departed.

~

Colin entered his home, opening his mouth to apologize for the mess, before closing it to find it remarkably tidy. He motioned for Araminta to sit, watching her settle on the settee before he sat on a chair facing her. After a few moments of silence, he rose, heading to the kitchen. He returned with two glasses of apple cider.

"Here. I thought you might be thirsty." He handed her one before drinking half his glass in a few swallows. He sat again, crossing his legs in an attempt to appear calm, but his foot tapping the air belied his nervousness.

She took a sip and set aside her glass.

"What did I do wrong, Ari?" he asked, wincing at the near-begging tone of his voice. "I know I waited too long to show you how much I care for you, but I thought, once I did, you'd want me too."

Araminta sat with her hands clenched in her lap, her gaze averted. Her pristine wedding dress was now wrinkled with a torn hem, while her veil had been forgotten at the church. The beautiful bouquet ruined in her pique of fury as she had railed against Colin remained clenched between her fingers. However, her placid detachment had vanished, and she trembled with pent-up emotions.

Colin hissed out a sigh of frustration. "Why would you agree to marry such a man?" He held up a hand. "I understand in the beginning that I hadn't offered yet, and that makes me an idiot. But afterward, after we were together, why would you still agree to go through with it?" He clamped his jaw shut as his voice shook with hurt and betrayal. "I love you, Ari. The thought of you with such a man ..." He shook his head.

"You don't really love me, Colin. You're just afraid that your life will change when I marry another."

Colin leaped forward, looming over her and caging her on the settee with his body. "Don't you dare tell me how I feel. I've never told a woman that I love her before. You're the only woman who could have provoked me to such madness as to interrupt a wedding." His eyes shone with fierce intensity and unshed tears. "You believe because you're an orphan that you are unworthy of love. And you were willing to accept a man who would treat you as nothing more than a servant in his home." He raised a trembling hand to trace her eyebrow. "Why would you accept that when you know how precious you are?" He waited for her gaze to meet his. "To me?"

She shook her head as tears poured out. She leaned forward, butting her head into Colin's chest and almost knocking him off balance.

He plopped onto the floor and pulled her down with him until they sat in a tangle of legs, with her half on his lap. "Tell me, Ari. Tell me why you turned your back on us," he entreated, kissing her head.

"I didn't." At his incredulous scoff, she reared back and hit him in the shoulder. "I had to marry him to protect you!"

Colin watched her, thunderstruck. "What? That's preposterous."

"He ... He says that you are a German sympathizer, and that he has proof. He says he can send you to jail due to that new law," Araminta said between her sobs.

"He thinks to use the Sedition Act to coerce you into marriage?" He shook his head in confusion. "I don't understand." He cradled her head between his two strong hands. "I love you. You know I do. But I can't imagine wanting to send a man to prison so as to marry anyone. Why?"

Araminta shook her head in confusion. "I have no idea. But I couldn't let you go to prison, Col. I just couldn't." She looked down. "I love you too much to see you harmed."

His hold on her tightened at her words. "I'll need you to repeat that for me, Ari."

She raised fearful eyes to meet his hopeful gaze. "I love you, Colin, but I don't know how that will aid you." She gasped as he tugged her to him, holding her tight and rocking her in his arms.

"We'll fight this together, Ari," he said, his voice triumphant. "That's what it means." He groaned. "God, all I want to do is make love with you. But I need to talk with Pat and Gabe about what you told me." He leaned back and met her gaze. "Stay with me tonight?"

Araminta smiled, joy finally reaching her eyes. "Of course. The town already thinks I'm a harlot."

Colin sobered at her words. "Then they're misinformed. You'll soon be my wife, and you are an honorable woman." He smiled mischievously. "Who happens to anticipate her vows." He winked at her as he rose and offered her his hand to help her off the floor.

～

Gabriel watched as Clarissa snatched a few letters from the front hall table and then followed the children upstairs to help them change into clothes they could romp around in outside. When he heard them overhead, he faced his brother-in-law. "Did you see anything disturbing at that wedding?"

Patrick met Gabriel's concerned stare and nodded. "Any idea why he would be here?"

303

Gabriel shook his head, momentarily distracted as he heard Billy shriek with delight upstairs. "Why should my bastard of a cousin care who Bartholomew Bouchard marries?"

Patrick shook his head. "I don't know, but I'm certain he's still in cahoots with Mrs. Smythe."

"Will we never be free of their meddling?" Gabriel muttered.

Patrick shook his head again in frustration and then smiled as Fiona entered Gabriel's house with Rose. "Hello, my loves." He kissed them both on the cheek.

Little feet clattered down the stairs, and Rose chased after her cousins as they raced outside. Patrick stopped his instinctive inclination to follow and play with them when his sister called his name.

"Fee, would you watch the children?" Clarissa asked. "I'm sorry, but I have to speak with Patrick, and I need Gabriel."

After Fiona departed, Gabriel ran a finger over Clarissa's ashen cheeks. "It's all right, Rissa. We already know my cousin was at the wedding."

"No," she rasped, holding up a letter. "Oh, it's so much worse." She fell to her knees.

Gabriel was at her side in an instant. "Tell us, love."

She gripped his hand and met her brother's worried gaze. "It's Melinda. She's … She's dead."

"Dead?" Patrick asked as a tremor ran through him, the only outward indication of her words' effect on him. "How?"

"Influenza," Clarissa said as a sob burst forth.

Patrick backed up until he hit a chair and then collapsed into it. "My … Melly," he whispered, his gaze shattered. Suddenly he rose. "I will be with the children."

"Patrick," Clarissa croaked, but he stormed from the room to the backyard.

"Let him go, love," Gabriel soothed as he held his wife still dressed in her wedding finery. "We all have our own ways of mourning."

She sniffled as she clung to her husband. "But he doesn't believe he has the right to mourn," she cried out. "I received Lucas's letter that he was rushing to Boston because Melly was sick, but I never realized it

304

would be this serious. She's too young to die!" Her wail was muffled against Gabriel's shoulder, as she took comfort from his quiet presence. After many minutes, she eased away. "I need to change. I need a little time."

He ran a hand over her shoulder. "Take what you need, my darling."

~

Colin gripped Araminta's hand as he attempted to stand still on Clarissa's front porch. He shared a chagrined smile with Araminta as he shifted from foot to foot. When he felt Araminta's soft caress down his back, he relaxed as he raised his hand to knock on the door.

Gabriel flung open the door, a menacing glower on his face. He attempted to soften his expression, but sorrow clung to him. "Thank God you came." He pulled Colin into the front hallway, clasping him in a hug for a moment. He then embraced Araminta.

Colin tensed at the undercurrent of despair in the house. He raised his head, cocking it to one side at the quiet weeping coming from upstairs. "What's happened?"

"Go to Rissa," Gabriel said. He cleared his throat as his voice thickened. "I know you have every right to be angry with her but please." He paused as it looked like he fought tears. "Go to her."

Colin nodded, gripping his shoulder a moment before taking the stairs two at a time. He entered her room, closing the door behind him. "Rissa?" he whispered.

She sat in her rocking chair, curled over herself as she sobbed. He crouched beside her and ran a hand over her back and arm. "Rissa, tell me what happened."

She toppled out of the chair into his arms, and he held her as she was incapable of speaking. When her tears calmed, she hiccupped and sniffled. Pushing away from him, she dug into a pocket for a handkerchief. "Why are you here?" Her red-rimmed eyes continued to leak tears.

Colin stiffened and backed away from her. "Araminta and I need my brother's aid and found that he was not at Jeremy's house. I'm sorry to break your command not to set foot in your home." He rocked onto his heels and moved to rise.

"No!" She grabbed at his hands, holding him in place. "Don't go. Not when there's so much I need to say." She swiped at her face. "Oh, Colin. I know the conversation we must have." She met his hurt-filled gaze with one riddled with shame. "I know an apology will never suffice ..." She stuttered out a breath.

"Were you weeping because I interrupted Araminta's wedding?" Colin asked.

A startled laugh emerged before tears tracked down her cheeks again. "Heavens no. I would attempt to bake a three-layer cake in celebration of what occurred." She looked down, and he followed her gaze, belatedly seeing a letter by the edge of the rocking chair.

"What is it, Rissa?"

"I received a letter today. From Jeremy. I should have thought it strange to receive a letter from him and not Savannah." She sighed, raising her head to look outside as the day slowly darkened toward night. "I hoped he'd be more forthright with information about how Savannah fared."

"Has something happened to Sav?" Colin's terrified voice snapped his sister's gaze to his.

"No." Her voice cracked. "Sav is fine. He wrote to tell me Melly ..." Her voice thickened with tears. "Melly died. From the Spanish flu."

Colin's hand dropped away, and he fell backward until he sat on his bottom on the floor. "She can't have. She's young and strong and vibrant. She ... She ..." He shook his head in denial. "She has her whole life in front of her."

As Colin fell apart, Clarissa gained strength in soothing him. "She *had* ..." she whispered.

"Dammit, Rissa," Colin croaked. He raised his hands, covering his face as his shoulders shuddered. She ran a tentative hand down one of his arms, and he opened them wide, pulling her close as he cried. "She can't have died."

Tree branches scraped the side of the house as a soft wind blew outside. Footsteps sounded downstairs, and children's laughter echoed through the house.

"I can't imagine she's gone. That she won't see her nieces and nephews grow up," Colin whispered as his voice cracked. "That I won't hear her imitate another of Mr. Pickens's misspoken words." His attempt at a chuckle transformed into a sob that he immediately attempted to muffle.

"I should have known that someone in our family would be vulnerable after reading about that horrible illness," Clarissa said.

"No one wants to envision such a tragedy befalling those they love," Colin said. After a few moments, he asked, "Where's Pat?"

"Outside, entertaining my children with Fiona's and Gabe's aid. He barely seemed affected by the news."

Collin sighed. "And still he holds himself separate. He should be here, mourning with us."

"If you came here today, I think Patrick wanted to give us a chance to finally speak." She held Colin close when he acted as though he would ease her away. "Forgive me, Col. Forgive me for allowing my fears to override what I knew was true. From acknowledging the truth."

He leaned against the wall while Clarissa backed up against her bed. "How soon afterward did you know you'd made a mistake?"

"As soon as I left your house and was walking home, I felt sick. And I knew something else explained what had happened." She flushed with embarrassment. "I was too stupid and prideful to turn around and ask your forgiveness."

"Did you encourage Ari to marry another?" he asked, his blue eyes shining with a deep resentment.

"No. I tried to talk her out of it. However, her mind was set, and I didn't want to make her feel as though we weren't supportive. Although I wasn't." Clarissa sighed and rubbed at her forehead. "And Gabriel was most displeased. Didn't you know from my note on the invitation how I wanted you to act?"

"Why bother sending me an invitation if you don't inform me of the new time?" Colin asked, his cheeks flushed and eyes flashing.

"I did, but you weren't home, or you wouldn't answer the door. I had to stuff the note under your front door this morning."

He closed his eyes and shook his head ruefully. "I only used the back door this morning," he mumbled. "Why did this stupid argument between us last more than a day?"

She hit him on the arm. "First of all, you changed your lock so I couldn't barge in and force a reconciliation the day after I accused you." She paused and bit her lip. "Then Minta asked me to keep you barred from the house. She didn't want to see you. Didn't want the possibility that you could drop by the house at any time. She implied it was the smallest of favors after all she'd done for my family over the years." She blinked but tears fell. "I didn't want to agree, but I didn't want to lose her too, Col. Gabe and I didn't know what to do."

Colin exhaled. "You don't hate me?"

"Of course not!" She brushed at her cheek as another tear fell.

"You don't fear I'll hurt your children?"

Her eyes filled. "Never. They've missed you desperately."

"Why did you glare at me at the wedding?" he asked, his brows furrowed in confusion.

She gave him a gentle kick. "I thought you were aware of the new time, and I couldn't believe you'd arrive so late." She rolled her eyes in exasperation before she saw his confused expression. "I wanted you there, outside the church, when Gabe arrived with Minta, so that you could cause a scene before she entered the church." Clarissa attempted a smile, although her eyes still remained sorrowful. "Although it was quite entertaining to watch you march down the aisle and force them off the altar. I think you're Billy's hero. He was despondent this morning that Araminta wouldn't be his aunt."

Colin smiled, and his sorrow lifted for a moment. "I can see them again? The children?" At Clarissa's nod, he sighed with contentment.

"I hate that there was such animosity between us. I hate that we lost that time. Especially now ..." Her fingers slid over the letter, and Colin nodded.

"How is Savannah?" Colin asked.

"Terrible. Jeremy worries for her health and the health of the baby." She bit her lip. "He doesn't explicitly write it, but I believe he worries that she'll become ill and die too."

Colin paled at the prospect. "But the doctors there are certain they can save her and the baby?"

Clarissa shrugged. "As certain as a doctor can be before they perform an operation." She closed her eyes. "I hate that they are so far away. Although I know Aidan and Delia will be there to support them, I still wish we were there too."

Colin nodded his agreement. He looked around the room, belatedly realizing the sky outside had almost completely darkened. The sounds downstairs had increased as the children played inside. "Come," he coaxed his sister. "Let's join the others." He heaved himself from the floor and reached a hand down for her. She stood and paused at their departure from the room.

"Are we all right again, Col?" she whispered.

He flashed a quick smile and nodded. "We are, Rissa. Although I need your help if I'm to marry Araminta and remain a free man."

～

Araminta watched Colin depart upstairs and buried her resentment at being left behind. Gabriel sat despondently on a chair as she moved quietly through the living room.

"Araminta, what are you doing?" Gabriel asked in a hoarse voice.

She turned to face him with her arms crossed over her waist. "I thought I'd begin preparations for dinner, seeing as there are so many of us here tonight."

Gabriel watched her with fond amusement and motioned her toward him. She perched on the edge of the settee with her ankles crossed. "Do you even realize you are still in your wedding finery? Did you think to be so efficient as to create a masterpiece in the kitchen in such a fine dress?"

She flushed at the gentle teasing note in his voice. Her fingers picked at the simple lace at the wrists of her dress before smoothing down a crease along her leg. "I'd wear an apron."

Gabriel smiled. "Fiona's in the kitchen, and, although I'm sure she'd welcome your aid, I think you should be free of such duties on your wedding day."

Araminta glared at Gabriel. "This isn't my wedding day. I will only ever recall it as the day I was saved from a great folly."

Gabriel outstretched his legs, his smile softening as he heard his children shrieking with laughter outside. "It's wonderful for them to have time with their uncle Patrick."

Araminta nodded, her gaze wandering to the stairs. She frowned as she imagined what was being said upstairs. "I would think that conversation will take a while."

Gabriel nodded before sighing and placing hands on his belly. "For more than the obvious reasons. Rissa had news today that ..." Gabriel broke off and stared into space. As the silence lengthened between them, Gabriel focused on Araminta. "You do know I'm not an employer to you. I've always considered you family, and finally you will be. Ask me questions. Tell me when I'm being an idiot. That's what families do." He gave her a small smile. Then his smile faded, and any trace of levity leached away. "Melinda died, Araminta. From that influenza that's in the East."

Araminta froze, her eyes widening in horror at the news. Tears leaked out, and she shook her head in denial. "She can't have. She's only seventeen."

Gabriel nodded. "That's what we've been thinking since Rissa received the news." He cleared his throat and stared into space again. His attempt at relaxation failed as his jaw flexed, and he clenched and unclenched his fists.

"What else are you not saying?" She reached out her hand, as though to clasp his, before retracting it and holding it on her lap again.

Gabriel's blue eyes were haunted as he met her gaze. "Word is that it's spreading west. What if it comes here? Melly was young and healthy. What if … ? What if … ?" He shook his head, unable to finish the sentence.

Araminta's breath caught at the implication of his words. "I know you'll do everything you can to keep your family safe."

Gabriel cleared his throat and donned a welcoming smile as the children barreled in the back door. He fell to the floor to play with Billy while Geraldine and Myrtle flitted about Araminta, marveling at her dress. Rose was in the kitchen with her mother.

After a while, Colin and Clarissa descended from upstairs, and the children raced to their uncle. He lifted Billy high, dangling him upside down a moment before giving each of his nieces a hug.

After dinner, when the children were tucked into their beds and Rose was asleep in Gabriel and Clarissa's bed, the adults gathered in the living room. Fiona snuggled into Patrick's side on one of the two settees and smiled as she looked around the room. "'Tis wonderful to have us all together."

Patrick snorted with amusement. "Yes, it is, although I think the next time we are together we should endeavor for it to be brought about in a less dramatic fashion."

Colin failed to blush or look repentant. "The results were what I desired. Thus I cannot feel badly about the outcome." He squeezed Araminta's hand. "However, I need your help."

Clarissa smiled. "Of course we'll help you plan another wedding. Do you desire one as grand as today's ceremony?"

Araminta shook her head no. "I haven't given much thought to the ceremony. That doesn't matter to me. Marrying Colin and being his wife is all I care about. The truth is, I felt I had to marry Mr. Bouchard."

Gabriel, who had sat next to Clarissa, tracing patterns on her palm, became alert. "Why?"

"Bartholomew informed me, if I broke off our engagement and approached Colin, that Bartholomew would utilize information he'd gathered showing Colin was sympathetic to the Germans," Araminta said.

Patrick eased Fiona away, leaning forward to rest his elbows on his knees. He peered at Araminta and Colin, his eyes a molten fury. "He'd use the Sedition Act against you? Lie, even, to coerce you to marry him?"

"Yes," Araminta stammered. "I don't know why he was so intent on marrying me. I am no beauty." She continued over Colin's protest. "I have no wealth. This is no fantastical Dickensian tale where I'm an heiress lost to the wilds of Montana. I'm a poor orphan. What would he want with me?"

Gabriel sat back, his gaze filled with fury. "Once I recover from my anger that anyone would threaten our family with such a vile accusation, I believe I shall relish the challenge of discovering why he desired to marry you, Minta."

"Anyone with half a brain would want to marry her," Colin snapped as he glared at Gabriel. He refused to be calmed by Araminta's soothing noises and caresses down his arm.

"I meant no disrespect," Gabriel murmured as he flushed. "I meant that I hoped to discover a nefarious plan and thus prevent him from following through on his threat." He met Colin's irate gaze.

"I think the question is whether or not Colin said something incriminating that could have been overheard," Fiona said.

Patrick looked from his wife to his brother, and his gaze sharpened. "What did you say, Col?"

"I can't remember saying anything. There are a few nights I don't recall. Ari had determined to marry Bouchard, and I went to the pub. I might have said something stupid." He shook his head. "What I don't understand is, why wait until now? In all the cases I recall reading about, the charges were instantaneous once someone spoke against the war, the president or the flag."

Araminta shifted in her seat. "I'm sure that had to do with me. Bartholomew promised you would be safe as long as I married him."

Gabriel tapped his fingers on his thigh. "Which brings us back to my original question. Why is he insistent on marrying you, Araminta? Men marry for love. For monetary gain. For social prestige." He shook his head. "There was no monetary or social gain, although he would have had fine company in all of us." His sardonic smile was met with scoffs and rolls of the eyes from most in the living room.

"Did he love you?" Clarissa asked.

Araminta squirmed, only settling when Colin placed a hand on her clenched fist. "I don't know. I think he cared for me. But I don't know if he loved me."

"There's another reason," Patrick murmured, meeting Gabriel's inquisitive gaze. "For as much as he tried to blackmail Araminta, he could have been equally as manipulated."

Gabriel's eyes flared with understanding as he communicated silently with his brother-in-law. "Minta, what did you learn about Bartholomew's business dealings?"

She shrugged. "Not much. He boasted about how generous his uncle and their bank were in loaning money to farmers during the War. It's something the Council of Defense desires, since they want plenty of food to feed the troops."

Gabriel frowned. "Do you know if he is an associate, or friend, of a man named Samuel Sanders?" At Araminta's blank stare, he said, "He's also called Henry Masterson."

Colin jerked at the name of Gabriel's cousin and Patrick's nemesis.

"No," she whispered. "He liked to preen about knowing the governor, but he rarely discussed business associates with me."

Colin asked, "Why should he be involved?"

"That's what we're trying to determine. You probably failed to notice as you had a singular focus, but Sanders was at the wedding today. Made a point of smiling at Fiona, Rose and me as we walked in," Patrick said as he held his wife's hand.

"Bouchard was in Butte. When I visited in July," Colin whispered. "I saw him in a pub, a short time before I left to catch a train to Missoula. To Ari." He squeezed Araminta's hand.

"He said his trip to Butte was unsuccessful," Araminta whispered. "I ... tried to break with him upon his return, but he was insistent we remain engaged."

"He blackmailed you as he was blackmailed," Fiona whispered, her lilting Irish accent even more pronounced than usual. "If he saw that man, that would have been the outcome." She fought a shiver as though envisioning Samuel Sanders in his office.

Gabriel looked at his family and shook his head. "The question remains—Why? He hates the McLeods, but he has never paid much attention to the Sullivans, unless he could garner information about us from such a connection."

Clarissa rubbed at her head. "If Mrs. Smythe is still working with him"—she raised an eyebrow at the dubious term *working*—"then there is every reason for Colin to be a target. She wreaked havoc on my life. On Patrick's. But never on Colin's. I imagine she relishes the opportunity."

Gabriel nodded at his wife's insight. "But I still don't understand why."

Fiona looked at Gabriel with compassionate impatience. "You are thinking and acting rationally. Like a decent person would. That is not the way of your adversary, Gabriel. You would need a reason for your actions. Mrs. Smythe only has a hoped-for outcome. Chaos and pain."

Araminta shivered next to Colin. "What can we do to help Colin?"

Patrick sighed. "Until we know what you are accused of, we won't know what to do."

"It's a waiting game," Colin murmured.

~

Fiona sat on the bed in a cotton nightgown and watched with unveiled curiosity as her husband entered the guest bedroom at Savannah and Jeremy's house. Rose had not woken as they carried her from Gabriel and Clarissa's, and she was sound asleep in a bed next door to their room. "How long can we remain here?" She patted the bed next to her and curled into Patrick's side when he settled in bed.

"I have a few days off from work." He kissed her on the forehead. "It will be nice to help Colin if we can." He pulled on a strand of her hair, playing with it absentmindedly.

She broke into his quiet contemplation. "I refuse to believe you are as unaffected by Melinda's death as you'd have your siblings believe." She freed her hair from his hold and leaned over him, her hands on his chest, her long hair acting as a veil, shielding him from the outside world. "She was your daughter."

Patrick nodded. He began to speak, but his throat was clogged, and he cleared it. "Yes, I believe she was. And yet I barely knew her." He met his wife's worried gaze. "I mourn for what I never had more than for what I lost."

Fiona sighed, resting her head against his chest. "I'm sorry, my love." She held him as he trembled in her arms, silently mourning the child he'd had no hand in raising or cherishing. After many minutes, when his breathing was again steady, she raised her head in expectation of finding him asleep. Instead he met her concerned gaze.

"I'm rotten company tonight, Fee," he whispered. "I'm filled with this impotent rage, and yet the only person I can truly be upset with is myself." He ran a hand over her back, tugging her closer. "What if I'd never left? What if I'd told my siblings the truth from the beginning? Might I have had a chance to be her father?" He closed his eyes as tears leaked out.

"You gave her a great gift by allowing her to remain secure in the knowledge of the love of the people who raised her as their own. Who had saved her from the orphanage." She kissed his jaw. "From the moment you returned in 1913, you could have caused problems, demanding that she be returned to you. Instead you allowed her to live an uncomplicated life, filled with joy, wonder, laughter and unconditional love."

He shook his head. "You speak as though I acted out of concern for her, when, in reality, I was a coward. More concerned for myself and fearful of losing my family again." He would have slipped from her arms and the bed, but she clung to him, wrapping her arms and legs around him.

"Stay, Patrick. Take comfort when you need it."

He groaned, collapsing back into the soft mattress.

She watched him with wonder, tracing his jaw so he looked at her. "You love your nieces and nephews. You love Rose. I know you adored

Melinda, even though you tried to keep your distance because you didn't want to cause any problems with Jeremy and Savannah. You cherished every letter from Melinda, every window into her life." She traced her fingers up and down his cheek. "You feel much more deeply than you want any of us to know."

He leaned forward and kissed her. "You have no idea how your words affect me," he whispered. "I know I haven't been alone for five years. But to know the depth of your regard ..." He looked into her eyes and shook his head.

"I love you, Patrick. I have since those early days in Butte before everything became complicated." She flushed at his chuckle.

"Only you could call your interaction with Samuel Sanders by such a mild word as *complicated*." He kissed her again, reaching down to peel her nightdress off her. He stilled as her words sunk in. "You love me?"

She nodded, as though unable to speak.

He kissed her cheeks, her chin and then her lips. "Only you could banish the despair I feel today. I love you too, Fiona. I always have."

She gave a small sob as she flung her arms around his neck and buried her face in his chest.

CHAPTER 17

A pounding on the door the following morning roused Colin from bed. He groaned as he was cocooned under the covers with Araminta, and he had hoped to spend a leisurely Sunday with her at his house. When the pounding intensified, he heaved himself out of the bed, kissed Araminta on her shoulder, and pulled on a pair of pants and a shirt. He shut the bedroom door behind him and walked barefoot to the front door, rubbing at his hair and yawning as he jerked open the door.

He glared at Gabriel, standing on his front porch. "Don't you have any sense? This was my first full night with Ari." When he saw Gabriel's panicked expression, he immediately focused on Gabriel. After Gabriel pushed his way inside, Colin whispered, "What's happened?"

Gabriel thrust a telegram at him. Colin stilled as he read it, freezing in place. "This is a joke, right?" he asked.

Gabriel shook his head. "No, I must leave this morning. I have a ticket on the train, and I hope to be in Boston with minimal delays. Will you watch out for Rissa and the children?"

Colin nodded. "I'll stay there if you prefer." At Gabriel's slap on his back, he pulled Gabriel into a hug. "I'm certain all will be fine. They'll think you overreacted when you arrive." Colin cleared his throat as his mind raced with possibilities.

"I pray what you say is true, but I have to be there for Jeremy," Gabriel said. "Wish me well. I'm sorry I won't be here to help you as you face what is coming."

"None of that matters now." Colin raised dazed eyes to meet Gabriel's impatient, terrified gaze. "You have to go."

Gabriel nodded, patted Colin on the shoulder, and departed for home and his goodbyes with his family.

Colin collapsed onto his dilapidated sofa, his gaze distant and his hand still gripping the yellow telegram. He jumped when warm hands rubbed his shoulders.

"What is it?" Araminta whispered. She sat next to him and snuggled into his side.

"Savannah is ill," Colin said in a dazed voice. "Jeremy's already lost Melinda. I don't know what …"

"*Shh*, Colin. You mustn't think like that. They'll be fine. They'll return with a strong, healthy baby, and we'll have a celebration." She kissed him on his cheek. "Was Gabriel here because of the gossip?" She blushed. "He can't have approved of finding me here."

"He won't make much of a fuss as long as we wed soon. And there is no gossip yet." He shared a chagrined smile with Araminta. "As long as we don't spend every night together. I can't be seen sneaking from your home, and you can't be seen scurrying from mine."

She ran her fingers over his cheek. "Thankfully Clarissa brought over my going-away suitcase, and I have a change of clothes. It would be shocking if I were to emerge in yesterday's wedding finery." She kissed him. "But we will be cautious."

"And we will wed soon," he whispered. His expression brightened at her ready agreement.

"Why was Gabriel here?"

"He's catching the train back East. He wanted me to look after Rissa and the children. Will you mind staying at their house for a while?" He attempted a smile and failed. "I know you must look forward to returning to your home, but I don't want you living alone right now. I would worry too much about your safety." He paused as she remained quiet. "I'm sorry. I know you'll wonder why you opted for me."

She ran a finger alongside his whiskered cheek. "This is exactly why I've always wanted you. You love your family. You cherish them. You worry about them. I've always considered them to be the luckiest people in the world because they had your love."

He tugged her close. "Oh, Ari," he whispered into her hair. "Now that I finally have you, never leave me." He shuddered as he fought deep emotions.

"How can you not understand, after all this time, there's nowhere else I'd rather be?"

～

Gabriel boarded the train that would take him to Minneapolis. The car was not overly crowded, and he sat next to a window, waving to Clarissa and the children as the train heaved into motion. He smiled as Billy chased after the train, eluding Clarissa's grasp. Only when he ran into a fence did Billy stop his pursuit of his father. Gabriel sighed, his heart aching at leaving his family behind. He focused on the farm across the river, its produce harvested and fields roughly tilled in preparation for the coming winter. The river sparkled in the sunlight before the train curved into the canyon and away from Missoula.

"You always were a sentimental fool," a man said from across the aisle, his voice derisive.

Gabriel jerked his attention from the passing scenery to the man who had settled across from him. "Henry." He glared at his cousin. "I'm sure there are other seats for you in this car."

Henry raised a mocking eyebrow. "But where else could I sit and catch up with my beloved cousin?" Henry Masterson had reinvented himself in Butte as Samuel Sanders and now worked in an elevated position for the Anaconda Copper Company. He never forgot his McLeod cousins or the shame their mother brought the family by marrying Gabriel's father. "Seems a pity you are leaving your wife and family unprotected. Is this a short trip?"

Gabriel glared at him mutinously.

"If you believe that pathetic Sullivan will aid your wife and children, you'll be proven wrong." He smiled with evil intent. "I have plans for him."

"Why would you take an interest in Bartholomew Bouchard's wedding?" Gabriel asked. "He seems beneath your notice."

"Bart has always been like a trainable puppy, and I've found him a delightful source of information since he arrived in Montana." His smile broadened as Gabriel frowned. "You can't imagine he sought out the cripple's attention because he actually craved her affection?" He snorted derisively. "Only your pathetic brother-in-law seems fascinated by her."

"Why harm her?" Gabriel tilted his head as he studied his cousin. "She's done nothing to you."

"All women are a means to an end, dear cousin. Even you must know that." He crossed his thin legs and smiled at the passing porter. By all outward appearances, a successful businessman had deigned to have a conversation with a laborer. "Your wife understands that, even though she clings to her illusions about suffrage for women."

"It's not an illusion," Gabriel hissed. "Women vote in Montana."

Henry shrugged his shoulders. "And what great effect has it had on the state?"

Gabriel leaned forward, his blue eyes gleaming with enmity. "Soon you will not be able to buy a drink." He frowned as Henry rolled his eyes.

"You don't expect Butte to follow that law, do you?" He shook his head as he stared at Gabriel. "You can't be that innocent to believe that they'd allow over two hundred businesses to lose their livelihood overnight. Or for the owners to lose a way to keep the men docile?"

Gabriel's jaw ticked as he stared at his cousin. "No great change will occur in Montana until the Company ceases meddling in every aspect of our lives."

Henry smiled. "The Company has the power and the fortitude to wield it. And it will be a long time before anyone in Montana stands up to us." He shrugged before his smile turned calculating. "I was delighted to hear that Jeremy's wife might die with the birth of their child. It always brings such comfort to know that you pathetic McLeods continue to suffer."

Gabriel clenched his hands together to prevent attacking his cousin. "They are well." He cleared his throat, refusing to speak of Melinda's death with the man who had allied himself with Melinda's birth mother, Mrs. Smythe.

"Perhaps they will decide they enjoy Boston more than Montana and never return. I doubt they'd miss your company."

Gabriel reached forward, gripping Henry by his tie and yanking him forward. They were virtually alone in this part of the train cabin, and Gabriel no longer cared about keeping up appearances. "One day, dear cousin, all of your plans, all of your plots, will fail. And you will have nothing." He thrust his cousin back into his seat, where Gabriel watched Henry impassively as he gasped for breath.

"You've never learned your place, cousin. One day, by God, you will."

Henry rose, but Gabriel gripped his wrist. "On the contrary, cousin. I know who and what I am, and have no need to present a persona to the world. I wonder how many will stand by you when they discover what a fraud you are?" They shared a loathing glare before Henry wrenched his arm free and strode down the aisle and into another car.

～

The following day Colin walked through town with Araminta on his arm. A cold front had moved through the previous afternoon and evening, and the hills were covered in the first snow of the season. "Are you certain you want to do this?" he murmured to her as he smiled at acquaintances. She nodded, and he continued their purposeful movements.

They arrived at the bank moments after it had opened. Colin eased them through the front door, surprised to see the secretary's desk vacant. "Where is his office?" Colin whispered.

Araminta pointed to a partially closed door and followed him.

He pushed open the door, ushering Araminta inside before closing it behind him with a loud *click*.

Bartholomew looked up from the papers he had been blindly staring at and rose to his feet in indignation. "How dare you barge in here!" he sputtered. "I have every right to throw you out."

"But you won't," Araminta said in a cool, collected voice. "Because, no matter what was said the other day and how you tried to coerce me into marrying you, I know that you cared for me." When she saw the tensing of his jaw, betraying the truth of her words, she shook her head in consternation. "Why have you acted as you have?"

"You have no right to ask me questions, madam." He glared at her. "Seems your ancestry bred true."

"Say one more disrespectful thing to Ari, and I'll finish what we started on Saturday," Colin declared. "You should give thanks that a woman as fine as Araminta even deigned to speak with you, never mind allowed you to court her. You're a damn fool."

"I'm a fool? Look at you, Mr. Sullivan. The town buffoon. Having to resort to interrupting a man's wedding to reunite with your harlot." His head jerked back as Araminta slapped his face.

"You have no right. Not after what you attempted to force me to do." She breathed heavily as she shook her hand to ease it of the sting of slapping him. "You, who would have forced me into a farce of a marriage."

He leaned against the edge of his desk. "It wouldn't have been a farce," he whispered. "I really care for you."

Colin watched Bartholomew, seeing in Bartholomew the despair he had felt when he had believed Araminta lost to him. "Would you have gone through with your threat to accuse me of being a German sympathizer?"

Bartholomew watched him speculatively. "Do you think there aren't men watching your every move, watching everything you say with the hopes you'll trip up? Many would love to gain control of your smithy."

Colin rocked back as though he'd been sucker punched. "You'd accuse a man of such a vile act simply for monetary gain?"

Bartholomew laughed. "There isn't much most men wouldn't do for monetary gain. I wouldn't have had to whisper in too many ears to entice your so-called friends and neighbors to speak out against you. We all know your sister is a radical suffragist."

Colin shook his head in confusion. "What's in it for you? You'd gain nothing."

Bartholomew rubbed at the cheek Araminta had slapped. "I have many enemies. And those who call me friend have expectations."

Colin shared a confused glance with Araminta. "I don't understand," Colin murmured.

"Why marry me?" Araminta whispered. "Why should you want to marry me?"

"Because, if I didn't, I would have faced unpleasantness from a man I'd rather not spend much time with. Which is now what I must do." Bartholomew sighed and shrugged. "At least I negotiated not having to kill you once I married you."

Araminta paled, edging closer to Colin. "You wouldn't have," she breathed.

He shook his head, his eyes troubled and reflecting a deep sadness. "No. I found I had no interest in becoming a widower. Not when it meant depriving the world of your loveliness."

Colin clenched his jaw and frowned. "That's one of the most convoluted sentences I've ever heard. It's as though you're congratulating yourself for not agreeing to murder Ari."

"Who would suggest such a horrible thing?" Araminta asked, clutching at Colin's arm.

Bartholomew looked from one to the other, sighing at the united front they presented. "All I would say is that my friends are your enemies. I'd be careful who you trust."

Colin shared a long look with him and nodded. He ushered Araminta out of Bartholomew's office and out of the bank. When they stood on the boardwalk, he began to shake. "Come," he rasped, walking as fast as she could toward her home.

When they arrived at her home, he waited impatiently for her to open the door. When he slammed shut the door behind them, he pushed her against it, kissing her. "I'm sorry," he whispered, continuing to rain kisses over her cheek and neck. "I ... I needed to remind myself you're well. That I can still hold you in my arms, no matter what was threatened."

"Colin," she stuttered, tears pouring down her cheeks. "I ... Forgive me."

"*Shh*," he murmured, kissing her more gently but just as passionately. "There is nothing to forgive. We were manipulated by a master con artist." He ran a hand through her hair, his desperate gaze roving over her. "I only give thanks that he came to love you and thus saved you."

He moved to sit on her sofa, and she followed him. He lay down, and she crawled onto the sliver of space left, dangling off the edge of the sofa. "Come here. You won't crush me," he said, his voice filled with humor for the first time since they had left Bartholomew's office. "Yes, let me cuddle you." He kissed the top of her head and held her as his thoughts drifted.

The sounds of the city permeated their quietude, with the rattle of carts, the whinny of horses and the increased honking of horns echoing through the air. "You know what this means?" When he felt her shrug her shoulders, he continued tracing patterns on her back, tangling his fingers in her loosened hair. "This means that some of those people accused of sedition could be innocent."

"Why would you say that?" Araminta asked, raising her head to meet his gaze. "They were tried by a judge."

"Judges are human, Ari." He held her close. "If I, a man who's been a member of this community for over fifteen years, am threatened by such a law, imagine what it must be like for true immigrants." He huffed out a humorless chuckle. "And I'm Irish!"

"They aren't only going after Germans. You know the Irish in Butte raised enough ruckus last year. Besides, many are concerned about their loyalty to the war effort as they see a potential benefit in Great Britain's loss to Germany."

Colin shifted so that he was more comfortable with Araminta resting on his chest. "That's true, but I wasn't born there. I don't have a brogue. I don't even know what county my father came from." He frowned. "I wonder which of my men would betray me."

Araminta reached for his other hand and laced her fingers with his. "Who do we know who could help us determine Bartholomew's relationship to Gabriel's cousin?"

Colin shook his head. "I don't know. Who should care? Any journalist worth his weight is in Europe or reporting on the flu. Not concerning himself with a family squabble."

"I'm such a fool," she whispered as she flushed, ducking her head against his chest. "I should have known no man would be interested in me."

He growled and urged her to meet his gaze. "Last I checked, I'm a man, and I am very interested in you." He waited for her to smile and then nodded. "Perhaps in the beginning Bartholomew showed interest in you because he felt compelled by his bargain with Gabriel's cousin." He ran a hand over her back as she shivered. "However, the regard he felt for you could not be feigned."

"What does this all mean?" Araminta whispered.

"It means that we have a wily opponent I don't fully understand while all three McLeod brothers are in Boston." He sighed as he encouraged her to snuggle into his embrace. "I'm at a distinct disadvantage."

"We'll figure something out," she whispered.

"I wish we had a cabin in the woods, and I could escape with you for a week." He chuckled. "A month."

"I wish we could too," she said as she kissed his jaw. "But we can't leave Rissa alone. Not when she'll be desperately worried about Savannah."

He hugged her tight in a full-body embrace. "I would be lost without you, Ari."

~

A week later Colin sat at a desk in the committee room, facing the three members of the Missoula County Council of Defense Committee. He forced himself to appear calm. He rested his hands on the desk in front of him, gently clasped together. His smile was warm but impersonal, and he stared at the three men in front of him with mild curiosity. Someone had propped open the windows, due to the warmer-than-usual day and the stifling number of pungent townsfolk crammed into the small room. Sunlight streamed in through the windows, illuminating Colin and the committee members. He sat up even straighter as his name was spoken.

"Mr. Sullivan, you have been called forth to answer the committee's questions regarding doubts of your patriotism." The rail-thin committee leader shuffled around papers in front of him until he found the slip of paper he looked for. "There are also concerns that seditious remarks were heard at your blacksmith shop."

Colin stared at the man with a blank expression. Silence lengthened in the room, the sound of bodies creaking in chairs reverberating in the air.

"Mr. Sullivan?" The man peered at him over a pair of wire-framed glasses.

"I have come to answer questions. I've yet to hear one, Mr. Caine."

The man slammed down the paper in front of him. "Is this the sort of insolence you show to those in positions of power?" When Colin remained silent, Mr. Caine removed his glasses, shaking them at Colin as he spoke. "You'd better learn your place, young man."

Another member of the committee cleared his throat and began a barrage of questions.

"How much have you spent purchasing Liberty Bonds?"

"Around $500," Colin said, the large amount earning a gasp from the gathered crowd.

"Do you have plans to purchase more?"

"If I can afford to."

"Do you contribute to the American Red Cross or the War Service League?"

Colin nodded. "When I am able to, I donate a few dollars here and there."

"So you do not donate on a regular basis?"

"No, sir."

"Do you believe your personal comfort is more important than supporting the government in its attempt to eradicate the menacing Huns?"

"No, sir, but I do believe in paying my debts, which includes paying well the men who work for me. I contribute what I can to the cause." Colin spoke deliberately with little inflection in his voice.

"You live in a grand house across the river. How do you justify such an expense when our boys are fighting in the trenches and freezing in their poor excuse for shelter that has been erected?"

"I live in a modest home. I fear you have confused me with someone else." Colin met the man's intent stare with no sign he would break under his questions.

A gavel hit the desk, jolting members of the committee who had been studying Colin as he answered each question. "Please enumerate for the committee all of your assets."

Colin tilted his head as he studied Mr. Caine and then each member of the committee who had leaned forward with avaricious interest at the question. "I believe that is no business of the committee. If the Honorable B. K. Wheeler, a federal district attorney, declined to answer such a question to the State Council of Defense Committee in Helena this spring, I see no reason why I should be compelled to answer."

"You are in contempt!" Mr. Caine roared. "You must answer."

Colin leaned back in his chair and shook his head. He swiped his palms over his pant leg and sat with a forced calm.

"You have been accused of seditious remarks." Mr. Caine watched Colin in confusion as his comment failed to rouse any reaction. "Did you say in your shop that it would be better for business if Germany won?"

"No."

Mr. Caine glared at him for his one-word answer. "You categorically deny saying such a comment?" At Colin's subtle nod, Caine held up a piece of paper. "I have sworn testimony from one of your workers stating you said such comments numerous times along the same vein."

"Was it Mr. Booker?" When Mr. Caine nodded, flushing at Colin's question, Colin took a deep breath. "I'm not surprised he swore to such a thing, considering he truly works for you, Mr. Caine. You have attempted to undermine my business for the past two years since you've been unsuccessful in purchasing it from me in a legal manner. It seems rather coincidental that I'm sitting in front of your committee, where you hope to fabricate charges against me and then swoop in to steal my business."

Loud gasps filled the room, and low "Boos" were called out by many of the men. The gavel sounded again, although it took many minutes for those present to calm down and to quit whispering among themselves.

"How dare you accuse me of such maleficence?" Mr. Caine said, his face beet red.

"And how dare you drag me in front of your committee, accusing me of sedition and of not supporting my country's cause? I've given more than most in this town in support of the war in Liberty Bonds. I've supported families when their breadwinner sons were called up and their parents no longer had a way to support themselves. I've followed every Meatless Tuesday and Wheatless Wednesday. I believe in my country, and I am a proud American. How dare *you*, Mr. Caine."

Mr. Caine took a deep breath as though to respond but turned to face a colleague on the committee who tugged at his sleeve. He conferred with the man who had asked Colin the rapid-fire questions, and the discussion between the committee members became heated. After a few minutes, where the murmurs inside the committee room had grown into a small roar, the gavel sounded again.

"You are a successful business owner, and, as such, you should have found a way to better support the war effort. Thus, let it be known that Colin Sullivan is a money slacker and deserving of any and all public censure. Those with sense will avoid association with his business." The gavel sounded again as a few more "Boos" rose from the audience, and then the committee members rose and departed.

Colin sat in stunned silence a moment before rising. He met Araminta's gaze and shook his head, grabbing her hand as he pushed through the crowd and out onto the boardwalk.

"Colin Sullivan!" a voice called out.

Colin walked as fast as he could without forcing Araminta to walk at an uncomfortable pace.

A squirrelly young man jumped in front of him, impeding him from walking farther. "Do you have a comment for the *Daily Missoulian?*" When Colin remained silent, the reporter wriggled with energy. "I'm Herman Talbot, one of the reporters. I was just at your hearing. I want you to know I'll publish what I can about what happened, but my editor has final say."

Colin nodded. "And I understand that you must publish what won't cause you to sit in front of that committee." He slapped Herman on the shoulder in a friendly manner and then pushed him to the side. "Thanks," he called over his shoulder as he continued to walk toward Clarissa's house.

~

Colin opened the door for Araminta and followed her inside Clarissa's home. They had been staying here since Gabriel had left, which had the unexpected benefit of protecting Araminta's reputation in town. Rather than be seen frequenting his house, she was at his sister's. Due to Clarissa's husband's absence, it was not out of the ordinary for Colin to stay with Clarissa to lend his aid. Although the townsfolk most likely knew that his relationship with Araminta deepened each day, none other than the Bouchards and Vaughans made disparaging comments.

Clarissa looked up from the dining room table where she wrote a letter. She frowned when she saw them. "I fear it did not go as well as you had hoped." She set down her pen and waited for them to join her in the well-lit room. The older children were at school, and Little Colin played with trains on the floor in the play area Gabriel had constructed for him.

Colin sat, smiling his thanks as Araminta emerged from the kitchen with cups of coffee for them all. "I was not charged with sedition, although they want it noted that I am a money slacker." He nodded ruefully as Clarissa hissed in a breath. "I think they hope it will prevent the townsfolk from coming to the smithy."

She glowered. "We won't allow this to ruin you, Colin. You aren't a slacker."

He sat, staring dazedly into space. "They didn't care that I'd bought $500 in Liberty Bonds. Nothing I could have said would have been enough for them. I would always have been seen as a slacker."

"Damn them," Clarissa muttered and then flushed as she rarely swore. "I hate that they are targeting you simply because you love Araminta."

Colin shook his head. "It's not just that." He gripped Araminta's hand and squeezed it. "I think Mr. Caine also acted because he saw an opportunity to take my blacksmith business. I discovered through the help of my loyal men that he had planted Mr. Booker in my shop in an attempt to discredit me and spy on me. Mr. Caine's plan backfired, though. He hadn't expected so many in attendance who supported me."

"You are an upstanding member of this city," Araminta said.

"Yes, but that doesn't matter when such laws are on the books. Thank God I'd read about Mr. Wheeler's testimony last spring when he was called in front of the COD and could use Mr. Wheeler's reluctance to answer their questions as part of my defense." Colin took a sip of coffee and then relaxed into his chair. "I hate to think what it would have been like had public sentiment not been in my favor."

"We have money saved, Col. You won't lose your shop." Clarissa shared an intense look with her brother, and he nodded.

"I know. And, if the worst happened, I think I could swallow my pride enough to wire Aidan. I know he would help me." He focused on his sister as though attempting to forget the morning's activity. "Who are you writing, Rissa?"

She beamed at him. "Oh, I've had the most wondrous letter!" She held it up and then read from it.

My dearest Clarissa, Colin, Araminta and children,

I am finally writing you after the birth of my darling son, Breandan Martin McLeod. We wanted to remember Jeremy's grandfather and my father, and it seemed the perfect name for our son once we met him. I can't wait for you to meet him too! I know all babies are beautiful, but I think he might be the most beautiful baby I have ever seen. When the nurse placed him in my arms, it felt as though a fissure in my heart healed. I still have others that will never heal, but at least one has.

Jeremy is beside himself with joy, although he was terribly worried when I had a slight fever after the surgery. I fear they were overworried and sent a telegram to Gabriel. I have heard that he is en route to Boston, and I will be delighted to see him and have him hold his nephew. However, I am sorry to have left you without his company, dearest Clarissa. I know how much I hate my time without Jeremy.

I am uncertain when Jeremy, Breandan and I will return home. I need to have time to spend at Melinda's grave. I cannot believe she is gone. So many times during the day I call for her or turn because I think I hear her voice. I reach for her hand, delighted to tell her something or giggle with her, only to be reminded that she is no longer with me.

How can my heart be so full of love for Breandan and yet turned to ashes at the loss of Melinda? I fear you will find me a mixed-up muddle when you see me again, dearest cousins.

Much love,

Savannah

Clarissa swiped at her cheeks and saw Colin wiping at his eyes as Araminta leaned into him, hiding her face in his shoulder. "I ... I'm so glad that Gabriel will arrive for something joyous. There has been enough grief."

Colin nodded and let out a deep breath. "Yes. They have enough sorrow to deal with without having to worry about Savannah."

Araminta cleared her throat and then raised her head off Colin's shoulder. "Have you had any word from Gabriel?"

Clarissa nodded. "He was marooned for two days in Buffalo after a train derailment, but he hopes to arrive in Boston soon. He sent a quick telegram, as I had thought he'd be in Boston by now."

Colin smiled at his sister as he held the woman he loved in his arms. "We should celebrate tonight with the children. Savannah and her babe are well, and I am not going to jail for sedition."

Clarissa beamed at him and Araminta. "Yes, we have something to celebrate."

Araminta giggled. "I'll bake the cake."

CHAPTER 18

Boston, October 1918

en days after the birth of their son, sunlight streamed into the room Jeremy and Savannah shared at Aidan and Delia's house. A bassinette with a fresh blanket and rattle sat in one corner, while a rocking chair was in another.

Jeremy knelt on the floor, holding Savannah's hand. He whispered to her about his dreams for them, what he hoped they'd do once they returned to Montana, about how excited Clarissa would be to see her again. He spoke until his voice was raw, and then he held her hand to his mouth as it moved silently with a litany of prayers.

"Jeremy," Lucas whispered as he eased inside. "You have to let her go." Lucas rubbed at his face, his palms scratching against his unshaven cheeks. His shirt was misbuttoned; he'd lost his waistcoat hours ago, and he couldn't remember where he'd misplaced his jacket. His brown eyes were a fathomless pool of grief.

"She's going to wake up, Lucas. You'll see." Jeremy squeezed her hand in encouragement. He growled when Lucas grabbed the hand that held Savannah's and tugged, severing his connection with her.

"She's gone, Jeremy," Lucas said, his voice cracking. "You have to

—" His head jerked backward as Jeremy slapped him and then launched himself at him. Lucas tumbled to the floor with Jeremy on top, pummeling him. He head-butted Jeremy, earning a moment's reprieve from the beating, and pushed Jeremy off him.

"What in God's name?" Aidan demanded on a roar as he burst into the room. He saw the toppled chairs, the smashed ceramics on the carpet and his devastated nephew on the floor. Now that the instinct to fight had left, Jeremy laid curled on the floor, deep sobs bursting forth. Lucas patted him on the back but nodded when Aidan motioned for him to leave.

Aidan knelt beside Jeremy, waiting until the worst of his sobs eased. "Come, Jeremy," he murmured, waiting until he heaved himself into a sitting position before pulling his nephew into his arms. He held his nephew as he continued to shudder.

"I know you believe you have some words of wisdom," Jeremy gasped out, "but they don't exist. Not for me."

Aidan's grip on Jeremy's back tightened a moment. "Don't give up on this life, Jeremy. It's the only thing I'd ask of you right now. Please." He eased his hold on Jeremy as his nephew pushed away from him and attempted to rise.

Jeremy faltered and ended on his knees. "There is nothing left for me." He stared dazedly into space, his gaze glassy with grief. "No wife. My Melly ..." He swallowed a sob as he swayed in place, tears pouring down his cheeks. He dropped to sit on the floor again with a stupefied expression, silent tremors racking his body. "I don't know what I'll do."

Aidan cupped Jeremy's head with his fingers at the back of his nape. "You don't have to know right now. No one expects you to."

The door burst open, and Gabriel and Richard entered. "Uncle? What's happened?" Gabriel asked as he looked around the room. His gaze moved from Savannah's lifeless form on the bed to his brother on the ground, shaking and swaying, and Gabriel's jaw tightened. "I'm sorry I was too late." He knelt on the floor before Jeremy. "Jer, we're all here. You're not alone."

"That's where you're wrong, Gabe. I am alone. Just as I will be forever."

Gabriel joined his brother on the floor, moving to sit beside him. He nodded as his uncle rose and noted when Richard moved to sit on the other side of Jeremy. "You have your son, Jer. And you have us. We're here with you. We'll not leave you."

"You can't promise that, Gabe. No one can," Jeremy said in a deadened voice. "My Savannah, with so much to live for." He shook his head, pursing his lips as he fought his emotion. "Our baby, still ill with the influenza. I can't bear it if he dies too."

"Don't give up hope for him, Jer," Richard pleaded.

Jeremy hit the wall behind him with his fist a few times as another sob burst forth. "How could she have an easy birth and then die from the influenza?" He laid his head on his knees and hid his face.

Gabriel slung an arm over his brother's shuddering back and pulled him close. "I don't know, Jer. It makes no sense. And it sure as hell isn't fair." He ignored the tears tracking down his own cheeks.

Richard leaned in on the other side. Together the two older McLeod brothers tried to form a cocoon around their distraught brother. "We will help you through this, Jer."

"I wish I could die too, and then it would all be over," he whispered.

Gabriel growled and moved with sudden speed. He let go of Jeremy and knelt in front of him again, holding his brother's head between his hands. Gabriel's eyes were lit with a desperate anger as he looked into his brother's eyes that seemed to hold an eternity of grief. "Dammit, Jer. You will not die. You will survive this." He waited for some kind of acknowledgment from his brother. "You ... You can't die."

Jeremy's head was listless on his neck, and it fell to one side after Gabriel eased his grip on it. "Nothing matters. Not now."

"You matter," Gabriel said.

"Your son matters," Richard snapped. "He needs you."

"I can't ... I can't watch another die." He met their gazes with an almost irrational desperation. "I wouldn't survive it."

Gabriel gripped his youngest brother's shoulder, and Richard nodded. "Then we will be there in your stead. He will never doubt he is loved," Gabriel said. "And, when he is better, he will know you, Jer. He will know his father and the love you had for his mother."

Jeremy fell forward into his brothers' arms as another sob burst forth, taking what comfort he could from the men who had always supported him.

Sophronia wore black crepe as she sat on the settee in her rear study. When her sitting room door creaked open, she *thump*ed her cane down with disapproval. "I demanded not to be disturbed today," she barked. She turned to find Lucas, bruised and mourning, standing in the doorway. "Oh, my boy. Come in." She pushed herself to her feet, holding him to her a moment. "How are you?"

She frowned as he swayed from side to side in front of her, his gaze distant. She pushed him into a chair and waited for him to speak.

"I thought nothing could take away my desire to compose. To perform. To see some reason to find beauty and to create music," he whispered. He raised dazed eyes to Sophie. "How could this have happened?"

Sophie gripped his hand. "Too often there is no reason for tragedy." She blinked rapidly although tears fell. "How is Jeremy?"

"I fear I'm soon to lose a brother too," Lucas rasped. He lowered his head and sobbed. He held a hand to his eyes as he attempted to control his emotion. "Forgive me." He took a stuttering breath and battled to control his grief.

After a moment's silence, only broken by the chiming of a hall clock, he burst out, "How can they both be dead?" He glared at Sophie with a deep anger. He rose, pacing to the mantel.

Sophie shook her head. "It is cruel of fate." She rubbed at her cheeks. "That one as old as I should live and the young such as Melly die. That Savannah ..." Her voice cracked.

Lucas shot out a hand and gripped Sophronia's. "Don't for one minute think we wouldn't miss you." Lucas shook his head at the thought of losing such a stalwart of support.

She smiled, but sorrow tinged her expression. "I know I spout my nonsense about wanting to live to vote, but I'd rather have had Melinda vote. Or Savannah." She blinked as a tear rolled down her cheek.

"There should never have been a need to choose. To wish it were someone else," Lucas said as he rubbed at his head. "Jeremy is inconsolable. I think he forgets he still has a son."

"He fears to hope," Sophie said and met Lucas's gaze. "For, if he hoped for Breandan's improvement, and then he died too, I fear it would be more than he could bear."

"He shouldn't already act as though he's lost him," Lucas muttered. "The poor baby is struggling."

"Who cares for him?" Sophronia asked.

"Oh, Aidan is terrifyingly efficient. He has maids and doctors and nurses who are helping, but it doesn't replace the love of a parent." He rubbed at his chest.

"You worry," she murmured, "for your own wife and child."

"How could I not? I've heard reports it is heading west. That it has already arrived in Montana." He scrubbed at his eyes. "I've written Vivie, begging her to remain at home. To not go out in public. To avoid any public gatherings. I think she fears I'm a madman who wants to keep her locked away."

Sophronia frowned. "You should have sent her a clipping of what was occurring in Boston. Then she would understand."

He shook his head and sighed. "I had one of my rambling fits in a letter, and I didn't have the sense to do that." For a moment, he shared a chagrined smile with Sophie before he sobered. "I ... I don't know what to do for Jeremy." He collapsed onto his chair and looked at Sophronia plaintively.

"Love his child as he is unable to at this moment. Ensure that he is well taken care of. You know Aidan is doing all he can, but I've found children need to be held. To be touched. Sometimes those we hire aren't as affectionate as children need them to be."

"As a doting uncle can be," he whispered. He saw her smile at his statement. "Thank you, Sophie. For everything you did for Savannah. For giving her a place of refuge all those years ago. For encouraging her to be brave. To live a life free of Jonas." His eyes gleamed with unshed tears. "She lived a wonderful life, with a man she loved, because you supported her and believed in her when she didn't believe in herself."

~

Rowena slipped her key into the lock of a house on Marlborough Street. It was a block from the Public Gardens and only five from Aidan and Delia's. She wandered the downstairs rooms, empty of furnishings, and envisioned what she wanted to do with the space. A formal living room with a bowed window was at the front of the house. Pocket doors separated it from the dining room but also allowed for a larger living room if desired. A private sitting room was at the back of the first floor, with wall-to-ceiling windows. The kitchen and servants' quarters were downstairs, with a dumb waiter to bring the food upstairs. There were three more stories, with three rooms on each floor. She twirled around and let out a giggle as she tripped and toppled to the floor.

A soft knock on the door caused her heart rate to speed up, and she rose. She opened the door a crack and then flung it open when she saw Perry standing on the steps. "Come inside," she said, grabbing his arm.

"Ro, what are we doing in an empty house?" He stood rooted in place in the entryway.

"I want you to look at this house with me." She tugged on his hand, pulling him into the well-lit living area. "What do you think?"

"It's lovely but an unnecessary extravagance." He frowned as her joy dimmed. "What is this, Ro?"

She wrung her hands together. "I want us to have our own home. I thought this could be ours."

He shook his head and looked at her. "This is big enough for a family of ten. We don't need something like this." He frowned as the rosy bloom on her cheeks faded. After a moment, he paled. "You already bought it, didn't you?"

She nodded. "I wanted to surprise you." A tear leaked out at the admission. "I had hoped you'd be as excited as I am."

He took a quick step toward her and held her face between his large palms. "I want a home with you." He looked around dazedly at the large space. "But I envisioned a small place with two or three rooms and a piano crammed in a corner and a desk for you to write on in another."

"I'm sorry," she whispered. "I should have talked with you."

He shook his head and pulled her to him, wrapping his arms around her. "I'm afraid how much this will cost."

"I have more money than I know what to do with," she said in his ear. "My mother left me a sizeable inheritance, and it has tripled since I gained control of it. I never told you, but I'm a bit of an heiress."

"I don't want your money, Ro. I want you," he growled as his hold on her tightened.

She leaned back so he could see her smile. "I know. But now that Teddy is helping me, I have more money than I could spend in this lifetime. Why shouldn't we have a nice home?"

He stiffened at Teddy's name. "I don't want people to believe I'm living off my wife."

She smiled at him. "You're not. You sing. You earn quite a bit from that. Anyone looking at the two of us will always wonder what a man like you is doing with me."

"If they have any sense, they'll know I'm smart as hell to be with a woman like you," he said. "What is there between you and Goff?" He flinched as she stilled in his arms.

"You sound jealous, and there is no need for it. I was ... infatuated with him." She flushed. "For lack of a better word. He was a wall-flower, like me, and I thought two wallflowers could bloom together." She turned a brighter shade of red at her words. "But then he met Zee. And I realized I would forever be a friend."

"Why would you pine for a man who wasn't smart enough to see your charm and beauty?" he asked as he kissed her forehead.

"Perry, you've met my friends. They sparkle while I look like dulled copper next to them." She bowed her head. "And I'm a writer. I found it easier to live in my head than in the real world sometimes."

"Well, I'm glad you decided to venture into the world long enough so that we met. And I still think Teddy was a fool, but I'm thankful he was." Perry smiled as she glowed upon seeing the truth in his expression. He bent his head and kissed her passionately. "God, I've missed you."

"And I you," she said as she stood on her toes to deepen their next kiss. "I'm afraid there's no furniture in the house yet." She gasped as his mouth dropped to kiss her clothed body.

"We don't need furniture, love," he murmured as he tugged her farther into the house, away from the windows and any potentially prying eyes.

She giggled. "Except for ..." She grabbed his hand and tugged him up two flights of stairs to a back bedroom. Breathless from their quick walk upstairs, she spun to face him with a triumphant smile. Along one wall stood a large bed with a down comforter and pillows piled high. "Except for a bed," she whispered.

"You're brilliant," he said as he picked her up and set her there, earning a delighted shriek. Diaphanous blinds covered the back windows, letting light in but affording privacy.

"I wanted something for us before we decorated the house together," she whispered as she arched into his touch.

He stroked a hand over her hair, now loosened from its pins and cascading over her shoulders. "Together," he whispered before lowering his mouth to kiss her more deeply.

～

S he played with his long fingers as they lay in bed spooned together after their passionate lovemaking. She smiled as she heard him humming the song "*K-K-K-Katy*" in her ear. "I love your voice," she whispered.

"You'll always be my favorite audience," he murmured.

"How long are you in town?"

"For as long as you would like me," he whispered in her ear.

She rolled over and faced him with a frown. "I'm serious, Perry. How long are you here?"

He ran his fingertips over her chin. "I am serious too. I've postponed my tour. I have no desire to chase influenza around this country, and I'm certain that all public gatherings around the country will be canceled. It would be a needless expense to travel someplace and not perform."

She hugged him to her. "I want you safe and healthy."

"I think Boston may be the safest place right now, my darling. It was hard hit, but the illness seems to be waning here. For the rest of the country, it's just starting." He met her gaze and smiled. "Let's decorate this home together. Build memories here. I can already see a large piano in the living room window."

She smiled. "Wait until you see the whole house. There is a beautiful room on the second floor that would be perfect and, more private, for your music studio." She frowned. "Although I'm uncertain how we'll move a large piano up a flight of stairs."

He laughed. "That's for the piano company to worry about, darling."

She swallowed and bit her lip. "I ... I'm not sure I'm brave enough to live with my lover."

He sobered and stared into her glowing amber-colored eyes. "Marry me. Marry me tomorrow."

She giggled. "I'll marry you any day, Perry. Yes!" She kissed him, tracing her fingers over his cheeks and then into his hair.

"My friend Lucas is in town. I received a forwarded letter from him at the hotel. He thought I was still touring and doesn't know I'm in Boston. I'll look him up and see if he will be my best man. I was his at his wedding in Minneapolis."

Rowena frowned and stared at Perry. "Why should Lucas Russell be here?" She shook her head. "I've neglected my friends with everything going on in Washington. And with you." She relaxed as he stroked a hand over her arm.

"I'm sure everything is fine. We'll pay a visit tomorrow to see how they fare. I believe he is staying at the McLeod mansion only a few blocks from here."

She pushed away from him and sat up. "Will you go there with me now? I have a sense something is wrong."

He kissed her hand and nodded. "Of course."

After they rose and hastily dressed, he watched as she battled to pin up her hair in a respectable style. When they departed the house, he held his arm out for her, and they walked arm in arm down the cobbled sidewalks. The mid-October afternoon was warm but still had a bite to it that warned colder weather was coming.

"What should we do for servants?" Rowena asked.

He shrugged. "I have no idea. I've never had any." He met her amazed look and raised an eyebrow. "This is what comes from buying too big a home."

"We would need a cook no matter where we lived!" she protested.

He chuckled. "We will figure it out, love. No need to fret. Ask your friends what they do."

She chuckled. "If I ask Zee, she'll advise me to speak with Delia, and we'll have a houseful of former orphans working for us." She looked at him and smiled. "I can think of worse things." She squeezed his arm and then sobered as they approached the imposing McLeod mansion, twice the size of neighboring homes.

After they knocked on the door, they waited a few moments for the butler to answer. Before they could speak, he intoned, "I am sorry, but the family is not receiving guests at this time."

Perry nodded and held out his card. "Could you do me the favor of delivering this to Mr. Lucas Russell? I will wait here for his response."

The butler glared at him before snatching his card and slamming the door in his face. They shared a perplexed look and then turned to stare at the other homes on the street.

"I fear you are correct," Perry murmured. "Something is wrong."

The door wrenched open, and they turned to find Lucas, disheveled and with bloodshot eyes, swaying on the doorstep. "Perry!" he exclaimed as he pulled him into a fierce embrace. He slapped him on the back a few times. "I had no idea you were in Boston." He ran a hand over his unkempt hair. "Forgive me. I had forgotten I was not dressed for guests."

"You know I don't give a damn about that," Perry growled. "What is going on? Why won't you invite me—us—in?"

"There's illness in the house," Lucas whispered. "I don't want you to get sick."

"Who?" Rowena asked as she grabbed his arm. "I beg your pardon. I'm one of Zylphia's friends. Rowena Clement."

Lucas nodded as though vaguely recalling her from the days when he had loved Parthena and then seemed to crumple in front of them. "My niece Melinda died over a week ago. And … now Savannah. My sister, Savannah, just died last night." He stilled as he heard a yowl of pain and then the crash of something heavy upstairs. He shook his head and looked at Perry. "Her husband," he whispered.

Perry gripped Lucas by the shoulders. "Your sister?"

"My only sister," Lucas said dazedly.

Perry pushed Lucas backward, into the house and into the front sitting room. He ignored the rich furnishings around him and focused on his friend. "We'll be fine here," Perry said, ignoring Lucas's protest. "How?"

"She had a baby. A short time after her daughter died." He stared into space as tears slowly coursed down his cheeks. "Sav was happy and heartbroken at the same time. And then the fever struck. We thought it was from the childbirth." He raised angry, defiant eyes to Perry. "The papers said the influenza epidemic was waning in Boston."

Lucas let out a stuttering breath. "But her fever wasn't from the birth. It was the influenza. At first it seemed a mild case, and she looked like she was improving. The doctors told us she was lucky and not to worry. She wrote letters, laughed, held her baby." He shook his head. "And then she was as sick as Melly."

"Lucas," Rowena whispered, taking his hand.

"She died, with Jeremy begging her to live. To live for them. For their baby. To not leave him alone." Tears poured out. "I know she fought. She fought so hard. But there was nothing she could do."

"There was nothing you, or anyone, could do," Perry said. He pulled Lucas close, holding his friend as he sobbed.

After a moment, Lucas pushed away as though embarrassed. "I beg your pardon."

Perry shook his head and sighed. He gripped his friend's shoulder. "I'm so damn sorry. I wish there was something I could do."

Lucas looked at him. "Will you sing? Sing at her funeral? I want there to be beauty because she deserves more than a somber group who can do little more than sob."

Perry nodded. "Of course. Let me know what song and consider it done." He squeezed Lucas's shoulder one more time, and then he gripped Rowena's hand, leading her from the house.

When they were a few blocks away, Rowena stumbled, and he looked down at her. "My love," he whispered, finding her silently sobbing. He pulled her close, ignoring the stares of others walking past. "*Shh*, it's all right."

"Did you hear?" she whispered into his chest. "Did you hear that scream of agony?" She shuddered. "I hate to think about how Savannah's husband suffers right now."

Perry kissed her head, his hold on her tightening. "I know," he rasped. "For it is what I would face were I to lose you." He stood there, holding her for many minutes.

～

Zylphia sat in her studio, curled on her settee, her mother's most recent missive on the table in front of her. She considered rising to find Teddy, but a listlessness pervaded her, and she pulled a blanket over her, curling into herself on the sofa. She ignored the maid who entered with her afternoon tea, shaking as she fought deep emotions.

"Are you ill?" Teddy's terrified voice broke through her malaise. "Zee! Tell me at once, and I'll ring for the doctor."

"No," she croaked. "I'm not ill. I'm fine." She sobbed, curling further into herself. "Everyone else is dying." Teddy pushed against her legs so that he could join her on the settee. Soon she found herself lying half on her husband's chest, his calming touch soothing her.

"What more has happened?" he whispered. "I've been worried about those at your parents' house since we were not invited back after we saw Savannah after the birth of the baby."

"Savannah died. The baby's ailing and will probably die." She buried her face in his neck as she sobbed. "They're all dead!"

"How can that be?" Teddy asked, hugging his wife closer as though to ensure she were still with him. "How can Jeremy have lost ..."

"Everyone," Zylphia breathed. She raised her gaze and met his. "What is he to do? How, how ..." Her voice cracked as she was unable to finish her sentence.

"*Shh*, my darling, Zee. Let me hold you. Let me comfort you." He sighed. "For I fear we are unable to venture there to comfort them. I refuse to risk your health entering the home of such illness."

Although in Teddy's arms, her shuddering intensified. "What if my parents become ill? What if I lose them too?" she whispered. "I can't bear the thought of any more loss."

"I know, love. I know."

"Promise me that you'll stop your meetings," she said as she clung to him. "I don't want some man to bring illness into this house. I can't lose you, Teddy."

"Darling, we will be fine," he protested.

"Promise me." She clasped his face between her hands. "No business dealings are worth what Jeremy is suffering."

He met her panicked gaze and nodded. "I promise, Zee."

She settled into his arms and fought another shudder. "I thought the worst was over," she whispered.

"The worst might be over, but that doesn't mean illness doesn't continue or that people still won't die." He sighed, kissing her head.

After a moment, his gaze settled on the painting on the easel. His breath hitched as he saw the portrait of a quietly contented Savannah holding her baby. Jeremy sat beside her on the bed, his arms around his wife and son. The colors were gentle while the soft brushstrokes gave a dreamlike feel to the painting. "Zee," he breathed as he stared at it. "That is a masterpiece."

She rubbed her cheek against her husband's chest. "Do you see how he holds them? They are cherished, and he is determined to protect them at the same time." She swallowed a sob. "I don't know what seeing this would do to him."

He kissed her head. "Give him time. He will want this painting, Zee."

"I was going to give them this at the christening."

His arms tightened around her. "You must continue to hope and pray that the baby survives, Zee. And when Breandan does, I think this will be the perfect gift."

He held his wife for long moments, as the shadows lengthened in the room while he studied the painting and the last glimpse of Jeremy's happy family.

J eremy stood at the cemetery, flanked by his brothers, his uncle, Delia, Zylphia and Teddy, and his wife's family. He bit back an inappropriate huff of amusement. He had no wife. She lay in a box in front of him, waiting to be lowered into the earth. Next to his daughter. He shrugged off the hands his brothers placed on his shoulders, shaking his head at their show of solidarity. He was alone even though those around him refused to acknowledge it.

He gripped his hands and fought tears as Lucas's friend, Perry Hawke, sang a haunting version of *"Ave Maria."* When the last note faded over the cemetery, the priest resumed his intonations of prayers and platitudes in Latin. Jeremy closed his eyes as he wondered if the words would bring any solace if spoken in English. When the casket was lowered into the gaping hole in front of him, Jeremy opened his eyes and swayed.

Gabriel gripped his arm. "Don't even think about it," Gabe whispered in his ear.

Jeremy nodded, swaying forward once before regaining his stoic balance.

At the long silence after the casket was settled in the grave, Jeremy raised his dazed gaze to look at the other mourners. He flinched at the naked pity in the priest's expression and then frowned as the priest made a shooing motion. Jeremy moved forward, filling his hand with dirt and clutched it in a clasped fist, holding it at the level of his heart for a moment. After closing his eyes and murmuring a prayer, he held his hand over Savannah's casket, sprinkling her with dirt. "I will always love you," he whispered as the last of the dirt left his hand.

He stood near the grave as each mourner murmured inconsequential blather about the loss of one so vibrant and young, never acknowledging their words. When they had finally dispersed, he took a deep breath and knelt in front of Savannah's grave. He bowed his head, watching as the gravediggers filled in the yawning hole, knowing that nothing would ever fill the devastation wrought by the loss of his Savannah.

～

G abriel and Richard stood to the side of the cemetery as they watched their youngest brother mourn. "I can't stand by much longer and do nothing," Gabriel muttered.

"I'm afraid you have to. He needs time to say goodbye," Richard said, kicking at a pebble and peering out from underneath his lashes as he watched a motionless Jeremy in front of the now packed-in grave. "I know I'd need to do something like this."

Gabriel shuddered. "Don't even think it." They shared a look, the pain of each having lost a child in their expressions. "I pray, every day, that I never have to live without Rissa."

Richard gave a humorless chuckle. "You're as selfish as I am. I pray the same. Flo is …" He shook his head. "What can we do for him?"

Gabriel's gaze filled with panic. "I don't know. I can't stay here forever. Although I will remain here until the christening."

Richard nodded. "Florence will want to see you, as will the boys." He let out a deep sigh. "We were fortunate we didn't lose any of them to the influenza, but Ian and Thomas remain quite weak."

Gabriel gripped Richard's shoulder. "I'm sorry I've focused all my energies on Jeremy. I never considered what you were suffering, Rich."

Richard shook his head. "I know you'll always be there for me, Gabe. Thank God, baby Agnes remained healthy."

They hugged Zylphia as she approached them. "Gabriel, this is Teddy," she said. "I can't believe you're finally meeting at a funeral."

Gabriel shook Teddy's hand and shared a remorseful smile with him. "I wish it were any other occasion." He looked into Teddy's anguished silver-colored eyes. "I want you to know how happy I am at your safe return from the Front and your marriage to Zee. I'm a few years late saying this, but welcome to the family, Teddy."

Teddy gave a faint smile. "Thank you." Unable to hide his concern as he stared at Jeremy still kneeling by Savannah's grave, he asked, "Will you remain in town for a while longer?"

Gabriel nodded. "Until the christening." He met their gazes and their unspoken concern that they might find themselves at another graveside service rather than a church blessing.

Two nights after he buried Savannah, Jeremy paced his room. Sleep eluded him, and memories of Savannah and Melinda tormented him every time he shut his eyes. He slipped out of the room to wander the halls of his uncle's large house, his stockinged feet quiet as he walked up and down the hallways.

Unthinkingly he walked down the wing where his son struggled for life. He paused outside the door and was on the verge of continuing his middle-of-the-night ramble when he heard a baby's squeal.

He clutched a hand at his heart and eased open the door. The nurse, immediately alerted to his presence, relaxed when she saw who entered the room.

He tiptoed to his son's crib and peered down. He stood rigidly a moment as he watched him breathe, and then he held out a trembling hand to touch his downy black hair. "Hello, my love," he whispered as his voice thickened with tears. "For I do love you."

Breandan turned his head at the sound of his father's voice and looked at him through eyes barely open. Breandan kicked his legs a few times and then gave another squeal. Jeremy ran a finger over a chubby cheek and marveled at him. Raising dazed eyes, he looked at the nurse. "He seems ..."

"Better," she said with a tired smile. "I believe he will be fine."

Jeremy collapsed onto the chair beside the crib and dropped his head down as a sob burst forth. "*Fine*," he whispered. "I never thought such a simple word could mean so much."

He sat there, watching as his son was lifted from the crib and brought behind a privacy curtain to be nursed. After Breandan was changed and burped, he was returned to the crib, where he was fast asleep. "Hello again," he whispered.

Jeremy stared at his son, watching him sleep, unaware of the time slipping by. He started as a hand clasped him on his shoulder and met the worried gaze of his father-in-law. "Sir," he whispered.

Martin pushed on his shoulder so that he remained seated and pulled another chair beside Jeremy. "I often come here in the middle of the night when I am unable to sleep. I didn't expect to find you here."

Jeremy traced a circle on the baby's blanket near Breandan's shoulder. "I ... I know. I've been a horrible father," he whispered.

Martin made a sound of disagreement in his throat. "You have not. You've needed time to mourn." He settled into his chair. "He seems more peaceful tonight."

"The nurse said she thinks he will be all right." His fingers clamped down on the mattress. "I couldn't ... I couldn't watch him die too."

Martin gripped his shoulder. "I know. I understand. And I do not blame you, Jeremy."

Jeremy shook his head. "You should. If I had never brought your daughter and your granddaughter here, they would still be alive. They'd be healthy and well in Missoula."

Martin sighed. "You know that Savannah would most likely have died in childbirth if she hadn't had that surgery." He waited for Jeremy to give a small nod, acknowledging his words. "You know that the Spanish flu is moving west. It's probably already arrived in Montana by now. No place will be safe, Jeremy."

"I brought them to danger." He lowered his head as he let out a deep breath.

"Yes, you did. Unwittingly." Martin stared at his newborn grandson a moment. "I will never be angry with you, Jeremy. I know how much you loved Savannah. How much you would have sacrificed for her."

"I blame myself."

"I know, son," he said. "I know."

They sat in silence, watching as little Breandan slept, each passing moment giving them hope.

CHAPTER 19

*A*idan sat in his study, reading the newspaper, as a fire crackled in the grate on a late October morning. Scattered lamps were lit around his dark paneled office, and he sat in a comfortable chair near the fire rather than behind his desk. He frowned as he focused on the report of the sinking of the steamer *Princess Sophia* near Juneau, Alaska. His jaw ticked at the firsthand reports from survivors and rescuers. He turned toward the door as it opened and lowered the paper. "Zee," he said with a broad smile. He rose to embrace her. "It has been far too long since I've seen you."

She squeezed her arms around his back and then sat in the other chair in front of the fire. She smiled as she realized Teddy's study was remarkably similar to her father's. "I was here just three days ago." She grinned as her father chuckled. "How are things?"

He picked up the paper again. "It appears the American Expeditionary Force finally had success in France. I hope the Germans will see sense and realize they will not win with our added numbers to the Allied troops." He tapped at the front page of the paper. "We've broken through the Argonne Forest and are pushing forward past their lines."

She nodded. "Finally something other than carnage in that horrible stalemate." She shivered. "What else?"

"Over 350 died in Alaska in a maritime accident. A steamer ran into a reef."

"Oh, how tragic," Zylphia gasped. "All of my focus is on the War, and yet there is tragedy everywhere."

Her father squeezed her hand, his mouth in a grimace.

"How is Jeremy?"

Aidan focused on his daughter. "Hurting. I think he will never fully recover, but Breandan is thriving. That brings Jeremy great comfort."

Zylphia let out a sigh of relief. "I had feared it would be like with Savannah, where she appeared to improve and then worsened again. I feared Breandan would die too."

Aidan shook his head. "No, he truly seems better and is a wonderful baby." He gave a chagrined smile. "Although all babies are wonderful. The christening will be in a few weeks."

She bit her lip, her expression worried as she met her father's concerned gaze. "I … I'm uncertain what I should do, and I want your advice. I've already spoken with Teddy, but I want your opinion too." At his nod, she sighed. "Before Savannah died, I did a drawing of Savannah, Breandan and Jeremy. I don't tend to do portraits, but Jeremy had asked me to do one of them as a family."

Her father tilted his head as she squirmed with unease. "Now you are uncertain if you should complete the commission he requested?"

"No. I painted it. Before I knew she died." She met her father's shocked look. "I don't know if I should give it to him."

Aidan sat back in his chair, his gaze remote as though reliving distant events. "It is a pain that you believe is beyond bearing. Losing a spouse, especially a beloved one. And then to lose the child too …" He shook his head, the echoes of just such losses reflected in his eyes. "I would have cherished any such painting of my first wife and child. A reminder that what I'd had wasn't a dream."

"Oh, Father," Zylphia breathed as she clasped his hand. "I don't mean to cause you pain."

"You don't, Zee. You bring me joy and hope and love. Never doubt that." He ran a hand over his daughter's raven hair. "And you will bring that to Jeremy too, when he sees that painting." He sobered.

"Although I would give it to him privately. I fear he may need time alone with it as he continues to mourn."

She sniffled and nodded. "Thank you, Father. Teddy said much the same, although I was thinking of waiting a year or two to give it to him."

"No, my darling daughter, give it to him now." He sighed and stared into the fire.

"What bothers you, Father?"

He sobered. "I fear that Gabriel will leave before the christening. He is worried about Clarissa and his children in Montana, now that the influenza is heading west."

"I shouldn't want to chase that dreaded disease across the country, but I can understand his desire to be with his family." She shared a long look with her father. "Especially after seeing how Jeremy has suffered." After a moment she frowned. "Will Lucas return with him?"

"No, although I think he wishes he were. He will remain for the christening as he is to be Breandan's godfather." He frowned. "I'm uncertain why Jeremy insists on having the christening here, when I know Savannah wanted Clarissa as godmother to her child."

Zylphia frowned. "Do you think he truly wants the christening here?"

Aidan shook his head. "I think, at this moment, he doesn't care much about anything, except his son. He's constantly in the room I set up as a nursery, and he rarely speaks at dinner." Aidan nodded as though making a silent decision. "I will speak with him to ensure this is what he wants."

Zylphia rose, kissed her father on his forehead and left to return home.

Gabriel clapped Richard on the back before being ushered into the three-story home Richard owned in Dorchester. He and Florence now lived on the bottom two floors while they rented the third. Rather than lead Gabriel into the living room, Richard brought his eldest brother to the large kitchen at the rear of the house, where Florence moved with grace as she prepared dinner.

"Flo," Gabriel said, opening his arms as she squealed and threw herself into them. "I can't believe it's been five years since I've seen you." He backed her away and looked at her. "You look wonderful."

She gripped his arm and squeezed. "And you're as charming as any McLeod." She shared a smile with her husband. "I'm so glad you're finally visiting and that you can meet all our children at last."

Gabriel nodded. "I hate that they are already so grown up and have no memories of me."

Richard chuckled. "Oh, they have memories of you, Gabe. I've told them plenty of stories about our antics when we were younger. About how we tormented our cousins." He shared an amused smile with his brother and then turned as his boys paraded in, from tallest to shortest. "Ian, Victor, Thomas, Gideon and Calvin, this is your uncle Gabriel."

Gabriel smiled. "Hello, boys." He grunted when they attacked him like players in a rugby scrum, as they all tried to hug him at once, and he tumbled to the ground. "You are fine McLeods," he said as he laughed.

"Come play with us like Zee does," Gideon said as he tugged on Gabriel's hand.

"Boys, Uncle Gabriel is here to visit all of us," Florence said. "Please allow him to stand, and apologize for acting like a herd of wild animals."

Gabriel rose and patted them on their heads. "You've fine spirits. I can't wait for you to meet your cousins." He focused on Calvin. "I think you and Billy would get into many adventures."

Calvin faced his parents. "Can we travel to Montana? Please?"

"It's cruel we don't know our cousins," the eldest, Ian, said.

Richard cast a quick glare at Gabriel and then shook his head at his children. "Not right now. You've already missed enough school due to the influenza, and you must finish this year before we have any discussion of trips." He ignored their groaning and watched them file out of the room to finish homework before dinner.

Gabriel sat, accepting a cup of tea from Florence. Soon he held baby Agnes in his arms, and he rocked her as she mewled. "There, there, little love. No need to make a fuss."

He smiled at his brother and Florence. "You don't know what it means to me to sit here in your kitchen and to see that your life is as I had imagined it. Chaotic and filled with contentment, surrounded by your children." His eyes glistened as he stared at his brother.

Richard nodded. "We hate that we are so far away from you and Jeremy." He took a sip of tea and then turned to Florence and kissed her cheek. "But our home is here. Our businesses are here."

Gabriel spoke to include Florence. "Richard showed me around his blacksmith shops yesterday, and I couldn't be prouder of all that he's accomplished. And you, Florence, have created a wonderful home for your family."

Florence watched Gabriel with curiosity. "I still have trouble believing you like me," she murmured, "after I misled you and your brothers about my acquaintance with your cousin Henry Masterson and your aunt Masterson."

"Of course I like you," he said, clasping her hand a moment. "I was a stubborn idiot, and I'm only thankful that my brother was not as blinded by his animosity as I was." He winked at her. "Besides, I've come to realize that my cousin will manipulate and hurt anyone he can to harm me. I'm glad that you and Richard overcame what he and his mother attempted to do." He smiled at her. "What do you do for yourself?" He saw her confused look. "Clarissa works at the library with her friend Hester. I think, if Rissa were solely at home, she'd slowly go mad for lack of adult conversation and friendship. What do you do, Flo?"

"I'm at home. But I'll try to find something that is just for me. I've finally agreed to Richard's badgering to hire someone to help me with the children a few days a week."

"Good," Gabe said with a nod, smiling at her news.

Richard frowned and focused on Gabriel. "What did you mean about the Mastersons, Gabe? I know what Henry did to Patrick's wife. What more has he done?"

Gabriel shook his head with frustration and then *coo*ed to the baby who had become restless with his agitation. "He wants to harm Colin for some reason. Clarissa thinks Mrs. Smythe is behind it, but it's impossible to know their motives." He shrugged. "I had to leave the day after I saw him at a botched wedding in Missoula." He laughed as his eyes lit while remembering the scene of Colin marching up the aisle. He told Richard and Florence an abbreviated version of that day's events and then of Gabriel's precipitous departure the next day. "I saw Henry on the train, but it's always a chess match, where neither of us reveals more than we have to."

Florence frowned. "Why should Henry have this much animosity toward you?"

"They lost almost everything in the Panic of 1907, and I know he resents Uncle Aidan. The Mastersons always took comfort in the fact that the McLeods were worthless nobodies, but that's not the case anymore." He shook his head with frustration.

"It's too much to hope he'd grow up and leave us in peace," Richard said.

Gabriel shook his head. "He'd never be that generous." Gabriel kissed Agnes's head.

"If it's any consolation, I've had no contact with Mrs. Masterson in years," Richard said. "She came by the blacksmith shop a few times after I bought it, preening about me beggaring myself." He shook his head. "I never saw her again."

"I wonder if she's still alive," Gabriel mused and then shrugged and shared a long look filled with memories with his brother. "I would not mourn her."

"Oh, I'm sure she's alive," Florence said. "I'm sure she's filling that cousin of yours with venom so he keeps his hatred for you fresh."

Gabriel sighed as he stretched his legs in front of him with baby Agnes on his chest. "I wonder what happened to cousin Nicholas?"

Richard shrugged. "I have no idea."

Gabriel smiled as his gaze became distant. "All this talk only makes me think about Clarissa and the children. I hate being so far away. I don't know how they fare."

Richard's frown deepened. "You're leaving," he whispered. "It's why you're here."

Gabriel nuzzled his niece's forehead. "Yes. I have to return home. There's every possibility that Colin needs my help. And I must be there with Clarissa in case the influenza strikes Missoula. I cannot leave her to face such a calamity alone."

Florence shook her head. "Of course not. Not when you know what it is like to lose a child. The fear alone is …" She shook her head again and let out a long breath, reaching to grab Richard's hand. She only calmed as he squeezed it and stroked his strong fingers over hers.

Richard sat in angry silence. "I can't blame you for going, but I'm damn sorry. I'll miss you. I hate living so far apart."

Gabriel smiled at his brother. "I do too."

Florence looked at Gabriel. "Let's make a promise. When the amendment passes, and women are granted the right to vote, we will gather as a family. We will rejoice together."

Gabriel smiled. "I already support all that Clarissa does, but now I will be an even more ardent proponent." He kissed his niece's head and shared a rueful grin with his brother. "I hope it is soon."

Perry stood in the hallway outside the small room decorated with white and yellow roses. A beautiful song played on the piano, but he could not decipher if Lucas or Parthena played. After taking another deep breath, he rolled his shoulders as he attempted to free himself of tension. He stiffened as a hand slapped him on the shoulder.

"You'll be fine. Zee's with her, and she'll be here soon," Teddy said with an understanding smile.

"I have this sense that something will go wrong." Perry shook his head with embarrassment.

Teddy laughed. "Something probably will, but that's what makes life enjoyable. Embrace the unknown, Perry. It's what I've learned to do with Zee, and it's made life more rewarding." He turned as he heard his name called from the top of the stairs. "That's my cue." He pushed at Perry until he stood in front of the small crowd that had gathered.

Lucas rose from the piano and stood beside Perry after shaking his hand and clapping him on his back. Aidan, Delia, Morgan and Sophronia made up the intimate group who had gathered to see Perry's wedding.

The minister cleared his throat, and then Parthena entered the small living room. She winked at Perry and then skirted the chairs and sat at the piano to play gentle music. Zylphia took slow measured steps as she approached the makeshift altar in a light-blue dress that highlighted her blue eyes and raven hair. Perry barely noticed her, his gaze riveted on Rowena at the doorway. She stood alone, her shoulders back as she waited for Parthena to change the music.

When the slow wedding music started, Rowena raised glowing eyes to meet Perry's ardent gaze. Her ivory-colored dress clung to her curves and enhanced her subtle beauty more than a white dress would have. The scalloped hem and short train made him think of European princesses, and his breath caught. When she reached him, he clasped one of her hands and kissed her palm.

They turned to face the minister, and Perry attempted to focus on the words, but his mind was filled with gratitude. When they turned to face each other to recite their vows, he traced a finger over her cheek and jaw before speaking in a loud, clear voice. She did the same, and soon he leaned forward to kiss her.

He backed away, far sooner than he wanted to, whispering in her ear, "Finally I am yours, and you are mine," and he smiled at the small group of friends who had gathered to celebrate with him. Lucas hugged him, while Zylphia and Parthena pulled Rowena close. Sophronia waved her cane about and nearly whacked him in his leg, but he deftly caught it and leaned down to kiss her cheek.

"About time one of you girls was sensible," she intoned, her aquamarine eyes lit with joy. "None of that dillydallying that your friends suffered from."

Rowena laughed and pulled her friend close. "Thank you, Sophie."

Soon they held glasses of champagne, and toasts rang out through the room. A small wedding feast awaited them in the dining room, and they moved there before Perry and Rowena were to leave on a short honeymoon. They had not informed anyone, but they planned to remain in their new home on Marlborough Street. Perry prayed for no interruptions.

As they walked to the dining room, the front door opened with a clatter. He frowned as Mr. Clement stormed in, his dark coat swirling around his ankles as he approached them. "Mr. Clement, you are just in time to wish us well," Perry said with a jovial smile. His head jerked to the side as Rowena's father slapped him.

"You insolent fool. I warned you to leave town last month. How dare you believe you can marry my daughter?" He glared at Rowena, who stood proudly beside Perry, and grabbed her arm. "You are coming with me, and this folly ends now."

"No!" Rowena screamed, yanking on her arm. However, her father tightened his hold to the point she grimaced in pain. "I am married to him."

"It will be annulled," her father growled.

Aidan, Morgan, Teddy and Lucas formed a circle around the three of them, all glowering at her father. "Let Rowena go, Reginald," Aidan said. "You must admit when you have been defeated."

"Defeated? Defeated by this son of a whore?" He sneered at Perry. "I would rather die than see my daughter defile herself in such a manner."

"Perry is a good man," Rowena said as she trembled with anger.

"He's nothing but a charlatan, and you're the fool for falling for his lies. He grew up in a whorehouse! Did he tell you that? That he peddled himself in order to survive? You're marrying nothing more than a two-bit whore."

She screamed and kicked, lashing out with such force that she shocked her father and freed herself. "Have you no shame? No decency? Perry is the best man I have ever met. He might have had a … a troubled childhood without the support of parents as I did, but I will never judge him for it. I will never find him lacking." She sniffled and swiped at her cheeks. "I will always find you inadequate because you are incapable of love or of any depth of feeling for something or someone you cannot control." She shook her head and backed away, placing her hand on Perry's arm.

Her father glared at her and then at those surrounding her like an honor guard.

Zylphia now stood beside Teddy, and Sophronia appeared eager to wield her cane.

"You are all fools, taken in by his shiny looks and melodious voice. You won't be able to say I didn't warn you." He turned on his heel and stormed out of the hall, slamming the door behind him.

Air *whoosh*ed out of Perry's lungs, and he collapsed to his knees. Rowena fell down with him and wrapped her arms around his shoulders. After a few moments, they were the only ones in the hallway. "Perry?" she whispered. She clung to him as he shook.

"I'm sorry," he whispered.

She cupped his face. "I should apologize. He's my father."

He shook his head and closed his eyes. "I knew he'd use my past against me."

She tilted his face so he had to look at her. "I know about your past. I know that you are embarrassed by some of the things you had to do." She brushed at his cheek, uncaring as tears coursed down hers. "I have not lost any regard for you, my love."

He sighed and turned his face into the crook of her shoulder. "What he said was true, Ro. Except for my mother being a whore. Or that I sold my body."

She met his gaze filled with shame and embarrassment, and she cupped his cheeks between her palms. "I trust you, Perry. You told me the truth, and I know you would not lie to me." She saw the truth of her words echoed in his eyes, and her smile softened. "Our friends will not think any less of you. They will ensure my father is the one to suffer for interrupting our wedding day."

"I hate that my past tarnishes you in any way."

She stared into his eyes with a fierce intensity. "Nothing you could have done would ever change how I feel about you, my love. Nothing you have done has tarnished me or my love for you." Her fingers stroked his cheeks. "I have no idea what it is to be alone and young and vulnerable with no one to care if I survive or not." She waited until she saw his acceptance of her words. "Rather than becoming a bitter, cruel, miserable man, you are ..." She stared at him with wonder and love. "A marvel."

She pushed herself up and reached a hand down for him. "Come. We have our wedding to celebrate with our friends."

He rose and tugged on her hand to prevent her from rejoining the others. "You can annul our vows," he whispered. "I ..."

She blinked away tears. She stood on her toes and kissed him. "I love you and want you and need you. Never doubt that." She beamed at him. "I refuse to be miserable like my father. Please celebrate life with me." She met his searching gaze, hers unguarded and filled with hope and love.

He pulled her close, his breath catching at her singular scent and the comfort of her arms around him. "God, yes, my love. Always."

~

A few days later Jeremy stood with his family in Aidan's front parlor. Aidan and Delia had opted to use that room because it was the largest and had a huge fireplace to keep the room warm on the cold early November evening. Jeremy held his son in his arms, although he would soon hand him to his aunt and uncle before Breandan returned to the nursery. "Thank you for having a gathering, Uncle," Jeremy said.

"I want to celebrate our family as you prepare to leave us." Aidan cleared his throat as though it were thickened by tears. "I will miss all of you and will travel to Montana soon with Delia to see how you and Breandan fare."

"I hope you are not upset that I decided to wait to have the christening in Missoula," Jeremy said. He watched Gabriel and Richard laugh as Richard's boys played on the floor with Zylphia.

"No. I had wondered at your decision to have anyone other than Clarissa be godmother."

Jeremy nodded and blinked a few times to clear away tears. "I know she would shower Breandan with her love even if she weren't his godmother, but this is one way I can honor Savannah's wishes." He nodded to his uncle and joined his brothers.

Richard slung an arm over Jeremy's shoulder, and the three tall McLeod brothers stood to one side of the room as they watched their family gathering. "I'll miss you both," Richard said. "Please continue to write. I hate when there is a lapse in communication between us."

Gabriel nodded. "We will. And I will keep to the promise I made Florence." He smiled as Zylphia joined them, breathless and red-cheeked from playing with her cousins. "You always were a bit of a heathen, Zee."

He laughed as she belted him on his arm. "I am not. I just refuse to be restrained by what society deems the necessary decorum for a woman." She sobered and looked at Jeremy. "I know you leave in two days. I was hoping to speak with you."

He frowned and nodded. "You can speak in front of the family."

She shook her head. "No. I have something for you, and I think it's best if it's shared in private." She grabbed his hand and tugged him into motion as she led him from the front sitting room, down the long hallway and into the back room that was a glass conservatory. The palms that had died in a blight had been replaced, and it resembled a tropical oasis again.

His brows furrowed as she wrung her hands. "Whatever it is, Zee, you can tell me. I've been through hell, and I'm still here."

She nodded. "I don't want to cause you more pain, Jeremy. I would never mean to do that." After another deep breath, she moved into the room and sensed him following her. When she approached a sheet-shrouded painting, she paused. "This is my parting gift for you." Her breathy voice was barely audible as she lifted the sheet.

His confused gaze flit from her to the canvas, and then he froze. He studied the fine brushstrokes of Savannah with their babe cradled in her arms, the joy in her gaze, her cheeks rosy as she flushed after he had teased her. The inherent promise of tomorrow in the painting. He looked at himself, a satisfied man with the world in his arms. A man he no longer recognized. He fell to his knees as tears leaked out. "Oh, God," he whispered.

She stood there, wringing her hands as he stared with unflinching, unblinking eyes at the painting. "I didn't know if you would want it. If it would bring you too much pain."

"It hurts," he rasped. "But it would be so much worse not to see it."

She squeezed his shoulder. "It's yours, Jeremy. To bring home to Montana."

He collapsed forward as he was racked by sobs. "I ..." His voice broke off.

Glancing toward the door as it eased open, she let out a sigh of relief to see Richard and Gabriel poking their heads in. "Please, come in and help me." She swiped at her cheeks. "I gave Jeremy a gift, and I fear it is too much."

Gabriel and Richard stilled a moment as they beheld the painting before focusing on their brother. Gabriel dropped to his brother's side and pulled him against him, murmuring words of comfort to him. Richard did the same, and Zylphia watched in wonder at the brothers' ability to soothe some of Jeremy's immediate pain.

Jeremy looked up and reached a hand out to Zee. "Thank you, Zee. Thank you for giving me such a gift." He shook his head. "I never thought you'd paint it after ... after she died."

She nodded as tears coursed down her cheek. "I painted it before I knew. I don't know if I could have painted it after ... after ..." She shrugged as her voice broke. She fell forward and was soon enfolded in a hug with all three of her cousins.

Gabriel eased away and ran a hand over Zylphia's head. "I hate that we will be separated soon." He looked at the small circle of his family around him. "You are like a sister to us, Zee, and it seems wrong to have us separated from you too."

Richard cleared his throat. "It's unfair to leave me behind alone in Boston. This way, there are two of us in Boston, and two in Montana."

He attempted a smile as they gave Jeremy time to recover from his deep emotions. "Remember your promise, Gabe."

Gabriel nodded, one hand on Jeremy's back and the other clasping Zylphia's hand. "We will have a family reunion and celebration when women are finally allowed to vote."

Zylphia's eyes lit with the promise of a family gathering. "Oh, yes. That would be wonderful."

Gabriel squeezed her hand. "Keep working hard so that it won't be long."

CHAPTER 20

Missoula, Montana, November 1918

Gabriel eased open the door to his home and breathed a sigh of relief. He cocked his head to one side, listening for his children. When he heard their calls to each other coming from the backyard, he walked with stealthy quiet through the house and to the kitchen's back door. He peered out the window to see them playing chase. Myrtle and Billy collided and fell to the ground. Rather than crying with displeasure, they shrieked with laughter. His breathing stuttered as he caught sight of Clarissa standing to one side, laughing and cheering them on as they played. Her chestnut-brown hair had been loosened in the soft breeze, and her eyes were filled with joy as she watched their children.

He opened the door and was immediately engulfed in a hero's welcome. He tumbled to the ground under his children's exuberant delight at having him home, laughing and kissing them on their heads as he held them each a moment. He rose, pulling Clarissa close, clinging to her as he battled a sob.

"What is it?" she whispered. "When I heard no news ..." She leaned back, running a hand over his face, frowning at the lines that appeared to have formed in his short absence.

His gaze roved around the backyard and lit on Araminta, standing to one side. "Minta," he whispered. "I hate to ask this of you, but can you watch the children?"

She narrowed her eyes as she studied his appearance. Her joy at his arrival dimmed, and she nodded soberly. She called to the children, planning out another game for them to play and distracting them from their father's hasty retreat.

Gabriel reentered the house, holding Clarissa's hand. He led her upstairs to their bedroom, where he shut the door behind him. Rather than speak, he tugged her into his arms and rocked her from side to side. A sob shuddered forth, then another.

"Oh, my darling," she whispered. "Is it Jeremy?" She held Gabriel tight, her arms wrapped around his back.

He pulled away and swiped at his cheeks. "Forgive me. I … I don't know how to say this." He grabbed her hand and led her to her chair and pushed on her shoulders so she sat.

Her breathing picked up to the point she was almost panting, and her gaze had become panic-struck. She gripped his hand as her gaze locked with his.

He opened and closed his mouth, before finally rasping, "Savannah …"

He nodded as Clarissa shook her head in confusion and then cried unabashedly as Clarissa let out a keening wail. She leaped at him, hitting him on his shoulders and beating at him. He wrapped his arms around her, stilling her erratic, bruising motions, and pulled her to him. "I'm so sorry."

"No," she howled. "No." She butted her head against his chest and squirmed until he released her arms. "I don't believe you. She can't be." She bit off the word, refusing to say it. "Jeremy took her to the best doctors. They were going to save her. I received a letter from her. She had a beautiful, healthy baby boy!"

"It wasn't the birth." Gabriel fell to his knees in exhaustion and grief.

"It was the influenza." He raised eyes with an echo of anguish she had not seen since their son Rory's death, and she collapsed to her knees in front of him. "She was weakened after the birth and got sick. So did the baby."

"The baby," she gasped.

"But he survived. I think he's the only reason Jeremy is sane right now." Gabriel shuddered as he thought about his brother.

Clarissa shook as though the shock was too much for her mind and body to assimilate at once.

He tugged her into his arms, holding her close. He nestled her between his legs, murmuring soft words as the heavy heaving sobs began. He did not ask her to stop, nor did he attempt to forestall her crying, for the grief was too great for any partial lamentation.

Clarissa had just begun to calm in his arms when the door burst open. Gabriel looked over his shoulder to see a sweaty, breathless Colin in his dirty work clothes. "Gabe," he panted. "'Bout time you returned home after not writing for so long." He stilled when he took in Gabriel's anguished gaze and Clarissa gasping for breath in his arms.

Gabriel motioned for him to enter.

Colin shut the door behind him and knelt by them. "Is it the baby?" he asked, grasping Clarissa's hand.

Gabriel gave Clarissa a moment to speak but realized she was still too far into her grief to form a coherent sentence. "Savannah perished due to the influenza," Gabriel whispered. "The same outbreak that took Melly."

Colin fell to his bottom in a *thud* and sat, dazedly staring back and forth between Gabriel and Clarissa. "You must be mistaken. Sav is strong. She'd survive the influenza."

"That's what we said about Melly," Clarissa whispered, clinging to Gabriel. She buried her face in his shirt, pulling him as close as she could hold him. Gabriel tugged her closer, his soothing hands moving up and down her back.

Colin sat there for a few minutes, his expression vacant. "I keep thinking how we were so worried about the birth. And, in the end, that's not what should have concerned us." Tears tracked down his cheeks, and he sniffled. "I need Ari."

"The children don't know," Gabriel whispered. "We must tell them." He attempted to ease away from Clarissa, but she clung to him.

Colin nodded, resting a hand on Clarissa's shoulder a moment. "We'll wait for you. If I can hold Ari a moment, I'll be able to control myself for a little while." He paused when he got to the door. "How is Jeremy?"

Gabriel shook his head. "I doubt he'll ever fully recover. He's lost his wife and daughter. In a matter of a few weeks. He blames himself for traveling to Boston. For exposing them to the illness."

Colin closed his eyes. "He couldn't have known. He did what he thought best."

Gabriel nodded and met Colin's gaze, Gabriel's terrified. "It's coming west, Col. It's in Butte and Anaconda."

Colin nodded. "I know. It's starting here too." He paled and slipped from the room.

Gabriel moved away from Clarissa, but she protested and linked her hands behind his back, refusing to release him. "Ah, my love," he whispered into her ear. "Thank you for letting me comfort you. I will comfort you, cherish you, forever."

"How long is forever? Didn't Jeremy want forever with Savannah and had that denied him?" She buried her face against his chest.

"Yes," he said as he kissed her head. "We, none of us, want to be the one left behind."

She reared back and poked him in the chest. "If you get sick, Gabriel McLeod, you fight. You fight for me. For our children. For the life we've made." Her eyes flared with desperation.

He ran a soothing hand over her shoulder. "You know I will. When haven't I fought for us, love?" He kissed her and sighed when she fell into his arms as more tears leaked out.

"When did she die?" Clarissa stuttered.

"A few weeks ago," Gabriel whispered. She allowed him to ease her back enough so he could bracket her face with his wide palms and swipe at her cheeks. Her eyes were tear-swollen and continued to leak tears. "I couldn't write. Not something like this. I needed to be here with you when I told you. To hold you in my arms."

She heard his unsaid words, and her fingers dug into his back as though she could hold him closer to her. "You feared I wouldn't allow you to comfort me." She sighed, kissing his neck. "I've learned that I need you, Gabe. More than you could ever know." She traced a new worry line by his mouth. "Where is Jeremy?"

Gabriel turned into her soft touch. "He remained in Butte, with Lucas. He'll be there a few days before returning to Missoula. He dreads entering their house."

She nodded. "I wish I could do something."

He smiled. "You do enough, my darling. Although I know he will ask you to be godmother. It's what Savannah wanted and why we didn't have the christening in Boston." He traced away another tear. "Lucas will be godfather."

"You aren't upset?" She frowned. "That one of the brothers isn't godfather?"

"Whether or not I have that title will never augment nor diminish my love of Breandan. He is my beloved nephew and will always be precious."

She sniffled and rested in his arms for another moment before pushing away. "Come. We must face this. We must tell the children."

Gabriel took a deep breath and rose. "I will rely on your strength, Rissa. I couldn't do this without you." She nodded, leaning into his side.

Lucas pushed open the door to his home in Butte and peered around. The trip from the train station had been eerie as the usually crowded, teeming streets of Butte had been empty. Only those with a purpose appeared to have ventured outside. However, the mines were running at full steam as evidenced by the smelters and smokestacks pumping out clouds of gray ash. As he hung up his coat, he sighed with frustration. Vivie was nowhere in sight, and his shoulders stooped in disappointment. His father and cousin were exhausted after the trip from Boston, and he had showed them upstairs to guest bedrooms. After finding Lizzie's bassinette for Breandan, he left Jeremy to relax as Lucas wandered downstairs. When he entered the living room, Genevieve emerged from the rear of the house.

"Lucas!" she shrieked, throwing herself into his arms. She clung to him and then backed away as her hands ran over him, as though ensuring herself that he was well. "Oh, please tell me that I'm not dreaming. I thought you were to arrive tomorrow ..." She leaned on her toes and wrapped her arms around him, pulling him close for a kiss.

"God, Vivie, how I have missed you," he whispered as he tugged her closer, kissing her over and over. After a moment, he shuddered and rested his mouth on her head. "I needed you so much."

She stroked his shoulder and jaw. "*Shh*, my love. I'm here for you now." She pulled back and brushed away tears that flowed down his cheeks. "I wish I had been there to support you."

"I thought to support Savannah as she mourned Melly," he whispered. "I never realized ..." His eyes closed, and he dropped his head to her shoulder as he fought a sob.

"I know, my darling," she said, her voice tear-thickened.

He nodded. "You lost a sister too." His shiny gaze was despondent, understanding their shared pain.

She blinked away tears. "I, ... yes. Isabel." She turned her face into his palm. "I missed you so much, Lucas."

He nodded and kissed her forehead. "How is Lizzie?"

She began to answer but then saw movement in the shadows near the door and jumped.

Lucas spun and then relaxed. "Vivie, this is my father, Martin Russell. He has sold his store in Boston and will be here with us for a while."

Genevieve flushed and held out her hand to her father-in-law. Stockier than Lucas, he and Lucas were about the same height, and both had brown eyes, although Lucas's were a lighter shade, resembling amber. However, there was no doubting their relationship. "It is an honor to welcome you into our home."

He smiled. "And it is a joy to finally meet Lucas's wife." He kissed her cheek and moved into the room to sit on a comfortable chair.

"How was the journey?" she asked, her hands fidgeting with her plain at-home skirts. Her gaze roved over her father-in-law's fine linens, and she fought a grimace at her simple clothes.

"Long but delightful. I never imagined our country was as big and diverse as it is." Martin smiled at her. "You have a lovely home."

Genevieve nodded to Lucas. "We do." She smiled as Lucas excused himself to go to the kitchen to find a snack for him and his father. "I was devastated when I heard the news."

Martin nodded. "You can imagine the difficulty Jeremy is having right now. Only little Breandan is keeping him sane. Thank you for having us as guests."

"Of course. You are Lucas's family, and he takes great delight in all of you. I know how much he has missed you in particular these past few years." She smiled at him.

"Your separation from your family must be equally as difficult."

"I miss my sister, Parthena. However, I never had a close relationship with my parents. And I have found great joy in my marriage with Lucas."

He watched her with a delighted curiosity in his gaze.

She noted it and flushed. "I beg your pardon for not welcoming you right away. I ... I was surprised by Lucas's return and overwhelmed. I had thought you were to arrive tomorrow."

Martin smiled. "You adore him as he adores you." His smile broadened as she nodded, her blush intensifying. "You cannot fathom what it means to a father to know that his two children found spouses as dedicated to them as they are. Who love them."

She blinked away her tears.

"Thank you for making Lucas so happy."

"I fear you have that backward, Father," Lucas said as he reentered the room. He beamed at his wife, handing a plate of cheese and fruit to his father before sitting beside his wife. "She's the one who brings me joy."

Martin smiled as he saw his son so contented with his wife. When he heard pacing on the second floor, Martin frowned at the ceiling. "Jeremy is restless, even with Breandan thriving. The nights are difficult for him."

Lucas pulled Genevieve close, and she snuggled into his side.

"I have a favor to ask of you, and I know it is not fair."

Lucas frowned after he swallowed a bite of cheese. "What is it, Father?"

"Will you come to Missoula? I know you will come next week for the christening, but I had hoped you would come for an extended visit. It would help Jeremy if the house he had shared with Savannah were not so empty."

Genevieve shuddered and then looked to Lucas. "What do you think?"

He squeezed her hand. "I don't like being on a train with Lizzie as there is still a great risk of influenza. However, there is no other efficient way to travel to Missoula."

She smiled at him. "It is waning here in Butte. They are on the verge of reopening the schools again."

He let out a deep breath. "Well, as I've learned from Jeremy, no decision is a perfect decision. And that, no matter how hard I try, I can't ensure everyone remains healthy. But I'd like to travel and spend time with him." He smiled. "Although I must find space for a piano in his house."

Martin smiled and relaxed as he ate the small snack Lucas had brought him. "Thank you, Lucas. I did not want Jeremy traveling alone, but I did not want to leave you just yet either."

Lucas smiled at his father. "Tomorrow you will meet Lizzie. Perhaps you'll see Patrick too."

∾

A few days later Jeremy walked the deserted streets around Patrick's house, having slipped out of his cousin's house and the family get-together. He was desperate to become so fatigued that he would have no choice but to sleep tonight. His dreams continued to haunt him. To taunt him with what would never be. He firmed his jaw as he bumped into a plump woman. "Pardon," he muttered.

She belted him with her handbag, and he paused under her attack, finally focusing on her. "Mrs. Smythe," he breathed.

"I find it hard to believe that you should ignore your daughter's mother in such a callous manner," she whined in her simpery voice. "Do you have no decency?"

He shook his head in confusion as he examined her. Her coat was well made but worn, as were her boots. Her gray-blond hair remained in ringlets, as though she were clinging to her youth as tightly as her hair to its fabricated curls. "I would never call upon you."

"Do you think I wouldn't want to see my own daughter?" she glared at him. "You may not like me, but I do have some rights."

He shook his head. "You gave them all up when you left her at the orphanage."

"I was out of my mind with grief at the loss of my husband!"

He snorted. "You mean, you were out of your mind with grief at the loss of his income." He firmed his jaw and nodded in a mockery of a deferential manner. "If you will excuse me?"

"No," she hissed as she grabbed his arm. "I demand to see my daughter. I have the right, if not legally, then morally."

His cheeks reddened with anger. "Morally? You would have sold her to some man to earn you coin the last time she was with you! How dare you suggest you have any moral right to ... to ..." His voice broke, and he shook his head. "It doesn't matter anyway."

She stomped her foot. "It does to me. I have friends on the Butte Police Department. If you continue to act in such an uncharitable manner, I will ensure you are visited by them."

He glared at her for a long moment. Finally he spoke in a low, lethal voice. "You want to see your daughter? Fine. Then I suggest you travel to Boston."

Surprise lit her gaze.

"She's buried there."

Shock and disbelief warred in her expression. "But she's young."

"Yes, and this influenza likes the young." He clamped his jaw shut and then whispered, "Whatever unfortunate association we may have had has now been irrevocably severed, Mrs. Smythe." He pushed past her and continued his walk, any hope of sleeping that night lost in the turmoil of his thoughts.

~

Patrick sat on his front porch, his feet propped on the cement railing as he waited for Jeremy to return. Fiona entertained Genevieve, Lucas, Martin and the two children. When he saw his cousin striding up the street with as much pent-up energy as when he left, he sighed. "Sit, Jer," Patrick said before Jeremy could reach for the door.

"Pat." Jeremy was slightly out of breath from his walk. He leaned on the banister and faced his cousin. "I'm sorry I'm not more sociable."

Patrick shook his head. "You know none of us care about that." He sat in silence a few moments, a cool wind blowing with the promise of snow in it.

"I'm sorry, Pat," Jeremy whispered. "I never meant for Melly …" He closed his eyes and ducked his head.

Patrick leaned forward and gripped Jeremy by the shoulder. "Don't you apologize to me. You raised her. Loved her as your own. You will never have to apologize to me for anything." His brown eyes glowed with sincerity.

Jeremy nodded and rubbed at his eyes. "Thank you." He took a deep breath. "For loving her enough to not rip her away from Savannah and me. For allowing her to remain in the only home she'd known." He met Patrick's tormented gaze. "She knew you cared for her, but I think she would have been miserable here."

Patrick nodded. "I know she would have been. She loved her life in Missoula, near Clarissa and Colin and Araminta. She would have hated it here." He cleared his throat. "And I had no right to rip her from what she knew."

Jeremy shook his head. "That is because you are honorable, Pat. Unlike some." He paused and listened to the faint sound of a streetcar passing a few streets over. "I ran into Mrs. Smythe on my ramble." He smiled sardonically as he heard Patrick's intake of breath. "She was irate I wouldn't let her see Melly."

Patrick sighed. "We never did tell her about Melinda. Or Savannah. It's none of her business."

"I imagine it would have been in the *Daily Missoulian*. That they died." Jeremy shrugged. "Although, in the end, what does it matter? They're gone, and no announcement will ease that pain."

Patrick gripped Jeremy's arm. "I'm sorry, Jeremy. I'm so damned sorry."

Jeremy took a deep breath. "So am I." He looked into the house. "But I have to go on. For my son's sake, if not my own."

Patrick rubbed a hand over his chest. "The pain of loss will ease," he whispered.

"But it will never go away." Jeremy rose. "I must see how Breandan is."

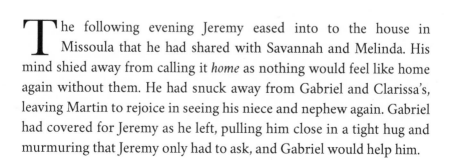

The following evening Jeremy eased into to the house in Missoula that he had shared with Savannah and Melinda. His mind shied away from calling it *home* as nothing would feel like home again without them. He had snuck away from Gabriel and Clarissa's, leaving Martin to rejoice in seeing his niece and nephew again. Gabriel had covered for Jeremy as he left, pulling him close in a tight hug and murmuring that Jeremy only had to ask, and Gabriel would help him.

The door *click*ed shut behind him, and he took a deep breath. Breandan slept in his arms and did not stir as Jeremy waited. Waited to hear Savannah call out to him in welcome. For Melinda to shriek with joy at his arrival home and to skid down the hallway. For the aroma of dinner wafting from the kitchen. For the subtle scent of lavender that had filled the house. He took a stuttering breath as he forced himself to walk through the downstairs, moving from the living room to the dining room and then the kitchen. All were clean but had a sense of staleness from disuse. Moonlight shone into Savannah's rear sitting room, and he shuddered, unable to force himself to enter that room.

Spinning on his heel, he walked down the hallway and up the stairs. He froze at the top, uncertain where to go. "Not the bedroom," he whispered as he fell back against the wall in the hallway. He looked up and down the hallway before sinking to his haunches. Images of Melinda prancing from her room, showing off new clothes, flitted through his memory. Of Savannah grabbing his hand and coyly smiling as she led him to their bedroom. Of holding Melinda in his arms when she was sick, battling fevers or demon dreams. Tears cascaded down his cheeks, and he sat until his legs had gone numb.

Breandan stirred, and Jeremy rose, taking a deep breath. He pushed open the door to his bedroom and paused. Her dressing table sat in expectation of her, with its stool vacant and her hairbrush waiting to be used on her long locks. He forced himself inside, his gaze searching for the bassinette for Breandan.

A soft hand touched his arm, and he spun, white as a sheet.

"Begging your pardon, sir, but I fell asleep while you were at your brother's," the woman said. She held her arms out for Breandan as he fussed more.

"Of course," he gasped, handing Breandan to the nurse who would help him care for his son. In his return to this house, he had forgotten about her. "How did you ... ?" He shook his head as his voice trailed away.

"Your cousin let me in. He could tell I was tired from the journey and had little interest in a family reunion." She nodded to Jeremy and headed to another room to tend to Breandan.

Jeremy watched the nurse walk away and moved downstairs to his office. He sat at the desk, shivering in the darkened room. A soft lilting song wended its way down the stairs, and he held his head in his hands, wishing it were Savannah singing to his child. Savannah whose breast gave Breandan nourishment. Savannah smiling in accomplishment at him as Breandan grew a little more each day. He lifted his head at the draft in the room. "Gabe."

"And Colin." Colin squeezed Jeremy's shoulder before sitting in a chair on the opposite side of Jeremy's desk. Gabriel remained standing as he studied his brother.

"What can we do, Jer?" Gabriel asked.

"There's nothing to do. My wife and daughter are dead, and I have to accept that." He rubbed at his head, keeping it bowed.

"Jer," Colin whispered. "I'm so sorry." He cleared his throat. "I feel like my joy in seeing Uncle Martin drowned my sorrow tonight. Forgive me if I was insensitive."

Jeremy shook his head. "No. If there's one thing I'm learning from Breandan, life must go on. And it was a relief not to be the focus of everyone's pity."

"How are things with the nurse?" Gabriel asked with a nod upstairs as the singing continued.

"Fine. She's here to do a job and takes little interest in me. Which is a relief." He looked at his brothers and shrugged.

"She told me that her name's Nora when we walked here tonight," Colin said. "Seemed a bit reluctant to talk about herself."

Gabriel rolled his eyes at his brother-in-law. "What does that matter as long as she does the job she was hired to do?" He stooped in front of the fireplace, fiddling with it until a small fire erupted. He fed it a few pieces of wood and rose. "Do you want to be in that room again, Jer?"

He shook his head. "No. I ... tried for a few minutes tonight, and I can't."

Gabriel nodded. "Colin and I'll be by tomorrow. We'll help you empty it."

"No!" Jeremy shook his head, his gaze frantic. "Just let it be. I need … I need her things still."

Gabriel froze as he watched his brother battling his grief. "Of course. Let me know what I can do, so I don't do something that brings you pain rather than eases it."

Jeremy nodded. "Thank you," he whispered to both of them. "For ensuring I was all right tonight."

Colin rose and squeezed Jeremy's shoulder. "Someday, Jer, you'll be much better than *all right*." He shared a worried look with Gabriel as Jeremy sat in a dazed stupor, disbelieving Colin's words.

P atrick walked through the long hallway in Savannah and Jeremy's house, looking for Fiona and Rose. He paused as he found Fiona asleep on a wicker chair in the back sitting room. Her red-gold hair had slipped from its pins and now framed her face. He frowned, in deep concentration, as she never rested during the day. "Fee?" he whispered.

He gave her a concerned smile as she forced herself awake. "Fee, love," he murmured as he squeezed her hand. "Are you all right?"

"Forgive me," she said around a huge yawn. "I should be at Clarissa's, helping to cook tonight's dinner. There is such a horde of us here for the christening tomorrow." She moved to rise, but he motioned for her to remain where she was.

"Where is Rose?" Patrick pushed her hair behind her ears.

"She's with Araminta. She stopped by a little while ago on her way to the park with the other children." She looked down. "I shouldn't have felt such relief at a few moments of rest."

"Why are you tired, Fee? I thought you slept well last night." He paled. "Are you ill? Is it the influenza?"

She shook her head and blinked away tears. "No, 'tis nothing like that." She clasped his hand and kissed his palm. "I meant to tell you last night, but then we were celebrating being together as a family. 'Tis selfish of me, but I wanted my own moment."

His brows furrowed as he studied her. "You're with child. You're to have my child," he breathed. His eyes widened with wonder as she flushed, her gaze a mixture of pride and remorse. "I should have known. You haven't had your courses in a few months."

"Patrick!" she said on an embarrassed laugh, tapping him on his shoulder.

"I'm right, aren't I?" At her nod, he *whoop*ed and pulled her into his arms. "Oh, my darling, thank you." He held her close, his arms roving over her back as though pulling her even tighter to him. After a moment, his body shuddered, and her hold on him tightened.

"Oh, my love," she whispered as she felt a sob burst free of him. "We miss her. We will always miss her."

"It's not right! Melly should know our child. She should have tutored her in the ways of Mr. Pickens and taught her to be just and strong, like she was." He shuddered as another sob burst forth. "Our child should know her aunt Savannah."

"Cry, my love," Fiona whispered into his ear as she rocked him.

After long moments, he pulled back, his eyes a fathomless depth of grief, joy, sorrow and hope. "I rejoice at our news, Fee." At her nod of understanding, he sighed and rested his head on her shoulder. "I wish …"

"I know," she whispered. "But nothing will change what happened, my darling."

~

Clarissa entered the front door to Savannah and Jeremy's house and paused. "*Jeremy's* house," she whispered to herself as she fought tears. She battled memories of hearing Savannah calling out to her from the kitchen, of Savannah singing in her back room, of Savannah's laughter at Melinda's antics. After a deep breath, Clarissa forced herself to climb the stairs to find Jeremy.

She poked her head into the room he had shared with Savannah and found it eerily empty. It looked as it did when they had departed for Boston and as though no one had ventured inside since Jeremy's return. She turned away and knocked on another door after hearing Jeremy's deep rumbly voice within. When he opened the door, holding a squirming Breandan in little more than a diaper, she fought a laugh.

"Here. Let me," she said as she reached for the baby she considered her nephew. After kissing his dewy soft black hair, she carried him to the bed, where his christening outfit was laid out. "Where's Nora?"

Jeremy shook his head in exasperation. "Like a fool, I told her that I didn't need her help. She's off somewhere, enjoying herself."

Clarissa smiled and tickled Breandan's stomach. "I'll change him first and then get him in his clothes." After adeptly changing his diaper and swaddling him in his christening gown, she smiled at Jeremy. "There. All done." Her smile faded at Jeremy's frown. "I'm sorry to have intruded."

"No." He held out a hand to forestall her rushing from the room. "I stare at you and how easy this is for you. And I wish …" He closed his eyes. "I can't stop yearning for what can never be."

Clarissa held Breandan in her arms as she approached Jeremy. "I can only imagine what you suffer, and the imagining is beyond bearing." She lost her battle with tears, and they formed a silent stream down her cheeks.

"Why don't you hate me?"

She stilled, her hold on Breandan tightening to the point Breandan gave a little chirp of disgruntlement. She met Jeremy's intense, fierce green eyes, lit with self-loathing. "I could never hate you, Jeremy. You did everything you could to protect those you loved most." She sniffled and kissed Breandan's head. "The influenza is a tragedy no one knew was coming."

"If …" He shook his head.

She reached forward and gripped his hand. "You can't live life that way. Savannah only knew love and devotion and joy the fifteen years she had with you. You shared sorrows. You had arguments, but you showed her what love and honor truly are." She blinked, and two more tears fell. "I could have asked for no better man for Savannah."

He pulled her tight, squeezing Breandan between them. "Thank you, Rissa. I thought ... I thought I'd lose your regard after I lost them."

"Never, Jeremy."

~

The large family gathering after the christening took place in Jeremy's house, as it was the only home large enough to hold all of them with ease at one time. Clarissa, Araminta, Genevieve, Hester and Fiona worked at a feverish pace in the kitchen, although Clarissa was largely relegated to washing pans and chopping produce. Children ran through the house, while the man of the hour slept in a crib in Jeremy's study, impervious to the noise made by his older cousins. The men sat in the front living room, close enough to hear Breandan if he cried, and far enough away from the kitchen to avoid being put to work.

"I still can't believe Uncle Martin is here," Clarissa said as she scrubbed a saucepan. "He looks marvelous." Her eyes glowed with momentary delight as she recalled seeing him at the train station, her disbelief transformed into joy in an instant. His strong embrace eased a small fraction of the agony she felt at the loss of her cousin and sister.

"He seems a wonderful man," Genevieve said with a smile. "I have enjoyed my conversations with him."

"He is, and he's quite different from his wife. He will take pride in anything Lizzie does," Clarissa said with a smile. She looked at the small mound of pots and pans that needed washing up and glared at them. "I fail to see why all this needed to be dirtied!"

Araminta laughed. "You only say that because you're doing the washing up."

"When's the wedding, Minta?" Fiona asked.

"We thought we'd marry next weekend." She beamed at the women she considered family. "Colin wanted to wait for everyone to return from Boston before holding our wedding. Plus now the Armistice is signed, and the War is over. Time for celebrating many things."

"Isn't it hard to believe the War is over?" Genevieve asked. "I thought it was rather tidy, having the notice on the eleventh of November at 11:00 a.m."

"Thank God, it is over," Clarissa said. "I lived in fear that Colin or Gabriel would be drafted. It ended soon enough that they never were. I heard from Amelia that Nickie is well, although it may be some time before he returns from France."

"France," Genevieve murmured. "Can you imagine? I would think that he'd have trouble adjusting to small-town life again in Montana."

"Amelia just wants him home," Clarissa said with a shrug.

All of the women nodded in understanding.

"Savannah visited Paris," Clarissa whispered. "On her honeymoon with her first husband." She fought tears as she sniffled.

"Keep telling us her stories," Genevieve urged. "You're the one who knew her the longest, and we should not silence her memory in a shroud of grief."

Clarissa nodded. She turned as Billy entered the kitchen, disgruntled by Myrtle taking over his favorite toy. Clarissa wiped her hands and moved with him to the living room, where the men had gathered. She stood in the doorway a moment, watching as the men chatted and told the tale of Mr. Pickens being chased by a moose. Ronan motioned with his arms as he told about Mr. Pickens climbing a tree while naked, and the men's laughter filled the room.

Jeremy sat next to Uncle Martin and Gabriel, his gaze somber but not as devastated as in recent days. He appeared to enjoy the storytelling, although he did not join in. Uncle Martin leaned forward, avaricious in his curiosity about life in Montana and the stories they had to share. She bit back tears as he knit his way into their Montana family.

Lucas slung an arm over her shoulder and pulled her close. "Why the tears, Rissa?"

"I'm already dreading when Uncle Martin has to return to Boston."

Lucas chuckled. "He doesn't. He sold the store. I suspect he'll be here forever."

She let out a deep breath. "Good. We've been separated long enough." She turned, burying her face in his shoulder. "We can't forget her, Lucas."

"Never," he whispered, holding Clarissa close a moment.

Soon the women had deemed their work completed in the kitchen, and they joined the men in the living room. The room was crowded but filled with joy as Breandan's christening was celebrated.

After a moment Gabriel stood, and everyone quieted. "This has been a year of tremendous joys and sorrows. We have been blessed by the arrival of Lizzie and Breandan, and we will continue to mourn our beloved Savannah and Melinda. Colin will hopefully cease dithering ..." Gabriel laughed as Colin chucked a dishtowel from Araminta's arm at Gabriel. "... and we will soon have a wedding to celebrate."

He looked at his family and cleared his throat, raising his glass high. "To the bonds that tie us together. To abiding love. To family."

NEVER MISS A RAMONA FLIGHTNER UPDATE!

Are you afraid of missing out on updates about the Saga? Sign up here to be included on Ramona Flightner's mailing list! You'll receive new release alerts, gain access to bonus material written only for Ramona's mailing list, and hear about sales and freebies first!

Don't forget to follow Ramona on Bookbub to be notified of freebies and sales!

ALSO BY RAMONA FLIGHTNER

Never fear, there will be one more book in the Banished Saga! My goal is to have it ready for September 2019. If you want to remain up to date on all my releases or specials that I only share with my newsletter subscribers, sign up for my newsletter.

The Banished Saga: (In order)

Banished Love

Reclaimed Love

Undaunted Love (Part One)

Undaunted Love (Part Two)

Tenacious Love

Unrelenting Love

Escape To Love

Resilient Love

Bear Grass Springs (In Order)

Montana Untamed

Montana Grit

Montana Maverick

Montana Renegade

HISTORICAL NOTES

As you can imagine, there was quite a bit of research required for *Abiding Love*. In fact, I never envisioned writing an entire novel about 1918. My original plan was to write one novel encompassing 1917/1918, but then, as I dug into research, I realized the novel would be too long, or I'd have to scrimp on the story I wanted to tell. Thus, *Resilient Love* and *Abiding Love* were born.

During my research, I learned about the Sedition Act. Although I am from Montana, I had never learned about it while in school. As I learned more about the Act, and how difficult it was for ordinary citizens living under such a law, I knew I wanted to have that be a focal part of the novel. The scene where Colin is grilled by the committee members is quite similar to the way B.K. Wheeler was interrogated (although B.K.'s lasted for hours).

The word "slacker" was popularized during WWI for those shirking their patriotic duty or who were not willing to join the Army.

The Influenza (or Spanish Flu) started in the United States in Boston in August 1918 at a military hospital. It raged throughout the city in September, and finally waned in October. It was one of the hardest hit cities in the U.S.

Although Savannah did not choose to use Twilight Sleep, it had been in use for a few years in Boston by 1918.

ABOUT THE AUTHOR

Ramona is a historical romance author who loves to immerse herself in research as much as she loves writing. A native of Montana, every day she marvels that she gets to live in such a beautiful place. When she's not writing, her favorite pastimes are fly fishing the cool clear streams of a Montana river, hiking in the mountains, and spending time with family and friends.

Ramona's heroines are strong, resilient women, the type of women you'd love to have as your best friend. Her heroes are loyal and honorable, men you'd love to meet or bring home to introduce to your family for Sunday dinner. She hopes her stories bring the past alive and allow you to forget the outside world for a while.